**DARING MEN, PASSIONATE WOMEN
CLAIMED A PLACE ON THIS WILD WESTERN
FRONTIER FOR GOLD AND FOR GLORY.**

JOHN COOPER BAINES—The Hawk. Mighty owner of the Double H Ranch in Texas, a man proud of his family and his land. When the woman he loves becomes the target of an assassin's bullet, he wants most is a chance for revenge.

FRANCISCO LÓPEZ—Last survivor of a band of renegades. His black soul embraces ___ easily as his arms embrace beautif___ ___ he has called on the devil h___ ___troy the Hawk.

*DOROTÉA*___ ___ghter of a wealthy Arg___ ___veliness brings new hope to ___ ___an, but will a sacred memory be tar___ ___ e makes her his bride?

JEREMY GAIGE—A grizzled old prospector ready for one final try at finding a fortune. The lost treasure of the San Saba River is the lure, but death may be the only prize waiting there.

SISTER EUFEMIA—A courageous Dominican nun. She and her band of sisters are willing to walk to Texas with their message of love even though it means risking the ravages of nature and ruthless men.

ANDREW AND ADRIANA—Two devoted young teenagers. Their innocent hearts may be broken when good-byes come too soon and last too long.

A Saga of the Southwest Series
Ask your bookseller for the books you have missed

A Saga of the Southwest
Book V

NIGHT
OF
THE HAWK

Leigh Franklin James

Created by the producers of
White Indian, Children of the Lion,
Wagons West, and
The Kent Family Chronicles Series.

Executive Producer: Lyle Kenyon Engel

BANTAM BOOKS
Toronto • New York • London • Sydney

NIGHT OF THE HAWK
*A Bantam Book / published by arrangement with
Book Creations, Inc.*

*Produced by Book Creations, Inc.
Executive Producer: Lyle Kenyon Engel.*

Bantam edition / September 1983

ISBN 0-553-23482-X

Published simultaneously in the United States and Canada

*Bantam Books are published by Bantam Books, Inc. Its trade-
mark, consisting of the words "Bantam Books" and the por-
trayal of a rooster, is Registered in U.S. Patent and Trademark
Office and in other countries. Marca Registrada. Bantam
Books, Inc., 666 Fifth Avenue, New York, New York 10103.*

PRINTED IN THE UNITED STATES OF AMERICA

H   0 9 8 7 6 5 4 3 2 1

The author wishes to acknowledge the inspiration and aid of the gifted Book Creations, Inc. team for critical suggestions and research, which vastly improved this book.

In addition, he wishes to express his gratitude to Fay J. Bergstrom, whose tireless work and helpful notes in transcribing the manuscript immeasurably strengthened it.

Also thanks to Saul Joseph at Chicago's Lincoln Park Zoo, for his valuable data on the animal life in Argentina.

The Southwest
1826

----- The Santa Fé Trail
- - - El Camino Real
······ The Nuns' Journey

© BOOK CREATIONS INC. 1983

· The Miromar ·

FROM NEW ORLEANS

CUBA

PUERTO RICO

LEEWARD ISLANDS

Atlantic Ocean

Venezuela
Colombia

EQUATOR

Ecuador

Brazil

RECIFE

Peru

SALVADOR

Bolivia

CAMPOS
RIO DE
JANIERO

Paraguay

Uruguay

PORTO ALEGRE

Chile

Argentina

BUENOS AIRES

Rio de la Plata

Pacific Ocean

MISSOURI
FRANKLIN

Missouri

Arkansas River

Territory

Red River

Trinity River

Sabine River

La.

NACOGDOCHES

NEW ORLEANS

Gulf of Mexico

The Voyage of the Miromar to South America

RON TOELKE '83

One

To most men, a new year brings hope for the future and for the realization of dreams and ambitions. On this first day of January 1826, however, the tall, hawk-featured, black-bearded man who rode into the little village of La Piedad, some fifty miles southwest of Nuevo Laredo, could only brood over his accursed luck. He had been thwarted in his obsession for money and power, and for this he blamed John Cooper Baines, the man whom he had marked as his most bitter enemy.

Francisco López, who had been a colonel in the Mexican Army, now found himself no better than many of the rebellious *peones* whom he had mercilessly hunted down and slaughtered in the name of Mexico—he who had been personal aide to the opportunistic General Santa Anna and who had been sent on a mission to steal a hidden cache of silver, which John Cooper Baines had discovered in the isolated mountains near the Jicarilla Apache stronghold in New Mexico. López now found himself dishonored, penniless, declared an outlaw with a price on his head, and forced to take refuge in this miserable little hamlet of La Piedad.

But last year he had been so certain of success when he left his sumptuous villa near Mexico City to undertake this mission. Santa Anna had told him how a former lieutenant, Carlos de Escobar, had been under his command and had knowledge of the silver hoard of his brother-in-law, John Cooper Baines. López had then gone to the Double H Ranch in Texas as a spy: He had pretended to be disillusioned with Santa Anna's greed and cruelty and asked for refuge. The Mexican had aroused John Cooper's suspicions, and after he had tried to molest one of the young female servants, he had been ordered to leave. But before his departure, he had eavesdropped on a conversation held by John Cooper, his fa-

1

ther-in-law, Don Diego, and foreman of the ranch Miguel
Sandarbal, concerning the disposition of the many ingots of
silver, which were worth a fortune. He had relayed word to
Santa Anna to have troops sent to meet him along the trail
John Cooper Baines would travel with his Jicarilla escort,
carrying the silver that he intended to deposit in a New Orleans bank.

Then fate had dashed his hopes. The valiant Jicarilla
braves and John Cooper, having been forewarned, routed the
Mexican soldiers, and Francisco López barely escaped with
his life. A second attempt to acquire the silver also ended in
failure when Santa Anna's former aide assembled a malig-
nant army of American renegades, Comancheros, and
Comanche warriors to attack the ranch itself, which the *trabajadores* and other workmen defended valiantly. When
López saw his army decimated, he blasphemed and swore in
a pact with the Devil that he would get his vengeance against
this accursed *americano* who seemed to lead such a charmed
life.

That had been in December, and alone, near madness
from frustration and hunger, López had ridden for many
days and nights, doubling back on his trail to throw off any
pursuers. He had lived on only water and a few berries, driving his frothing gelding to exhaustion till at last, his horse
staggering under him, he rode into the tiny village of La
Piedad.

Dismounting, he sank down on all fours and dragged his
body toward the little well in the public square and began to
drink. Wearily his horse staggered a few steps; then with a
horrible retching sound, the beast toppled, shuddered convulsively, kicked, and died.

Roused by the noise, the crippled, nearly blind, old *alcalde* of La Piedad came out of his *jacal*, the largest adobe
hut in the village. He could dimly make out the figure of a
man in a tattered uniform, wearing the sword that Santa
Anna had once given him, crouching near the well, and the
dead horse just beyond. *"¿Qué pasa, hombre?"* he called to
the stranger.

Bone-weary and crazed with his obsessive hate, López
nonetheless had the good sense to realize that what he needed
most of all at this moment was a place of refuge till, having
regained his strength, he could concoct a way to obtain that
treasure. In truth, he no longer had any intention of acquir-

ing the silver for Santa Anna, who thought his colonel had been killed anyway. No, López wanted to be rich himself, rich enough to buy an army that might even take the field against his own commander and defeat him. Then it would be he who would be ruler of Mexico, not Santa Anna.

So when the old mayor of the town questioned him, López had enough presence of mind to make himself welcome in this humble little village, where no one would think of finding him. He answered in a wracked voice, *"Amigo,* I am Capitán Manuel Ribeiro, attached to the *federalistas* in Chihuahua. My *coronel* had sent me on a mission with a troop of fifty *soldados* to track down two outlaws who had killed their masters' *peones* and stolen *mucho dinero.* But my men betrayed me, and after they had captured the bastards, my *teniente* went over to the side of the *gringos* across the Rio Grande in Texas and took with him the money he had confiscated from his captives."

"But that is treason, *señor capitán,"* the old man wheezed, dolorously shaking his head. "And you, I can see that you are ready to drop in your tracks, as your poor horse has done."

"Es verdad, viejo," López hoarsely acquiesced, drawing in great gulps of air and clenching his fists. "I, an officer in the army of our great Commander Santa Anna, to be so treated, humiliated by *gringos,* and even shot at by my own soldiers when I ordered them to return with me to Chihuahua! I am undone. Can you give me shelter, *viejo?"*

"Pero seguramente, I am the mayor of the town. We are poor here, *señor capitán,* but there is always a little food and water and a *jacal.* One of the young men of our village went off to Nuevo Laredo to help his uncle with his cattle. You are welcome to use his *jacal.* I will take you to it. You would do well to sleep. Have you had food and drink on your journey?"

"Very little, *viejo.* May *el Señor Dios* reward you for your kindness to a *soldado de México."* With this, López crossed himself and the old man imitated him, murmuring, "We are all in His hands, *señor capitán.* I cannot see very well, but I know my way. I have been *alcalde mayor* here for twenty years and more. Take my hand and I will show you the way."

"May your sight be restored and your health as well with it, *viejo,"* López unctuously declared.

When he reached the little hut, he flung himself on the

straw pallet and slept almost till the next noon. He was too weary to think of food or drink, but when he awakened, a comely woman in her mid-thirties, wearing a plain, dark-colored wool dress, was bending over him, staring down with compassionate anxiety.

He blinked his eyes and then slowly sat up. "I have surely gone to Heaven. It is a vision of an angel I see. . . ."

The woman blushed, lowered her eyes, and stammered, "You are alive, *señor capitán.* You have slept all day and all night. I have brought you some broth and some *tacos.* We do not have much meat, but this morning my uncle, the mayor, had one of the men kill a goat, so that you might have nourishing food to give you back your strength."

López gulped down the broth and greedily attacked the *tacos.* He had been ravenously hungry; after he had satisfied his hunger and thirst, he felt resuscitated. With this, he could look at the woman who had so charitably tended him, and he found her intensely appetizing. What he would learn in time was that the niece of the *alcalde* was named Benita Marcado and had been a widow for the past three years. She had longed for a child, but, though married for a dozen years, she and her husband had not been so blessed. He, like the young man whose *jacal* Francisco López now inhabited, had gone to Nuevo Laredo to become a *vaquero,* so that he could bring back money to the poverty-stricken little village. But he had been killed during a stampede, and at about that same time, Benita's old uncle had become nearly blind with cataracts; she had stayed on to look after him.

Swiftly, López decided to conquer her. She was mature and handsome and she could certainly give him back his *macho* manhood. Without it, he might begin to have grave doubts over his failures, and now that he had sworn his pact with the Devil himself, López passionately yearned for the restoration of all his crafty mental and physical powers. He said, with an oily, humble voice as he stared up at Benita Marcado, "You are very kind to a man who has lost everything, señora. I do not wish to be a bother to you."

"You are no bother, *señor capitán.* Now lie still. You must rest and get back your strength." She shook her head compassionately. "My uncle has told me how your *soldados* deserted you—*¡qué lástima!*"

As she visited him each day bringing food and watching him convalesce, López played the role of supplicant for her favors, piously assuring her that he was weary of military ambition and that he desired only the love of a decent woman, a home, perhaps children, if *el Señor Dios* so willed it. Benita, bereaved and lonely, found him handsome and virile and fascinating. Shyly, in bits and pieces, she told him her own story.

He quickly convalesced from his exhaustion, trimmed his pointed beard, and regained his suavity. She was bemused by him: No such man had ever come to La Piedad. Her husband had been a good, earthy, uneducated man who had loved her in his way, but without frills or frippery.

Francisco López found it amusing to play the reformed rake who sought redemption through the love of a decent woman. Besides, for nearly a year he had enjoyed no carnal gratification. Sadly, he remembered the loss of his lovely, compliant *criadas* who had worked for him in his *villa*, now no doubt abandoned or put up for sale by the Mexican government.

A scant two weeks after he came to La Piedad, on a warm January evening with a full moon, he reached for Benita's hand as she turned to leave after having brought him supper, and plaintively murmured, "*Querida*, forgive me if I go too fast—but I'm in love with you."

"*Señor capitán*, do not play a joke on poor Benita—" she stammered, crimsoning.

"I have done many bad things in my life, my dear one," he said with a self-pitying tremolo, "but of one thing I am certain: I have fallen in love with you because you are good and kind and beautiful. I am lonely, I begin my life over again, and if you would but share it with me, I could again be rich and powerful, as once I was."

"But, *señor capitán*—"

"Please, it would make me get well the sooner if you would call me by my name," he slyly interposed. "It is Manuel."

"M-Manuel. I am only a peasant woman; I am not good enough for you—"

"You are wrong!" He emphatically shook his head and took a firmer hold of her hand as she stood beside his pallet. "I have been to Mexico City, and I have seen the fancy daughters of the *ricos* in their beautiful, expensive gowns. I tell you, Benita *querida*, that not one of them is worthy of you. You are a woman. They are only pretty puppets. I swear to you that I love you."

She trembled and was lost. Never in her life had any man addressed her so passionately.

He saw the play of emotion on her handsome face and smiled to himself as he ardently pursued his courtship. "I swear to you by all that is good and holy that I have never before met a woman such as you, my dearest Benita. Say that you care for me a little. I beg this of you."

"Oh, no, señor—I—I mean, Manuel, a man like you must not beg! It is not worthy. Oh, Manuel, yes, I want you, too! I cannot help myself. Be kind and gentle with me, I beg of you!" she plaintively entreated.

"I shall be gentle with you, that I swear to you on my honor," he said as he drew her down to him on the pallet. Her arms linked around his neck, and López tasted the willing sweetness of her mouth. He shuddered with desire. For the first time in a long while he felt himself a man again, capable of all prowess, yes, even keened to the razor-sharp purpose of paying back that damned *gringo* in Texas the Indians called *el Halcón*—the Hawk. As he contemplated her face, soft and lovely in the acknowledgment of her desire, he murmured, "Is there a priest in this village, *mi corazón?*"

"Oh, yes, my dear one—Padre Luis Caldorna, the cousin of my uncle."

"He can marry us, Benita. Tomorrow I will ask him to read the banns. That is, if you will have me as your husband?"

She uttered an ardent sigh and, for answer, gave him her mouth as her arms locked the more tightly around him. So overwhelmed was she by this incredible wooing by a man she believed to be unattainable above her that she offered only token protest when he began to disrobe her. With her enticing, large-breasted, and large-hipped body naked beneath his, he possessed her, and she whimpered only, "Oh, Manuel, it is a sin. We are not yet married! Oh, please—oh, I want you so much—Holy Mother, forgive my sin—aah, oh, Manuel!"

Restored to all his sensual powers, Francisco López once again began to plan. This time, he resolved, he must be cautious and cunning. To begin with, he would need the best horse he could find. He had already noticed two fine geldings in the little stable behind the mayor's *jacal*. He also needed a stake so that he might purchase the best possible rifle and a brace of pistols and plenty of ammunition. What his army of renegades, Comancheros, and Comanche had not been able to do, he, Francisco López, would do by himself, utilizing the element of surprise. His conceit permitted him to see only the positive side of this desperate venture.

The first thing he had to do was cement his union with Benita Marcado. Accordingly, on the day after his seduction of the widow, López visited the tiny church at the end of the small public square. When he entered, his lips curled contemptuously: It was hardly worth the name of church; there were barely any decorations. There was an ordinary brass crucifix at the altar, resting on a threadbare cloth, and no stained glass or religious statues. An old priest, frail and white-haired, knelt at one side, then rose, crossed himself, and went to the altar, where he again genuflected.

López cleared his throat and waited till the old priest slowly turned. "Excuse me, *padre*," he began in a genial tone with an ingratiating smile. "I did not mean to disturb you."

"You are the newcomer to La Piedad, my son, are you not? My cousin the mayor told me of you."

"Yes, *mi padre*. I am weary of the military life and the political struggle in Mexico City. I wish to settle down here and to become a villager of La Piedad. Also, I have been blessed by the love of a fine woman, and I have come today to ask you to read the banns between us. It is Benita Marcado."

The old priest stared at López; then he beamed. "God's ways are inscrutable, my son. She is indeed a wonderful woman, and she lost her good *esposo* through an accident. All this while, she has remained here to care for her old uncle—but it is a lonely life for a young woman who should be fruitful and bear many children. You say you and she are affianced?"

"She accepted me last night, *mi padre*. I am honored and privileged. I will make her a good husband. Bless me, *mi padre*." López knelt in the aisle of the little church and bowed his head sanctimoniously while the smiling old priest said his orisons, then murmured, "Go, my son, with His blessing. On Friday, at vespers, I will read the banns between you and the Señora Marcado."

"I look forward to the happy day when you will unite us

as man and wife, *mi padre*. Thank you again. *Vaya con Dios.*"

"You also, my son." The old priest made the sign of the cross, and López solwly rose, nodded toward him, then turned and left the church.

That night, lying on his straw pallet with Benita in his arms, he told her that he had asked to have the banns read, and boasted about what a good husband he would be. Then he fell sorrowful, and she, quivering with ecstasy, awakened to the pleasures of the flesh as never before, not even with her husband in their early years together, wistfully murmured, "Why are you so sad, Manuel?"

"It is because I realize how poor I have become, my dear one," he said with a long sigh. "I wish I could take you from this little hamlet to Mexico City and dress you in jewels and fine silk gowns, as you deserve."

She kissed him, stroking his cheeks with her soft palms, and whispered, "The thought is sweet, but, *querido*, I do not ask for this. No one in La Piedad has much *dinero*. It is a hard life. We farm a little, and once in awhile, we sell a pig or a cow, if we are lucky. Only my uncle has saved a little from his years as *alcalde*."

"You say that your uncle has put away some money?" López assumed a casual tone.

"*Sí, querido*. Besides my dead father, he had another brother, Hermano Bensadón, who was a *capataz* for a *hacendado* many miles south of Nuevo Laredo. When Hermano died, he left the money he had made from his little ranch to my uncle. He keeps it now, hidden away. If things go badly with us, if the crops do not come in and we do not sell anything to the *soldados* who come through the village on their patrols, then he takes a few *pesos* and buys what food we need. Oh, he is a good man, *querido*."

"Is this village ever attacked by *bandidos, mi dulce?*" López asked as his hands began to stroke her breasts and thighs. He felt her passions roused again and knew that she was like a harp on which he could play whatever tune he desired.

"Ah, how you stir me, *hombre!* Oh, it will be so good between us! I could never have a child, but perhaps with you, Manuel, if *el Señor Dios* so wills it! How wonderful it would be to have a son by you!" She moaned, arching herself as he again possessed her.

After he had made love to her, Santa Anna's former aide went on with his cunning questions. "The reason I asked about the *bandidos, mi corazón,* was that it would be well to have some weapons to defend ourselves, in case we are attacked. Does anyone have a rifle or a *pistola* in La Piedad?"

Benita, her eyes closed, her head tilted back, panting from the effects of their lovemaking, said, "Only my uncle—he was given a fine Belgian rifle—ah, Manuel, what a lover you are—it is a Belgian rifle—it was given to him by another *capitán* of the *federalistas* about five years ago. It happened when my *tío* rallied the other men of his village and beat off an attack by *bandidos.* One of them had a price on his head—I do not remember his name—but that was why he was given the rifle. Oh, Manuel, must we talk now? I'd much rather you make love to me again. Such joy, such bliss—hold me tightly—have me!"

"Of course, my sweet one," López murmured. "I ask these things only because I am eager to keep you safe in my arms like this. Hold me and kiss me—just so—now, my dove, my perfect treasure, my wife-to-be!"

Late in the afternoon of the next day, Benita went out with the other women to the little garden at the western edge of the village to gather vegetables for a stew. This would be the main dish of a feast to which all the village had been invited for the celebration of the union between the handsome captain and the mayor's niece. Meanwhile, Francisco López stealthily intercepted Mayor Oswaldo Bensadón just as he was about to go to the church to pray.

"A word with you, *señor alcalde,*" Santa Anna's former aide smilingly requested. "What I have to say to you should be for no other ears except yours. Shall we step inside your *jacal?*"

"As you wish, Manuel," the old man said, smiling and patting López's shoulder. "You are practically one of the family now, you see, so I call you by your first name. Now then, what have you to say to me?"

López cast a swift look outside and saw that the few men of the village had gone to the fields to help the women. The square was deserted and the sky was darkening with an oncoming rainstorm. He had buckled on his sword and now swiftly he drew it from its sheath and put the tip to the old man's throat. *"Señor alcalde,"* he growled, "you are going to tell me where you have hidden the sack of *pesos* and that fine Belgian rifle which the *federalistas* gave you."

"But I don't understand! Why do you threaten me with a sword? You are going to marry my niece—"

"So I wished you to think," López interrupted.

"But this is unheard-of—we are so poor—"

"Do you take me for a fool, old man? Your niece told me that you have saved some money. I need it. You will give it to me, and the rifle as well."

"I won't—by what right do you dare—we took you in when you were nearly dead of fatigue and hunger and thirst, and this is how you repay us?"

"One does not talk of debts at such a time, you old fool. I'll find a way to get what I want!" Casting his sword to one side, López seized the frail old man, bound his wrists behind his back with his sash, and took a bandanna from his pocket and gagged him. Then he flung the mayor down on his straw pallet and retrieved the sword.

"Now then," López announced as he put the tip of the sword on the old man's groin, "you're going to show me where you've hidden the money and the rifle. Nod your head to tell me that you're ready to talk, and then you will show me where they are. If you play me false, I'll cut off your *cojones*!"

Oswaldo Bensadón writhed as he shrank back from the sharp tip of the shining sword, his eyes goggling with horror at this sudden, unexpected treachery. Cruelly, López pressed the point of the sword into the old man's upper thigh, drawing blood. "Be quick; I have little patience with a fool like you," he insisted, and then drew blood from the other thigh.

Agonized, shuddering, the old *alcalde* at last vigorously nodded his head, his tear-blurred, rheumy eyes fixing on a colored cloth mat at the other end of the room. Comprehending, López grinned. "It's hidden under there, is that it? You'd best be telling the truth, or I'll cut them off for you—not that they do you any good now, at your age."

Thrusting the mat to one side, López scrabbled at the dirt floor with both hands, then uttered an excited cry. "I feel something!"

Under a thin layer of soil was a little trapdoor covering a hole in the ground. Lifting the trapdoor, López reached into the hole and drew out the Belgian rifle, then a pouch of ammunition and powder. Under these was a brown cloth sack with a drawstring, which he lifted and shook, grinning to hear the jingle of coins. "*Gracias, amigo.* For these things I'll let you keep your useless life. Only, so you won't get loose and raise an outcry, you'll forgive me if I put you to sleep for a little while."

Reversing the sword in his hand, he brought the heavy hilt down on the old man's temple. Oswaldo Bensadón slumped back, inert. López straightened, replaced the sword in its sheath, and, carrying the rifle and the sack of *pesos,* strode to the little *jacal* of Benita Marcado.

He had found a box of cheap cigars in the drawer of a battered little desk in a corner of the *jacal* of the old *alcalde,* and he lit one now and waited. After leaving the mayor's hut, he had visited the little stable at the back and the two fine geldings. He would take the roan; it was the fastest and the strongest. Then he would go to Nuevo Laredo, enjoying a week of good food and drink and the company of a *puta,* a really talented one who could be bought for some of the silver *pesos* in the sack. He chuckled sardonically to himself: Perhaps Benita might even accompany him.

As he puffed at the cigar, he saw in his mind's eye the details of how he would ride back to the Double H Ranch at night, wait in ambush for that damned *gringo,* take him by surprise, and knock him out with the butt of the rifle. Then he would torture him—perhaps he would even heat the sword and touch the white-hot point to the *americano*'s flesh, till the latter agreed to take him to the silver. Then, of course, he would kill him.

His smile was diabolic, and the flux of madness seized him again as he dreamed of how he could recoup his good fortune, after all the disasters the *americano* had caused him.

Out in the field, Benita excused herself to go back to her hut to get her shawl, for the evening had suddenly turned cool. As she entered, she started to see López seated on her pallet, grinning and puffing at his cigar. "Manuel—I thought you'd be in your hut!" she exclaimed.

"I've decided to leave La Piedad, *querida.*" He rose, took a long puff of the cigar, and blew the smoke at her.

She glanced down at the pallet and then drew back, a hand on her mouth, her eyes wide with disbelief as she saw the sack and the rifle of her uncle.

"Yes," López said, "I persuaded your uncle to lend these

to me. He has no use for money or a rifle. Now, *mi corazón*, take off your clothes. If you please me, I may take you with me."

"You robbed my uncle! How could you, Manuel? We trusted you!"

"Enough of such stupid talk!" he growled. "Woman, you serve only one purpose, to satisfy a man's desire. Take off your clothes, or I'll tear them from you!"

"No! What a fool I was, to be tricked by your promises! Now I can see it all—and I was the Judas who betrayed my poor Tío Oswaldo—I told you about the money and the rifle, and you—oh, *Dios*, did you kill him—?"

"No, I didn't kill him. He's sleeping and he won't bother us. Now, for the last time, do what I told you to, *mujer*! I want you naked!"

"No, I will call for help, I will—stop—stop!" As she turned to the doorway of the hut, López seized her, planted a hand over her mouth, and dragged her back to the pallet, flinging her down upon it. Then, kneeling, brutally clenching his right hand, he struck her violently on the cheekbone, stunning her.

"Now then, *puta*, you don't say no to me. By the testicles of the Devil, I've had better women than you in my day!" He ripped at her cotton dress until she was naked. She closed her eyes and whimpered in shame and fright.

Then, brutally mounting her, he threatened, "If you promise to obey me, I could take you with me—"

"I'd rather die! Oh, you're hurting me! Let me be! I loathe you! Oh, you hurt; you hurt me so—" she groaned as he ruthlessly forced himself upon her.

When at last he had satiated himself with her, he rose and buttoned his breeches, then moved swiftly to retrieve the rifle and the sack of *pesos*.

"You won't come with me? A pity," he taunted her as he moved toward the doorway. "You're not too bad in bed. Your last chance, Benita."

The marks of his fingernails streaked her flesh as, half fainting from his brutality and from her own shame, she raised herself on an elbow and panted, "Now I see what a liar you are, how full of deceit and hatred. I'll wash away the contamination of your flesh against mine. I'll ask Padre Caldorna to pray for my salvation."

"Do so, if it pleases you, woman. I've done with you."

"So you have. But you, Manuel Ribeiro, I swear you'll have no peace on earth. Yes, God Himself has turned His face from you. I shall pray to Him to strike you down."

"I deny God, *mujer!*" Francisco López burst into jeering laughter, then strode back to the widow, bent down, and slapped her across the mouth. "I renounce Him for the Devil. He'll serve my purpose better. *Adiós*, Benita!"

With a last burst of laughter he walked out of the hut and to the mayor's stable. He selected the roan gelding and mounted it, after having placed the sack of *pesos* in an old saddlebag that he found atop a bale of hay. Then he rode out of La Piedad as night was approaching and the rain began to fall, even as the men and women were returning from the fields, laughing and talking of the feast that would celebrate the banns.

As he headed the roan gelding north, López's eyes glittered as he thought of his revenge against John Cooper Baines.

Two

On the January day when Benita Marcado first yielded to Francisco López in the distant Mexican village of La Piedad, there was joyous celebration in Texas at the Double H Ranch, known also as *Hacienda del Halcón*. It was the wedding day of Teresa de Rojado and Carlos de Escobar.

The day was bright and sunny, with a cloudless blue sky. Throughout the day, the great new bell from Belgium pealed from its steeple, its joyous sound proclaiming the happy tidings of this union that Carlos had so ardently sought for over two years. The wedding would take place shortly before sundown, and young Padre Jorge Pastronaz would preside in the newly rebuilt church, whose ravages from the fire set by López's attacking Comanches and Comancheros had been swiftly repaired by the *trabajadores*.

Don Diego was ecstatic over this promise of new happiness and new life for his beloved son, who had lost his first wife, Weesayo, but who had found renewed love with Teresa. Don Diego had given orders that there should be a great feast and had enjoined the old cook, Tía Margarita, to commandeer all of the *criadas* and the wives of the *trabajadores* themselves to aid her in preparing food and drink. Ernest Henson and Matthew Robisard, who had come to visit the Double H Ranch on their return from a trading trip to Santa Fe, had remained as welcome guests at the urging of Don Diego. As he gruffly told them, trying not to show too much pride over the happiness of young Carlos, "It is only fitting that you have a place of honor among our wedding guests because of your valiant part in the defense of our *hacienda* last December."

Out near the bunkhouse of the *vaqueros*, the workers had erected two huge spits and ovens. They had slaughtered six lambs and six steers, expertly butchered them, and were turning them on the spits over the crackling fires. Large wooden tables had been brought out into the courtyard of the ranch house, and the *criadas* had covered them with the finest tablecloths, using silverware and napkins imported from Delft in Holland. There were wine goblets, and Don Diego had contributed two cases of Madeira, one of port, and two of wine from the Canary Islands, as well as several excellent bottles of old red Bordeaux.

Tía Margarita had been busy from noon of the day before, baking pies and cakes, making *tacos, enchiladas,* and *chile* with sweet red peppers, kidney beans, and her own special spices. As the *pièce de résistance* of her heroic culinary efforts, she had baked a special three-tiered wedding cake covered with white frosting, while Esteban Morales, assistant *capataz* of the ranch, had artistically carved little figurines out of sweet, hardened icing. Esteban's wife, Concepción, had adorned the figurines with bits of cloth to represent the bridegroom and the bride, with a remarkably lifelike result.

There would be dancing, too, and six of the most musically talented *trabajadores* would play the accordian, the violin, the flute, the guitar, the mandolin, and the drum. Don Diego had instructed them to play many of the old dance tunes he remembered from his days at the court of Madrid, years ago before he had been wrongfully exiled to the New

World and had found a new life. He himself had rehearsed the musicians.

Jeremy Gaige, the old prospector who had come along with the two St. Louis traders, had spruced up for the wedding and the feast to follow. He had trimmed his straggly beard and scrubbed himself at dawn, having gone to the kitchen to entreat Tía Margarita to let him have several wooden tubs of hot water and, at the same time, asking her to be silent about it. "You see, ma'am," he awkwardly explained, "t'ain't right for an old prospector like me to be dandified up, you understand. But this is somethin' special, and it's 'cause Don Diego's son is gettin' hitched to that cute filly. Just the same, I'd be much obliged if you keep mum about my takin' me a bath so early in the day."

"Your secret will be safe with me, Señor Gaige," Tía Margarita said, almost choking with laughter but managing to keep a straight face. She liked the old man, for he had endeared himself to the children of the *hacienda*, telling them colorful anecdotes of his early prospecting days, of how he had fought a bear with a knife and lived to tell the tale, and how a tribe of Blackfoot Indians had taken after him and chased him over a plain, where he had found refuge in a secret cave and lived three days and nights on bark and berries. What was more, having lost her husband some years before, Tía Margarita herself was glad for the old prospector's amiable companionship.

Ernest Henson and Matthew Robisard, dressed in their best, came out to join him as he smilingly watched the musicians assemble at their bench and saw the *criadas* piling the table with food. "Well, Jeremy, it's a far cry from our trading days, isn't it?" Ernest chuckled.

"Sure is, Mr. Henson. You know, I've been thinkin'. You and Mr. Robisard there, you've both been mighty kind to me, and I ain't never gonna forget it. But I've got a hankerin' to stay in this country. It's big and beautiful. You see, I'm gittin' older by the minute, and I ain't up to snuff when it comes to ridin' all the way back to St. Looey with you. I'd like to try my last hand at prospectin' some out here, 'cause I think it'd make me young again. Would you feel it mighty bad iffen I was to stay here a spell? That is, if Don Diego'll put up with me?"

He cast a hopeful, wistful look at the white-haired *hidalgo*, and Don Diego, overhearing, came up to the three men, put his arm affectionately around Jeremy Gaige's thin shoulders, and declared, *"Mi amigo*, it would be a pleasure to have you as a longtime guest. You have earned your keep the way you divert the children with your exciting stories. They would miss you if you left, so be assured that our hospitality will continue."

"That's mighty kind of you, Don Diego, mighty kind," Jeremy muttered.

In the little chapel in the *hacienda*, Teresa de Rojado knelt in prayer. She would go from there to her bedroom to put on her wedding dress, and Catarina, Don Diego's lovely daughter and John Cooper's wife, would be her matron of honor.

She clasped her hands and bowed her head before the little statue of the Christ that an old Indian had made and that a rich *hacendado* had refused to pay for on the grounds that it was sacrilegious, a statue that Don Diego had bought because he could appreciate the feeling and the devotion of the old Indian's handiwork. "Holy Mother, blessed of our dear Lord," the beautiful widow prayed, "I ask You to guide me, that I may make my husband Carlos a good wife. I love him, Holy Mother. I did not hold him off all this time because I wanted to test his love for me, but because I was not certain myself that it was proper for me to marry after my husband's death. Yet I know now that my life and his will be inseparable, for we have so much in common, and we have fought together side by side like gallant comrades. He has suffered far more than I—my husband was old, and I expected his death, but Carlos lost that beautiful Apache girl who was so young and vital and who gave him children. Holy Mother, let me be a wise and loving mother to them. Grant me also, though I am past thirty years of age, the blessing of childbirth, for I wish to give my husband a child of love as proof of the devotion and the tenderness I feel toward him. Hear me, be sure of my humble gratitude for Your compassion and concern for me during these last years."

She crossed herself and rose, her face aglow with joy and the anticipation of what this day truly meant to her and Carlos de Escobar.

As she straightened, crossing herself again before the statue of the *Cristo*, she heard the tolling of the bell, and she blushed. She was remembering that day, only a few weeks past, when she had at last agreed to marry Don Diego's gallant son. . . .

It had been on the day before Christmas just last month, when the young priest had drawn on the bell rope to ring out the thanks of everyone on the Double H Ranch to Him Who protected them from the terrible danger of López's attack, as well as to express their joy at the birthday of the blessed Son of the most merciful God.

Teresa had stood side by side with Carlos, and they had looked up and listened to the wonderful, clear, joyous sound of that bell. She had looked at him with grave eyes, and they had both been silent a long moment, till at last he had taken her hand and murmured, "Teresa, come with me to the little creek. There is something I must say to you."

She had crimsoned under his gaze, and her heart beat faster. She knew Carlos as a man who would lay down his life for her, who had fought side by side with her on the journey from New Mexico when they had been attacked by López's band. He had been wounded as she had been.

She nodded, and when his fingers entwined with hers, she made no sign of protest but went with him till they were alone under the blue sky.

"Teresa, I love you truly and deeply. I wish to spend the rest of my life with you; I wish you to be the mother of my children, those who exist and those who, may the good God grant, may come of our union. I swear to you constancy, respect, and the purest love, if you become my wife."

She turned away, trembling with an emotion she could no longer suppress. She knew how truly he had been devoted to her and how constant he had been in that devotion these past two years and more. Now that they had shared hardship together, had faced danger and the risk of death, had fought side by side like true *compañeros,* she could no longer deny that she returned his love.

There was nothing for her in Havana, only the wealth her first husband had left her and some of which she had brought from her own family. Also, there was nothing for her in Taos, where she had come after her husband's death to live with Don Sancho de Pladero, an old friend of her father's, and the good friend of Don Diego, as well. It was there in Taos that she had first met Carlos, about two years before the death of Don Sancho.

As Carlos squeezed her hand and stared wordlessly into her eyes, Teresa de Rojado knew that there would be an aching void in her heart if she again rejected his proposal and went back to Havana.

"You are courageous and good and kind, and no woman could ask for more," Teresa said softly. "But are you truly sure that it is not loneliness that makes you ask me to marry you, Carlos?"

His face had hardened with resolve, and the warmth had gone out of his eyes. There was a kind of hopeless anguish in his voice as he went down on his knees and brought her hand to his lips and kissed it, then said, "I truly love you; I desire you. I love your mind and soul and spirit that will always keep me trying to better myself to be worthy of you. I do not ask you to marry me because I have no mother for my children, Teresa. I am still young enough to desire you as a woman, to want to be your lover and your companion, to know all of you, to bring you joy, and to give you no pain or sorrow. I pledge you on my honor and with all my soul that it is as if I loved for the first time, Teresa."

She closed her eyes, then said, "You mustn't kneel to me, *mi* Carlos. I married a man old enough to be my father, and I did so for my own father's sake. So truly I have not known love. My husband respected me, was kind to me—but here I am a mature woman at an age when most women already have their children. You have proved yourself to me many times over, *mi* Carlos. If you will have me, I would be proud to be your wife, and I will try to be all the things you wish me to be, because I do love you."

He had uttered a joyous cry and taken her in his arms, and from there they had gone to see the priest to arrange for the banns, and to set their wedding day for three weeks hence. . . .

Now she headed for her bedroom, for it was time to don her wedding gown. It could not be white, since this was her second marriage, but it was of a beautiful blue silk that she had bought in Havana.

Catarina was there to help her with the gown. Teresa's eyes were wet with tears as John Cooper's beautiful dark-haired wife hugged her and exclaimed, "You look absolutely wonderful, Teresa! You will make my brother so happy! I know how much you love him."

"I do, with all my heart and soul! And I couldn't ask for a sweeter sister-in-law, dear Catarina!"

Outside on the *patio*, the children shared in the excitement of the celebration. They had been rehearsed in the parts they would play in the church. Don Diego told them they must be very good and do exactly as Padre Pastronaz instructed. The young priest, who had hitherto been known as Fra Pastronaz, had received a letter from the bishop of Santa Fe only last week announcing that he had been accepted into the priesthood because of his admirable acts of faith and his devotion as a lay priest. Henceforth, he could be called *padre* and have all the authority of a priest of the church.

Diego, Carlos's stalwart twelve-year-old son, was waiting outside the church, talking to Francesca de Escobar, age eleven, the child whom Doña Inez had given Don Diego and who had brought them such great joy in their old age. At first, Francesca had found Diego something of an overbearing, loud-mouthed bully, but he had given her one of his prized toy soldiers in a gesture of reconciliation. Since then, they had been inseparable friends. She said to him now, "I am so happy that my big brother is going to marry Señora de Rojado!"

"Yes, she's very pretty. She'll be my new mother."

"I know. But she fences and rides so well; she won't be the usual kind of mother."

"You're right about that," Diego said, grinning boyishly. "She's promised to teach me how to fence. Of course, Miguel Sandarbal has helped me a little, but it would be fun fencing with her with the button foils."

"Well now, Diego," Francesca could not help twitting him, remembering how earlier he had treated her so condescendingly, "you mustn't expect to beat her just because you're a man and she's a woman. She's a very fine swordswoman. My father and Miguel both say so, and they should know. Remember, Miguel had his own fencing school back in Spain, before he came to America with my father."

"I don't think she'd be easy to beat because she's a woman. And now I also think you can do things just as well as I can, even though you're a girl."

Francesca realized that this was high praise from Diego, and she accepted it without protesting further. She rewarded him with a smile, then turned her attention to the growing crowd now assembling outside the church in the bright January sun.

The hour had come, and the spectators filed into the church. When they were all seated, full of anticipation, Bess Sandarbal, Miguel's blond-haired American wife, began to play the wedding march on the church's spinet piano, and Don Diego, looking proud and solemn, escorted Teresa de Rojado in her blue silk wedding gown down the aisle to where Carlos awaited her before the altar.

The ceremony was simple and beautiful. Carlos placed the ring on Teresa's finger, and when it was done, the priest blessed them and made the sign of the cross over them. They turned and went back down the aisle as one of the *trabajadores* began to pull the bell rope to announce the completion of the ceremony.

"My wife, my beloved Teresa," Carlos murmured, and he took her into his arms and kissed her tenderly on the mouth.

"*Mi esposo, querido* Carlos," she whispered back. She returned his kiss.

Miguel Sandarbal, the elderly *capataz* of the Double H Ranch, now joined his Bess, who was awaiting the birth of their fourth child. They smiled as the handsome young Spaniard took Teresa in his arms and imparted a long kiss on her lips. Miguel sighed deeply with satisfaction. It seemed to him that the cycle of his life had come to completion, and yet, if the good God allowed it, there would still be a few more years in which to indulge himself in the love of a beautiful young wife, children from her loins and his, and the satisfaction of knowing that he had served Don Diego de Escobar and the latter's son, Carlos, and daughter, Catarina, with unswerving fealty and courage. Bess saw his beaming face and teasingly whispered, "One would think it was your own wedding, *mi corazón.*"

Wishing to show her that despite being sixty-one, he was still *macho*, he leaned over to whisper into her ear, "*Querida,* when I am beside you, I feel as if it is my wedding night all over again." He was rewarded to see her delicious blush and to feel her hand squeeze his in decorous rebuke.

Outside the church, Teresa and Carlos found that many of the little children of the *trabajadores* had gathered in opposite rows and were throwing flowers at them. Turning to one of the brown-eyed, black-haired little girls, who was not more than six, Teresa took her up in her arms, kissed her, and said, *"Gracias, mi dulce."*

"You are welcome, señora," the little girl gravely replied. "It was the Señor Morales who showed us how to do this. We want to wish you *felicidad."*

"You darling!" Teresa exclaimed, and there were tears in her eyes as she kissed the child again before setting her down. Then she turned to Carlos and took his hand and held it firmly as she whispered, "I have prayed to the Holy Virgin that I may bear you a child, *mi esposo."*

Carlos trembled and could not speak for a moment as he escorted her to the place of honor at the outdoor tables where the feast would take place. When he seated her, he put his hands on her shoulders, kissed her cheek, and whispered, "I, too, have prayed, my sweet one. I have thanked *el Señor Dios* that you said yes to my unending proposals, because I know how fortunate I am."

The others followed them to the tables, and Don Diego, observing this tender exchange between the newlywed young couple, gruffly turned aside so as not to intrude. He said to Doña Inez, "My dearest wife, how good it is to see Carlos happy again! It is all that I have prayed for ever since that terrible day—" He fell silent, remembering Carlos's desolation of heart when his first wife had died, which had prompted him to join Santa Anna in the vain illusion that he would be fighting for the independence of Mexico. Now, all that was past, and it was well to banish such sorrowful memories. This evening heralded a wonderful new life for his son.

The feast began and the six musicians began to play cheerful tunes, recalling the courtly dances of the Old World. There were the *paso doble,* the *malagueña,* and a jaunty *bolero.* Later, after they had eaten and drunk their fill, they danced. There was a full moon and stars twinkled in the dark blue, cloudless sky. Don Diego looked up at the sky and then put his arm around Doña Inez's shoulders and whispered, "I am so content with my life, now that you are with me to bless it and to guide me, my dearest Inez. Ah, when I left the presence of His Majesty that terrible day in Madrid, how could I have dreamed that God would have consoled me for my loss of Dolores by giving you, her faithful sister, to me?"

"My dear one," Doña Inez said, turning to him and putting her soft palm on his cheek. "And I thank God daily for giving you to me. I have had years of happiness."

"Ah, *mi* Inez, we have other joys in store. Only today I had a letter from Padre Madura in Taos. It appears he had word from the mother superior of a small group of Dominican nuns whose abbey is in Parras. The town has fallen on evil times, and she wrote Padre Madura, asking if he could give them a mission in Taos. He felt that the unsettled conditions under their new *alcalde* in Taos made it unwise, and so he suggested that they journey here, believing I would help them."

"It would be a wonderful thing if you would, dear Diego!" Doña Inez enthusiastically answered. "To have a mission here and a school with it—why, it would draw all of us, the *vaqueros* and *trabajadores* and the new settlers and their families, closer together."

"I knew you would feel that way, my dearest. So of course I wrote back to Padre Madura that when they come here, I shall do everything to make them welcome and offer them the opportunity to establish a mission here at the *Hacienda del Halcón*."

"You are such a kind, generous man, *mi corazón*," Doña Inez whispered as she gave him a quick kiss.

"Ah, how happy I feel tonight—my only regret is that conditions are so unsettled in Taos. With my old friend Don Sancho gone, and with the new *alcalde mayor* governing the land with an iron hand, I am afraid there will be much civil strife, and even rebellion of the Pueblo Indians there. But enough of such gloomy thoughts on this of all nights."

Andrew and Charles, John Cooper's strong young sons, were seated on either side of their two younger sisters: almost eight-year-old Ruth and three-year-old Carmen. Across from them were little Inez and Dawn, Carlos's two daughters by his first wife, the Apache girl Weesayo, who had died by her own hands after being kidnapped by a cruel *hacendado*. Teresa sat next to his children and Carlos to her left. His heart was full, and when his father rose to propose a toast to the happy couple, Carlos lifted his glass and made a sign with it to Teresa, then to his children, and called, "Diego, I toast you, for now you have a wonderful new mother."

"I know, *mi padre,* and I am very happy for you and for myself," Diego smilingly retorted. Then, getting up from his place at the bench, he went around to Teresa and asked, "*Mi madre,* may I kiss you?"

Don Diego had to clear his throat several times to continue with his toast, so moved was he. When he looked to another side of the table, he could see Catarina, who had her youngest, little Coraje, in her arms, seated next to his son-in-law, John Cooper Baines. It was like a dream, he told himself. How indeed could a man have believed that after having been cast out of the king's favor, to return home to find his wife dying, he would have come all the way across the Atlantic to the dusty little town of Taos, only to meet this unusual *gringo* who had also traveled so far to find a new life, in his case with Don Diego's daughter Catarina. All that was so many years ago, and they had grown in love and prospered, coming to this new land of Texas to make a home for their families, free from the harsh restrictions of Mexican dictators and generals.

So, aloud, his eyes misty with tenderness, Don Diego called out in a hearty voice, "*Amigos,* eat and drink and then let us dance to the music of these good *caballeros,* these loyal *trabajadores* of ours, who are part of our great family, and who prove that God has made all of us to be brothers and friends, never enemies!"

Loud huzzahs acclaimed this generous accolade, as Miguel and Esteban Morales, the assistant *capataz* of the ranch, acknowledged the toast on behalf of the *vaqueros* and the workers. Each, in turn, goblet in hand, proclaimed the worthiness and goodness of Don Diego as the best *patrón* in all of this new, growing country.

Darkness had settled by the time they finished eating and drinking. Carlos served Teresa, but he himself was abstemious, for tonight was one of unbridled joy, and nothing must cloud his senses in the final realization of his dreams of love.

"To the dance, all of you," Don Diego cried, reveling in his role as master of ceremonies. He rose somewhat unsteadily from the table, goblet filled and eager to make another toast. Doña Inez smiled to herself: She would not remonstrate with her elderly husband, for she knew how deeply he was moved by his son's wedding.

Don Diego turned to her, tendering his arm as an *hidalgo* of old Spain would have done at court, and with the polished manner of the *hidalgo* he had once been, graciously demanded, "Will the grand lady whom most I love in all this world do me the honor of this dance?"

As she rose, Doña Inez smiled tenderly and tapped his hand with her fan. He took her beyond the tables into the clearing to begin the dance. The musicians began to play a stately waltz, and Don Diego and Doña Inez for a moment were the center of all attention as the *trabajadores*, the children, Carlos and Teresa, John Cooper and Catarina, and Bess and Miguel, watched entranced to see the white-haired old man lead his wife with a polished elegance that would have done credit to a man half his years. There was applause, and now Carlos invited his beautiful wife to join his father and stepmother; the others waited as the two couples danced side by side.

"Let Concepción hold your baby for a moment, my dear one," John Cooper whispered to Catarina, and she joyously assented. Concepción Morales took little Coraje and cradled him in her arms while the tall American's black-haired, green-eyed wife rose and was escorted by her blond, bearded husband to the dance floor.

Soon, the clearing was filled with other couples, and they danced the *sarabande*, and finally, because this was a night of love and passion, as well as of celebration, the *zapateado*.

Teresa and Carlos took part in every dance. They did not speak, but each watched the other in the soft night, and their eyes spoke a language known only to lovers, mystic and adoring, with the promise of untold rapture and total surrender. Finally, when Carlos could bear this sweet torment no longer, just as the last dance ended, he whispered, *"Mi corazón*, shall we take leave of our friends and our family and begin our marriage?"

"With the greatest eagerness in the world, *mi esposo*," was Teresa's faint reply.

He offered her his arm, and they walked sedately back to the *hacienda*, while Don Diego, ever tactful, again filled his goblet and proposed a toast to his loyal *capataz*, Miguel Sandarbal, ". . . to felicitate him on his beautiful wife, the Señora Bess, who will soon bring another Sandarbal into this happy world!"

Faintly, the strains of music wafted toward the spacious bedroom of Carlos de Escobar. He, wearing his *calzones* and a red silk robe that Don Diego had given him as a Christmas gift, went to the little chapel to say a final prayer before his long-yearned-for union with Teresa. He was almost as terrified as a schoolboy, for although they had mingled their blood through the wounds they had sustained in fighting off Francisco López's attackers, though they had known adversities and sorrow and bereavement, he remained a stranger to her sweet intimacies. He was anxious not to do anything that might offend her. He crossed himself and went back to the bedroom.

Teresa had been grateful for the privacy to prepare both her person and her thoughts. She had carefully hung up the blue silk gown and chose her finest white silk chemise trimmed with lace at the hem and bodice. A single candle burned on the bed table, and its flickering glow touched her cheekbones and eyes and made her face exquisitely enigmatic, partly that of a young girl who is fearful, yet eager, partly that of a mature woman who is in control of herself, yet has doubts.

She moved toward the huge bed and drew aside the hand-embroidered quilt to uncover the soft white sheets. She started to blow the candle out but then straightened and, with a proud smile, refused to avail herself of this subterfuge. There was no need to play the prim, timid novice at love. Let him see her as she was, and let him initiate her as he desired.

He entered, closing the door softly and drawing the bolt. She straightened, her arms at her sides, a tender smile on her face. He moved toward her, his eyes glowing with adoration. All her last fears were swept away by that look of ineffable longing and joy, mixed with the most poignant devotion. Her heart went out to him with a great wave of tenderness as she held out her arms and murmured, *"Mi esposo querido, mi* Carlos."

His arms went around her, and he sought her mouth as they kissed each other hungrily yet with great tenderness and love. The music had stopped, and all the *trabajadores* and the others had gone to their repose in the silence of the night. Teresa and Carlos de Escobar came together in the blessed sacrament of love, each feeling reborn into the new life that was promised to them by Padre Jorge Pastronaz.

Three

In this new year of 1826, John Quincy Adams was ending his first year as President of the United States, but there was already talk of electing Andrew Jackson to the presidency. The hero of the Battle of New Orleans had become very popular, and his policy of forcing the Indians of the Southern states to move north and westward had begun to win favor, especially with the land-hungry settlers who were pouring into the new country.

Shortly after the wedding of Carlos and Teresa, a young, thickly bearded courier rode into the Double H Ranch, dusty and weary from his long journey, with a letter for John Cooper Baines from Fabien Mallard, the rancher's factor in New Orleans. John Cooper had gone out to exercise his palomino gelding, Pingo, riding the horse several miles along the Frio River, the wolf-dog Yankee accompanying them. They were coming back now, Yankee trotting obediently at his master's side and glancing up with his gleaming yellow eyes, his pink tongue lolling. When he saw the young courier dismount, he bared his teeth in a low growl, but John Cooper, also dismounting, gently cuffed him and muttered, "No, *amigo,* Yankee, *amigo!*"

Leading Pingo by his reins, he approached the rider and said, "I'll wager you've come all the way from New Orleans, judging by the way you and that tuckered-out mare of yours look."

"That's right, mister. Be you Mr. John Cooper Baines?"

"That's the name I was christened with, yes, sir," John Cooper said humorously. "Now, then, if you're from New Orleans, you must have a letter for me."

"I do. It's from Mr. Mallard."

"Well, that's a surprise. I didn't think I'd hear from him until this spring, closer to the time when we make our cattle drive to New Orleans." John Cooper took the letter. "Thanks. Now, why don't you go into the kitchen around the back of the *hacienda* and tell Tía Margarita that I told you to get a good meal. After that you can go to the bunkhouse and rest up. Stay with us as long as you like. I'll have one of the *vaqueros* look after your mare."

"Mighty kind of you, Mr. Baines. Sure do appreciate it." The young rider tipped his hat and headed in the direction John Cooper had indicated, while the tall Texan led both Pingo and the mare to the stable. There, two of the younger *vaqueros* hurried up to take the reins from his hand, one of the men looking after the mare, the other man looking after Pingo, who was led to a nearby stable where John Cooper's palominos were quartered.

John Cooper, leaning against the stable wall, opened the letter and observed that it had been written by Fabien Mallard ten days ago. The courier had averaged forty miles a day on horseback to reach him, and that alone meant that the news from his factor was urgent.

He frowned after he had read it because he knew Catarina would not be pleased. She had not forgotten how he nearly missed the birth of Andrew and now, just a month after she had given birth to little Coraje, he would have to leave her and go to New Orleans. He made an exasperated sound with his tongue, shrugged, then reread the letter:

Monsieur Baines:

I have a pleasant surprise for you, and that is why I am sending Andy Harkimer, a very dependable and enthusiastic courier, to you as quickly as his mare will carry him. The six short-horned pedigreed bulls that you ordered from the East have unexpectedly arrived, several months ahead of when I myself had told you they would come. You will recall that I said to you last month it would be early spring. Happily, I have already inspected them, as has one of my good friends who himself is a *hacendado* with a small ranch some fifty miles upriver, and he tells me that if you do not want them, he will buy them at any price I ask.

Of course, they are yours, and I am wondering if you wish to come back quite so soon for them. If you like, you can send word back by the same rider, and I shall be happy to hold them for you, until such time as is convenient.

If you do decide to come on to New Orleans at once, I have some other news for you, which need not be mentioned in this letter, but which may be of eventual interest to you, regarding your palominos and long-horned cattle.

I have the honor to be, your privileged and devoted servant always,

Fabien Mallard

John Cooper carefully folded the letter and thrust it back into the pocket of his buckskin breeches. Those bulls he had ordered were real prizes, and the sooner they were back at the Double H Ranch, the sooner he could mate his best heifers with them and produce calves that would grow up to be the finest beef in the Southwest.

He shook his head as he thought what a singular destiny it was to have begun as a boy from Illinois, orphaned by a brutal and needless tragedy, and to have come so far that now he was a serious-minded property owner and a man of great wealth, ever since marrying Catarina and then finding this land in Texas for the Baines and de Escobar families. The silver he had found in the mine, now safe in the vault of the New Orleans bank, would enable him to lead a life of luxury for as many years as God decreed he had left, but it was his feeling that he should live off the capital coming from his main purpose in life, and that was the *Hacienda del Halcón*. With a growing population in San Antonio and New Orleans and indeed in the entire United States, there was a need for good beef and hides; thus, it was very sensible to develop his cattle breeding so that he could meet the growing demand. There would be money enough just from the operation of the ranch for his children, for the defense of the ranch and for improvements, and perhaps even to help some of the new, worthy settlers who would be coming to Texas to build this young country into a sturdy bastion of freedom.

As he walked away from the stable, he saw Miguel Sandarbal coming out of the paddock where he and a few of the *vaqueros* were roping a recalcitrant young mustang that had recently been caught and which they were attempting to tame. Miguel had thrown himself into the contest with the horse as energetically as the youngest *vaquero*, and his prowess and agility were amazing in a man his age.

John Cooper called to the *capataz*, "*Hola*, Miguel, *aquí!*"

Miguel sauntered toward him, a broad smile on his weather-beaten face. "*Mi compañero, buenos días*, I greet you."

"How would you like to come to New Orleans with me?" the blond Texan asked.

"I'd like it very much." Then Miguel's face fell. "But my Bess is going to have her baby in March and I'm not sure we'd be back in time. Why do we have to go there?"

"Just a short while ago a courier rode up from New Orleans from Fabien Mallard, telling me that the six bulls I'd asked for from the East had come in several months ahead of schedule. It's a good time to pick them up so we can start breeding them."

"I agree, *mi compañero*. But do you think we can be back in time?"

"I think so," John Cooper replied. "We can put the six bulls in *carretas* and come back in perhaps three weeks. That would be five weeks coming and going. I plan to take both Andrew and Charles with me this time. Charles felt a little unhappy that he didn't accompany us the last time. But now I think it would be a good occasion because we're not driving a lot of cattle, and yet it will give him a feel of the land."

"I follow you, *mi amigo*." Miguel nodded and chuckled. Then he sighed deeply. "I'd certainly like to accompany you one last time to share your enthusiasm. Well then, I'll break the news to Bess." Miguel grinned and winked sympathetically. "And you'd best break the news to your lady."

John Cooper glumly nodded as he reached down to knuckle Yankee's head. The wolf-dog immediately sat down and enjoyed the rub, looking at his master with luminous, yellow eyes. Like his predecessor Lobo, who had become old and left the ranch to return to the wilds, Yankee was a cross between a wolf and an Irish wolfhound. There had always been such a dog on the ranch to act as protector and defender, and in the kennel was Yankee's littermate Luna, as well as his wolfhound sire.

At this moment, Charles, Andrew, and Diego came out of the *hacienda* and, seeing John Cooper, hurried to him with cries of joy. To Charles and Andrew, age ten and twelve, their father was their idol, and Carlos's twelve-year-old son Diego also revered his uncle. John Cooper squatted down, and the three boys ran to him and began to wrestle and box with him playfully.

"I tell you what," John Cooper said as he rose, "you go to the palomino stables. The horses I gave you need exercise, so have a little ride for yourselves. I've something to talk over with Catarina."

Andrew grinned. "Come on, Charles and Diego, I bet I can beat you in a race."

"Bet you can't, either!" Diego yelled, and Charles, the youngest, was already on his way. John Cooper watched them run to the stable and grinned to himself. "I think," he said aloud, "Carlos and I have some fine boys there. Now, if I can just convince Catarina of that, I'll be fine."

"Coop, I'm beginning to think you want to be away from me," Catarina peevishly said as she cradled little Coraje. Sitting on the edge of the four-poster, canopied bed, she looked up at her husband with a reproachful frown. "I nearly died last month when I gave birth to your son and we had that terrible attack against the ranch. Now, with Coraje hardly a month old, you want to traipse off to New Orleans again. Do you have a fever in your blood, that you can't stay with me and be my love?"

"Catarina, my dear one, you know better than that," he softly remonstrated as he reached for her hand and brought it to his lips. "I swear to you, I had no idea that the bulls would be ready this soon. I thought it wouldn't be till March or April. But now's a good time. There won't be any cattle to drive. I'll just go there to pick up the bulls and bring them back in carts. We can make good time. Why, I'll be back by late February or early March for certain. Then, I promise you, you and I will have lots of time together."

Catarina softened. She put her arm around his neck and drew him to her. "You know that I don't want to hold you back, my dear one. You mean so much to me now because we've been through so much together. You can understand that, can't you, *mi corazón?*"

"Of course I can. And you mean the world to me. I'll tell you what: I'll bring a wonderful gift for you from New Orleans."

"Oh, Coop, that's not what I meant," Catarina retorted.

"I want *you*, not gifts. But, very well, I won't protest anymore."

"I'd like this time," her husband began tentatively, "to take Charles. It's his turn to be initiated, just like Andrew was last year. They're two fine boys and they've got lots of spunk and grit. The sooner Charles has his first outing with me, especially with Andrew along, the better it'll be for him. You know I'm right, darling."

"You always are, Coop. Oh, well, if you've made up your mind already, there's no sense arguing with you. Besides," her voice softened as she leaned forward and kissed him on the mouth, "I'm still so much in love with you; I can't say no to you."

"You're a wonderful, understanding girl, my dear one. We'll leave in a day or two so I can be back all the sooner. Then, you've my word of honor, I'll spend lots of time with you and the children," John Cooper promised.

That same evening, Miguel had his own domestic challenge. Standing with Bess in the large, main room of their cottage, Miguel asked his lovely, blond wife whether, despite her advanced pregnancy, she would mind if he accompanied John Cooper, promising that he would be back in time to hold her hand during their child's birth.

"I could deny you nothing, my dear one, not after you did so much for me," Bess said as she stirred a pot of stew that was hanging on a hook over the fire. Then turning to Miguel, putting her hands on his chest, she added, "Do you know, I still remember how years ago I was the prisoner of the Indians, and how you and Don Diego intervened to save me. Then you offered me marriage and a home and since then I've truly been blessed. You gave me such love and understanding that few women have. Go then, my dear one; but be careful. I want you to come back to me, and I want you to sit beside me when I bear our child. Perhaps this time it'll be a daughter."

"If only she's as beautiful as you, *querida*," he gallantly replied, taking her hand and kissing it fervently. Bess stroked his head with her other hand, smiling benevolently upon him, and there was an intimate tenderness in her blue eyes.

The next morning, while Catarina was still drowsing, John Cooper put on his buckskins and went over to their bed to kiss her on the forehead. She stirred and reached out to him in her sleep.

"Go on sleeping, *querida*," he said. "Pretend it's just a dream. I swear to you I'll be back before you even miss me. I'll take good care of the boys; you needn't worry about them. Yankee'll be along and four of my best *vaqueros* and Miguel. Now go back to sleep, dearest Catarina."

He turned quickly and went out of the bedroom. Charles and Andrew, who had been up since before dawn and had raided the kitchen for as fortifying a breakfast as a sleepy Tía Margarita could offer them, patiently awaited their father. Miguel was there, having already saddled two sturdy young geldings, which the boys would ride. They would not take their palominos on such a long journey. Four *vaqueros*, Antonio Lorcas, Pedro Martínez, Jaime Portola, and Bartoloméo Mendoza, had saddled their mustangs and were ready. Food, pots, and other necessities were already loaded on the back of the packhorse they would take with them.

Leaving the *hacienda* with the others, John Cooper went over to the shed where Yankee slept. The wolf-dog joyously bounded out, growling and barking, wagging his tail, jubilant, as his master called him.

They mounted their horses and were soon on their way, John Cooper riding between his two sons. They had traveled only a few miles from the ranch when the rancher addressed his younger son. "Charles, I hope you can kill some game for us on the journey. I've given you a musket, and Miguel and some of the *trabajadores* have given you some practice with it. Now you'll show me how much you've learned."

"I'll bet I'm a better shot than he is, Pa," Andrew spoke up.

He was quelled by his father's stern look. "That'll be enough of that, Andrew. Everybody has to start sometime. Don't forget, I started with a musket; then I learned to use my Pennsylvania rifle 'Long Girl' because it was do that or be killed. Just be thankful that you and your brother are coming along with four fine *vaqueros* and Miguel, who's worth a regiment of men."

"You give me too much credit, *Halcón*," retorted Miguel, who was riding just behind John Cooper and his sons.

"I say only what is your due. But what I'm getting at, Andy," John Cooper said, gently, turning to his oldest son again, "is that you and Charles had best learn to get along with each other on this long trip. I don't want any talk of superiority, understood?"

Both boys, chastened, warily eyed each other, then simultaneously nodded to their father.

Suddenly Miguel called out, *"¡Cuidado, es un buitre!"* He pointed upward toward the sky off to the southeast.

John Cooper glanced up and scowled, seeing the ominous black outline of a vulture slowly circling and descending. "He's after carrion, that one. Wonder what's been killed, an animal or maybe some poor *indio?* Let's go find out. But just so the vultures won't be too greedy, I want to show you that 'Long Girl' still won't let me down on a long-distance shot."

Swiftly drawing his father's Lancaster rifle out of the sheath, having primed and loaded it at the outset of the journey, John Cooper took careful aim at the descending scavenger and squeezed the trigger. The buzzard seemed to leap in the air, then plummeted out of sight.

"Caramba, what a shot that was, *Halcón!"* Miguel exulted, while Charles and Andrew cried out admiringly at their father's marksmanship. "That was at least five hundred feet away."

"Yes, but there wasn't any wind," John Cooper said modestly. Then, patting the rifle stock affectionately, he primed and reloaded the weapon before thrusting it back into its sheath.

"All the same," Miguel muttered as he glanced back to see the *vaqueros* eagerly talking among themselves to compliment the *patrón,* "it's an ill omen, a very ill omen." Reverently, he crossed himself.

Feeling better at having warded off the ill omen by a fervent prayer, Miguel Sandarbal galloped toward the site where he had seen the vulture fall. Reining up short, he stared down at the ground, then turned to call back, cupping his hands to his mouth, "It's a young doe!"

John Cooper and his two young sons rode up to join Miguel, and all four of them dismounted. "Now that's odd. I don't see blood or any marks that would have been caused by an arrow or a rifle ball."

"Perhaps it was a snake, *Halcón,"* Miguel muttered. "Yes, that's what it is; see there on the poor thing's flank? A swelling, and it's discolored there. It must have been a rattlesnake—"

Suddenly there was a shot behind them. Both men turned, and there was Charles, his musket still smoking, staring at the ugly, grayish body of a large rattlesnake at the base of a boulder.

"Good for you, *hombre!*" Miguel joyously approved. "You blew its head away. Now there, *Halcón*, was a shot to match yours!"

John Cooper strode up to his younger son and clapped him on the back. "I'm proud of you, son. That's keeping your eyes open."

Charles modestly lowered his eyes, not without first stealing a quick glance at his older brother.

John Cooper turned to Miguel, while the *vaqueros* drew in their horses and circled young Charles, tipping their *sombreros* to him, the accolade due a skillful marksman. "Well," John Cooper said, "we'd best be going on. Miguel, you and I have wives to come back to, and if the boys can keep up with us, we could make it to New Orleans in ten days. The more time we save going, the sooner we'll be back."

"That's what I'm thinking, *Halcón*," Miguel said, feeling uneasy over the omen of the buzzard and then the snake-bitten doe. He glanced back along the trail he had come and then suddenly let out an astonished cry. "*Hombre*, someone is riding hard to catch up with us! *Por todos los santos*, it's the Señora Catarina!"

John Cooper, his eyes wide with astonishment, saw his beautiful black-haired wife, wearing buckskins, riding the palomino mare Corazón, which he had given her for Christmas. It had been sired by old Fuego, the noblest and the first of John Cooper's superbly bred horses.

Mounting Pingo, he galloped out to meet her. "Catarina, what are you doing riding out like this?" he asked as he and his wife rode side by side to where the others were waiting.

"*Mi amor*, you didn't take proper leave of me as a husband should, so I came to say a real good-bye. And to wish Charles and Andrew a safe and happy journey." She reached out her hand to him, and he took it, staring adoringly into her eyes, which danced with merriment.

Miguel doffed his *sombrero*, made a low bow, and said, "Señora Catarina, you're a fine rider, to have covered all this distance in so short a time."

Catarina made a saucy face at him. "I have a message for you, Miguel. Bess says I'm to tell you to behave yourself and not to forget that you're past sixty."

The *vaqueros* could not help a mild titter of laughter, which they hastened to suppress the moment Miguel turned to glare at them, his brows bristling with indignation. Then he tilted back his head and laughed. "That indeed sounds like my Bess. Well, now, *vaqueros*, let's go on ahead a ways and let the *patrón* and his lady have their privacy."

The four *vaqueros* nodded and rode off toward the southeast. Miguel mounted his horse and followed them, while Andrew and Charles, standing beside their horses, lingered, curious that their mother had dressed in buckskins and ridden so swiftly to overtake them.

"You aren't angry with me, Coop?" Catarina inquired.

"How could I be? What a lovely thought it was for you to come to say good-bye to me on the trail. Now I know you've forgiven me a little for taking the boys."

"Not entirely. Not until you promise that you'll come back as quickly as you can, certainly no later than early March. Coraje will be wanting to recognize his father by then, you know."

"Yes." He reached for her hand and brought it to his lips; the two palominos nickered as they stood side by side.

Turning to her sons she asked, "Well, Charles, are you enjoying your first ride with your father?"

"Oh, yes, *mi madre*," the boy excitedly answered. "I shot a rattlesnake!"

"A rattlesnake!" Catarina shrank back in apprehension, then turned her dilated green eyes on her husband. "I don't think he should have come; there's so much danger for a boy so young—"

"There wasn't any danger. As a matter-of-fact, Charles saw the snake before any of us did," her husband smilingly assured her.

"Well, that was wonderful, Charles," Catarina said dubiously. "All the same, boys, you're not to take any unnecessary chances. Do what your father tells you, and you look after him, too."

"We will, Mother," Andrew soberly promised.

"Boys, get on your horses and go ride ahead to join Miguel and the *vaqueros*," she now urged.

"Come on, Charles," Andrew importantly exclaimed, "Mother wants to be alone with Pa; don't you know that?"

John Cooper and Catarina watched the two boys ride off, then turned to smile at each other. "Andrew is trying to imitate you all the time, and it won't be long before Charles does the same thing," Catarina laughingly commented.

"They'll be their own men in good time, my darling." His face softened, and he reached for her hand again and kissed it.

"How I wish I could come with you," she said, holding on to his hand, loath to let him go. "Wouldn't it be the way it was when you took me to the Jicarilla Mountains, to the stronghold?"

"Yes, Catarina," he said with a nostalgic sigh, remembering that wonderful first year of their meeting, the stormy courtship, and finally his audacious abduction of her. If it hadn't been for that, he thought to himself, perhaps he and Catarina might never have been wed, never have had such fine children. That was the heritage of Catarina's blood, merged with his; their union was that of the Old World and the New.

Now he took both her hands in his and stared steadfastly into her eyes as he said gently, "My darling one, I'm happy that you came out to overtake me. But now it's time for me to ride on, sweetheart. Go back, take care, and when I come back, I promise I'll stay for a good long while."

"*Vaya con Dios, mi corazón,*" she whispered as she leaned over to kiss him a last time. Then, wheeling the mare around, she headed toward the Double H Ranch. She did not look back, but when she reached a slight bend in the road, she lifted her right arm and waved at him. John Cooper stared after her, a bemused smile on his handsome, bearded face. Then, with a sigh, he turned Pingo back along the trail ahead and galloped till he had caught up with his sons, Miguel, and the four *vaqueros*.

Late afternoon on the tenth day of their journey, John Cooper's party rode into New Orleans. Miguel went to find quarters for them at a pleasant little hotel in the French Quarter, while John Cooper rode directly on to Fabien Mallard's office.

The Creole factor was just about to leave when the tall rancher rode Pingo up to the one-story frame edifice that

housed Mallard's office, dismounted, and tethered the palomino's reins.

"*Mon Dieu*, I hadn't expected you so quickly, Señor
Baines," the mustached and bearded middle-aged, dapperly
dressed Creole exclaimed. He strode forward and offered his
hand. "You're certainly eager to get those bulls. I put them
away in an old warehouse on rue des Jardins, with two of my
best workers to guard them. I also have two large carts avail-
able for you to transport them in."

"I'm anxious to get them tomorrow, then, M'sieu Mallard," John Cooper genially replied, "because I want to go
back to the ranch just as quickly as I can. You know, Catarina gave me another son last month."

"That's happy news, indeed," the Creole declared.

"You've met my oldest son, Andrew, but you haven't yet
met Charles," John Cooper said, putting an arm around the
younger boy's shoulders.

"A pleasure, Charles," the factor said, shaking hands
first with Charles, then with Andrew. Then to John Cooper
he said, "Would you do me the honor of dining with me—
you, your sons, and the men you've brought with you, as
well?"

"Yes, Miguel Sandarbal and four of our best *vaqueros*,"
John Cooper smilingly interpolated.

"I've happy news for you, myself. Since you were last
here, a lovely widow, Mme. Hortense Colombard, did me the
honor of accepting my hand in marriage, and tonight is our
second anniversary. It is the end of the second week."

"I'm delighted to hear it, M'sieu Mallard! That's very
kind of you to invite us."

"Make it at seven o'clock. My address is on Greenley
Street, just above Chartres. It's the first house on the corner,
with the second-floor balcony and the wrought-iron fleur-de-
lis design. Now, I'll go home ahead of you and tell Hortense
and the cook. I hired a man from Jamaica who is an absolutely perfect *cordon-bleu*. He'll outdo himself tonight in your
honor."

"That's most gracious of you. See you at seven, then."

Hortense Mallard was not quite forty and was very
beautiful, with an oval-shaped face and large, widely spaced,
dark brown eyes. Her dark brown hair was coiffed with a
fringe of curls along her high-arching forehead and drawn

back in a large bun in which she wore a comb made of silver
and set at each end with a huge pearl. John Cooper was fascinated by this ornament, and his host smilingly explained,
"It is an heirloom from my grandfather, M'sieu Baines. He
owned a sugarcane plantation in Haiti, and one of his workers, wanting to please him, dived into a cave in the sea and
brought back two huge oysters. In each, there was a magnificent pearl. For this gift, the worker was given his freedom
and later made assistant foreman of the plantation. I thought
that it would be a worthy decoration for my beautiful wife."

"You were right, M'sieu Mallard," John Cooper said gallantly as he took Hortense Mallard's hand and brought it to
his lips with the polished bow of a courtier.

"I have heard so much about you from Fabien," she declared in a soft, sweet voice. "Yet, you are not at all as I pic-
tured you. Though you wear the buckskins of a frontiersman,
and I know that you have lived with *les sauvages rouges*,
what you have just now done would be appropriate at the
court of a Bourbon king."

"I can understand why M'sieu Mallard waited so long to
give up his bachelor's freedom," John Cooper smilingly complimented her.

Dinner was lavish, and what the Creole factor had
promised of his Jamaican cook was more than fulfilled. To
start with, there was a delectable shrimp jambalaya, accompanied by a bottle of white Bordeaux, then young ducklings
in an orange and brandy sauce, vegetables of the season, and
a *bombe surprise* for dessert. Fine port and cognac were
served with strong chickory-strengthened coffee, a favorite of
the Creoles of New Orleans.

Andrew was allowed a small glass of port, as was
Charles. John Cooper was pleased to see that both his sons
showed excellent table manners, and made a mental note to
compliment Catarina when he returned. When he thought of
this, he smiled to himself, remembering how she had called
him a savage at their first meeting.

The house was large, and Fabien Mallard genially suggested that there was room enough for Miguel, the two boys,
and their father to stay overnight instead of going back to the
hotel late at night. In the carriage house there would be room
for the four *vaqueros*.

The journey to New Orleans had been swift and yet
wearisome, so John Cooper was glad to accept the factor's in-

vitation. Fabien Mallard's majordomo, a stately, grave mulatto named Antoine, showed the boys to the room they would occupy and Miguel to his, then ushered the *vaqueros* to the carriage house, while Hortense Mallard took her leave of her guests.

As the Creole walked with John Cooper to the latter's room, he said, "By the by, M'sieu Baines, I received a letter a few weeks ago that will be of considerable interest to you. It's from a Señor Raoul Maldones, who has a huge ranch on the *pampas* of Argentina, near Buenos Aires. I've sold him some pedigreed bulls, just as I have you. In the course of our correspondence, I happened to mention the superb palominos that you raise on your ranch in Texas. Well, you can see from this letter that he would like very much to buy some of your best steers, as well as a bull and a heifer, and one or two of your palominos. In exchange, he offers you two of his very finest *pampas* bulls, as well as an appreciable sum of money."

John Cooper glanced at the letter, nodded after having read it, then folded it and put it into the pocket of his buckskin jacket. "That's interesting. I don't know anything about Argentine cattle, I'm afraid, M'sieu Mallard. At the moment, I must admit I'm thinking only of the six fine bulls you've kept for me and of getting an early start tomorrow, with your permission. I don't want to seem ungracious, but I'm anxious to get back to the ranch. But I'll certainly write this Raoul Maldones a reply in due time."

"I understand. Well now, I'll wish you a restful sleep. My cook will have breakfast ready for you as soon as you awaken. You've only to pull that bell rope there by the bed. It was a pleasure having all of you for dinner this evening."

Yankee, who had slept overnight in the small courtyard in the rear of the Mallard house, wagged his tail and uttered a low, gentle growl as Charles and Andrew came down to play with him. They squatted and knuckled his head, as their father had taught them to do, and he licked their faces. At this moment, Miguel also came out of the house, and he chuckled with the sheer zest of being alive, as he saw the boys playing with the wolf-dog.

Hortense Mallard, in her peignoir, came to breakfast with her husband, and the tall, blond Texan thanked her effusively for her hospitality. The Creole smiled at his wife.

"M'sieu Baines is a man of action, *ma chérie*. He's eager to be off and about his business." He rose and kissed her on the cheek, as John Cooper bowed.

After bidding his wife good-bye, Fabien Mallard rode with John Cooper and the two boys back to the old warehouse where the six pedigreed bulls were guarded by two of his stevedores. Miguel and the four *vaqueros* followed on their horses.

When the Texas rancher saw the fine livestock, he smiled his approval. "I'll write you a bank draft for the cattle, the carts, and the horses to draw them."

"Quite satisfactory. I'm happy I was able to arrange this for you. Do you think you'll be coming to New Orleans again in April?"

"Perhaps. I'll have a few thousand head to sell by then, but I may take them to San Antonio. For sure next fall, M'sieu Mallard, I'll have plenty of cattle for you, thanks to these bulls which I intend to mate with some of my Texas heifers."

"Don't forget about Señor Raoul Maldones. I'll write him and tell him that I've shown you his letter, and that you're thinking about it, if that's all right with you."

"It's fine. Well now, the *vaqueros* and Miguel will load the carts. I'm off to town to buy a few things."

Hearing this, Miguel perked up and exclaimed, *"Mi compañero,* since I'll be busy with the bulls, could I commission you to get something very nice for my Bess?"

"Of course, and I'll stand treat," John Cooper replied. "You just leave it to me. When you come back with it, she'll hug you and kiss you and make you a very happy man." Miguel, weather-beaten and white-haired though he was, blushed like a schoolboy at John Cooper's teasing.

John Cooper bade Andrew, Charles, and the men good-bye. Then, mounting Pingo, he rode off on his errand.

It was almost nine o'clock in the morning when he reached the French Quarter and tethered the palomino to a hitching post. When he had been in New Orleans on the cattle drive the previous fall, he had stocked up on supplies for the ranch, loading a wagon with foodstuffs they could not make or buy in Texas—some new guns and knives, clothing material, and even some surgical tools imported from Europe. These last had been particularly beneficial, for just after Christmas, a trained doctor from Mexico City, Dr. Pablo

Aguirrez, had taken up residence at the ranch. Thus being so well stocked, John Cooper had no need to burden himself with a wagonload of supplies on this unexpected winter trip, though he did want to get a present for Catarina, as he had promised, and also fulfill the commission Miguel had given him.

He had also decided to reward Charles for his courage in killing the rattlesnake. He would buy him a Pennsylvania long rifle, like his own "Long Girl," just like the rifle he had bought for Andrew last year. He knew just the shop where he could purchase the rifle, and after doing so, he was on his way to carry out the much more difficult task of finding presents for Catarina and Bess.

John Cooper sauntered down the timbered sidewalk, pausing at a millinery shop, then a jewelry shop, and finally a dress shop. As he did so, an elderly man with white sideburns and a neatly cropped Vandyke beard beamed at him and gestured. "Come in, m'sieu, I am just opening my shop. May I offer you a cup of coffee? I have some excellent values, and you seem like a man who would appreciate such."

"Thank you, m'sieu. I'm looking for gifts for two very beautiful ladies, both wives."

The elderly man chuckled. "Not yours, I trust? We have come a long way, but I do not think that America is yet ready for more than one wife per husband."

"Actually, m'sieu, one gift is for my wife; another is for the wife of a very good friend of mine."

"Ah, that explains everything. *C'est bien, alors! Entrez, soyez le bienvenu, m'sieu.*"

John Cooper, chuckling at the elderly Creole's banter, followed the latter into his shop. Though small, it was elegantly furnished, and the counters and decor made the most of the limited space. His eyes fixed at once on an exquisite red silk scarf, with tassels at each end. That would be perfect for Catarina and he at once gestured to it. "I'll take that, m'sieu. That's for my wife. Now for my friend's. She's blond, much younger than he, and very wonderful, for she's given this friend of mine new life at his age."

"*Vive les femmes!* Your friend is lucky, for there is nothing better than the love of a good young woman for an older, considerate man. I think I have just exactly what she would like. Perhaps a little music box?"

"Perhaps," John Cooper drawled.

"Ah, but this is a special music box, m'sieu. Inside are thimbles, needles, and thread, so that it is both romantic and useful."

"I'll take that, too, then. Now I'd like to get something that has neither rhyme nor reason, but simply is lovely enough to be worthy of a beautiful woman," John Cooper declared. He had in mind to make Catarina an extra present, for he felt so much in love with her, remembering how she startled him in riding out to say good-bye in her buckskins.

The old Creole said, smiling, "If I read you aright, I have just the thing for her." With a triumphant cackle, the old man turned to the back of his shop, opened a teakwood chest, and drew out one of the most beautiful chemises John Cooper had ever seen. It was made of green silk, with a tasseled belt, mother-of-pearl buttons, and a demure yet suggestive bodice. He was sure that Catarina would blush when she put it on.

"That, too, I'll take," he at once decided. "Now, for the reckoning, m'sieu."

They agreed on a price, and John Cooper drew out his wallet and paid the old man in notes of the bank of the United States.

"Thank you very much, m'sieu. It has been a pleasure to serve you, and you would do an old man a great kindness if, when you reach home safely, as I pray *le bon Dieu* you will, you will write me and tell me how the ladies take to these gifts."

John Cooper smilingly agreed as he took the Creole's card and placed it in his pocket along with the folded letter from the Argentinian ranchowner.

They left a little after noon. Miguel, delighted with the gift John Cooper had purchased for Bess, told his friend, "With three bulls in each *carreta*, we should be able to make at least twenty miles a day, perhaps more. They seem sturdy, and there are partitions in the carts so that they will not jostle one another."

Each of the carts was pulled by two sturdy workhorses, and a *vaquero* sat at the front of the cart, holding the reins. The two remaining *vaqueros*, bringing up the rear, led their companions' horses. The four men would take turns cleaning out the carts, also making sure the bulls were well fed and watered. Bales of hay and grain were kept in the front of each cart, and water was stored in closed barrels attached to the sides.

They traveled rapidly, and at the end of the first week, John Cooper was not only content with their progress, but also proud of both his sons, who had stood their watches without complaint.

Charles beamed when John Cooper presented him with the new rifle; it was the best gift he had ever received. Andrew, far from showing any jealousy, seemed genuinely pleased that his younger brother, like himself, had been awarded such a fine Pennsylvania long rifle. Andrew even took part in the brief practice sessions John Cooper held whenever their little caravan stopped for a rest. Andrew listened as his father told Charles how to shoot, how to allow for the recoil, and he even gave Charles a few tips that he had learned.

John Cooper was happy to see that Charles had almost as much stamina as Andrew, despite his youth. On the tenth day, a good shot from his new rifle brought down a jackrabbit, on which Yankee feasted.

By the eleventh day, John Cooper was optimistic about their early return and said to Miguel, as they made camp at noon for a brief lunch, "If this keeps up, we'll be back by the first or second day of March."

"I hope we can, *mi compañero*," the *capataz* said with a chuckle. "That way, I'll be sure to be there when Bess has our child."

If both men had not been so concerned about returning to their wives, John Cooper would have stopped at the American settlement near the Brazos that the impresario Eugene Fair had founded the previous year. John Cooper would have enjoyed renewing acquaintances with old Mr. Hornsteder, Simon Brown and his Naomi, and Jack Sperry and his Nancy. But the bulls had traveled so well in the carts that the *vaqueros* were able to increase their pace to almost twenty-five miles a day, with pauses.

They had met no hostiles, nor even any Mexican patrols on the way back. That was indeed good. Yet nevertheless, Miguel Sandarbal had an uneasy feeling—perhaps an evil presentiment from seeing the vulture swoop down upon the snake-bitten doe—as they started on the last lap of their journey back to the Double H Ranch.

Four

After Francisco López left La Piedad, he rode directly to the flourishing town of Nuevo Laredo. In the money sack that he had forced the crippled, nearly blind old *alcalde* to turn over to him, he had found some six hundred silver *pesos*. But the rifle was defective and the ammunition was moldering from having been in the earth so long. Infuriated, he flung them away.

On the outskirts of Nuevo Laredo there was a shop run by a man who had once been a bandit and who sold contraband to anyone who had the price. His name was Sebastian Navarro, a lean, bearded, black-haired rogue nearing forty, who recognized in Santa Anna's former aide a fellow opportunist.

From him, López purchased an excellent Belgian rifle, a brace of French pistols, and ammunition for two hundred fifty silver *pesos;* he paid fifty more for a uniform with the epaulets of a captain.

When the shopkeeper, content with the day's business, decided to close his doors, López invited him to the nearest *posada* and stood treat for the best *tequila* in the house. Casually, he inquired of news, saying that he had been busy with a detail of troops in the province of Chihuahua and had resigned his command because he could not agree with the garrison officer.

The shopkeeper was mockingly sympathetic. "I shan't ask your business, *amigo*. News? There's a struggle for the presidency, but that's far away in Mexico City, and no one cares up here. Santa Anna? He's biding his time, and one day he'll take the field with a large army and probably rule all of Mexico. But it won't matter to me in Nuevo Laredo, so long as I can do business with men who have silver *pesos* to spend,

44

like you, *amigo*. To your health!" With this, he toasted his companion.

"And yours as well, *mi compañero*," López muttered as he took a sip. "I have a matter of honor to settle, though it's a story that won't concern you. Perhaps, though, since you've been here some time, you might tell me of some little village where I may rest up. You see, in the last campaign, I was wounded, and I haven't quite recovered. When I get back my health, then I'll go about getting even with a *gringo*."

"There are too many *gringos* in Texas, that's for certain, *amigo*," the storekeeper growled as he poured himself another glass from the nearly empty bottle. "One day, we're going to have to fight them and send them all to hell. They're not good *católicos* like ourselves, and they don't respect our traditions. Devil take them all!"

"I agree to that. Especially one I have in mind. There's a certain Texan—well, never mind—" López realized that he was talking too much. Then, in a jocular tone, he pursued, "As I said, perhaps you know some little village where I can rest. One where there are no military troops, where there are a few *mujeres lindas,* and where I can enjoy a *siesta* whenever I take a fancy."

"That's the way of it, is it?" the storekeeper said, giving him a shrewd wink. "Well then, *amigo*, you'd do well to head for Acuña. That's near the border, in the province of Coahuila. Only a few miles from the Rio Grande, to be exact. Beyond, not too far north, you'll find the Frio River."

López started, his eyes fixing on the storekeeper. "The Frio River, yes, it would be close by, wouldn't it? Let me buy you another bottle of *tequila*."

"A man who spends so many *pesos* with me in a single afternoon is worthy of attention, señor," the storekeeper chuckled with another broad wink. "The *posada* of the Toro Rojo, down the street from here, has many *putas* who are pretty and not too badly used."

"I'm grateful to you. Ah, here's the other bottle—and here's the reckoning for it. I wish you good fortune."

"And to you. May your mission, whatever it is, be successful!"

"If the Devil so desires, yes. *¡Buenas noches!*" López abruptly rose, curtly nodded, and strode out of the *posada*.

He was beginning to believe that his renunciation of God and his allegiance to the Devil had brought him luck.

Thanks to the *pesos* he had stolen from the old *alcalde*, he now possessed weapons and a new uniform. He could make an imposing entry into the village of Acuña and there plan his vengeance against the hated *americano*. Moreover, he had a few hundred *pesos* left, and with this he might perhaps buy the allegiance of a few young men who would form his new army. Where a large force had failed, he reasoned, a small, well-trained group might wreak havoc against that accursed *gringo*. Also, since a man of his passionate nature needed assuagement by a woman, he might find some handsome wench in Acuña who would be as appetizing as Benita Marcado. If she had not had that final outburst of piety, he might have taken her with him, for she had satisfied his lusts as well as any of his lovely young *criadas*.

Remembering what he had lost, the *villa* and his servants and the confidence of the man who one day was going to rule Mexico, López gnashed his teeth. He lifted the rifle, testing its heft and balance, squinting along the sights, imagining that even now that bearded, infernal meddler of a *gringo* was in range. The dry click of the trigger as he pulled it gave him almost an erotic thrill.

It was nearly a hundred miles from Nuevo Laredo to Acuña, and Francisco López, enjoying the luxury of a fine horse and having ample provisions, made the journey with several pauses for rest and food. On the evening of the third day, he rode into the outskirts of Acuña and saw at once that it was a poor village. Though the *posada* was reasonably large, the church was small and unassuming. There was a public square near a well that was used by both villagers and horses alike. Most important was that he was some sixty miles from the Double H Ranch and its boundary, the Frio River. This meant that, after he had formed his plan, he could ride northward and wait until the damned *gringo* was within the range of his fine new rifle.

Before he had left for the village, he had availed himself of the services of a handsome, buxom *puta* named Mercedes. He had treated her to supper in the best restaurant of Nuevo Laredo, bought her a cheap red cotton dress, and she had given him an intoxicating night of love. She had exclaimed over his virility, good looks, and military bearing. This fanned his ego, and now he felt himself capable of great deeds that would obliterate in one fell swoop all the ignominy of his past failures. He had named his roan gelding Diablo, by way of cynical acknowledgment of his pact with the powers of darkness, and he lived only to strike back at John Cooper Baines and to lay hold of the silver treasure so that he might surpass Santa Anna.

Dismounting at the trough, he let his horse drink, then led it to the *posada*, where there was a tethering post. He entered slowly, surveying the interior. There were four low, somewhat dirty tables and a nondescript bar at which a fat, thickly mustached man in his early fifties stood polishing glasses with a weary expression on his flaccid face. There were two customers, young *peones*, who were contenting themselves with the cheapest of beers and muttering to each other. He studied them and his lips curled in scorn. He had seen far too many of this type during his work with Santa Anna—shiftless, lazy dreamers, who hoped that the independence of Mexico would bring about a reversal of their drab, squalid lives. They were fit only to fight and die and be forgotten—and to be used by someone like himself who could manipulate men to achieve his own ends.

The two young men glanced at him, goggling at the splendor of his uniform, then went back to their conversation. Diffidently, López approached the bartender and declared, "I have ridden here from Nuevo Laredo, and I was told by a friend that I might find a room and a good supper. Can you provide these for me, *amigo?*"

"Of a certainty, señor, for I have the only inn in Acuña. There is a room on the second floor at the back, with a good view of the hills. You can see the sunset from there—though, of course, tonight you are much too late for it. As for supper, my daughter, Rosa, will serve it to you. I can give you *chile rellenos*, some *tacos*, and a little *carne asada*."

"That will be very satisfactory, *mi amigo*. How are you called?"

"My name is Rodrigo Nuñez, *su servidor*."

"And I," López said deprecatingly, "am Capitán Felipe Lorrengar, equally *su servidor*. I'm on leave from my service with the regiment of Mexican troops in Durango. My friend in Nuevo Laredo recommended Acuña as a peaceful village where I might recall the happy days of my boyhood in the country."

The owner of the *posada* scratched his head, then fatuously grinned. "It is country, to be sure, *señor capitán*. We do some farming here, but most of the men work for a *hacendado* who has many *ganado* and whose ranch is some twenty-five miles to the southwest of here. Some of them stay all week long there in their little *jacales*, then come home to spend the Sundays with their *esposas*."

"Just what I was looking for. Well then, whenever you wish to order my supper I shall enjoy it. If you have some good *tequila*, I should like to have a glass and treat you to one."

"Thank you, *señor capitán*." The fat proprietor produced a bottle of *tequila*, deftly opened it, drew out two glasses that were somewhat flyspecked, and poured a liberal portion into each. Then he pushed a dish of salt and a cut lime before López. The tall, black-bearded former officer tossed off his drink and smacked his lips. "That is excellent *tequila, amigo*. If your supper is of the same quality, I shall have no complaint. Now, if you like, you may show me my room. I trust there is some water for me to wash with?"

"My daughter, Rosa, will bring you some hot water directly. Your room is at the top of the stairs there. I shall go at once to the kitchen and tell her to prepare your supper, *señor capitán*."

López nodded and then, perceiving the narrow stairway at the back of the little tavern, ascended to find his room. It was small, with a wooden bunk over which a pallet of straw had been placed. There were a little table and a chair, a porcelain bowl on the table, and broken shutters hanging on a small, narrow window. Wearily, he opened these to see that there was a full moon that cast its light upon the low, jagged hills to the northwest. Beyond there was Texas, and over the Rio Grande was the man whom he had vowed to pay back for thwarting him.

He flung his saddlebag upon the table. In it were the few hundred *pesos* he had left, a new razor, the best shirt he could find in Nuevo Laredo, and underdrawers. He had also bought a pair of boots; these he wore. Also, out of vanity, he had bought himself a small, silver-framed handglass, so that he could study his face while shaving.

There was a faint tap at the door, and when he turned to call out, *"Entre,"* an attractive girl of about nineteen timidly crossed the threshold with a bucket of hot water. She had large, dark brown eyes, a heart-shaped face, a small but ripe mouth, and an opulent figure, dressed in a blouse and long green cotton skirt.

"Thank you, *querida*," López purred. "If you will pour some of the water into that bowl on the table, I can shave and be more presentable. You are Rosa, are you not?"

"*Sí, señor capitán.*" She approached, eyes downcast, but he could sense that she was sending him covert looks from under her thick lashes. "My father has told me that you have ordered supper and are going to stay with us. How long will it be, *señor capitán?*"

"Why, as to that, *mi linda,* I am here for a rest in the countryside. I was told that your father had the finest *posada* south of the Rio Grande."

"That is very flattering. Alas, *señor capitán,* there is not too much commerce these days. There is no *dinero,* and the men who work do so for the *hacendado* far away. He sells them things there, as well as the *cerveza* they drink, so when they come back they do not have much to spend with *mi padre.*"

She raised her eyes to his and her expression was one of fascination. Rosa Nuñez had long dreamed that one day a handsome, rich *caballero* would come to take her away from this dreary little town, just as her father entertained hopes of becoming a wealthy innkeeper. He had married late in life and his wife had died in childbirth; he had brought Rosa up, jealously guarding her from making a hasty match with some poor *peón* because he felt that she was worthy of greater things, as he was himself.

López watched her pour water into the bowl and effusively thanked her.

"*De nada, señor capitán.* My father tells me you came from Durango. That is a long way from here."

"It's true," he admitted. "But I wished to come to a quiet place where I might relax and enjoy myself. Now that I've seen you, señorita, I am happy that I made the choice of Acuña."

She blushed, then turned to go. At the door, she turned back to send him a hopeful, provocative glance that made him chuckle to himself. She would be as easy as Benita. Moreover, she was younger and tastier.

Slowly, deliberately staring at her, he took off his uniform coat, to which the shopkeeper had added a few medals that had little meaning but would impress *peones.* He could see her shiver and draw in a deep breath, and then she blurted, *"Señor capitán*—I—I'll go prepare your supper. Would you like me to bring it here to your room?"

"That would be most kind, *querida."*

She colored vividly. "I'll go prepare it right away, *señor capitán."*

"Gracias. Meanwhile, I shall freshen myself. Take your time. It will taste all the better when you bring it with your lovely hands," he said in his most intimate tone and flashed her a dazzling smile.

Half an hour later, Rosa brought López his supper and hovered about him as he complimented her floridly. He had trimmed his beard and shaved, and his brown eyes were soft as they fixed on Rosa's rounded figure. But when she finally left the room, his eyes grew hard and narrowed into pinpoints of rage as he thought again of that damned *americano.*

He took out a packet of cigars that he had bought from the gregarious storekeeper in Nuevo Laredo and mulled over several modes of action. If he could get three or four young men from the village to accompany him, he could use them as scouts. Perhaps he would be able to take the *gringo* by surprise, knock him unconscious, take him out into the woods far from the ranch, and torture him until he revealed where the silver was hidden. Then it would be a simple matter to keep him hostage while his accomplices went to get it. He would force the *gringo* to write a note saying that these men had orders to bring back a portion of the silver. He could pretend that the military commander in the area had levied a tax against this wealthy family of *gringos.*

By the time he had finished two cigars and summoned Rosa back to his room to bring him a bottle of *tequila,* some limes, and a dish of salt, he was in a much better humor. This time, he would go very slowly with the *puta.* He could tell that she was impressed with him and that she probably had never had a man before. He knew that, ultimately, she would yield to him. As he bade her a smiling good night, he took his right thumb and forefinger and firmed the point of his crisp beard. Again, he saw her shiver and flush.

He slept till nearly noon of the next day and woke with a bound, refreshed. Good food and rest, the acquisition of weapons and money, and this tempting opportunity of seduction that he was certain he could achieve had refreshed him greatly. He smiled to himself, and just as he did so, there was a timid knock at the door. *"Entre,"* he called. He wore only his underdrawers, and as the door opened and Rosa entered, she stopped dead in her tracks, her eyes very wide, her face crimsoning. "I beg—forgive me, *señor capitán*—" she stammered, and made as if to withdraw.

"Oh, no, *mi dulce,* it's all right. Have you never seen a man before?"

"Never—never one so strong and tall and handsome as you, *señor capitán,*" was her ingenuous reply in a faint, quivering voice. Her bosom rose and fell, and she put a hand to it as she stood nonplussed.

"That's most flattering and it's a lovely way to start a morning, Rosa—may I call you that, *querida?"*

Rosa was nearly swooning with ecstasy at being so addressed, so flatteringly treated, as if she were a great lady. But being practical she reasoned that if she could win the favor of this astonishingly good-looking man, she might earn herself the opportunity of leaving Acuña forever. Her father would be equally grateful for the chance to leave this peaceful, depressingly dull hamlet.

"I am surprised, Rosa, that you are not yet affianced to some fine young man in this village," López suavely declared.

"I—I have no *novio, señor capitán*—"

"To my friends, I am known as Felipe," he gently chided her, moving forward and taking her soft hands in his. Rosa was trembling so violently that she could scarcely stand, for she saw his naked, strong shoulders and his hairy chest. Only the short underdrawers covered his manhood, which was already beginning to manifest its prominence, thanks to her own delectable young beauty. Her eyes were downcast and her face was scarlet as she tremulously responded, "But you are too kind, *señor capitán.* I could never call you by your first name—it would not show enough respect for an officer who is so fine and elegant."

"You have a pretty turn of phrase, *mi corazón,*" he chuckled, drawing her hands closer to his body, his lips only a few inches away from hers. "But you must call me Felipe because we are growing closer to each other. You see, you've just told me something that delights me, that you have no sweetheart yet. Would you think it too bold of me, if I said that I find you *muy linda,* very sweet and a girl with whom I could very easily fall in love?"

"Oh, *señor capitán!*" she incredulously gasped, trying to draw her soft hands from his steely grip.

Her eyes half closed as her bosom rose and fell with nervous irregularity. Her warm olive skin was vividly flushed with carnal awareness; virgin though she was, her secret fantasies had often been about such a man as Francisco López, coming out of nowhere, martial and splendid in his courage and manhood, to take her away from this dreary prison.

Wily even in his madness, López savored the delicious perversity of drawing this ingenuous girl to the brink of total surrender, yet halting her before she could take the plunge. "Forgive me, Rosa. It's only because I've been so lonely and I've had such hardships these last months. I must apologize to you. I hope I didn't frighten you—I would never do that, *mi linda.*" His voice was softly pitched, caressing, and persuasive. He loosened his grip on her wrists, but his fingertips, still touching her arms, seemed to caress her flesh with such an unctuousness that it was almost as if he were making love to her. "There will be time enough for both of us. But you must be sure. I am sure already, but it isn't fair to you, since you've known so little of me. But already, Rosa, I feel a great passion for you. Perhaps, if you so wish, you can share my future."

"Oh, *señor capitán*—I mean Felipe—I never heard anyone talk like that to me. I don't know what to say. I do like you, terribly much—I shouldn't tell you so soon. What must you think of me—"

Her babbling, almost incoherent words betrayed the confusing diversity of her emotions, fear mingling with desire, caution and shame merged with an almost intoxicating yearning.

"What I think of you?" he echoed with a persuasive smile as he put his left arm around her shoulders and kissed her chastely on the cheek. "I think that you're good and virtuous and sweet, all a woman should be. That's why I've fallen in love with you. But let us not hasten matters. I shall be here some time. I wish only to say to you that I should be proud and honored to court you, and I shall tell your father to put his mind at ease, that I mean you no disrespect."

"Oh, Felipe—I—I'm so happy—I never dreamed a man like you, so important, so handsome, could want a village girl like me—"

With his right hand he took one of hers and lifted it to

his lips and kissed it solemnly. "This is to show you that I mean what I say, dear Rosa. Now, if you have any chocolate, I should like it very much for breakfast. I slept long, you know, because I've had so many dangers and troubles lately. But here I feel so much at peace in your little village, and it's partly you who have brought this about, like a healing angel."

"I'll get your chocolate right—right away, Felipe—" she stammered as she reluctantly disengaged herself from his embrace, then hurried out of the room.

During the next few days Francisco López learned from Rodrigo Nuñez that the *alcalde* had died two months ago and his successor had not yet been chosen by the villagers. Moreover, the priest had died eighteen months ago and had not been replaced. Although the then *alcalde* had written to a friar whom he knew in Mexico City to obtain a successor for the little church at the northwestern end of the village, no one had been found willing to come to a desolate village. It was, to be sure, the same problem that Taos in Nuevo México had faced all through the days of Spanish rule and, even more so, after the Mexican revolution, when distant towns and provinces were estranged from the capital so far as direction, guidance, and even military support were concerned.

This suited López perfectly. If the village was so disorganized and impoverished, he could recruit several loyal, adventurous young men who would willingly risk the danger of death as against the dreary, monotonous life that they led in Acuña.

By means of spending several silver *pesos* for the information that the fawningly obsequious innkeeper provided, López quickly became accepted as a salvation to both father and daughter. The former had dreams of a grand tavern with elegant fixtures in the heart of Mexico City; the daughter dreamed of making a romantic match far beyond her station.

López became familiar with the terrain and especially the trail to the north that led to the Frio River and thence to the ranch of the damned *americano*. It would be, he calculated, two days of good, hard riding.

On the fifth day of his visit Rodrigo Nuñez himself proposed a solution to López's immediate concern, that of establishing sufficient status in Acuña to recruit young *peones* for his plan.

This particular evening he had taken his supper at a table at the rear of the *posada*, served by Rosa, who lingered as she bent to place a plate before him, so that he might admire the rounded, dimpled curves of her shoulders and the lovely throat with a hint of the deep cleft between her full breasts. Her father, polishing glasses at the bar, cleared his throat and, after she had gone back to the kitchen, declared, "Capitán Lorrengar, what would you think of remaining here and serving as our *alcalde*? We would feel confident here with you, even if you could not stay very long."

López stiffened, straightened his shoulders, then smiled ingratiatingly. "I should be honored, Señor Nuñez. To be sure, since I am on vacation and expect to return to my command when I have received orders, it can only be temporary."

"That's no matter. Since you've come, the village has taken on new life," the innkeeper said. Then, leaning over the counter of the bar, he murmured in confidential tones, "I see also that my daughter is quite smitten with you, *señor capitán*."

López stroked the tip of his beard. "I confess I find her very beautiful and very sweet, Señor Nuñez. Nothing would please me more than if she returned my affection."

"But she does, *señor capitán;* she does indeed! Why, only last night she told me so herself."

"Well now, I'm very flattered. I've only been here a short week or so, and already I find myself at peace in your charming village."

"Then you will accept the post of *alcalde*?"

"Yes, with the humblest motives in the world. So long as I'm here, I shall protect all of you. Perhaps, Señor Nuñez, I shall soon have a serious proposal to make to you, father of the girl whom I find most charming."

At this, the innkeeper puffed himself up, a smile spreading from one corner of his mouth to the other. He reached under the counter and produced a bottle of old brandy. "I wish to drink to your health, *señor capitán*. I had a feeling, when first you came here, that fate had brought you to Acuña. Now I know it's true. Our destinies are intertwined."

Behind López's smile was withering contempt. Things were going his way now; he would have the girl, and he would have men who would work for him. When he had killed the *gringo* and that damned wolf-dog, when he had found the treasure, he would be general, president—perhaps emperor! Well, why not, did not Iturbide proclaim himself emperor of all Mexico? Nothing was impossible, and especially when one had the wealth of those silver ingots!

The next day, when Rosa brought him his breakfast, López, with a benevolent smile, bade her close the door. "I have something to tell you, my dearest one. Last night I talked with your father, and he has told me that he would not find it amiss if I were to court you."

"*Señor capitán*—Felipe! This is so wonderful!" She was trembling and her voice wavered as she stared at him, her eyes large and moist with desire. She had dreamed of him last night, and she had seen a romantic phantom of herself in a wedding gown and him in his resplendent military uniform, in the great cathedral in Mexico City, before the venerable bishop, who blessed them and united them. Then she saw herself carried in his arms to a four-poster bed with a canopy, and after that, the ecstasy of what she anticipated surpassed even her power to conceive it. So now, as he came to her and held both her hands in his, she saw again that marvelous dream and believed that perhaps it could be realized.

"Your father also asked me if I would accept the post of *alcalde* of Acuña, and I told him I should for so long as I can be here. You see, my dearest one, I have affairs. There is a score I must settle with an *americano*. He tricked me, he killed many of my men, and he owns something which should be mine. Once he has paid his debt to me, then I shall be free to tell you what is really in my heart."

"Oh, Felipe! I know what you're going to say—and—and I want you to know—I—I'm in love with you. Oh, Felipe, please say that you mean it—"

"But I do, *mi corazón*." He pressed his hands against his heart and then leaned forward and kissed her on the mouth. Rosa started, tried to withdraw, and then closed her eyes as a sweet fervor overwhelmed her senses.

"I want you very much, *mi* Rosa. But first, I have some work to do. I shall need some of the young men of this village who will come with me on this errand. Once it's done, then you and I can begin to think of the future. I have a *villa* near the great blue Gulf of Mexico, and we could live there and be happy."

"Oh, yes, Felipe, I could be happy anywhere with you—oh, yes, I do want you so!" she stammered. "Oh, Fe-

lipe, you must think me shameless, but I've never known a
man, and yet I want you so!"

How easy it was, he told himself. It would be a pretty
little game to lead her on until she practically gave herself to
him. First, however, there was something he must do. With a
heroic smile, he sighed and said, "Alas, dearest, I have sworn
to avenge myself. Only afterward can we be married. Till
then, think of me and wish me well." With this, he took her
by the shoulders and, kissing the nape of her neck, solicitously ushered her out of his room.

The next day, just before the noontime *siesta*, Rodrigo
Nuñez called a meeting of the villagers in the public square.
López, standing on a raised platform, preened himself; he
was resplendent in his sparkling uniform, his medals on his
chest, his sword at his side. Rosa, behind her father, wearing
a blouse and a short skirt and sandals, sent him yearning
glances. When he looked at her and smiled, she blushed and
looked down at the ground.

Briefly, without too much florid commentary, realizing
that these ignorant *peones* could not comprehend too many
details at one time, he explained that he was an officer from
the province of Durango, that he was on vacation, but that
he felt that the tumult and strife in Mexico City were estrang-
ing him from further military service with a unit that did
only useless patrolling. He was happy to be here in Acuña,
where he felt at home, and best of all, his *host*—he turned to
Rodrigo Nuñez, who made a deprecatory shrug as if to indicate that he was not worthy of such a term—had done him
the honor of offering a mere guest the post of *alcalde*.

There was a murmur of curiosity in his gaping audience.
He could see that there were perhaps some fifty young men
and women in their twenties and thirties; the rest were older.

Having their attention now, he spoke slowly and suc-
cinctly. "If I am to accept this post, I will make you the best
alcalde you ever had. But if you accept me, then I must
make you part of my sorrows and grievances, for all of us
should work together to eliminate these and make our village
one of harmony and peace and fruitful labor."

There were a few desultory cheers, and before continuing, he waited until the audience fell silent. "Some years ago,
when I was only a *sargento* attached to the regiment of General Arredondo, who, as you may remember, bore himself so
valorously in the first battles for Mexican independence from

Spain, I spared the life of a *gringo*. He was only a boy, badly wounded, his weapon was useless, and he wished to surrender. We had been told to take no prisoners. But because I was humane, I spared his life."

The murmur was louder this time, and he knew he had his audience in the palm of his hand. "It is said in the Holy Bible that if we cast our bread upon the waters, it will return to us a thousandfold. Alas, such was not the case with the *gringo* whose life I spared. Only last year, when I was commanding a patrol near the border, he fired at me and wounded me. My men went off on a futile chase because there were other accursed Texans opening fire on them from an ambush. When the *gringo* came to kill me, having seen me fall from my horse, I recognized him as the boy I had spared. Before I could draw my pistol, he struck me on the forehead with the butt of his, stunning me. Then he bound and gagged me, robbed me of what *pesos* I had in my uniform pocket, and told me that I was a filthy Mexican swine and that the next time he would kill me on sight. It was an insult to my glorious country and to my uniform, *mis amigos*."

Now the murmur was louder and there were approbation and interest in all those stolid peasant faces.

"What I'm getting at is that if I accept this post of *alcalde*, I should like to have as volunteers three or four of your bravest young men who wish adventure. I will pay them well, and since I hold command as a captain, I am authorized to begin them as corporals."

A tall, raw-boned young Mexican, not much older than twenty, stepped forward, clearing his throat. "*Mi capitán*, my name is Luis Pedrosillo, *su servidor*. What do you wish of me?"

"My compliments, Corporal Pedrosillo. I will tell you. This *gringo*, this man who bore me so little gratitude for having saved his life that he robbed me and threatened me with death, lives across the Rio Grande near the Frio River. He is now a *hacendado*, and he drives *ganado* to New Orleans and to San Antonio. He is *muy rico*, and he has many *criadas lindas* who are slaves to him, decent young Mexican girls, who should be married with families of their own, instead of catering to the degenerate lust of this cowardly *americano*."

The young Mexican nodded, his face hardening. "Such a man deserves death, *mi capitán*."

"You are right. But all I ask of you and those others of

you who will follow Corporal Pedrosillo is to ride toward that ranch and report to me whom you see riding away from there. I wish to know if my enemy is so protected that it would be useless to try to give battle. But if by any chance he should go out alone, then I could meet him man to man and settle our debt of honor."

Three others now stepped forward and eagerly demanded the privilege of serving their new *alcalde*. López smilingly handed each of them three silver *pesos* and, raising his right hand, proffered the military oath, which all of them took. "Now you are true *soldados* of Mexico, *mis amigos*. Do any of you have horses?"

"I do, two of them," Luis Pedrosillo proudly spoke up.

"*¡Bueno!* Then you will ride your favorite, and you will lend the other to your three compatriots. They will take turns. Every other day I wish one of you to go forth and to report on the terrain and what you find there."

"It shall be done as you command, *mi capitán*." Luis Pedrosillo saluted smartly; López chuckled to himself as he returned the salute. This was better than he had expected.

By the last week of February, López, as *alcalde* of Acuña, was gratified by the adulation he received in this impoverished little village. The four young men whom he had sworn in to military service took turns riding the trail north every other day and returning with reports from the Double H Ranch. They saw *trabajadores* working the herd or engaged in building a new little house and a shed beside it, but nothing of much interest. The last day of February, however, Corporal Pedrosillo rode back into the village, out of breath and excited, tethering his horse outside the *posada*. He hurried in to find the supposed Capitán Felipe Lorrengar conversing with Rodrigo Nuñez. "*Mi capitán*, I've seen someone wearing buckskins as an *indio* might!" he exclaimed.

López turned to the excited young Mexican. "Someone in buckskins, you say? The accursed *gringo*? Pedrosillo, I shall promote you to *sargento*! Here are two silver *pesos*, to reward you for your vigilance."

"But, *señor capitán*, I mean, *señor alcalde*—" the young man stammered.

"Since this is a military matter, I am your *capitán*. Tell me, was it a man?"

"No, *mi capitán*, it was a *woman*. Black-haired, riding a

palomino mare. She rode toward the south, almost to the Rio Grande, and she waited awhile and seemed to talk to her mare, then finally headed the horse back across the Frio."

"*¡Diablo!*" López swore, a crafty look twisting his sinisterly handsome features. "I know who that is—it is the wife of that accursed *americano!*"

"I do not know, *señor capitán*. But Joaquín Suarez, who is my cousin and got back yesterday from his trip to the ranch, tells me he saw the same woman, dressed the same way, and riding out almost to the Rio Grande. She let her palomino water at the bank of a creek and then turned back."

In a hoarse, trembling voice that betrayed his pent-up hatred, López declared, "You've done very well. Tomorrow, I shall go out riding myself. I thank you, Corporal Pedrosillo, for your vigilance."

That night he ate his supper ravenously and went up to his room to smoke a cigar, his face aglow with a demoniac cruelty. "If I cannot have the *gringo*, I can at least have his wife. I will kill her. Then he will suffer, far more than if I injured him. I have only stupid *peones* to help me; I cannot expect to raise an army to attack the ranch. But I can take something from the *gringo* far more precious even than his silver!"

He went back down into the *posáda* after having smoked his cigar and seated himself at the farthermost table at the rear, while Rosa hovered attentively about him and her father obsequiously brought out his best *tequila*. "This time, *señor capitán, señor alcalde*," the barkeeper said flamboyantly, "allow me to treat you to the best *tequila* in all Mexico. I am grateful to you, Capitán Lorrengar, Alcalde Lorrengar, for the spirit you've aroused in the young men. One day you will go back to Mexico City a hero."

"Yes," López mused as he poured himself a liberal glassful and stared amorously at Rosa. "A hero. But there are deeds to be done. If I succeed, *viejo*, I myself will buy you the finest *posada* in all of Mexico City, and that's a promise made in front of your beautiful daughter."

"Do you know, *señor alcalde*," Nuñez slyly insinuated, "I realize that my daughter has caught your fancy. She's pure, a sweet, innocent girl, and she would make you a good wife. Consider it, I pray you."

"I understand that already, *viejo*. Tonight, with your permission, I mean to speak to her about it."

"*Señor alcalde,* you do us great honor, and my family would be eternally grateful if there could be an alliance between you and Rosa," the *posada* owner said with a dreamy sigh.

"I will take her to Mexico City along with you, and we shall be married in a cathedral in the great square near the *palacio* of *el presidente*," López boasted. At this, Rosa clasped her hands to her bosom and gave him a passionate look. She had already made up her mind to visit this fascinating suitor late tonight, when her father would be asleep—all the more reason now, since he had declared his intention to marry her and to make her his wife.

Thus it was close to midnight when Rosa tiptoed up the stairs, clad in only her night shift and robe, barefooted, her heart pounding wildly as she thought of the ecstasy awaiting her. She believed that if she did not capture this man at the full flight of his ardor for her, he might vanish like a dream, as swiftly as he had appeared out of nowhere, and then there would be no prospect for her except to marry one of those dreary young men who had neither ambition nor *dinero* nor anything else, save the will to possess her flesh and to make her a breeder of many children.

Almost fainting with excitement, she knocked softly. López grinned to himself and sprang out of bed. He had anticipated her and opened the door, wearing only his underdrawers. She saw his hairy, lean chest and ribs, and she put a hand to her mouth and drew back, but already he had seized her by the wrists and drawn her in, closed the door with his other hand, and swiftly, almost in the same movement, taken her in his arms. "I knew you wanted me, as I want you, *querida*," he murmured in her ear as his hands roamed over her rounded, resilient young body.

Rosa was undone. Nothing had prepared her for such ardor. True, she had dreamed of a romantic, poetic courtship, but she had never realized that the passion of the flesh would render her powerless.

Reassuringly, even as she submitted herself tremblingly in his arms, she remembered his words before her father, that he would wed her in the cathedral near the great palace of *el presidente*.

Sobbing, she felt his lips trace a delicate, erotic pattern against her thin shift as he opened the robe. She felt her nipples stiffen, and when his hands gripped her hips and drew her against his body, she felt the obdurate root of his maleness. Against this, she had no defense; nor did she wish any.

Much later, she turned to him, wistfully, tearfully, and murmured, "Oh, Felipe, will you truly marry me? I'm all yours now, you know that; there's never been a man till now. I want you as *mi esposo!*"

"Of course, my little dove," he cynically whispered as his hands explored the satiny warmth of her nakedness. She had abandoned herself, and she had almost died of ecstasy as he had possessed her. "You heard what I said to your father. Let me do what I have to do, *querida,* and you'll be *mi esposa* and perhaps, one day, the wife of *el presidente* of all of Mexico!"

As he spoke this, he truly believed it. Not that she would be at his side, but that he would attain the highest glory in the nation. First what had to be done was to punish that damned *gringo,* and now he knew how sweet his vengeance would be, even sweeter than killing John Cooper Baines!

"Oh, Felipe, oh, yes, oh, *mi corazón!* Aaah!" she moaned deliriously as he possessed her again with skill and finesse, savoring his triumph as but another proof of his total superiority.

Five

John Cooper, the four *vaqueros,* Miguel, and young Charles and Andrew made excellent time on the way back. The weather favored them, and Miguel, as he made camp two nights before they were due to arrive at the Double H Ranch, exulted as they sat by the campfire, "By all the saints, I'll be there to hold my Bess's hand when she gives me another son!"

"Or a daughter as beautiful as she is, *mi compañero,*" John Cooper chuckled, clapping the white-haired *capataz* on the back. "As for my part, Catarina will be as eager to see me as I am to see her." He paused and smiled. "I might also have a litter soon from Luna, if her mating with the Irish wolf-hound took this time. Then Yankee would have lots of wolf-dog cubs to look after."

At the mention of his name, the wolf-dog emitted a soft, low growl and crept up to his master, bending down his head to be scratched. "Yes, boy, you know your name, don't you? You've done very well on this journey," John Cooper compli-mented him. "You've flushed out mallards, some quail, and even a small deer. We've eaten well this time, Miguel, haven't we?"

"That we have, *Halcón!* And your boys have covered themselves with glory."

John Cooper looked fondly at his sons, who, trying to act modest, lowered their eyes. "That's right. Catarina will learn that she's got two strong, fine boys."

Miguel nodded happily, then called, *"Hola,* Antonio, what are you making for our supper tonight?" The amiable *vaquero* smiled, squatted down, and stirred the large kettle hanging over the fire. "A stew," he replied, "with some of our dried vegetables and the deer we shot this morning. It's al-most ready, señor; would you care for a taste?"

"I certainly would," Miguel responded, taking the spoon from the *vaquero.* "Delicious!" Miguel pronounced with all the gusto of a gourmand. "Tía Margarita might have some stiff competition from you as cook for the *hacienda!"*

Catarina was sure that John Cooper would come back today. For the last five days, riding her gentle palomino mare, she had gone beyond the Frio River toward the Rio Grande, following the same trail he had taken. After their tender parting scene, she felt that he would return to her even more swiftly than he had originally believed. She wanted to surprise him again.

She remembered the rapt smile on his face when he had seen her come riding after him, and she remembered also their tempestuous courtship and the ecstatic joy they had shared at the Jicarilla stronghold in New Mexico—especially that time when she had persuaded him to ask Descontarti, the heroic chief and father of Weesayo, to allow them, for a sec-ond honeymoon, to occupy a secret wickiup and pretend that they had been married Apache-style. These memories made her glow with such a surge of love that it was almost as if they had begun their courtship all over again.

Eagerly hurrying out to the kitchen, she persuaded a sleepy Tía Margarita to prepare a cup of chocolate and to bake a pan of biscuits, which the fat, elderly cook had not planned to make until noon.

"But, Tía Margarita, I've a feeling that Señor Baines will be back today! I feel it so strongly I'm going out to ride after him and to surprise them all on the trail!"

Tía Margarita sighed and shook her head. "Ah, yes, querida, how wonderful it is to be in love."

Catarina hugged the fat cook and kissed her on the cheek. "I don't know what we'd have done if you hadn't come to Texas with us. I want you to live forever, so you can make me this wonderful hot chocolate for breakfast every morning. Only, after my esposo comes back today, would you mind serving it to us in bed tomorrow?"

Tía Margarita pretended to be scandalized and actually blushed. "Get along with you, young mistress!"

After eating, Catarina went to the stable, saddled her mare, and, breathing in the sweet, cool morning air, glanced up at the cloudless blue sky and rode off toward the south. Yesterday, little Coraje, as she held him in her arms, had pointed to a bluebell, and she had been struck by the delightful gesture. Already the baby saw the beauty of nature in this wild, magnificent country. So she had picked the bluebell, put it to the baby's lips, and pressed it between the leaves of her prayer book. The prayer book she carried with her now, in the pocket of her buckskin jacket. On the jacket were the beads and the figures sewn by the old women of the Jicarilla stronghold. They foretold a happy life with el Halcón, as indeed it had been and would always be.

The day was superb, and she filled her lungs with the sweet air, let her mare graze a moment near the bank of the Frio River, and then crossed it at the shallowest point. The plash of her mare's hooves and the song of the birds chirping in the nearby live-oak trees lifted her spirits. She rode easily, preferring to ride astride a horse the way a man did.

She had never before ridden quite so far this way, but because it was early and the air was still pleasantly cool, she felt that she could ride for hours. If John Cooper and the boys appeared, what a delight it would be to ride back with them and to twit him, as an old married woman might, about having to go looking for an errant husband!

The soft lapping of the Frio River, flowing placidly, made her turn back to look at it. One day, she thought, it would be delightful to have Coop, the boys, and Ruth and Carmen and little Coraje enjoy a picnic with her along the river, shaded from the sun by trees that stood along both banks.

By noontime, she was hungry and stopped at a little creek to eat the biscuits she had brought with her and to drink some of the pure clear water, while the palomino nuzzled at her.

It was, she estimated, about fifty miles from the ranch to the Rio Grande. Because of the effortless gait of her gentle mare, who had more endurance than she had suspected, she had covered nearly a third of the distance. The sun, though it was at its zenith, did not seem oppressively hot. She felt refreshed, with the feeling that she would encounter her husband and the boys coming back from New Orleans. Audaciously, she determined to ride as far as she could, till perhaps the first sign of twilight. It would be an adventure to find him on the trail in the evening, and to see how surprised he would be! She smiled happily to herself and, mounting the mare, directed it on toward the south.

Francisco López, feeling the flame of hatred consume his vitals, could think only of death and vengeance. He had left the village of Acuña early, and he rode his gelding with merciless speed, certain that he would find his quarry.

It was a pleasant day, ideal for riding, and he had crossed the Rio Grande at a fording point where the water was no higher than his horse's shanks, and headed toward the Double H Ranch. He rode with his features tautened and warped, his lips thinned and compressed to bare his teeth. From time to time, he patted the rifle sling attached to one side of his saddle. He prayed to *el diablo* for a chance to see the damned wife of the *gringo* and to have her in his sights!

He remembered how cool that uppity *puta* had been to him when he had tried to ingratiate himself at the Double H Ranch on his first fateful visit there. She would pay dearly for what her husband had done to him, impoverishing and disgracing him. Yes, he would settle the score once and for all.

He raised his eyes to the clouds, and a short, raucous laugh broke from him as he said aloud, "My words are for the evil one, the one who defies *el Señor Dios,* for he has already brought me good fortune, where God never did. I pray you now, lord and master of wickedness, to send the *esposa* of the *gringo* toward my path this day!"

From the distance, far to the west, there was a faint rumble of thunder. López's brown eyes glowed with a ferocious joy, and then he burst out laughing, so strange and horrid a sound in this stillness that his gelding whinnied.

"Yes, that thunder is the sign that *el diablo* has heard me!" he cried aloud, digging his fingernails into his palms. "Thank you, master of evil, thank you, lord of all creation! To you I dedicate my vengeance! Grant me the strength and the fortune to achieve it this very day!"

All this way, he had seen no patrols of Mexican troops. It was as if the world had become a solitary place in which he was alone with his burning hatred. The land was a series of plateaus, broken only by bunches of chaparral and the odd-shaped, prickly cactus; there were occasional copses of scrub trees and stagnant little creeks, dry gullies, and scattered boulders. Above, a hawk uttered a shrill cry, dived toward a starling, and killed it after a single swoop. The hawk bore it off in its beak and perched upon a stunted oak tree, where it consumed its prey.

That, too, was a sign. The hawk must surely stand for that damned *gringo,* called *el Halcón;* but he, Francisco López, would destroy the hawk. He drew the Belgian rifle out of the sling, swung his horse to the right, and took a snap shot.

The hawk plummeted to the ground and lay still. López brandished the rifle and shouted aloud, "So will perish the *esposa* of *el Halcón,* and once again, lord of evil, you have given me the sign I seek! Let me but accomplish my purpose this day, and I will live by your ways for the rest of my life!"

As he rode on the terrain became more fertile, with banks of high grass, trees, the winding tributary of a larger stream to the northeast, and more birds and wildlife. He saw a wild pig dash suddenly out of a thicket of brambles and make for a copse of trees and disappear.

He halted his gelding long enough to reload the rifle and to thrust it back into the sling. Then, leaning forward in the saddle, he urged the gelding on. His eyes were pinpoints of obsessive hate as he scanned the horizon. He wanted only a sign of the buckskin-clad figure whom Pedrosillo had seen.

Catarina heard the sound of the rifle shot, far to the south. Her eyes widening with joy, she kicked her heels against the mare's belly and urged her onward. Surely that must be John Cooper! She had felt so certain of finding him today! She could already hear his scolding, "What the devil do you mean, Catarina, riding out all by yourself this long way, just to meet me?"

She was smiling as she patted her mare's neck and crooned soft words of endearment to her. "Hurry, take me to him! If you do, you shall have all the sugar you can eat tonight when we come home; I promise you that! ¡Adelante, querida!"

The mare obeyed. Stretching her long legs, she galloped south, and Catarina exulted as she neared the Rio Grande.

Then she uttered a cry of joy, for, in the distance, she could make out the faint figure of a man on horseback.

"Let's hurry now; there he is, my dear one; give me all the speed you can, querida!" she urged the mare.

Francisco López galloped forward on his gelding, straining his eyes. He let out a joyous oath as he saw the buckskin-clad figure come closer. It was a woman . . . the dark-haired esposa of that cursed yanqui. He pulled his gelding to a halt near a thicket of mesquite, leaped off, drew out the Belgian rifle, and crouched low. Then, cocking the rifle, he waited, the blood pounding in his veins, roaring in his ears; his lips drew back in a savage grimace as he squinted along the sights.

Catarina halted her palomino, for she did not recognize the gelding as one of the Double H Ranch horses. She saw that the man had gotten off his horse and was crouching near a thicket of mesquite. That was not Coop! With a terrible flash, she recognized the swarthy, ferocious López. Wheeling around, she kicked her heels against her palomino's belly. "¡Adelante, adelante, ahora!" she cried out.

But López had her at his mercy. He aimed at her back as he cried, "Now, filthy puta of that hell-damned gringo, the devil take you!"

Frantic, Catarina swerved her palomino, but López's eyes were glued to the sights, and he squeezed the trigger.

Catarina stiffened, uttered a strangled cry, her eyes enormous with pain and shock, as the bullet smashed into her spine. Then, leaning forward, she sobbed hoarsely, "Oh, *Señor Dios*, not like this! Coop, Coop, help your Catarina!"

Behind her, the bearded, uniformed madman stood, the rifle clutched in both hands, watching with gloating eyes as the buckskin-clad woman toppled from the palomino, rolled over onto the ground, and lay with her arms sprawled forward, her head turned to one side. The palomino mare, startled, turned back to look at her mistress, then whinnied; but López had already reloaded the rifle and, swinging it up swiftly and triggering it, sent a bullet through the mare's head. She fell not far from her mistress.

López laughed, and the sound was satanic in the sudden, terrible silence, as dusk began to fall over the plain of southeastern Texas. "Yes, it's Francisco López, *puta*, and your husband will be next! I swear it by the devil!"

For a moment he thought of going over to her and seeing if she was dead. If not, he would give her the coup de grâce with his pistols. But then, chuckling, he reasoned that even if she was alive, alone here without food or water, she would surely die. Let her suffer, so that she would know whom she had dealt with and whom her husband had tricked and thwarted!

He walked back to his gelding, put the rifle in the sling, mounted the horse, and turned back toward Acuña. His eyes glowing with a demented joy, he beat at his chest with his free hand and shouted, "*¡Gracias, Señor Diablo, muchas gracias!*"

Six

John Cooper Baines and his two sons rode side by side, with Miguel watching like a mother hen over the two carts carrying the six pedigreed bulls driven by the two *vaqueros*. The other two *vaqueros*, on horseback, brought up the rear.

A rumble of thunder foretold a storm. There were several jagged bolts of lightning and then the sudden drench of blinding rain. As a wind rose, John Cooper wheeled his palomino around to cry to Miguel, "Take shelter, over by those hills—I know they have caves! It's useless to try to go on; we'll have to wait till the storm is over!"

As furious streaks of lightning daggered the dull, dark sky, the horses drawing the carts grew skittish and reared and whinnied. Miguel bawled to the *vaquero* drivers, *"Por todos los santos,* calm those horses, or the carts will overturn and do the bulls injury, and all our journey will be wasted!"

The two drivers pulled on the reins while the *vaqueros* bringing up the rear swiftly dismounted and ran up to the workhorses, slapping the frightened animals on the withers and urging them to trot to the sheltering row of little, irregularly shaped hills off to the east.

The caves were high and wide enough to permit the entry of the carts, and after unharnessing the horses, the *vaqueros* tethered their reins to trunks of gnarled live-oak trees. The lightning soon subsided, but the downpour continued unabated for nearly two and a half hours.

Miguel grumbled, "May the devil take this storm! We'll have to waste a whole half day in getting back."

There was another minor calamity when John Cooper discovered that their tinderboxes had been dampened even through their leather saddlebags, and a fire for cooking was out of the question. He and his companions had to make do with strips of jerky washed down with swigs from their canteens.

Then, as suddenly as it had begun, the storm died away, and there was only a warm dampness in the darkness of night and the sounds of insects and night birds in this isolated terrain. They were now within a day's journey of the Double H Ranch.

When suppertime came and there was no sign of Catarina, Don Diego and Doña Inez grew alarmed. Carlos and Teresa had recently come in to the *hacienda* after riding, and while she went to their room to change her clothes and freshen up, Carlos waited for her in the large, comfortably furnished parlor, drinking a glass of wine and reading a book of Spanish poems. His father burst in on him, anxiously exclaiming, "I do not know where Catarina can be, or what she is thinking of, staying out so long. One of the *vaqueros* told me he had seen her going out riding on her mare, but that was early this morning."

"Maybe she felt that John Cooper would be back today and rode out to meet him," Carlos said, looking up at his father's agitated expression. Trying to quell Don Diego's worry, he continued, "She may have met him and the others and decided to spend the night with them."

Don Diego nodded his head. "That may be, but even so, I would feel better if I knew for certain."

"I'll have Esteban Morales ride out in the direction she took and see if he can find her," Carlos proposed.

"Yes, do that! Tía Margarita told me that Catarina took along some biscuits, and that would mean she planned to be out for a while." Don Diego frowned and shook his head as Doña Inez came into the room and put an arm around his shoulders. Trying to allay his fears, she urged, "Come now, my darling, there is no need to be upset. Catarina is a fine rider."

"You are right, my dearest. Well, then, we shall have supper without her. But do go and find Esteban; that is a good son," he said to Carlos as the young man hastily left the parlor.

Carlos hurried out to the bunkhouse to find Esteban, who was in charge of the *trabajadores* in Miguel's absence. After Carlos described his father's concern, the sturdy Mexican saddled his gelding at once and rode off toward the southeast.

Catarina slowly raised her head and, her eyes glazed with pain, stared out into the distance. Darkness had fallen and she could only make out the shadowy outline of her dead mare. She had lain unconscious for an hour or two. She tried to move but could not. With one hand she gripped her prayer book and tried to put the other hand on her back to determine the nature of the wound. There was a torturing pain as she moved her arm. Uttering a sobbing groan, she pleaded, "Oh, please, Holy Mother, let me live until Coop comes back."

Suddenly there was a rumble of thunder and it began to rain. Catarina's throat was parched, so she managed to tilt her face upward and open her mouth. The falling drops revived her somewhat, and she tried to sit up, but she could not. The lower part of her body was numb. She clenched the prayer book in her right hand and again prayed.

If only John Cooper would come back along this same route, find her, and take her home! She wanted to be in her own bed, with her children around her. The bullet had taken her in the back, she knew, and there was the terrible fear of dying from loss of blood, though she could not even tell if she was still bleeding.

Irrationally, she wished she had saved some of the biscuits, instead of eating them at noon. She became feverish, then hallucinations seized her, and John Cooper appeared nearby. She feebly called to him but there was no answer. From afar, there was the wail of a lone coyote, and from the copse of trees from which López had made his ambush, there came the low hooting of a screech owl.

She closed her eyes, tried to lay her cheek on the prayer book, and prayed again. She could not move a muscle. There was no moon, and there was darkness all around, and the ground reeked of dampness.

Esteban had seen Catarina ride off many a time during the past weeks. He knew that she had crossed the Frio River, because last week, in his hearing, she had told Don Diego that her beloved Coop should be back any day now, and she wanted to ride out to meet him.

Catarina's trail was not difficult to find, for the downpour had not reached the Double H Ranch; the prints of her mare's hooves could be plainly seen in the warm earth. Esteban Morales forded the Frio River at its shallowest place, just as Catarina herself had done.

When he reached the opposite bank, he found again the mare's hoofprints. He had an uneasy premonition; he could not forget the tragic night, when he had been on duty and when the *jefe de bandidos*, Jorge Santomaro, had come to the *hacienda* in Taos, ravished Catarina, and stolen the infant Andrew—though John Cooper Baines had tracked down the outlaw, as well as his treacherous accomplice, the former *capataz* of the de Pladero ranch, José Ramirez, and made them pay the supreme penalty for their crimes. Esteban had felt guilt for a long time over his self-accused negligence. Even though the former mountain man had repeatedly avowed that he had not held Esteban responsible for that vile attack upon his beautiful wife and the abduction of his oldest son, the assistant foreman continued to pray that one day he might erase that misdeed by performing a vital service for John Cooper and his family. He owed the man and his family so much. The rancher had once saved the life of Esteban's firstborn, Bernardo, by killing a scorpion with his knife as the baby crawled toward the creature. With night falling on him, his mind roamed through fantasies about the hidden dangers that might lie along this darkening trail. He leaned over his horse's neck, holding the reins tight, and spurred his mount onward.

It was nearly midnight when he reached that most fertile part of southwestern Texas, as yet unpopulated and uncultivated, which was in such contrast to the barren, cactus-ornamented hilly plain beyond the Rio Grande. The moon came out as the clouds drifted away. He was exhausted, but he did not stop. His only thought was to find Catarina or, even better, John Cooper reunited with his black-haired wife and both on their way safely back to the Double H Ranch.

His horse whinnied its fatigue, and Esteban compassionately brought it to a walk. Sitting erect in his saddle, squinting and cupping his eyes with his hands, he surveyed the terrain. Then, with a startled cry, he saw the outline of Catarina's mare, sprawled and lying inert two or three hundred feet away. With a hoarse encouragement to his mount, he made it trot in the direction of the fallen animal. Reining in, he stared down at the dead mare and the darkening red-rimmed hole left by Francisco López's rifle shot. Horrified, he dismounted, ordering his horse to stay docilely where it was. Then he saw Catarina lying sprawled on the ground, her hand still touching the prayer book, the other arm stretched along the ground in a kind of gesture of supplication.

With a groan of anguish, he crossed himself and prayed aloud as he hurried to her. Kneeling down, he put his hand to her cheek. Her dilated, swollen eyes opened and stared unrecognizingly at his face. Her lips tried to form words, but she was too weak.

"Señora Baines, can you hear me? Who has done this to you?" he gasped, for now he saw the clotted blood at the back of her buckskin jacket, the perforation of the ball from López's rifle. A sudden fury seized him and he dug his nails into his palms as he repeated the question.

Her mind was wandering, and her voice was faint and

weak as she quavered, "He—Francisco—López, he was the one—the one who shot me. It hurts so; I can't move; I've tried, but I can't."

Her voice trailed off and she closed her eyes. Esteban crossed himself again. "Señora Baines, I must carry you back home. I will be just as careful as I can, so I don't jostle you."

"You—you won't hurt me—" She forced herself to open her eyes to stare at him. Vaguely, she recognized his anguish-contorted features. "Esteban? You've come to bring me home? Oh, please, please take me home!" Then, mercifully, a wave of darkness swept over her, and she lay unconscious.

"I will; I swear it, Señora Baines," Esteban said, weeping, and praying he would not hurt her. There was no way of making a travois or any kind of support. He would have to hold her with one arm, as tightly as he could, and he must go swiftly, for that ominous blood-rimmed hole in the back of her jacket filled him with terror.

He seized control of himself, for he knew this was a formidable task. He did not know how long she had lain here, nor how much she had bled. Her voice sounded weak, and yet her mind was still clear. That, at least, was a good sign.

He now noticed the prayer book by her hand and, shaking his head sadly, placed it in his pocket. Then, with painstaking care and holding his breath, he knelt down and slipped his hands under her shoulder and knee hollows. Lifting her up, he walked toward his placidly waiting gelding.

The horse turned its head to watch him, nickering softly. "Gently, Valor, gently." He carefully draped Catarina on her stomach, facedown over the withers of the gelding, just in front of the saddle, and then swiftly mounted. The gelding pawed the ground with its left rear hoof and swished its tail. "Oh, please, don't move, it'll be over in a moment, and then we'll go home, and you'll have oats and sugar, everything you want. Do this for me, Valor; do it for Esteban," he begged. Then with both hands, he draped the unconscious young woman across his lap. His left arm supported her shoulders as he took up the reins. Then, kicking his heels against the gelding's belly, he called out, "¡A casa, pronto!" With good fortune, if he dared ride swiftly, he could be there by dawn. And every moment counted.

The moon shone down on the peaceful land. Catarina did not stir, and he tried to shift himself so that his lean, wiry thighs bore the brunt of her weight. Her face was pale and upturned and her eyes were closed, but he could see from the flickering of her nostrils and the rise of her bosom that she was still alive. May all the saints preserve her, he prayed.

In a spacious room of the Texas *hacienda,* Carlos woke just before dawn, refreshed and happy as he had not been since Weesayo's death. He turned to look at Teresa lying beside him on her side, one arm outflung on the pillow, a happy smile on her exquisite face. He gently kissed her hair, then her earlobe, just brushing his lips to it, and smiled, the solicitous smile of a man very much in love.

He rose and donned his shirt and breeches, then left the bedroom to go outdoors, to breathe in the cool morning air and revel in the joy of being alive and loved by someone whom he loved, yes, as much as gentle Weesayo. Yet the latter would never be absent from his heart until his death, for she had cherished him and made him understand the sensitivity and wonder of women. All of this had prepared him for his union with Teresa.

The sun was rising and the sky was gradually turning purple and red. He stood there entranced by the gradually brightening dawn, seeing the sun's first rays touch the rich, green grass, the trees, and the flowers, and dapple the waters of the little creek beyond. A gentle breeze began to blow from the east, and there was the promise of a very pleasant day, without the excessive heat that so often sapped the energy of the *trabajadores* working with the cattle or in the fields.

He stared southward, where he heard a faint sound. The clop-clop-clop of a horse's hooves came nearer and nearer. He wondered idly who it could be—and then he thought to himself that it must be one of the *vaqueros,* no doubt riding on ahead with the joyous news that Catarina and John Cooper were coming back with all the others.

He walked forward to meet the rider, his face aglow with eagerness. It would be good to have his brother-in-law back. Perhaps they would go hunting for deer or other game and take Yankee along. Come to think of it, he was anxious to try his skill with his rifle against John Cooper's, though he knew his brother-in-law would always win. Still in all, competition was good for the soul, especially when they were such good friends.

The sound of the horse's hooves grew louder and he could make out the dim figure in the distance. It was a lone rider, riding hard, and there was something—there was something—no, it could not be! The rider was holding someone in buckskins, an arm around his shoulders, guiding the gelding with the reins in his right hand. Carlos uttered a cry of horror.

"Oh, no! In the name of the most merciful God, no, not Catarina!" he cried out as he recognized the tumbled black hair, the pale white face tautened with pain.

"Esteban, what has happened to her? Oh, Catarina, my sister, my sister!" Carlos cried out, as he hurried toward the foaming gelding.

"Señor Carlos! She's been shot and left for dead! She fainted. For God's sake, wake the *médico*. He can save her!"

"She's been shot?" Carlos echoed, numb with disbelief. "Wait, let me help you take her inside."

They carried her into the kitchen, Carlos weeping silently as he stared down at his sister's wan, pale face. Esteban related that he found the palomino mare shot as well and that Catarina, before she had fainted, had told him that it had been Francisco López who had shot her from ambush.

"I'll kill him!" Carlos raged, keeping his voice low so as not to disturb the inert young woman. "I'll get a horse and go after him; I'll cut him to pieces with my sword; I'll make him pay for this! How could it happen; how could the dear God let my dear sister be shot by that spy, that traitor, that swine of a tool to Santa Anna?"

Esteban sadly shook his head. "Señor Carlos, if you can open the door, we'll gently lay her down on the bed on her side. Do you see that terrible wound? It's the ball of a rifle."

"Oh, no," Carlos groaned, "the noise has wakened my father. My God, what can I tell Don Diego?" His father, in his nightshirt, emerged from the bedroom down the hall and came slowly toward them, still drowsy with sleep.

"But what has happened? What is this? Catarina! Has something happened? Tell me, Carlos!" the old man urged in a trembling voice.

"Esteban found her, *mi padre*. She's been shot by Francisco López."

"Oh, no! My poor child!" Don Diego covered his face and burst into sobs.

"I'll go wake Dr. Aguirrez," Carlos said in a hoarse, trembling voice. "Stay with her, Esteban."

Distraught, tears streaming down his cheeks, Carlos ran from Catarina's room and out of the *hacienda*, toward the little cottage where Dr. Aguirrez, his wife, and young son were quartered. He hammered on the door with his fists, calling out, "Dr. Aguirrez, for the love of God, come quickly; it's my sister!"

A moment later, the door opened, and the Mexican doctor emerged, yawning and trying to summon his senses into order. At Carlos's repeated words that his sister had been shot, he came awake at once. "What monster would do such a thing? Wait a bit; I'll get my instruments. Can you have one of the maids heat some water? Get me some clean linens! They can be torn into bandages."

"I'll do it at once, Dr. Aguirrez. Please hurry, she's in her bedroom, and Don Diego is with her."

The doctor found Don Diego kneeling, his hands clasped in prayer, weeping like a child. Doña Inez, who had wakened to find her husband missing and then heard the uproar, had come to join him, and she, too, knelt and wept beside him.

"Forgive me, but I must examine her," the doctor said gently as he stepped to the bed. He saw the ugly wound and shook his head. "It is a very bad place. A rifle ball, I was told?"

"Yes, Dr. Aguirrez." Carlos uttered a soft groan. Esteban Morales had gone for the hot water and bandages, and now the doctor opened his bag and took out a sharp scalpel, then very deftly cut the buckskin jacket from the neck down. "Forgive me, but there is no time for false modesty," he said apologetically. "I must examine the wound. It is in a very bad place. Along the spinal vertebrae, at about the waist."

Don Diego said in a choked voice, "What tragedy has struck this *hacienda!* First Weesayo, and now, my own daughter." Overcome with grief, he bowed his head again and covered his face with his hands, as his shoulders shook with weeping. Doña Inez, putting an arm around his shoulders, tried to soothe him, but she, too, was dissolved in tears.

Dr. Aguirrez turned to Carlos. "I am afraid to probe for the ball, Señor de Escobar. Her pulse is very weak and she has lost a good deal of blood."

"Is there nothing you can do for her, Dr. Aguirrez?"

Doña Inez wiped her eyes with her handkerchief and looked up at the young doctor.

"She is very weak," the doctor gravely responded, "and I fear removing the bullet might cause her death. Lodged in such a place, it has already done irreparable damage to her. I should not be surprised if she was paralyzed from it."

"Oh, God, hear a father's plea and let her live, even if paralyzed!" Don Diego lifted his eyes to the ceiling and, his gnarled fingers twisting back and forth, prayed in a trembling voice. His face was ashen, and he seemed to have become more frail since he had learned of this tragedy.

Esteban and one of the *criadas* of the *hacienda* came in with a pan of hot water and some strips of linen. "Here you are, *señor médico*," Esteban said. "Is there anything else I can do?"

"Pray, as all of us shall," the doctor solemnly responded. "If only the bullet had been off to one side or the other, there might have been a chance. I'll try to make her as comfortable as I can, and sponge the wound and put on bandages. Yes, the bleeding seems to have stopped, but there may be an internal hemorrhage. When things like this happen, we learn how frail we truly are. But to shoot a woman! What an abomination!"

"I pray to God that she'll live long enough, at least, to see John Cooper and the boys again," Carlos fervently exclaimed.

Esteban turned to Catarina's brother. "Let me have a bite of something to eat and to drink, Señor Carlos. I'll ride out and see if I can't find Señor Baines and bring him back quickly."

"I'm very grateful to you, Esteban. But you look fatigued. Let one of the *vaqueros* go on ahead."

Esteban wrung his hands in helpless anguish. "I'll be all right, Señor Carlos," he insisted. "I owe the Señor Baines this news, and I can ride more swiftly than any of the other *vaqueros*. I could not rest, knowing that the señora is in such danger. I will go now and bring the Señor Baines and the others back; this I swear to you."

Seven

Esteban Morales changed horses, for he could not possibly expect his gelding to repeat that arduous ride almost to the border and back. He chose a piebald mare whose fleet-footedness he had tested on many an occasion, and headed directly along the same route that he had taken across the Frio River in the direction of the Rio Grande, where he had found Catarina.

It was almost noon and the sun was scorching. Esteban was a number of miles from the spot where he had found Catarina when he sighted the two carts, the four *vaqueros*, Miguel, and, at the head of the little procession, John Cooper on Pingo and his two boys on each side of him. Digging his heels into the mare's belly, he urged her on to her topmost gait, galloping toward John Cooper and waving his *sombrero* to attract the latter's attention.

John Cooper turned back to Miguel, a frown on his face. "It's Esteban, *mi compañero!*" he called. "He must have some urgent news, to ride that poor mare like that!"

"I agree, *Halcón*," Miguel anxiously replied, surreptitiously crossing himself.

"Esteban! What's happened? I never saw you ride so fast before!" John Cooper exclaimed as the panting assistant *capataz* galloped up to him and reined in the snorting mare, whose flanks were wet with sweat.

"It's the señora, Señor Baines—I found her last night not too far from here near the Rio Grande—she'd been shot—"

"Oh, my God! Shot?" John Cooper repeated, stunned, his face blank, his eyes widening. "But who would do that?"

"She said it was Francisco López, Señor Baines."

John Cooper uttered a hoarse cry of agony and rage. "That bastard! So that's how he took his revenge! Oh, God,

77

how badly was she shot, Esteban? Don't hide it from me; tell me!"

"Forgive me, Señor Baines, I wish *el Señor Dios* had not destined me to bring you such dreadful news. We were all worried about her at the ranch, you see, when she didn't come home last evening for supper, so I rode out and I came upon her. Her mare had been shot, too. It was dead, and it lay not far from her."

"Go on." In his agony John Cooper had forgotten his two young sons. Andrew and Charles stared at Esteban as if praying that he would disappear and his news vanish with him.

"It was a rifle ball, Señor Baines," Esteban haltingly informed him. "She had been shot in the back."

"Oh, my God, my God. I'll kill him! He's a monster to strike at me through poor Catarina! Is she back at the ranch now; is Dr. Aguirrez tending to her?"

"Yes, Señor Baines, I myself brought her back to the ranch on my own horse, just as gently as could be. And Dr. Aguirrez is with her now. Don Diego and his *hijo* Carlos sent me to you as fast as I could find you."

"Bless you, Esteban."

The assistant *capataz* could hardly see for the tears that welled up in his eyes. "She was in her buckskins and she rode out believing that you would be back yesterday. She wanted so much to meet you and her boys."

"Yes—oh, God, yes, I know." John Cooper bowed his head and ground his teeth as he fought his own tears. He drew a deep, shuddering breath, turned back, and beckoned to Miguel who had ridden up, concerned over the long dialogue between his assistant and John Cooper. "Miguel, we'll have to make all speed. Catarina has been hurt."

"Oh, sweet Jesus in Heaven, no, young master!" Miguel groaned. Then he listened as Esteban hastily repeated his story, and he told his assistant *capataz*, "You did all that any man could have done."

John Cooper nodded and reached out to touch Esteban's shoulder. His cheeks were wet with tears. He moved toward his palomino, and then halted, struck by a thought. "Esteban, do you remember exactly where you found her?"

"Yes, Señor Baines. A few miles from here, a little to the northwest."

"Then López must have been in ambush for her." John

Cooper spoke slowly. "Miguel, whom among these four *vaqueros* would you pick as a tracker, who could read signs of horses' hooves and of a man's footprints, and be able to trace on leaves and grass from which point a rifle was fired?"

"Why, I'd say Antonio Lorcas. Antonio, *ven aquí, pronto!*"

The young *vaquero* rode up and saluted his *capataz,* looking inquiringly at John Cooper. "Did you not live with the Toboso for a little time, *amigo?*" Miguel questioned him.

"*Sí, mi capataz.* One of their scouts showed me how to track and I still remember the things he taught me."

"*¡Bueno!*" Miguel turned to John Cooper. "Here is your man. I know what you are thinking, *Halcón.* That if you go back to the ranch to be with your *esposa,* the trail will grow cold. But Antonio can track this *bastardo* down and then come back to you and tell you where he is."

John Cooper rapidly explained to the *vaquero* what had taken place, then said, "Antonio, my prayers will go with you. Miguel, give him all the food you have left and the best horse we have."

Antonio Lorcas packed the food in his saddlebags and mounted a gray gelding, which Miguel himself had ridden and which seemed to have the greatest stamina. Then he conferred with Esteban, who gestured in the direction where he had found Catarina and her dead mare, and gave him what other information he could. The young *vaquero* saluted both John Cooper and Miguel and galloped off.

Telling Miguel and the other three *vaqueros* to bring back the bulls at their own time, John Cooper and his sons, with Yankee following, galloped back to the ranch. As they neared it, John Cooper outdistanced Andrew and Charles in his frantic desire to see Catarina and to learn whether she would live. His face hardened into a grim mask as he demanded the utmost of Pingo, who stretched out his long legs and seemed tireless. His mind was clouded and tortured by what Esteban Morales had told him of Catarina's words. Yankee's angry growls when López had first come to the ranch should have served as warning: He should have gotten rid of that treacherous bastard long before he had. Better still, he should have let Yankee go for the monster's throat, and perhaps then López would have babbled what was really his plan in coming to the ranch pretending to have renounced Santa Anna's service.

Oh, dear God, John Cooper prayed, *don't let it be too late!*" Then, because he had lived with Indian tribes from his boyhood to young manhood, and had learned their superstitions, their fables, and their lore, he was suddenly haunted by the remembrance of the vulture and the dead doe and the poisonous rattlesnake that had killed it. He thought of how Miguel had been worried about that curious scene: Had that been a kind of mystic warning that his journey to New Orleans would be fraught with disaster?

Yankee had started after his master when the latter had galloped ahead, but even he had given up the futile chase and lagged behind now, guarding the boys, who rode swiftly, but did not have the horsemanship to spur their mounts to such a mad gallop as their father had demanded of loyal Pingo.

When John Cooper reached the courtyard of the Double H Ranch, he flung himself off his horse and ran into the *hacienda.* Don Diego had just come out of Catarina's bedroom and saw him, threw up his hands, and said in a sobbing voice, *"Hombre,* there is no hope. Dr. Aguirrez has said he cannot remove the ball; she is weak, she has lost much blood, and she has no strength left."

The young Texan went to Don Diego and hugged him, and tears flowed down both their faces. Then John Cooper went into the bedroom where Catarina lay, her head propped up by two pillows. Dr. Aguirrez stood gravely at one side of the bed, and Doña Inez and Teresa and Carlos were on the other side, watching her intently, their eyes filled with tears.

"I'm here, *mi corazón,*" John Cooper hoarsely exclaimed as he flung himself down on his knees beside the bed and reached out to take Catarina's slim hands in both of his and bring them to his lips.

Her eyelids began to flutter, then opened. Wanly, she turned her head to see him. "Coop—you—you've come back to me. . . ."

"Yes, sweetheart. Don't try to move. I wish I hadn't gone away. Oh, God, how I wish it! I love you, Catarina. You must live; you have to, for the children's sakes and for mine. We'll care for you, my Catarina. I need you, sweetheart; I need you so!"

He felt the faint pressure of her fingers in his hands, and through tear-blinded eyes he stared up at Dr. Aguirrez, who shook his head, clasped his hands, and closed his eyes.

John Cooper forced himself to tease her. "I raced Pingo

home and I beat the boys all hollow, coming back to you, sweetheart. It'll be awhile before they get here. But they're fine; they're safe. They both did very well. I've a present for you, a wonderful present—two presents, in fact. So, after you finish sleeping and resting, we'll have a chat, and I'll show you what I have for you, my Catarina."

She had closed her eyes again, and he felt his heart constrict with the savage grief of loss. For the moment, he had driven out of his mind the identity of the man who had done this to her, for all he could think of was his wife. Again, he looked up at the doctor, who made the sign of the cross, and his lips moved silently in prayer. Doña Inez had turned away, an arm over her eyes, to hide her tears. Don Diego took her by the shoulders, murmuring to her, and he, too, was weeping. Teresa and Carlos, very pale, stared down at Catarina, their fingers linked together.

She opened her eyes again; they were bright with fever, unseeing. "Mamacita, please get Catarina the new dress. It's on the calle Descanso, you know the shop. I've been such a good little girl, please, Mamacita—"

John Cooper stared at the doctor, uncomprehendingly. The latter leaned forward and whispered, "It's the delirium of fever, Señor Baines."

He put her hands to his lips and held them tightly, wanting to share even this agony with her.

Catarina's head turned slowly, feebly, on the pillows. "I hope I won't be seasick. I've never been on a ship before. Carlos is showing off again. He's trying to climb the mast to show everybody how brave he is. What a lovely bird! I've taught him to say 'te quiero, Catarina' so I'll know that someone really loves me. Mi padre, must we have that savage at our table? He's lived with los indios, you know. I hope he won't try to scalp me. Where are you taking me, señor—oh, you're hurting me! Please don't! I hate you; I hate you! Oh, no I really don't. How beautiful it is here in the stronghold—"

The doctor whispered, "Her life is passing before her, Señor Baines. The fever should pass before—" He halted, turned away, aware that he had touched upon the cruel inevitability that would estrange this loving couple forever.

John Cooper wept unashamedly. He had not cried like this since he had discovered his family murdered by the renegade Shawnee just before his fifteenth birthday—a lifetime, an eternity ago. He was wrenched and twisted in his torment, and he clung to her hands as if believing that, by doing so, he could halt the approach of the grisly shadow-god who hovered over this bedroom and awaited his prey.

Her eyes opened and this time there was a strange clarity to them. He felt her fingers return the pressure of his own, and in a faint voice she murmured, "I—I'm—I'm going to die, Coop. I'm not afraid. Hold me; kiss me; tell me you love me. Please, *mi esposo*."

John Cooper drew a shuddering breath and leaned forward, his hands gently taking hold of Catarina's shoulders as he sought her lips.

With a final, supreme effort, her eyes already beginning to glaze with death, she forced herself to lift her arms and lay them limply around his neck, as she murmured, "You mustn't mourn me too much. I know you love me. Coop, I love you so much. Our children will remind you of me always. For their sakes, and for yours, too, I don't want you to be lonely, Coop. Please do this for me—find someone else who will love you—but always remember me—"

"No one will ever, can ever replace you, my Catarina." His voice was hardly audible as he fought back the flood of grief.

"My darling Coop, you—you can't live without love. I know what love is. Without your love, I'd have been only the spoiled little girl who didn't care for anyone, only herself, who thought you were a savage. Oh, Coop—you must find someone. I know there must be someone who needs love as I did, and you're so strong and good. Find someone. I promise I won't be jealous. I want you to be happy always—I—Coop—oh, my Coop—"

Her voice trailed off, her eyes fixed on his, and he felt a convulsive tremor of her fingers in his. As he stared at her, he knew that she had drawn her last breath.

He held her in his arms for a long moment, tears streaming down his face. There was a hush in the room, and no one spoke. Finally, he let her go and laid her back upon the pillows; he kissed her on the mouth and then on the forehead and then the cheeks. As he straightened, his face drawn and haggard, his lips grimly tight, he turned to Don Diego, who was sobbing openly, with his face buried in his hands. "Were you told who did this to her, my father?"

"Yes, that traitor, that spy of Santa Anna's, Francisco

López," Don Diego groaned, and Doña Inez put her arm around his waist and kissed him and solicitously whispered, "I will share your sorrow, my darling; let me bear most of your grief."

John Cooper closed his eyes and clenched his fists, then dashed them against his thighs till he winced. "Before I rode back, *mi padre*," he addressed Don Diego again, "I had Antonio Lorcas track that *cobarde*. When Lorcas returns, Yankee and I will set out to find Catarina's murderer."

"I would to God I could go with you, my son," Don Diego sobbed.

"Carlos, would you go to Padre Pastronaz and ask him to give a funeral service?" John Cooper asked.

Too overcome to speak, Carlos could only nod.

"Let her be buried near Weesayo," the Texan said in a choked voice, "for in many ways they were both alike."

At this, Carlos broke down and began to sob, and Teresa put her arms around him.

It was the doctor now who stepped forward to the side of the bed, bent over Catarina and examined her, and then gently closed her eyelids. "I think you may say that she was spared great pain, Señor Baines," he said softly, almost apologetically. "I would to God that I had more skill, but I do not think any doctor could have extracted that ball from her spine and kept her alive."

"I understand. I'm not blaming you, Dr. Aguirrez. I'm only glad that she was alive when I came back to her, my beautiful Catarina—"

He did not finish but went to Don Diego and Doña Inez and comforted them by gripping their hands. Then he went to Carlos and Teresa, putting an arm around each of their shoulders and murmuring, "Thank you for being with her, thank you both."

He turned and went out of the room, his eyes unseeing, his face hard and grim and relentless. He walked outside the *hacienda* and into the large, new church that had been repaired after the burning, another act of blasphemy that López had brought about in his pact with the powers of evil. There, he knelt and prayed, and he prayed also for the souls of his family, his mother and father and his sisters, and for Weesayo and all those who had been taken from him. In his prayers, he remembered those whose names the Apache would not speak after their deaths, the name of the former chief of the Jicarilla, Descontarti, and the name of the brave son of the present chief, Kinotatay, who had died in war.

When he was done, he left the church and waited for Antonio Lorcas to return, so that he might begin his own revenge, one for which he had asked the help of God Himself.

Eight

Antonio Lorcas rode back to where Catarina had been found, relying on Esteban Morales's directions. Aware that Catarina had been shot in the back, the *vaquero* determined that Catarina's murderer must have fired from near the mesquite thicket. He rode there, dismounted, and on hands and knees, stared at the ground until he found the trail of the man that had killed John Cooper's wife.

He mounted his horse again and carefully followed the trail south. By nightfall, he saw the dim lights of Acuña, and concluded that Francisco López had ridden out from that village on his diabolical and treacherous attack.

Though armed with a rifle, the young *vaquero* was cautious enough to realize that he would be no match for the Mexican officer; moreover, he knew that it was for John Cooper Baines to administer the rough, primal justice of the frontier.

Wheeling his horse back toward the north, pausing only for a few minutes to eat and to drink from his canteen, Antonio Lorcas galloped back to the *Hacienda del Halcón*.

Before noon of the next day, he rode into the courtyard of the *hacienda*, as exhausted as the horse beneath him. John Cooper Baines stood waiting for him, his face set in a bleak stare. Their eyes met, and the tall Texan said hoarsely, "You found him, then?"

"*Sí*, Señor Baines. The trail leads to Acuña. I am certain he is there, Señor Baines."

"May God bless you, Antonio. Pray for me. I will avenge her."

Antonio was about to speak, but he saw the grim, taut features of his *patrón* and knew that no word would comfort him. He crossed himself and, after he had stabled his horse, went back to the bunkhouse. Then he flung himself down to sleep.

Francisco López had ridden back to Acuña in high spirits. He thought gloatingly to himself that now he had truly destroyed the hated *americano*. From what he had learned at the Double H Ranch, the *Halcón*, that legendary, untouchable hero, who had lived with *los indios* and been revered by them, was nothing but a man, who would weep and tremble and lose his reason because he loved the woman López had killed. The *gringo*, destroyed by his grief and hate, would seek out the man who had deprived him of his *puta*. Well, let him come. He, Francisco López, hoped he would. Even if the *gringo* was successful in finding him, he would be so undone that he could be shot down as easily as his *puta*'s mare. Then it would be a simple matter to raise a faithful army of stupid peasants, greedy for booty, to raid the ranch that would be leaderless, and to seize the silver. It could not have been better planned if he had designed a chart on that first day when Santa Anna had commissioned him to learn the whereabouts of the treasure!

When he returned to the *posada*, he distributed a handful of silver *pesos* to the four men who had ridden out as scouts on his behalf. Grandiosely, flinging a handful onto the counter of Rodrigo Nuñez's bar, he ordered a lavish supper for three evenings hence. He told the smirking innkeeper, "*Mi compañero*, as your *alcalde*, I wish to celebrate. From this day forth, I mean to live at my ease, till the day when I take all of you to Mexico City and make your daughter my honored *esposa*."

John Cooper had decided to take Yankee with him on his quest for his wife's murderer, for Yankee had growled at the first meeting with Santa Anna's treacherous aide and would help flush López out of his hiding place.

The wolf-dog raced along, keeping pace with Pingo's galloping hooves. When John Cooper made camp at nightfall, he fed Yankee some strips of jerky and sat brooding as he chewed his own meager supper. By late afternoon the next day, he would be close to the village toward which, according to Antonio Lorcas, López had fled.

On a small *mesa* there was a curious, almost circular growth of trees. He tethered Pingo's reins to the trunk of one of the trees, then stretched himself out on the still moist ground.

Yankee lay down beside him. He knuckled the wolf-dog's head, and Yankee emitted a low growl of pleasure as he licked his master's face. John Cooper kept his rifle beside him, primed and loaded. He still had the Spanish dagger in its sheath tied around his neck; it reminded him of the hardships he had survived since his boyhood on the bank of the Ohio River, and it had saved his life on more than one occasion. He had taken along new pistols, the finest that he had been able to buy in New Orleans. These were primed and loaded. Before he fell asleep, he mused that López must by now have rallied others. He reasoned that, if that were the case, Santa Anna's former aide might very well send out scouts. But the wolf-dog's senses were keen, and John Cooper knew that if anyone came within a thousand feet of him during the night, Yankee would warn him.

He slept fitfully, and dreamed that he was back in the Jicarilla stronghold with Chief Kinotatay, and that the former chief's son, Pastonari, had become chief. Kinotatay was crippled with age and his hair was snow-white. They spoke freely with each other, as in the days of old. He dreamed that he led his horse to the farthest and highest point of the mountain in that stronghold, and there let the horse find its own way back to the Apache village while he, John Cooper, prostrated himself on the rocky ground and prayed aloud to be purged of his guilt in Catarina's death.

He woke after dawn, physically refreshed and eager for the hunt. He gave Pingo some oats that he had brought in the saddlebag, shared a strip of jerky with Yankee, and set forth.

John Cooper had estimated that he would arrive at Acuña in a few hours, but daytime did not suit his purpose. He intended to take López by surprise because, at nightfall, a man is more relaxed and his reflexes slower. His mouth set grimly as he thought of what he would do to the skulking coward, the accursed spy who had come to the *Hacienda del Halcón* with a lie in his heart and who had really planned to steal and to murder.

Thus, in no rush, he was content to walk Pingo for most of the next day and to watch the trail ahead, till at last he came within sight of the village. It was still daylight, and because López no doubt had either friends or allies, it was as well to find a hiding place until nightfall.

About two miles to the northwest of the village, John Cooper noticed a little clump of irregular trees setting off a grassy knoll and flanked by thick bushes of mesquite and chaparral. Mounting Pingo and beckoning to Yankee, John Cooper rode toward the copse and hid.

At the *posada*, Francisco López was holding forth in great good humor. Rodrigo Nuñez had added extra tables and chairs for the guests who wished to crowd into his tavern and drink the health of their new *alcalde*. He had engaged three women of the village to cook the lavish supper that López ordered to celebrate his triumph over the hated *gringo*. He carefully neglected to mention that this triumph had been the shooting of a helpless woman; instead, he boasted that he had slain the *americano* with his own hands and gloatingly heard the *cobarde* whine for mercy before he died.

The four *peones* whom López had commissioned to act as his bodyguards as well as scouts had been invited to the festive supper. Rosa, in her prettiest dress, sat beside the elegantly uniformed Capitán Felipe Lorrengar, or, to give him his current title, Alcalde Lorrengar.

Sweating profusely at the bar, Rodrigo Nuñez was a happy man. López had just made the announcement that he planned, by summer of this year, to resume his command, but this time of a regiment with headquarters in Mexico City itself. He would marry Rosa and he would take along her kindly father, whom he would stake to the finest and most luxurious *posada* in all Mexico. By now, Nuñez was practically out of *tequila* and only had a little *cerveza* left. However, there was ample food, and the villagers feasted on *chile con carne*, *chiles rellenos*, *enchiladas*, and *tacos*, as well as *nachos* and *tostadas*, which the women had just now brought in from their stone ovens.

In return for López's favors, Nuñez had a present for the new *alcalde*. In gratitude for what he was going to do for his daughter and himself, and to honor the importance of so famous an officer who was now the head of their village, Nuñez had the young men build a new *jacal* on the outskirts of the town. It was a fitting residence for the *señor capitán*. This evening, when he left the *posada*, López would sleep in his new little house and—though the innkeeper did not suspect it—Rosa would join him. Despite the sin, Rosa could no longer help herself. She was infatuated with López and dominated by him. Moreover, he had pledged to marry her in front of so many witnesses, including her own father, that she reasoned they were as good as wed.

At last, the roistering and feasting came to an end, and with an expansive gesture, López climbed onto one of the tables and declaimed, *"Mis amigos,* I must express my gratitude to all of you for your kind concern and for your hospitality. Tonight I shall sleep well in my new *jacal.* And I promise you this, that those of you who are the most conscientious shall accompany me to Mexico City. I have friends in high circles there, and we shall transport the very heart of this village to the capital, where all of you will be *ricos!"*

There were loud cheers, many of them inebriated. Rodrigo Nuñez sighed wearily, a smile on his face, as he mopped his brow. He had taken in more *dinero* tonight than he had in the past five years, and it was all due to this handsome devil of a *capitán*.

He turned to Rosa, who herself was weary from having waited on the crowd that had surged into the little tavern. "Best you go to bed, *mi hija,"* he said. "And devil take it, I'm out of spirits. Perhaps we can induce Pedrosillo to ride to the nearest town and see what *cerveza* and *tequila* he can buy."

"Yes, my father," Rosa dutifully replied. "But what a wonderful evening it was, *¿no es verdad?"* Here, she stretched her arms and yawned, feigning exhaustion. Her father, in a marvelous good humor, beamed at her with paternal approval, patted her on the cheek, and said, "Then by all means go to sleep. Soon, you will sleep with the blessing of Mother Church with that wonderful *alcalde* of ours."

"I truly hope so, *mi padre. Buenas noches,"* Rosa softly answered, as she kissed her father and then went into the rear part of the *posada* to her little room. There was a window that faced toward the northwest, and she smiled to herself as she glanced at it. When her father was asleep, she could sneak out and visit dear Felipe. She yearned for him, especially after the lovemaking they had already enjoyed!

*   *   *

John Cooper slid "Long Girl" out of its sheath and thrust the pistols into the pockets of his buckskin breeches, the butts projecting so that they could be drawn instantly. He beckoned to Yankee, whose yellow eyes gleamed in the darkness, to follow him.

Leaving Pingo tethered to one of the trees and well concealed from view, he and the wolf-dog moved silently toward the outskirts of the little village.

There were lights where the public square must be, and possibly the *posada*—every village had at least one such meeting place where poor men could drink and forget their sorrows and the hard lives they led. Now these lights were going out. He hoped some restless villager might take a fancy to a midnight walk to clear his head from too much *cerveza;* then he would seize him, describe Francisco López to the man, and learn where his enemy was lurking. To be sure, it was possible that López had taken flight. Yet, intuitively, he did not think so.

He put his hands to the butts of the pistols. His mouth was tight and thin as he waited for something to happen. Yankee lay beside him, his tongue lolling, his eyes keenly fixed ahead.

The night was still and oppressively humid. There would be a storm again tomorrow, judging from the faint rumbles of thunder in the distance.

Suddenly he flattened himself on the ground and bade Yankee to remain still. He had heard the sound of a horse's hooves coming toward him. He waited, holding his breath and staring into the darkness. From out of it came a lone rider, ambling along and calling in a slurred, thickened voice, "Not so fast, *estúpido,* wait till I get my bearings! *Ayúdame,* I've had too much *cerveza* tonight. But I must make the rounds all the same. Slowly now, you brute, I told you!"

It was Corporal Pedrosillo, who, lauded by his neighbors for having been appointed as the ranking aide of their new, noble *alcalde,* had forced himself to continue his nocturnal patrol. He would show Capitán Lorrengar that he was the best scout and soldier in all Acuña and should certainly soon earn the stripes of a *sargento.*

He sat unsteadily on a lean, aging gray mustang, his *sombrero* pulled down over one side of his face, blinking his eyes as he tried to squint through the darkness. His only weapon was an old fowling piece thrust through the sash around his waist, even though it had little accuracy and was in sore need of cleaning. Yankee, in spite of John Cooper's injunction, suddenly emitted a soft, menacing growl, and the mustang started, rearing up and pawing the air with his front hooves, unhorsing the inebriated rider.

John Cooper swiftly moved toward the sprawled young Mexican and, gripping him by the shoulders and staring down at him, said, "*Hombre,* I won't hurt you, but I want you to tell me the truth, *¿comprende?*"

Pedrosillo nodded, stricken with terror. "I'll do whatever you say, señor. Don't hurt me, *por el amor de Dios.*"

"That depends on you. Now then, I'm looking for a man named Francisco López."

"There's no such man in Acuña; I know that much," Pedrosillo declared. Yankee, beside the sprawled and helpless young corporal, uttered another menacing growl and moved closer. Pedrosillo shrank back from the savage jaws and the gleaming yellow eyes. "In the name of mercy, don't let that dog at me, señor. I swear on the grave of *mi madre* there is no such man in Acuña."

"It's possible he goes under another name," John Cooper said. "I'll describe him. . . ." He detailed the features and the build of the bearded, swaggering officer.

"*Pero sí,*" the man stammered, "but that's not his name; he's Capitán Felipe Lorrengar—and we made him our *alcalde.* He's going to marry Rosa, that's old Nuñez's daughter, *¿comprende?*"

"Yes, I understand you. Where can I find this *alcalde* of yours?"

"Do you see over there?" Frantic with terror and eager to be released, the young Mexican gestured toward the north-west. Mistaking this for a threatening gesture, Yankee suddenly sank his fangs into the corporal's palm. John Cooper clamped his hand over Pedrosillo's mouth to stifle the ago-nized, shrill scream, while at the same time angrily rebuking Yankee, "No, no, boy, let him be!"

Then, staring pitilessly down at Pedrosillo, he insisted, "Do you mean this *alcalde* of yours is in that *jacal* over there?"

"Oh, yes, señor, that's where he is. He left the *posada* about half an hour ago. We celebrated his paying back a *gringo* who cheated and hurt him, and—"

John Cooper again clamped his palm over the man's

mouth and, restraining his fury, said in a shuddering, raging tone, "I'm the *gringo* he's after. He shot and killed my wife and she had never done him any harm."

Pedrosillo, terrified and nearly fainting from the pain of his bitten hand, nodded, his eyes enormous and glazed with fear, as he stared at the bearded face of the scowling, blond Texan.

As John Cooper drew away his hand, Pedrosillo babbled, "Oh, please don't hurt me. Don't let that dog bite me again. I'll do whatever you want—"

"You'll do nothing. You'll go to sleep, *hombre*. I won't hurt you, but I won't have you interfering, either. And you'd best start looking for another *alcalde* tomorrow. Sleep well!" John Cooper drew out one of his pistols, took it by the barrel, and directed a vigorous blow against Pedrosillo's temple. The young Mexican slumped unconscious.

John Cooper quickly rolled him over onto his belly, bound his wrists behind him with a leather thong from his saddlebag, then gagged him with a bandanna and knotted it tightly at the back of his neck. Then he retrieved his rifle and beckoned to Yankee. He moved stealthily, crouching, toward the *jacal* on the outskirts of Acuña. Concealing himself behind a huge mesquite thicket, he gestured to Yankee to lie beside him.

There was a stillness in the night and the lights of the little village had nearly all gone out. But an oil lamp burned in the new *jacal*, and that pinpoint of light drew John Cooper's gaze with unwavering intensity. His teeth clenched, his hands gripping "Long Girl," he waited.

Suddenly he saw the shadowy outline of a figure make its way toward the *jacal*. He propped himself up on one elbow, holding the rifle in his right hand, and he saw the figure stop before the door of the *jacal*. An instant later, the door was opened, the light was brighter for an instant, and then the door was closed.

John Cooper's mouth twisted in a wry, grim smile. Perhaps that alone proved that it was Francisco López in the *jacal:* The figure was that of a female.

"*Querida*, I knew you'd come," López whispered as he drew Rosa into his arms. She wore only her nightshift and a robe and she was barefooted. She turned up her mouth to be kissed, her eyes closed, trembling with anticipation. As his mouth took hers, she uttered a stifled moan and locked her arms around his neck, pressing herself against him.

"It's the fitting way to end this magnificent day, *querida*," he told her with a chuckle.

"Tell me that you love me again; tell me that I'm going to be your wife—" she entreated.

"Of course, you are, *mi linda!*" he reassured her as his hands began to explore the soft, voluptuous contours of her thinly clad body.

John Cooper and Yankee had crept toward the *jacal*, and the former mountain man crouched under the window, putting one hand over Yankee's muzzle. He listened intently as he heard Rosa faintly stammer, "Be gentle, *querido*. You know I belong to you—but please, can't we first talk about the wedding? *Mi padre* is so proud to think that he will be your *suegro!*"

"You heard me promise that I'd marry you, Rosa. That's enough talk. Come give me a kiss. Now, let me take off this robe and this nightshift—"

"Oh, no, please not so quickly. I asked you to be gentle. You must respect me, if I'm to be your *esposa*, Felipe," she timidly protested.

Yankee, having heard López's voice raised in exasperation, had suddenly uttered a low, ominous growl. López started, cocked his head, then muttered, "What was that?"

"I didn't hear anything," Rosa stammered, for by this time she was caught up in the sensual vortex of her feelings.

John Cooper had caught the sudden alarm in his enemy's voice. He called, "Francisco López, come out!" As he did so, he moved in front of the doorway, the rifle at waist level, primed and readied.

"What is it, Felipe? Who is that who calls to you by that name, *querido?*" Rosa anxiously demanded of her lover.

"Who calls the name of Francisco López? I am Capitán Felipe Lorrengar," Santa Anna's former aide arrogantly called back as suddenly he husked Rosa of her filmy garments. She uttered a cry of shame and crossed one arm over her bosom and the other over her loins, as he drew out his pistols, cocked them, and waited pressed against the wall.

"You lie, López. You know why I've come, don't you?"

Rosa could not understand. "What is he saying to you? Who is this man? Why does he keep calling you López, *querido?* I don't understand all this. What are you doing? Please don't—"

"Shut your mouth, you stupid bitch," López hissed into her ear as he put the barrel of one pistol to the back of her neck. "Now you're going to do just what I tell you, if you want to live. We're going to go out there, and you're going to march ahead of me. I'll pull the trigger at the least trick you try; do you understand that, Rosa?"

"But I'm naked—" she quavered.

"You're at your best then, so let this idiot see you before I kill him," López cynically responded. Then he called out, "Yes, I know you. You're the *gringo*. I see you are as eager to die as your wife was, Señor Baines—I'll accommodate you. I warn you; I wouldn't start shooting that fine rifle of yours right away, for there's a very charming señorita in here with me, and your ball might hit her instead of me."

"Then come out, Goddamn your filthy soul!" John Cooper Baines hoarsely shouted. Yankee bared his fangs and snarled. "Are you coming out, López, or do I come in after you?"

"Oh, yes, I'm coming out. But as I said, I have a charming señorita here with me, so be very careful. You had best not let that savage animal of yours jump at me, or there might be an accident."

With this, López kicked open the door, and Rosa, sobbing, her face scarlet with shame, emerged, stark naked. López's pistol was pressed to the back of her neck; the other pistol was trained on John Cooper Baines.

Yankee bared his fangs in an angry growl and John Cooper commanded, "Stay, Yankee!" Then, to the Mexican, he said contemptuously, "I might have guessed you'd try a stunt like that, López."

"*Cuidado,* Señor Baines," he taunted the Texan, "be very careful about that rifle. If you pull the trigger, my trigger finger will send the ball into this *puta*'s neck."

"Oh, señor, señor, please don't shoot," Rosa hysterically pleaded. "Oh, please, Felipe, how can you treat me this way?"

It was all John Cooper could do to hold himself back. In a voice that shook with pent-up rage, he declared, "If you're a man, López, you'll let her go, and I'll fight you with my bare hands."

"I don't trust you. Everyone knows what an expert

marksman you are with that rifle, Señor Baines. So naturally
I wish to equalize matters and not give you the advantage,"
López responded. Then, jabbing the muzzle of his pistol
against the sobbing Rosa's neck, he growled, "Besides, you've
that infernal wolf-dog with you. No, decidedly, Señor Baines,
I don't propose to give you any advantage over me. Maybe,"
López taunted, "I'll let the girl go if you tell me where that
silver is."

"The silver is where it belongs, in a New Orleans bank
vault."

"What in the name of ten thousand devils are you telling
me, American dog?" López demanded. "I'll kill you! I swear
by the devil in hell, I'll kill you! All right, I agree to fight
you barehanded. Throw down your rifle and I'll throw down
my pistols and let the woman go!" López shouted.

John Cooper, trembling with fury, dropped the rifle.
López, with a sardonic grin, triggered off a shot with the pistol in his right hand. John Cooper, anticipating treachery,
moved swiftly to one side, so that the ball only grazed his
hip. He rushed forward, dragged the naked, sobbing young
woman out of the way, then kicked López in the belly, sending him sprawling. Both of his pistols fell to the ground, and
with a quick lunge, John Cooper grabbed them and flung
them off to one side. Quickly, he called to the dazed, hysterical young woman, "Get back into the *jacal!* Now it's a fair
fight between us!"

Rosa, a hand at her mouth, ran back into the hut and
donned her shift and robe, while John Cooper watched his
enemy slowly stagger to his feet, retching from the kick, rubbing his belly. "Come on, you yellow dog," John Cooper
cried, "all you can do is shoot helpless women! Defend yourself like a man!"

López lunged forward, butting John Cooper in the belly,
felling him, and the two men rolled over and over, kicking
and trying to gouge out each other's eyes. "I'll kill you,
chinga su madre," López panted.

His glazed eyes, burning with madness and hate, fixed
on the Spanish dagger that hung from his enemy's neck, and
freeing one of his hands, he tried to tear it off and use it. John
Cooper swiftly intercepted that sudden movement and twisted
the Mexican's wrist, till López howled in agony and kneed
him in the crotch.

Fighting the waves of blinding agony that surged through him, John Cooper managed to roll López onto his belly and to crawl astride him, grasping the Mexican's wrists in his left hand. With his right thumb, he reached forward and brutally thrust his thumb upward into López's right eye.

A frenzied howl of pain was torn from the writhing Mexican who, with a supreme effort, arched and then twisted himself with all his strength to unseat his foe. John Cooper was thrown to one side and López got to all fours, then rose. His eyeball was half out of the socket, blood pouring down his cheek, and his teeth were bared in a hideous grimace. He mouthed blasphemous oaths as he kicked out at the Texan, then hurled himself once again at John Cooper and seized his neck.

Rosa timidly emerged, a hand at her mouth, staring transfixed at the two mortal enemies as they battled to the death.

"I'll kill you; I'll kill you. I killed your wife and you'll be next!" López shrieked in his frenzy. He charged like a bull and knocked John Cooper to the ground. Possessed of demoniac strength, he tried to gouge out both of his adversary's eyes with his thumbs. John Cooper managed to roll out from under the other man, and jumping up, he grabbed López by the collar and brought him to his feet. Using all his strength, John Cooper punched him first in the stomach, then in the face. The breath went out of López and he fell to his knees.

Panting, the pain of the blows and his gouged eye becoming intolerable, López saw the discarded rifle a few feet away and made a lunge for it, seizing it by the barrel, even as John Cooper flung himself at the man. López was able to swing it, using the butt like a club. "A little closer, *por favor*," he taunted. "I'll smash your skull in, I'll cut your tripes out with your own knife, once I've beaten you down, and then I'll cut off your *cojones* and feed them to the buzzards! You can join your *puta* of a wife in hell!"

By these insults he hoped to set John Cooper into such a frenzy of rage that the latter would forget all cunning and judgment. But John Cooper, nimbly darting from side to side, evaded the furious sweeps of the rifle, which López swung back and forth as he would a heavy club. Then, just as the Mexican drew back the rifle to swing again, John Cooper lunged forward, head lowered, and butted his adversary in the belly, toppling him to the ground with a cry of pain as the rifle dropped from his hands.

"Now we're back to even terms again, López," John Cooper panted. Evading the man's thumb jabs that sought his eyes, John Cooper caught one of López's wrists, then dragged him to his feet and, with his right hand, delivered a tremendous uppercut to López's jaw, which felled him.

Rosa cried out as John Cooper sprang at his staggering adversary. Before López could recover, groggily shaking his head and rubbing his jaw as he tried to rise, the Texan swiftly got behind him. He knelt and circled López's neck with his left arm, then put his right palm to the Mexican's chin. Gritting his teeth, John Cooper tightened his grip and exerted all his strength to jerk López's chin. A raucous, prolonged shriek was torn from the Mexican as his one remaining eye bulged and glazed, and then there was the sound of a crack, and his body slumped inert. John Cooper had broken his neck.

He crouched on all fours beside his dead foe, drawing in great gulps of air. He lifted his contorted, sweating face and saw Rosa watching him, her eyes enormously dilated, her lips open, without the ability to speak.

"It's over. He killed my wife, señorita. He's tried several times to kill me and others with me, seeking treasure that didn't belong to him. He was a traitor and a spy. His name was Francisco López. He was a colonel in the army of Santa Anna."

John Cooper rose, and as he did so he swayed from pain and fatigue. Turning to Yankee, he said, "Come along, boy! We've finished here. We'll go back home. Home," he repeated the last word with a gloomy, tragic sigh. Then striding forward, he started back to where he had tethered Pingo.

He turned to stare down at the body of his dead adversary, and a wave of nausea took hold of him. The pain in his groin had become so torturing that tears stung his eyes. His chest was heaving from the exertion of that deadly duel, and suddenly Rosa exclaimed, "Señor, you're bleeding. The pistol, when it went off . . . your hip is bloody—you mustn't think of riding across the Rio Grande now—"

"I have to get home—don't worry about me, señorita—" His voice was hoarse, unrecognizable. He took a step toward the copse where he had tethered Pingo, and then sudden blackness engulfed him. Before he lost consciousness he heard the young woman cry out, "Oh, señor, you're hurt! You're hurt badly! Oh, *Dios!*" Then all was nothingness.

He woke to find himself on a straw pallet, and the woman whom López had tried to use as hostage was bending over him with a solicitous look on her lovely face. Beside her stood her father, Rodrigo Nuñez, who exclaimed, *"Gracias a Dios,* he comes back to the living."

John Cooper blinked his eyes, trying to adjust to his surroundings. "Where am I? What happened?" he hoarsely stammered.

"After the fight, señor," Rosa spoke up, "you wanted to get your horse and ride back over the Rio Grande to your home. But you fainted. I did not know what to do because that fearful animal of yours—"

"Yes—Yankee—where is he; what happened to him?" John Cooper tried to prop himself up on one elbow and grimaced at the wave of nausea and pain that it cost him. Yankee was standing beside the bed, and he licked his master's hand when he saw he had regained consciousness.

"He is a good dog," Nuñez said. "After my daughter ran to tell me what had happened, he let us take you inside this *jacal* to look after you. Rosa told me how you had called that man Francisco López and accused him of killing your wife—"

"He did. He shot her with a rifle, and in the back."

"¡Qué lástima! We had no way of knowing that he was not what he claimed to be, señor," Rosa's father interposed.

"I understand." John Cooper drew a deep breath and then lay back, closing his eyes for a moment. "My horse—"

"Oh, yes, señor," Nuñez smilingly broke in. "One of the four young men whom this man commissioned as his private scout could not find Corporal Pedrosillo, so he rode out and found him tied and gagged—"

"I did that because I had to come find the man who murdered my wife."

"I know that now, señor. Pedrosillo bears you no malice. He, too, has learned who this Capitán Lorrengar really was. Anyway, they continued on and found your horse. It is now in my stable and it is well fed. It is a fine horse."

Rosa softly spoke. "I nursed you through your fever. You've been here two days and three nights and this is the third day. You kept calling 'Catarina.' When I bathed you and gave you the medicine the *indios* use to take away fever, you reached for my hand and kissed it and said, 'I love you so, Catarina; don't leave me.' Señor, it made me cry."

John Cooper closed his eyes and turned his face to the wall. He had been quartered during his convalescence in the *jacal* that the villagers had built to express their gratitude to Capitán Lorrengar. The father and daughter respected his silence, and there was a long pause while John Cooper tried to regain his self-control and to thank his benefactors. "I am glad that no one else was hurt. This was between that man and myself, you understand," he finally said.

"Perfectly, señor," the innkeeper said, nodding. Then his face fell as he shrugged. "Well, for a time, I was as much a fool as any of them. I believed in him."

Now John Cooper slowly began to rise from his straw pallet.

"You must not be too much in a hurry to leave, till you feel well again, señor," Rosa hastily interposed.

"Thank you, señorita, you've been very kind to me. But if I've been here three days, then it's high time I was getting back home. I feel well enough, thanks to you. What is your name, señor?" he said, turning to the innkeeper.

"Rodrigo Nuñez, *su servidor.*"

"Señor Nuñez, when I get back to the ranch, I'll have one of my *vaqueros* bring down to you one of my Texas bulls and a heifer and three steers. Perhaps, with the heifer and the bull, you could begin your own herd."

"That's very generous of you, señor," Nuñez excitedly exclaimed. "God will bless you."

"It's a debt of honor I wish to pay, Señor Nuñez. Your daughter, who cared for me—is there no man in this village who would make her a good husband?"

"She will have none of them. Of course, now that they know that she was fond of this enemy of yours, the men in this village will have nothing to do with her, either. You see, this man promised before all that he would marry her. No one here will want a woman who was pledged to such an evil man."

"I have been thinking," John Cooper said slowly, now sitting up on the bed, "I have a large ranch just across the Frio River. We have many *vaqueros*, some *criadas*, and many *trabajadores* who have sent for their families. Perhaps your daughter would enjoy working at my ranch, where she could be a maid. I'm sure that, good and sweet as she is, she would find many of our fine *vaqueros* who would make good husbands, when it is time for her to make such a choice."

"Do you really mean that, señor?" Rosa's father incredulously asked.

"Of course, I do. If she wishes, she can ride back with me." John Cooper closed his eyes and sighed. "It will be a lonely journey, and I should be grateful for her company."

Rodrigo Nuñez turned to his daughter. "It is a new chance for you, my Rosa. Perhaps, as the señor says, you'll find someone who's an honest man and who will respect and love you. You have my blessing."

"She will be able to visit you many times during the year, Señor Nuñez," John Cooper said as he stood, turning the other way as he gingerly touched his groin where López had kneed him. He found that though it was still sensitive, the pain had almost entirely subsided.

Yankee wagged his tail and barked, then pressed his head against John Cooper's thigh. His master reached down to scratch his head and play with his ears, and Yankee uttered a growl of pleasure. John Cooper looked up at the innkeeper's daughter. "How long will it take you to get ready to go with me?"

The young woman looked first at John Cooper, then at her father, and then at the ground. "Could I ask you to wait until tomorrow morning? I would like to spend one last night with my father, if that is all right."

"Of course it's all right. And I don't think it'll do any harm either for me to rest up another night."

Rodrigo Nuñez suddenly remembered something. "This man who called himself Capitán Lorrengar, señor, he had a sack of silver *pesos*. There are quite a few left. Perhaps he stole them from you?"

"Oh, no," John Cooper said, uttering a sardonic little laugh as he thought of the much greater fortune in silver that had been responsible for all the tragedy. "No, I'm sure he stole the silver *pesos* from someone else. I suggest you keep them."

"Why, señor, I thank you. I have every reason to be grateful to you, señor, and so have the others of this village. All of us were deceived."

"At least he did no real harm. He only used you. But I'd best not think of that anymore. Well then, it's settled. Tomorrow morning, I'll ride back across the Rio Grande, and you needn't worry for your daughter's safety."

"By the way, señor," the innkeeper said, "we buried him, the morning after the fight. Because of what my daughter told me, we did not even put up a headstone to mark his grave."

John Cooper laughed again, a grim, bitter laugh. "That, Señor Nuñez, must have been for Francisco López the most dreadful failure of all. He had grand ideas and ambitions and was certain that he would carry them off. There's a saying, 'Man proposes; God disposes.' I think that about sums it up."

Nine

The next morning, with Rosa Nuñez riding beside him on her father's mustang, John Cooper Baines headed back to the Double H Ranch, with Yankee loping along beside them. But the tall Texan no longer smiled. His face seemed altered; there were lines in his forehead, and his eyes, fixed on the horizon beyond, were unseeing. He saw little except the face of the beautiful wife whom he had held in his arms till she had drawn her last breath.

When they crossed the Rio Grande, the innkeeper's daughter was startled by the vivid contrast between the desolate terrain of the northernmost part of Mexico and the sudden, fertile, lushly green plain that extended beyond the river, with its profusion of trees, wildflowers, and flowering bushes.

She wore her best, a long-skirted red cotton dress with sleeves to her wrists and a modest bodice. To facilitate her riding, she had tucked up the skirt, rolling it above her knees. She blushed to think that she was journeying so far with a man who had been a stranger to her until so recently.

He was taciturn throughout the journey. Uneducated and young though she was, Rosa sensed that he did not wish to talk, that he was preoccupied with his gloomy thoughts.

Remembering his delirium when he had spoken the name of his wife and recalled their courtship, she felt pity for him. Perhaps her compassionate gratitude for the man who had rescued her from the miserable village led her almost to wishing, in a wistful, fanciful way, that he would notice that she was desirable and young and that she could console him. But she dismissed the thought at once. So profound a love as he had shown for his murdered wife struck her with a kind of awe and an admiration, and helped her realize that John Cooper Baines was unattainable.

They crossed the Frio River and rode on, till at last, early the following day, she saw the church, the many barns, the bunkhouse, the cottages, and the large, impressive *hacienda*. Only then did he turn, reining in Pingo, to look at her and nod amiably as he said, "Here we are, señorita. You've done very well to keep up with me. I hope you're not too tired."

"Oh, no, señor, I'm fine, *gracias*," she said.

"Fine. Tell me, are you good at cooking?"

"*Mi padre* thinks so," Rosa ingenuously responded.

"Well, then, I'll take you to Tía Margarita. She's been our cook for years, and she's getting old. I think she'd take a liking to you, señorita. At any rate, I'll put her in charge of you. I hope you'll be happy here. I know I was—" He abruptly broke off and frowned, and Rosa knew that he did not intend to explain, nor did he need to. She felt her heart go out to him, but she knew that no words she could say would ease his hurt.

He rode ahead of her into the courtyard, dismounted, and then turned to see Miguel Sandarbal gravely contemplating him. "Thank God you're back, *Halcón*," the old *capataz* declared. "We've all said prayers for you."

"*Gracias*, Miguel. That bastard is food for the worms now. He'll never trouble us again. Oh, this señorita, Rosa Nuñez, lived in Acuña, where I tracked López down, thanks to Antonio Lorcas. She was kind enough to look after me while I was recovering from a few little injuries I sustained in a fight."

"I hope you weren't seriously hurt, *Halcón*!" Miguel anxiously asked.

"No," John Cooper said quickly, wishing to erase all the unpleasantness from his memory. "That's all past now.

Miguel, be kind enough to take Señorita Nuñez into the kitchen and introduce her to Tía Margarita."

"I'll see to it, *Halcón*." Miguel gave the lovely young peasant girl a courtly inclination of his head and added, "If you'll come with me, Señorita Nuñez, I'll be happy to introduce you to the best cook in all of Texas."

"You're most kind, señor. *Gracias,*" Rosa stammered as she flushed nervously. The smile and the twinkle in Miguel's eyes told her that she was welcome here, and for the first time since she had realized how cruelly Francisco López had betrayed her, she began to believe that perhaps there would be a new life for her.

Yankee was growling softly to demand attention from his master, and John Cooper reached down to knuckle the wolf-dog's head. Then he led Pingo to the stable.

As he left the stable, heading back to the main house, Don Diego strode out of the *hacienda*, his eyes bloodshot from weeping, his face haggard and drawn. "My son, my son, you are back safely; may all the saints be praised!" the white-haired, former *intendente* of Taos hoarsely exclaimed as he flung his arms around his son-in-law and kissed him on both cheeks. "I prayed that the man you sought would not lay in wait for you and shoot you down without mercy, as he did my poor daughter."

"No, my father, your daughter, my wife, is avenged. Her murderer died in Acuña, and the villagers buried him in an unmarked grave."

"A fitting end for the carrion that he was," Don Diego bitterly said.

"I shall try to forget him, but I shall never forget Catarina. Oh, my father, I did not mean to make you weep again. No, it is for me to weep for all of us." John Cooper was close to tears as the old man broke down again and, clinging to his son-in-law, let his tears flow unashamedly.

They stood together for a long moment sharing their grief, until at last John Cooper, trying to force his voice into a normal tone, inquired, "How are Andrew and Charles?"

"Good as gold, my son." Don Diego straightened, releasing John Cooper from his embrace, and took out a handkerchief and loudly blew his nose. "I declare, sometimes this Texas air has things in it that clog my nostrils. Well then, they have become closer than ever. Doña Inez has been looking after them, and both she and Teresa took care of little

Carmen and Ruth. Coraje, of course, is still being looked after by Concepción. And I must say that it is wonderful how Teresa has taken to Carlos's children. I should not be surprised at all if before this year is over I shall be a grandfather again."

"I hope so, for your sake as well as Carlos's," John Cooper replied. He turned to stare southward, and his face was bleak again. Don Diego anxiously regarded him, then murmured, "We must remember that we have her children to remind us of her, my son."

"Yes, that will help me. But I feel lost and empty, my father. I shall be with my sons and my daughters for a time, and then I'm going to go see Kinotatay, after I've gone up to one of the mountains near the stronghold to think things out clearly. You remember how Carlos did that, after Weesayo died?"

"Oh, yes, I shall never forget that. It tore my heart from my very breast, my son. But you will return to us?"

"Most likely. I must think about how I'm to take up my life again, Father. At the moment, I haven't the least interest in cattle or horses or anything else."

"Of course, you haven't. Come along now. Doña Inez will be eager to see you, and so will Carlos and Teresa," Don Diego encouraged him, as he put his arm around his son-in-law's shoulders.

John Cooper was sick at heart, and he knew that the kindly people at the ranch, from the *criadas* and the *trabajadores* to Don Diego and Carlos and his good friend Miguel, would try their best to console him; yet words, no matter how compassionate and sincere, were of little use.

He felt it would be wrong to inflict his deep anguish upon all of them, and most of all upon his children. He remembered how Carlos had gone off into the mountains to commune with a higher power, to find some reason for the needless death of his beloved Weesayo, and had gained strength from that spiritual isolation. He wanted that, too, and yet there was something else that still had to be done.

It would be, John Cooper thought to himself, the hardest task he had ever undertaken. He must bring his children together, even the baby Coraje, to explain why their mother would never be there again to comfort them and rejoice in their games and aspirations. It must be done immediately. Already little Carmen, who was nearing her fourth birthday, had run up to him as soon as he arrived home and asked him plaintively, "Why isn't Mama here, Daddy?" He had said, almost unthinkingly, "Because she's gone on a very long trip, darling." Then, seeing her questioning, hurt look, he squatted down, took her in his arms, and kissed her and murmured, "Daddy will tell you what it is, when we all have supper this evening. I promise, Carmen honey."

As the sun began to set and the reddish and purplish glows painted the horizon on a limitless canvas, he strove to collect his thoughts so that he might deal with this task in a way that would comfort the children.

He thought that it would be best to tell them what had happened out here under the sky, because the beauty of the land and of the sky and the green grass and the trees and the majestic church with its glorious bell would all remind them of the goodness of life.

That was what made him seek out Esteban Morales and ask, "Do you think you could bring out a long table, such as you use at barbecues and festivals, and put it to one side of the church? I'm going to eat supper with my children this evening and tell them what has happened."

"*Comprendo*, Señor Baines," the assistant *capataz* replied, "I'll see to it myself. Is there anything else I may do for you?"

"No, Esteban, whatever debt you thought you owed me was paid many times over, when you brought her back. God bless you and Concepción and your children."

"The *trabajadores* asked me—I do not wish to offend you; I understand what you feel now—but they asked me to tell you, all of them, how they pray for you and for her, who was so kind to them—"

John Cooper turned away for an instant. Finally, he said, "If you will tell them that I am very grateful for their thoughts and their prayers, it will please me, Esteban." Then, remembering the assistant *capataz*'s skill in whittling, he added, "I would ask only one more favor of you—could you make some new little toys for the children?"

"It would be my great pleasure."

As he neared the kitchen, John Cooper was suddenly accosted by a radiant Miguel Sandarbal, who hurried out of his cottage, his face aglow with delight, and cried out, "It's a boy, *Halcón!*"

He turned to meet the *capataz*. "My congratulations, Miguel. I'm glad you got back in time to be with your Bess and to see your child born."

"She says she wants to name it after me, and that's very flattering for a man my age, *Halcón*." In his pride and joy, Miguel had momentarily forgotten John Cooper's grief. Suddenly he clapped a hand over his mouth, then ruefully shook his head and mumbled, "I'm a stupid, pigheaded old fool, *mi compañero*. I ought to have had better sense—"

"No, don't apologize, old friend. I'm happy for you and for Bess. By the way, I want to ask a favor of you."

"Anything; name it, *Halcón!*"

"Tomorrow I'm going to ride to the stronghold because I want to be alone and think things out. I don't know what I'm going to do; I haven't any heart for anything right now—"

"Of course, you don't," Miguel sympathetically interposed. "I think that's the best thing for you."

"What I was going to say, Miguel, is that when I leave for a time, I'd be very grateful if you'd take both Charles and Andrew under your wing. Let them do some work around here and get the feel of things. Well, I'll see you before I go tomorrow." He gave Miguel a friendly nod, then walked to the kitchen.

The night was gentle, with hardly a wind, yet pleasantly cool. Near the church, Esteban and one of the *vaqueros* had set up a long, low wooden table and chairs for John Cooper at the head, with Andrew and Charles respectively at his right and left nearest him, and then Ruth beside Charles and Carmen beside Andrew. John Cooper held little Coraje in his lap. He wished Catarina's last child, despite his tender age, to be present at this family conclave; after he had spoken to them all and before they ate, he would take Coraje back to the Morales cottage for Concepción to nurse.

Tía Margarita had understood, and after John Cooper had asked her to prepare a special supper for his children and himself, she wiped her eyes with the corner of her apron as she confided to Rosa Nuñez, "He is such a good man, *querida*. I weep for him. Perhaps you would serve the food?"

"Oh, yes, Tía Margarita, I should like that very much! I shall never forget what he did for me!" Rosa herself began to cry.

"Now, now," said Tía Margarita consolingly. "Here,

take this tray of food. I have made some special things the children will like. Some little meat patties with vegetables, which will be good for them, not too spicy, and some nice little cakes. It would not be a picnic without cakes outdoors, you know. There you are!"

Rosa carried the tray from the kitchen out toward the church but, seeing that John Cooper had already begun to talk to the children, respectfully waited. She could not help overhearing what he was saying, and she began to weep silently. Ah, if only *el Señor Dios* would send her such a man as that one, so devoted to his wife, so agonized because of her death.

"My children," John Cooper began, clearing his throat and smiling down at little Coraje, who cooed and reached up for his father's beard with a tiny hand, "I have asked all of you to have supper with me, so that we may talk about your mother. You know how much I loved her."

At this point, little Carmen, more and more curious, broke in, "Daddy, you said she went away on a long trip."

"Yes, little one. A trip from which she will never return. God took her to become one of his angels."

"That man, that Francisco López, Pa?" Andrew turned to his father with hurt, questioning eyes.

"He has gone to meet his Maker, Andrew. You see, boy, we have no law yet, here in Texas. We're trying to make our own laws, but until that day a man must fight to defend his loved ones. Sometimes he has to punish those who hurt him or his family or his friends. That was what I did when I went to find López."

"Mama is dead, right, Daddy?" Ruth asked.

"Yes, sweetheart. You understand that, what death means, don't you?"

"Yes, Daddy. That was when the other day, they put Mama in the ground with her prayer book in her hands, and Padre Pastronaz said the beautiful words, and they put up a stone over where she is sleeping."

"Yes. That is exactly what happened. But you see, Ruth, the body dies, but the spirit goes on. I think that right now your mother is seeing us and listening to us. They say that the spirits of those who have gone on ahead of us watch over us and try to guide us. I want you to think that of your mother, children."

Carmen had begun to cry, at last realizing the enormity

of what John Cooper had been saying. Ruth's direct question had made her think about such things for the first time in her life, and she was both terrified and stunned.

John Cooper made room for her on his lap and kissed her and comforted her. Holding Carmen with one arm and the baby with the other, he went on to explain, "Now that she has become an angel, children, all of us must remember her, how lovely she was, how kind and sweet. Her love will always be with us, if we remember her."

They were silent, except that little Coraje again cooed in his father's lap and reached up to tug John Cooper's beard. He smiled and bent down to kiss the top of the baby's forehead. Then he resumed, "Andy, you're the oldest now, and you've already proved what you can do. As for you, Charles, you're a year younger, but you've also proved yourself, and I'm proud of you, too. Both you boys must look after your little sisters and, of course, Coraje. Just because Ruth and Carmen happen to be girls, it doesn't mean they're any less quick or smart or able to do things. They're just younger than you and need your support. One day, when you all grow up, you'll marry and have children of your own. That is the way all of us go on into a next life, you see. You, Andy, and you, Charles, will one day replace me, and I hope that you will be good, upright men and help those who are weak and sick and need your protection."

"I'll sure try, Pa," Andrew murmured. He tried not to show how affected he was, though his eyes were moist.

"I'm planning on that, son. Now we will bow our heads and say a prayer for your mother, children. Say it aloud, if you wish, or say it in your hearts. She will hear it, and so will God. Tell her how much you love her and that you hope she will continue to watch over you."

Rosa Nuñez turned to one side, for her eyes were blinded by her tears. She saw John Cooper, after a long moment of silence, rise from the table and heard him say, "I'll come back in just a few minutes, once I've given little Coraje to Concepción. Then we'll have our picnic." Rosa waited until he had gone toward the Morales cottage to set down the tray and to smile at all the children.

When he came back and seated himself at the table, he smilingly said, "Why, Señorita Nuñez, the food looks wonderful. Tell Tía Margarita I thank her very much. Thank you, too."

"De nada, Señor Baines." Rosa inclined her head and hurried back to the kitchen. She told herself that in the morning, she would go to church, if there was some time she could spare from her work with that fat, kind old woman who ran the kitchen, and thank *el Señor Dios* for the good things that had happened to her. She would also pray for the salvation and the happiness of this bearded man who had avenged his wife and yet whom she had just heard being so gentle in explaining the terrifying mystery of death to his children.

When they had eaten, John Cooper again addressed them. "Tomorrow, children, I'm going to ride back to the mountains where I once lived. I shall be gone a few weeks, but your Uncle Carlos and Aunt Teresa will look after you, and so will Don Diego, Doña Inez, and my good friend Miguel. I must go, for I want to pray and to think about what work I'm going to be doing here on the ranch from now on."

Then, rising, he said in a jocular tone, "Now, I think it's certainly your bedtime. Tomorrow morning, before I go, I'll say good-bye to each one of you. Charles, why don't you take your sisters into the house?"

"Sure, Pa." Charles rose with alacrity and offered his hands to Ruth and Carmen, who took them and walked slowly back to the *hacienda.* Both girls looked back over their shoulders and simultaneously called out, "Good night, Daddy."

"Good night, sweethearts."

He watched Charles take the girls into the house, then turned to Andrew and stared questioningly at him. "Do you want to say something to me, Andy?" he gently asked.

"Could I go for a walk with you, Pa? I don't want to talk, just to walk and be with you. I don't feel like going to bed early. Maybe we could take Yankee with us?"

"That would be fine. I think he'd like a romp. Come along then, Andy."

Ten

He said his good-byes to his children, to Don Diego and Doña Inez, and to Teresa and Carlos and the latter's children. Yankee was instructed to stay behind, to look after the families of the ranch.

Tía Margarita packed the food John Cooper had requested for his journey, and she had a parting gift for him. *"Es un ojo de Dios*—the eye of God, Señor Baines," she said in a tremulous voice. "Wherever you have it, it will look at you, and you will see and lose yourself in it and be close to Him Who makes us all."

Two polished little sticks had been made in the form of a cross and connected with colored woolen strands, red, green, and yellow, forming a bright knob at the meeting of the crosspieces. She added, mopping her eyes with the hem of her apron, "Padre Pastronaz blessed it especially for you, Señor Baines. It will keep away evil, even if it is in your pocket. *Vaya con Dios.*"

"It was kind of you, Tía Margarita. Now I must go."

"When will you be back, my son?" Don Diego asked.

"I am going to the mountain where I found the treasure. It is the place of ghosts now, but they are gentle ghosts, now that the treasure is gone. I want to be alone up there and to think and to pray."

Don Diego nodded, and Doña Inez slipped her hand into his and squeezed it, her eyes fixed on John Cooper's stern, taut features.

"After that—I must see Chief Kinotatay again. Then I shall return. I don't know how long it will be. I've talked to my children and they understand. I know you'll look after them."

Don Diego took out a handkerchief and blew his nose. "Of course, my son. The ranch goes by itself. With Miguel and Esteban to handle matters, we can sit back at our ease and not even think." Then, seeing that his jovial tone made no impression on his laconic son-in-law, he added gently, "I will pray, too, and so will Doña Inez. When you are there on the mountain and you look into the blue sky, my son, say a prayer for us also, and for my beloved daughter."

"I shall, *mi padre*." John Cooper offered his hand, and Don Diego shook it. Then the tall rancher walked to the stable.

Esteban Morales had worked all night long to whittle out the figurine of a hawk, and as he saw John Cooper lead Fuego, Pingo's sire, out of the stable, he showed it to him. "*Con su permiso, patrón,* I've made this for Carmen. Shall I give it to her, or do you wish to?"

"You give it to her, Esteban. But don't forget your promise to make toys for the other children. Now, God bless you. I shall never forget all you've done."

"I shan't forget, either, how you saved Bernardo from the scorpion. Now he's sixteen, already a man, and ready to help me with the herd. And he's had a good education, thanks to . . ." He had been about to refer to Catarina, for she had taught the children of the ranch about history and literature. "Well, I pray to God, Señor Baines, to keep you safe and bring you peace."

"I'm grateful, Esteban. Now I must go." John Cooper could hardly bear the kind words and the solicitude bestowed upon him, and he was harshly abrupt as he mounted Fuego and wheeled the great stallion to the west.

He rode slowly, alone with his thoughts. John Cooper remembered how years ago, when they all had lived in Taos, he had first ridden a mustang to *la Montaña de las Pumas,* the Mountain of the Lions, which was his destination now. With his first wolf-dog, Lobo, he had come upon the mountain through a valley well beyond Taos, a steep and precipitous mountain that towered six thousand feet above the valley floor. He had left the mustang midway and had ascended by hand and foot, and Lobo had followed him, till both of them had found the rocky ledge framed by two massive fir trees. That was where he had seen the six skeletons of Spanish soldiers on whose skulls were rusted metal morions, and whose bony fingers had clutched ancient harquebuses and muskets. There had been two rusted metal tripods for the harquebuses. There were other skeletons clad in bits of brown cloth and rotted cords—the skeletons of monks. He had seen flint arrowheads and the barbs of lances, whose wooden hafts had long since become rotted.

When he had slipped inside the narrow opening of the cave and felt the bitter cold, dry air, he had found a broad wooden table with benches around it, at which were seated the perfectly preserved bodies of forty dead Indians, hands bound behind their backs with rawhide thongs, clad only in breechclouts and moccasins. The bodies were so well preserved because the cave had been virtually sealed off from the outside air. Then John Cooper had found in the mine shaft the stacks of silver ingots and religious artifacts.

When he had married Catarina, it had been thirteen years ago—a lifetime on the rugged frontier of the Southwest. He shuddered to remember that this month of March, which was their anniversary and which should have been so rapturous, had been also the month of her murder. Almost unconsciously, he put his hand to the pocket of his buckskin jacket, into which he had put the eye of God that Tía Margarita had made for him. He rode on, the panorama of his life taking shape before him, as he recalled all that had happened since he had first come to the Jicarilla stronghold to escape the Sioux braves who had tracked him all the way from the Dakotas to Nuevo México. He remembered that epic battle, in which Lije had lost his own valiant life to save his master, and how the Jicarilla Apache had watched silently, as he carried the body of the great Irish wolfhound to a ledge and buried him. How long ago it had been, and yet it was still vivid in his mind.

Beyond him stretched the fertile grasslands of Texas as he rode toward that mountain in New Mexico that was at a distance from the stronghold, and yet accessible to the Jicarilla braves, who had so zealously guarded the treasure while he had moved from Taos to the Double H Ranch. He thought of his life and of what was yet to come. In December, he would reach his thirty-fourth birthday. For many men, that was the beginning of old age, illness, or even violent death if one's instincts for survival slackened in the least against all the risks and hazards of the still-untamed frontier.

He did not feel old but sadly nostalgic. Now he had no enemies left, so far as he knew, and yet at this moment he would have willingly given back to all of them their lives in exchange for Catarina.

At night, when he made camp, the great palomino,
Fuego, seemed almost human as he nuzzled at him and nickered. As he resumed his ride in the mornings, he saw here
and there the distant outlines of little farms, stables, and
barns, and yet the stretches between his ranch and these settlers were still so vast that it was as if all this land were unin-
habited.

In one large saddlebag John Cooper had presents for the
Jicarilla whom he intended to visit: two new rifles, some
knives, and ammunition. He had also taken "Long Girl" and
ample ammunition and powder for himself, as well as his father's old tinderbox. Each time he made camp and lighted a
fire to prepare his meager supper, each time he glanced over
at Fuego, who was placidly grazing on the rich grass, and
saw the long rifle in its saddle sheath, he was reminded that
the tinderbox and the rifle had been all that remained of his
father's legacy to him. When he thought again of the mountain and its treasure, now safe in the New Orleans bank
vault, he thanked God in having been able to provide for the
needs of his children, when he might not be there.

He wondered, too, whether, now that López had failed
to wrest the treasure away from him, the opportunistic Santa
Anna would make still another attempt. What he wanted for
his children now was peace, but so long as there were men
like Santa Anna, who believed that power was right and
might combined, there would be trouble between Mexico and
the United States.

There were nights when he dreamed that Catarina was
journeying with him, happy to share his life and asking only
to know that he loved her. There were times when the
dreams were so real that he groaned in his sleep, and called
her name aloud, just as he had done when Rosa Nuñez had
nursed him in the *jacal.*

The sun beat down on him by day, and he was lean and
wiry and so sun-bronzed that he resembled a Mexican or an
Indian. There were long periods of the day when he did not
say even a word to Fuego, meditating and thinking over all
that had happened. It was like sifting the grains of sand on
an ocean beach and hoping to discover some meaning to the
riddle of life.

Never before had he felt such a loneliness, nor, at the
same time, such a mystic affinity for the past. When he had
first left Shawneetown as a boy, he had prayed that he would

be able to forget that horrifying scene that had left him an orphan and altered his destiny. But now he was as grief-ridden as he had been then.

On an afternoon less than two weeks after he set out, he saw the Mountain of the Lions, with its top still covered by snow. As he approached it, he again remembered that he had had to leave the mustang tethered halfway up. As he recalled, there was plenty of rich, sweet grass for grazing all along the winding, tortuous trail. Thus, Fuego could graze to his heart's content, while he himself climbed to the top and found a niche where he would be protected from a sudden storm and be able to meditate and purge himself of the agony and the hatred that still lingered in him. He had only a few strips of jerky left; when it was gone, he would find berries and herbs to sustain him until he was ready to leave the mountain.

He came at last to the base of it and gazed upward. He asked himself why he had gone to this of all mountains, rather than to the one where Carlos had mourned his Weesayo or directly to the stronghold where surely the welcome of Kinotatay and the warm friendship of the Jicarilla villagers would have helped ease the hurt that dwelt in his spirit. There must have been a reason for this, but it would be revealed to him in God's own time, he felt sure.

Turning to stare all around the horizon, he saw not a living soul. It was as if this mountain had been isolated and reserved for him alone, after the long years that had passed since the soldiers who had guarded the Indian slaves had been surprised by the warriors of some hostile tribe to whom the mountain was sacred. Since those violent deaths, the mountain had retained its secret, and the legend had prevented the curious from reaching its heights. Destiny had led him there to find the silver.

He had never really been superstitious. As a boy, his gentle mother had told him that reality is all, and that God is truth and reality. She had warned him about not letting his mind dwell upon fantasies and legends, for a forthright conscience and disciplined toil are the surest ways to make a richly rewarding life. Yet the Indian philosophy he had absorbed during his sojourns with the Ayuhwa, the Skidi Pawnee, the Dakota Sioux, and finally the Jicarilla Apache, had added a mysticism that was now a part of his outlook.

Out of respect for Fuego's age, John Cooper led the palomino by the reins for several hours till he reached the midway point. He saw the huge oak tree to which he had tethered his mustang that first time he had ascended the mountain and found the silver. The grass was still rich, and Fuego dipped his head and began to eat.

Before he could leave the palomino there to his own resources, he must provide water. He recalled that there was a placid little stream running down the gentle incline, and he led Fuego to the water and let him drink, instead of tying the horse to await his return. He knew Fuego would understand. He stroked his nose and muzzle, and the palomino stared at him and whinnied softly.

"Good Fuego, *bueno, bueno!*" he praised the great stallion. Removing the saddlebags, he found a barren place of ground near where Fuego stood and spread out the oats he had brought along.

He took his rifle and the tinderbox, as well as his canteen and a deerskin pouch containing the few strips of jerky. Then, hardly knowing he did so, he patted the pocket in which the *ojo de Dios* rested. He began to search for the trail that he had first taken, and found it readily. The Jicarilla braves, who had guarded the mountain's treasure, had cleared away the bushes that had originally obliterated it, as well as the wildflowers. It was plain and clear and wider now. It wound up the mountain as it always had, and it was an arduous climb.

Doggedly he climbed until nightfall. He made himself a camp on a wide ledge that seemed to jut out to one side from the trail sheltered by a profusion of small fir trees. He did not wish to light a fire, not this first night. The air was cool and a half-moon climbed in the sky and cast its luminous glow. It was as if fingers of light searched him out, as they came nearer his resting place and illuminated the surroundings. There was quiet and peace. He closed his eyes and prayed. He prayed for Catarina's soul and he asked that she be granted the gift of watching over him and the children. He prayed to God to absolve him of the crime of murder, admitting that he had broken the commandment, "Thou shalt not kill," and not wishing to justify it because he had dealt out justice. He said only, "God, I'm just a man, and I loved her so much, and he was evil and he took an innocent human life for the sake of wealth and power. Forgive me my sin and do not visit it upon my children, I humbly pray You."

He sat for a long time on the ledge, watching the sky,

breathing in the pure air, listening to the faint occasional call of a nightbird. The emanations of the night were good, chastening, and calming. There were no evil spirits here. He felt a curious attunement with the night and the mountain and the air, as if he were the very last man on earth.

Then he slept, and when he woke, the sun was already high in the sky. He bit off a piece of jerky and chewed it, drank a swig of water from his canteen, and then knelt on the ledge and prayed again for guidance.

He climbed again. By the end of the afternoon, panting and exhausted, he reached the plateau some four hundred feet from the mountaintop itself. He saw the familiar rocky ledge about four feet above his head, framed by two giant fir trees.

He took a deep breath, summoned his strength, and carefully began to grip the rocks and draw himself up. That was where he had found the skeletons of the soldiers and the monks. Now there was not even the slightest trace. It looked as if the ground were undisturbed, as if no human had ever visited here. He remembered how Lobo had scrambled up to join him that first time, growling over the grisly remains of that ancient tragedy, and then stared at a huge slab of rock, weather-beaten and with curious, faded markings upon it. This was the slab of rock that concealed the opening to the cave.

He took out his tinderbox, broke off a long, dry branch from one of the fir trees, wrapped moss around the top, and kindled a fire to make a torch. He walked up to the opening and squeezed through the narrow passageway. The table was still there. But there was nothing, not even the dust of those who had died so many years ago. As he neared the mine shaft, he went in to see that it too was empty. The church relics, the silver crucifixes, the rosaries, and the great cross with the figure of Christ crucified upon it, which had been set upon a massive stand of gleaming silver with the most intricate and beautiful workmanship—all these things were now in the safekeeping of the priest of the church in Taos, who had replaced kindly Padre Juan Moraga.

There were no ghosts here. The souls of those poor slaves who had been forced to mine the silver and to work upon it, and who had been left to die of starvation and thirst—they had been laid to rest, buried by the Jicarilla Apache during his last visit.

At last, he could let the mountain remain as a legend for the Indians, for he knew that the descendants of the Jicarilla Apache would be told over the campfires of the taboo and the treasure, and how the treasure had been turned from evil usage into a force for good.

The second night he slept on the ledge where he had found the treasure, and he limited himself to only two strips of jerky and a swig of water three times a day from his canteen. The altitude, the pure cool air, and the isolation above the earth under the heavens gave him a sense of exhilaration such as he had not had since those days when he had lived with Descontarti and the Jicarilla high in their stronghold. What a simple life it had been, living by a code based on honor, respect, and trust. He had learned a lesson from the Jicarilla: One need not make war on the weak to prove one's power and force of will. For when the time came when they had to wage battle against their age-old enemies, the Mescalero, to endure, they had done so in defense of their stronghold, their old men and women, and their wives and children. They had won by defense and not by attack. They had learned how to live in peace with their neighbors, contrary to what so many of his own people contemptuously said against those who had been first on the land in this brave new world.

He thought about this most of the second day, and of the disquieting news that already in the southeastern part of the United States efforts were being made to drive away the Creek, the Chickasaw, and the Cherokee. His mother had once told him that Washington, soon after becoming President, wanted to send federal troops against the Georgia settlers who were stealing the land of the Creek and murdering them to obtain their holdings. But because the young nation was in debt from its victorious fight against the tyrannical British, such action could not be afforded. Now it seemed that the enemies of the Indians were growing in number. He hoped that the Jicarilla would never be driven from their stronghold.

He slept dreamlessly, and on the morning of the third day, he prayed that there would be a sign to tell him what he should do with his life. At noon, there was a violent windstorm and the ominous gray and black clouds were driven across the sky. An hour later, the sky was blue and serene once again, and the clouds became fleecy and drifted lazily across the broad blue panorama.

He sat cross-legged with his arms folded across his chest, silent and immutable, his eyes fixed on the sky. He remembered how Descontarti had gone off into isolation far from the stronghold where no one would find him, there to commune with the Great Spirit, until such time as he received some inspiration whereby he might guide his people. As he thought of this, he stared fixedly at the heavens.

Suddenly he started, for beyond him was a great cloud in the form of a horse. He saw the proud head and the arching neck, the long legs, even the tail and the sturdy back—and he uttered a cry at the incredible likeness.

He put his right hand to the pocket in which he kept the *ojo de Dios* and touched it. Mechanically, his other hand went to the other pocket, and he touched a folded sheet of paper—the letter that Fabien Mallard had given him in New Orleans.

Wonderingly, he drew it out, unfolded it, and read it again. It was from the Argentinian *hacendada*, Raoul Maldones, expressing his desire to buy a few palominos, some of the great long-horned Texas steers, and perhaps a pedigreed bull and heifer from this *americano* of whom he had heard so much.

He sprang to his feet. His mind was clear, his body refreshed, and his spirit renewed. It was a sign. He did not question by what method it had come to him, but he knew that he had suddenly found hope in the promise of that which might set his feet upon the proper trail. He would go to Argentina. He would meet Raoul Maldones and learn what life in this other country was like. It might mean new knowledge about ranching techniques for the *vaqueros* and *trabajadores*, and new opportunities for improving the quality of life for everyone on the Double H Ranch. It would give him a greater vision of the world, and particularly of a part of the world of which he had had no previous knowledge.

Picking up his rifle, the tinderbox, and his canteen, he began the careful descent down the mountain. The grimness had left his face, and the dull, glazed anguish in his eyes had brightened. He felt that he had made his peace with his Maker; he felt that Catarina understood and even now looked down upon him with prayerful love.

It was nightfall when he reached the level where he had

left Fuego. He uttered a cry of joy to find the great palomino placidly awaiting him, as if he had departed only an hour before. The stallion whinnied and came forward, thrusting his muzzle against John Cooper's chest. He stroked the palomino's head and then tears poured down his cheeks in gratitude, humility, and thanksgiving that he had been purged of hate if not entirely of grief.

He led the palomino down to the base of the mountain. He needed no sleep tonight, for he was impatient to see Kinotatay and to renew the bonds of blood brotherhood.

As the dawn broke on the fourth day of his lonely vigil, John Cooper Baines rode off in the direction of the Jicarilla stronghold.

Eleven

On the morning of the third day after he had left the *Montaña de las Pumas*, John Cooper Baines rode Fuego up the familiar trail to the stronghold of the Jicarilla Apache. His ascent had been noted by the scouts, who made the cries of the coyote and the owl to signify that a lone rider was coming to the village. Recognizing him in his buckskins, riding the palomino, the scouts came out of their places of concealment, from behind boulders, gnarled trees growing along the slope of the mountain, and bushes, and shouted welcome to him. He raised his right arm and made the sign of peace and friendship.

When he reached the plateau high atop the mountain, he dismounted before the largest wickiup, and Kinotatay emerged. This short, wiry man, with a stony and weatherbeaten face, was now fifty-five years of age, and yet he looked not a day older than he had almost a decade and a half ago when he had first met John Cooper, who had saved the chief's son, ten-year-old Pastanari, from death on a runaway horse.

John Cooper had just buried his great wolfhound Lije in a wide, deep hollow in the mountain slope. He had taken the wampum belt, which he had been given in the Ayuhwa village to announce to all tribes that he was a friend and hunter, wound it around Lije's neck, and covered the great shaggy body with rocks. Next he had followed the Apache scouts, and because he had saved Descontarti's son, he earned the friendship of the great Jicarilla Apache chief—a friendship resulting in blood brotherhood and, in its time, the union of his destined brother-in-law, Carlos de Escobar, with Descontarti's beautiful daughter, Weesayo.

All these memories flocked through John Cooper's mind as he saw Kinotatay, the present chief, come toward him, his face aglow with pleasure.

"It is good to have *el Halcón* back with us," Kinotatay said simply. Then he embraced the tall Texan and put his right palm over John Cooper's heart, an act that the latter imitated in token of their blood brotherhood. "What brings you back from Texas, *Halcón?*"

"I have been to the Mountain of the Lions, Kinotatay. I spent three days and nights there in meditation and prayer with the Great Spirit. I mourn the death of my wife." As briefly as possible, John Cooper told the chief about Catarina's death.

Kinotatay could say nothing for a moment. Finally, he managed to control his emotions. "I share your grief," he said, his voice choked. "How well I remember her, and how, after you were married in the faith of your people, you came here to follow our Apache practice of spending ten days alone together in the secret wickiup. She gave you children, strong sons and daughters. I shall not henceforth say her name, as is our custom, but you know that because we are bound by the ties of blood, my heart is filled with sorrow at your loss."

"I am grateful to you, Kinotatay. I would spend a little time with you, until I take up my life again. There, on the mountain, I saw a sign, and it tells me that I shall go far across an ocean to a land south from here, and take palominos and cattle to a *hacendado,* who lives on the *pampas* of Argentina, and who has written to say he would like to do business with me. Such a journey will help me live with my sorrow. I am curious to see this land that is part of South

America. They have different ways, and perhaps I can learn something of value to use on my own ranch."

"Tonight, we will have a feast to welcome you back with us, *Halcón*," Kinotatay said. "Our shaman will look into the sky and consult the signs to foretell what awaits you." After a long pause, his face expressionless, he added, "My days are numbered, *Halcón*. It will not be long before Pastanari becomes the *jefe* of our tribe."

"Why do you say this, Kinotatay? You look strong and vigorous as ever."

Kinotatay shook his head. "A disease gnaws at my vitals, as if it were a wild fox eager to tear me asunder. I do not think there is any cure for it, save the endless one of death, and I am ready for it, as all men must be. I can look back and say that my people have prospered."

John Cooper nodded. He said as gently as he could, "You will be honored long after your days are over, Kinotatay, and I pray those will be long and fruitful and that your health will be restored. Your people need you."

"When the Great Spirit calls, a man has no recourse but to obey. No, *Halcón*, I thank you for your good wishes, but the shaman has told me that it will not be long before I sing my death song. When it is time, and I will know it, I shall go somewhere high on this mountain to be alone, to sing the song and to await the setting sun. But enough of such talk. Come now and let me take you to a wickiup."

They had a great feast, at which John Cooper presented gifts to the chief. Warriors looked on with pleasure as they saw two fine rifles, six shining knives, as well as three sacks of powder and ball. "These are not for war," John Cooper exclaimed. "They are so you may be strong as a people and may live in peace."

A shout of approbation went up from the Indians assembled around the fire, and it seemed to John Cooper that he had never left the stronghold. He recognized old friends, and the years had dealt kindly with the Jicarilla, for there were few missing faces among those with whom he had competed in throwing the lance and drawing the bow. The shaman Marsimaya, father of Colnara, the young woman who had nursed Carlos back to health after he had been shot by Santa Anna's scouts, crouched before John Cooper to perform a ceremony honoring the Beloved Woman. As Kinotatay had explained in advance, because of their unbreakable law against mentioning the name of the dead, this ceremony would ostensibly honor Lismaya, a seventeen-year-old virgin who was the daughter of Teemueldo, one of the revered elders of the tribe. She had cared for the sick and cooked meals for them when they were too ill to provide for themselves; she had rescued a two-year-old boy—the son of Colnara and the young warrior Jisente—from falling into a canyon far below. Yet the shaman's words touched John Cooper, for he understood that they referred not only to this gentle girl, but also to Weesayo and to his own Catarina.

"Hear us, O Great Spirit," Marsimaya intoned as he lifted his face to the sky and raised his hands, palms upward with the fingers splayed. "Tonight we honor the Beloved Woman who has earned esteem for her kindness to the needy and the sick, her courage in saving human life, and her devotion to her father. The name of Beloved Woman is never lightly given, but must be earned. We have had many whose names may not be spoken, for they have gone into the Heavens to be with the Great Spirit. One of these was from our own tribe, and another was a *gringa* who loved our people and respected our ways and customs. Look down upon her whom we honor tonight, we pray to you, but remember also those of good heart and virtue whose spirits are already within your keeping. Let what they have done for the Jicarilla be remembered always, and may their example guide those who will come after us."

The shaman turned to him, and John Cooper wept unabashedly. All the pent-up loneliness and anguish that had been festering within him since he had ridden out from the Double H Ranch to the Mountain of the Lions now seemed to burst unleashed from within his very marrow.

There was a long silence, and those who watched the ceremony looked away from John Cooper, for they respected and loved him and did not wish him to believe that they found his emotion unnatural; the Jicarilla themselves were not demonstrative, but they could understand how this *wasichu* or "white eyes" who was their blood brother could be affected by great loss and sorrow.

The dancing fire flickered in its circle in front of the wickiup of Kinotatay as Marsimaya now drew a deerskin pouch from his beaded robe, shook it, then opened the drawstrings and shook out bones.

Through his tears, John Cooper stared at the bones that Marsimaya cast on the ground before him, saw the shaman squat down and touch each with a reverent forefinger, and then stare at him, his face almost grotesque as the firelight cast weird shadows upon the paints of red, yellow, and brown with which Marsimaya had daubed himself for the ritual.

At last Marsimaya spoke, and John Cooper felt the eyes of all upon him. "You have known great sorrow in your life, but these sacred bones tell me that you will know happiness again before another twelve moons have come to fullness and waned. You will go by water to the one who awaits you, unknowing though you are of her being. Your oldest son will find his happiness there also, so the bones tell. Because you are *el Halcón,* who strikes like the hawk against evil, you will be called upon to defend those whom you do not yet know but whom you will love. They will urge you to remain with them and live there to defend them, but you will come back to your ranch. You will never forget the blood brotherhood that binds you to us who love you also. This is what I see in the bones before me. The Great Spirit has marked you and is well content with you."

"I thank the shaman for this message. Before all of you," John Cooper said in a hoarse voice that betrayed his deep emotion, "I swear I shall never forget how I am bound to you by the blood oath."

John Cooper remained two more days and nights in the stronghold. He learned from Kinotatay of the unsettling conditions in Taos, where the Indians of the pueblo were being so sorely oppressed by the new *alcalde* that there was the possibility of open rebellion against the administration.

"And we of the Jicarilla," Kinotatay explained, "will fight beside our brothers in the pueblo, though we have lived in peace for so long now. We cannot stand idle, not when our own safety may also be at stake. For I fear the new mayor may even send soldiers to our stronghold in the mountains, in order to demand our allegiance to him."

"My gifts to you will make your people strong, Kinotatay," John Cooper said, and then he told the chief that he meant to ride into Taos to visit Padre Madura. The *jefe* took his blood brother's hands and pressed them against his own heart, then said, "My heart is heavy that you must leave us. It is the will of the Great Spirit whether you will see me again. I pray it will happen. Yet, if it does not and I am summoned, I ask you to think of me through the gift that I give you now."

He beckoned to Marsimaya, who had come out of his wickiup holding a little rawhide sack, which he now handed to Kinotatay. The latter, in turn, pulled at the drawstrings and bade John Cooper hold out his hands, palms upward. When the Texan complied Kinotatay turned the little sack over and let its contents fall into John Cooper's hands.

He stared incredulously at a turquoise necklace adorned with tiny silver bells, a work of the most exquisite craftsmanship. He raised his eyes to Kinotatay's and stammered, "It's magnificent—but surely it's too great a gift—"

"No, *Halcón*. It is an heirloom that has been in the tribe for over a hundred years. It is said that it came from Mexico City and once belonged to the wife of a viceroy. What is known is that it has brought good fortune to those who wear it. It has meaning for you, *Halcón*. The bells resemble those of the wickiup of mating, and you remember them well. They will remind you of the happiness you knew. The color of the turquoise is for grief, but it is also for the new life that the Great Spirit has in store for you, my brother. You may someday give it to someone who will share that new life. Go now and find your destiny."

John Cooper stared again at the necklace, shook his head, and sighed. He carefully put it into the pocket of his buckskin jacket that contained the *ojo de Diòs*. "I will prize it, and it will not be given lightly. I do not know if it will be given at all, Kinotatay."

"It is so written that it will be," Kinotatay almost defiantly responded. "In life there is always a balance between loss and gain, between grief and love, and so it will be with you. Marsimaya has spoken, and the sacred bones do not lie. Come back to us when you can, my blood brother. May your heart be lightened, your path sure, and your eyes clear along that path for whatever awaits you."

John Cooper and the ailing Jicarilla chief exchanged the embrace of brothers, and each made the sign unto the other of respect and honor. Then the Texan turned, mounted Fuego, and rode out of the stronghold.

He rode to Taos, and there he saw Padre Madura and told him how the silver ingots had been taken to safety. He now gave the priest a thousand silver *pesos* as a donation to the church; much more would be kept in the bank for when it would be needed by the poor of Taos, by the Pueblo Indians, and by those who were oppressed by the *ricos*. He told Padre Madura of the death of Catarina, and the priest held him as once again John Cooper wept over the great loss.

"It is well that you weep, John Cooper," Padre Madura told him. "Tears are truly the way God allows us to purge ourselves of heartache and pain."

Recovering, John Cooper said, "I go now on a long journey, *mi padre,* and I ask your blessing for it and your prayers that I may return safely for the sake of my children. If you have need of me in my absence, send word to my brother-in-law, Carlos. I have learned from my Jicarilla friends that conditions here have never been so unsettled, that your new *alcalde* is more corrupt and violent than any of his predecessors."

"It is true, my son," Padre Madura said. "Even *Los Penitentes* are powerless to stop the tyranny of this man, and I fear for *los indios pueblos,* who receive the brunt of his abuse."

"Not only will my family support you, Padre Madura, but the Jicarilla braves will come to the aid of the Indians here. You have only to send them a message if you need them."

The priest blessed him, and then John Cooper went to the *hacienda* of Doña Elena de Pladero, to tell her and Tomás and his Conchita of the death of Catarina and of his impending voyage to meet the Argentinian *hacendado*. Refusing their invitation of supper, he kissed the women and shook hands with Tomás, who indeed had taken effective charge of the de Pladero sheep ranch and looked after his wife and mother and children, providing them with all they wanted and needed. Gratified to see the happiness of this little family—such good and faithful friends to both him and his father-in-law—John Cooper took his leave, having been given ample provisions by Tomás.

That afternoon, pondering the words of Marsimaya and the extraordinary gift of Kinotatay, John Cooper headed back to the Double H Ranch along the trail that he had taken in his quest for solace of his grief.

Upon his return, it did not take long for John Cooper to put into effect his plans for the trip to South America. Everyone on the ranch—his family, his friends, the workers—quietly helped him with the preparations, aware that he had set for himself an undertaking that would compensate in some way for his recent loss.

A message was sent by courier to Fabien Mallard—who in turn would send the letter to Raoul Maldones in Argentina—that John Cooper would be leaving New Orleans for Buenos Aires within a fortnight. Miguel helped his good friend select the palomino horses—a stallion and a mare—that he would take, and the *capataz* had his *trabajadores* prepare the carts that would take the breeding bull and heifer to New Orleans, where, along with the long-horned steers, they would then be boarded on ship. At the same time, four of Miguel's best *vaqueros* were also chosen to accompany the blond Texan on his journey.

Don Diego and Doña Inez watched John Cooper engage in all these activities, and their hearts went out to him. They were taken aback when John Cooper announced that he intended to take Andrew with him on the trip, but they quickly came to realize how deeply Andrew was mourning his mother and that the journey would do him good. They, of course, would look after John Cooper's other children, as would Carlos and Teresa, and Doña Inez realized it would do her grieving husband much good to be surrounded by his grandchildren.

On the day before his departure, John Cooper received a small cloth-wrapped package and letter, brought by a man who had ridden all the way from Eugene Fair's settlement on the Brazos River. Jim Bowie, whom the blond Texan had befriended in New Orleans the previous year, had sent him a knife exactly like his own. It had a nine-inch single-edged blade, made of the finest tempered steel, and John Cooper had already witnessed how sensitive and accurate the Bowie knife was. He read the letter also contained in the package:

John Cooper:
I promised to send you one of my knives, didn't I? Well, here it is, with my best wishes. Remembering the way you handled that Spanish dagger of yours, I'm sure you'll get the hang of my knife in no time at all.
Also want to mention that me and some of my men (we've formed a kind of a police force to patrol the new settlements—call it the Texas Rangers) are going to be

heading out your way within the next couple of weeks. We'll drop by and pay you a visit. Sure looking forward to seeing that spread of yours.

Jim Bowie

John Cooper would not be there for the visit of Bowie and his men, but he would ask Miguel to give his regrets and say they'd see each other some other time.

Spending his last afternoon on the ranch before his departure, with everything packed and ready to go, John Cooper frisked about the yard with Yankee, along with little Carmen.

He watched with pleasure as his little girl threw a stick for the wolf-dog and cried delightedly as he brought it back to her, dropping it at her feet. Carmen grabbed the stick, and as Yankee bounded after her, barking, she ran to her father and held his legs, not sure if she was afraid of the big animal or not.

"He's not going to hurt you, honey, you know that," John Cooper said stroking her hair. "Yankee looks after you children, don't you, boy?"

Yankee barked, then sat at Carmen's feet, staring intently at the stick she held in her hand.

"Here you are, Yankee," Carmen said coming out from behind her father's legs and giving the stick to the wolf-dog. "I'm not afraid of you. I love you." Even after Yankee took the stick from the little girl, he waited patiently as she reached out and hugged him fiercely around the neck.

Later, John Cooper checked with Miguel about mating Luna. The last mating had not taken, and it would be several months before the wolf-dog would be in heat again and could be coupled with one of the Irish wolfhounds. He hoped, though, that the next mating would produce a litter of pups by the time he got back.

That evening, he had a farewell dinner. Don Diego, Doña Inez, Carlos, Teresa, Miguel, Bess, and all their children sat around the big table in the dining room, which was the heart of the *hacienda* at the Double H Ranch. Tía Margarita prepared a wonderful dinner, and the occasion was festive and happy.

Late that night, after everyone else had gone to bed, John Cooper and Carlos—as close as they had ever been— stayed up in the library to talk and reminisce. Carlos was drinking some of his father's fine Madeira; John Cooper elected to drink nothing. Suddenly the Texan rose and said to his brother-in-law, "Take a walk with me, if you're not too tired. I'd like to go for one last romp with Yankee before I leave."

"I'd like to do that very much," Carlos softly said, and as they left the house, he put his arm around John Cooper's shoulders. Yankee came forward, wagging his tail, and rubbed his muzzle against Carlos's leg. Carlos leaned down to rub his knuckles over Yankee's head. "You know exactly how to get on his good side," said John Cooper. "I'm going to leave Yankee in your charge. Keep an eye on the whelps, too, if they're born while I'm gone. We're going to have a large family of wolf-dogs on this ranch—as large as our own family!"

Carlos chuckled. "Of course I'll take charge of them, John Cooper." They walked in silence for a bit, then Carlos said, "Look at the sky—dark and hardly a cloud."

John Cooper glanced at his brother-in-law, then nodded. "There's a saying that it's always darkest before the dawn, Carlos. I hope it's true. If you had asked me a year ago whether I'd ever think about going to Argentina, or any country below the Rio Grande and beyond Mexico, I would have thought you were crazy. Now, it seems almost necessary."

"For your peace of mind—I know that. Don't you see, *mi cuñado*, you and I now share a loss, an irreparable loss. I lost Weesayo and you've lost Catarina. When I was a little boy, I hated my sister because she was so pampered and she gave herself such airs. Later on, I understood that she was lonesome and trying to prove that she was really a good girl. But after she found you, she became a wonderful woman."

"Gracias, amigo." John Cooper bent to rub his knuckles over Yankee's head and then straightened. "It's a night for reflection. They say that when a man's old, he sees all his life appear before him in scenes, as if he were about to die. I don't feel at all old, but I am thinking a lot about things that happened in the past."

"I, too." Carlos pensively shook his head. "But perhaps, if our lives are paralleled, you'll profit from my own example, John Cooper. I couldn't be happier than I am now with Teresa. It took me two long years to win her. What I feel for Weesayo hasn't diminished in the least—if anything, it's stronger than ever. Only, it doesn't come between us. Teresa understands this. What a wonderful woman she is! That's why I'm sure that before too much longer, you'll find someone who will help you not forget Catarina, but remember her in a very special, loving way. This new woman, whoever she may be, will give you joy and make you feel that life is worth living. That's the way Teresa makes me feel."

"I certainly hope you're right. Understand, I'm not looking for anyone, just a chance to change my outlook. It's so gloomy, and I feel so lost. The days and the nights on the mountain helped, but they didn't rid me of my pain."

They had come to a little creek, and Yankee went partway in it, lowering his head so that he could lap up the water. He came back up onto the bank and shook himself. Then he turned back to look at the two men, and uttered a soft, encouraging growl.

"The rascal," John Cooper smiled. "I think he feels that I'm going to be away from him for a spell, and that's why he wants to make the most of tonight. Well, I'm in a mood for walking and talking, if you are, Carlos. Except that—well, I'm sure the honeymoon isn't over, and you shouldn't keep Teresa waiting."

"Never you mind, John Cooper," Carlos smilingly reassured him. "Tonight's a night for brothers to be together." Once again, he put his arm around the Texan's shoulders and gave him a knowing look. "I hope when you write, you'll tell me all about Argentina. I'm very interested because long ago, when the *conquistadores* went down there for treasure, they changed the whole history of Spain."

"Carlos, you were a boy when you were back in Madrid with Don Diego. Do you remember anything about the Spanish court and the way people got along in those days?" John Cooper asked.

Carlos stopped for a moment to reflect, then replied, "I remember the elaborate costumes the *hidalgos* wore and how pompous and colorful the ceremonies were, and I thought even then that people in power were very selfish. That's still the case, you know. That's why there's still trouble with the Mexican authorities who really would like to take over Texas, as well as New Mexico, and revert to the old days when they had all the power."

"I know that, Carlos. What worries me is that this may lead to a war."

"Very possibly, *mi amigo*. If it should come, I would be on the side of the *americanos*, if only because you're my *cuñado*. Too, your country was founded as a democracy, as a bastion of freedom. We Spanish have not known what freedom is, not since our birth when we were under the monarchy, and then afterward when we were under Napoleon's tyranny with his brother on the throne and a weak king to replace him when at last Napoleon was beaten. Come, let's take a drink in the creek. My throat is parched from so much talking."

Both men knelt down, lowered their faces, and drank the pure, clear water. They sat on the bank for a spell, and John Cooper told Carlos all about the conditions in Taos, such as they had been described to him by Chief Kinotatay and Padre Madura.

"You know, John Cooper," Carlos said, "Teresa and I plan to make a little trip to Taos in the near future, a honeymoon trip. I want to take her to the stronghold in the mountains and introduce her to the Jicarilla braves, who are our brothers. We want to spend some time with the de Pladero family, too, of course, and see Padre Madura. Maybe when we are there we will be able to do something to help the situation."

"I hope so," John Cooper said. "Kinotatay, and Padre Madura, too, know they can call on you for assistance if they should need it, just as they would call on me if I were here."

Refreshed, having drunk and rested, Carlos gestured southward. "Let's see how far we can walk tonight. It's still early, and I'm not talked out yet." They both rose and walked for a time before Carlos broke the silence.

"If I don't see you again for a long, long time, *mi cuñado*," he said, "I'll devote myself to your children and to Yankee. Your children and mine will become close friends, just the way my Diego is with Francesca."

"That's as it should be, Carlos. It seems like a dream now, waiting until tomorrow to go all the way to Argentina," John Cooper mused.

"Miguel and I will keep the ranch for you, and we'll keep it strong. Our friends who have come to settle on the ranch, as well as any new settlers who wish to come here, will help make our community stronger still. Also, we'll open our hearts to the Dominican sisters from Mexico, who will be here within a few months' time."

"That's a good thing, Carlos. I know Catarina would have liked that." John Cooper found that he could pronounce the name almost in a level tone, but inwardly he still felt a surge of grief. He added, "I think it will be a fine thing to have the sisters here. We've a church, a fine young *padre* in Jorge Pastronaz, and the sisters will be an invaluable help as teachers in our school. How far we've come, with an actual schoolhouse and classrooms. I remember that when I was a boy I had to do my lessons in our cabin, before Pa would let me go fishing or hunting with Lije—"

"I remember my school days, too, at the *escuela* back in Madrid," Carlos said. "Well, I think we'll all be better off when the sisters get here, and they'll make even the *trabajadores*, as well as ourselves, look to our manners and especially our language."

John Cooper smiled, grateful that his brother-in-law had gotten him out of his bleak nostalgic mood. "I'll miss you, Carlos," he drawled with a boyish grin.

Carlos slapped him on the back. "I'll miss you, too, you long-legged, blond *gringo!* Now let's finish our walk with Yankee,. have another glass of wine, and then get a good night's sleep. I'll say this—if it weren't that I'm in love with my Teresa and still on our honeymoon, as you might say, I'd give a good deal to go with you."

"If you weren't married to her, I'd take you," John Cooper smilingly parried. They looked at each other; each had tasted sorrow and despair, and each had survived it. It had made them more than brothers-in-law; it had made them the most loyal and devoted of friends.

At dawn of the next day, John Cooper Baines and young Andrew joined the four *vaqueros* chosen to make the journey. Pedro Martínez, Jaime Portola, Bartoloméo Mendoza, and Enrique Saltanda were men in their mid-twenties who had proved themselves valorous and dependable, as well as being excellent marksmen and superb horsemen. Antonio Lorcas, who had been responsible for tracking down the murderer of Catarina Baines, would have been a logical choice to take with him, but the young Mexican had asked to remain behind, for he was growing very fond of Rosa Nuñez and was hoping to win her hand in marriage.

Now they set out. Pedro Martínez drove the dozen steers, riding a wiry, well-trained mustang and directing them with shouts and flourishes of his *sombrero*. The pedigreed bull and the heifer each went in its own cart, sturdily built by Esteban Morales, the four sides higher than the bull's head, so there would be no danger of its breaking free. Two dray horses were attached to each cart. A five-year-old palomino stallion rode in still another cart, while the four-year-old palomino mare was in another, and the walls of these were as protectively high. It was a slow way to go, and they could make no more than fifteen miles a day. John Cooper's concern was not so much for the steers, as for the bull and heifer and the palominos, for they were superb specimens, and he wanted the Argentinian *hacendado* to be satisfied with his purchase.

Andrew rode a strong gray gelding and carried his long rifle, the present from his father, in his saddle sheath. John Cooper watched covertly as his son patted the sheath and smiled, pleased with himself. The boy glanced toward his father and John Cooper was careful to look away just in time lest Andrew think that he was under surveillance. Nonetheless, the Texan could not resist a wry little smile; Andrew's appreciation of the gun was a symbol of his approaching manhood.

Twelve

Eleven Dominican nuns, headed by a tall, intrepid, white-haired mother superior known as Sister Eufemia, walked along the dusty road that led from the town of Parras, in the province of Coahuila. It was on the very day in early April that John Cooper had chosen for the start of his long journey to the ranch of Raoul Maldones, and they were heading northward. They had left their abbey that morning, taking their few possessions in a cart drawn by a wheezing, balky burro. Sister Eufemia told her little group, "I shall drive the burro, for I am used to obstinacy, having dealt with it so much of my life. It will be hardship enough for you, my sisters, to go on foot this long distance. When we reach the end of our journey, perhaps a blessed refuge will await us."

Over the past decade, the little abbey, which had once been patronized by the *ricos* of the community, had fallen into sad neglect. Some of the older families had moved away from the area, for there had been bandit raids, and the most prominent *hacendado*, Luis Rivera, with his wife and two daughters, had been murdered. His wealthy neighbors, terrified by the lack of military protection from the *gubernador* of the province, had deserted Parras and gone farther south, where they could be certain of the protection of *federalista* troops.

Only last year, Sister Eufemia learned that the slothful, fat, and corrupt *alcalde* of Parras was secretly linked to the *jefe de bandidos*, and by more than greed for gain: The two men were actually cousins. When she had braved personal danger by confronting the porcine, smirking Alonzo Cermada in his office in the town square, he had shaken a pudgy forefinger at her and shouted, "Sister Eufemia, don't meddle if you know what's good for you. How you found out about me and Juan Pordilla, I don't know, but the knowledge can be very dangerous to you. Besides, this town has no need of an abbey such as yours. Those who wish to pray may do so in their own chapels."

"But that is infamous, *señor alcalde*," Sister Eufemia had indignantly protested. "We do charitable work, and the produce of our garden we share with the poor."

"*I* do not need your charity, and *I* do not need troublemakers like you in Parras. I will tell you this, Sister Eufemia, if you and your nuns do not leave the abbey by the middle of this April, I cannot answer for the consequences. My cousin might take over the abbey as his headquarters, for he has a small army that needs a permanent roof over its head." He had grinned and leaned back in his stuffed chair, examining the rings on his fingers, rings with precious stones that had been stolen by his cousin and given to him as bribes.

Sister Eufemia understood that his threat was no mere show of words. She had feared something like this, ever since the assassination of the Rivera family, about which nothing had been done. That was why she had remembered the name of a friend, Padre Madura, who was now in Taos. She had written to him, telling of her plight and how she and her eleven sisters sought some place where they would be welcome to do the work of *el Señor Dios*. He had replied:

> I would bring you here to Taos gladly, Sister Eufemia, for when I was in Santa Fe the bishop showed me letters you had written to him of the good work you and your nuns did in Parras. Unhappily, we have an *alcalde mayor* who is even more wicked than yours, and thus I cannot recommend your coming here. But if you will cross the Rio Grande to the *Hacienda del Halcón*, which is beyond the Frio River and near Uvalde, you will find Don Diego de Escobar, who worships our dear Lord and is faithful to His Commandments. Go there with your group; you have my blessing.

With the letter had come a donation in silver, some of the silver that John Cooper had given to the church for the poor and the needy.

Using some of the silver, Sister Eufemia had bought the burro and a sturdy new cart, which was big enough to contain their belongings as well as the large silver crucifix that the chief patron of the abbey—the *hacendado* who had been murdered by the *bandidos*—had contributed when the abbey had first opened. It was concealed in a flour sack, for although Sister Eufemia was staunch in her faith that God would protect the innocent and the weak, she was also practical enough to know that the bandits who preyed on the little villages and hamlets all through this northern portion of Mexico, so poorly and infrequently patrolled, would not hesitate to steal a crucifix if they could turn it into *pesos* for *tequila* and women. The rest of the silver, she told her colleagues, would go toward the establishment of a new mission in whatever place they could find sanctuary.

Sister Eufemia had been a young novice in Mexico City, and had entered a convent there at the age of seventeen, after deciding she did not love her *novio*—a man whom her parents had arranged for her to marry. Her greedy parents had been furious with her for not having married the young *rico*, hoping that such a union would improve their own impoverished status. Thus, feeling that her duty was to God, she had taken holy vows.

She had joined the Dominican group because it seemed

to her, of all the orders of the Holy Church, the most piously dedicated and charitably inclined. Now in her sixty-first year, she had been rewarded for her good works and humility by having been named abbess at Parras over a decade ago. The Church was her life, but the abbey had been her favorite of all the places to which her work had brought her.

"My sisters," she had said to the small band of nuns on their last night in Parras, "perhaps this is a good lesson for all of us. We were taught, when we took our first vows, to form no lasting attachments, and particularly not to become covetous of material possessions. It is true that this abbey sheltered us, was a cheerful place, provided us with rooms for study and meditation, for the teaching of the young, and for the guidance and counselorship of those men and women who came to us with anguish in their hearts and sought solace. Now we have been uprooted because we fear for our lives. I do not think it wise to emulate the ancient martyrs, my sisters, because we can do more good living than dead. Since the *alcalde* himself has seen fit to declare in the boldest terms his affiliation with the bandit chief, we should seek a new home. God answered my prayers, and my old friend Padre Madura, who now presides over the church in Taos, wrote me that he could not offer us a home there."

The other nuns looked at one another, and a faint murmur was instantly silenced by Sister Eufemia's peremptory wave of her hand.

"He recommends, my sisters," she continued, "that we go to Texas, toward Uvalde and the Frio River. There is a ranch there owned by a certain Don Diego de Escobar, who was *intendente* of Taos, a man renowned for the justice he gave even the lowliest, yes, *los indios del pueblo*. It will be a journey of some five hundred miles by foot. We must go slowly, and because of the bandits we must be careful where we camp for the night. Like gypsies, we shall take the open road, and we shall share with the villagers and the farmers what they have to offer us in sustenance and also the strength of their prayers. Yes, my sisters, it will be a hard journey, but also it will be an inspiration to us to give of our very best."

The youngest of the nuns, Sister Rosalie, who was only twenty-four and had come to the abbey just two years before, protested. "But, Sister Eufemia, how can we be sure that this man of whom you have just spoken will give us land and help us with the building of an abbey? It is so far away, and there are such dangers. Worst of all, do you propose that we go across the Rio Grande and remain with those *gringos* of whom I am mortally afraid?"

"Oh, you of little faith!" Sister Eufemia smilingly rebuked the young nun, whose face, framed in its habit, looked like a child's. "All of us are in God's hands. He will look after us; never fear. As to the *gringos,* if Padre Madura, whom I have known for some years, tells me that this man is upright and charitable and kind, it suffices. If it is not so"—here she made an eloquent shrug—"we shall simply go on until we find a new home. You must not think, Sister Rosalie, that the *americanos* are heathens or creatures of the devil. Now, my sisters, let us go to the chapel and pray there for the last time that He who watches even the falling of a sparrow from the heavens will look after us and guide us to our new home."

The next morning, with the sun high in the sky beating down on them, in their black robes, they moved slowly down the dusty road. Sister Eufemia already began to regret her purchase of the burro. It was ill-tempered, and even switching it with a willow withe did not always quicken its footsteps. She looked back toward their abbey, murmured a silent prayer, and then called out, "Courage, sisters, see how beautiful the sky is and the sun and the heavens? That is the work of the Creator. At each new step we take along this road, we shall find more evidence of His greatness."

At noon of the second day after John Cooper's departure for New Orleans en route to Argentina, four men rode their mustangs at a leisurely pace as they neared the extensive holdings of the Double H Ranch. Heading them was a tall, square-chinned, blue-gray-eyed man just turned thirty who, very much like John Cooper himself, wore buckskin leggins and jacket, with a leather belt around his lean middle, to which the sheath of a knife was attached. Conversing with his companions, he said jocularly, "You're in for a surprise, boys, because John Cooper's a man after my own heart. It's men like him and me who are going to make this Texas territory into a great land; you watch and see."

The three men with him were about his own age. Carl Yeend was tall and lean, with a reddish-brown beard; Dexter Melton was stolid, muscular, and black-haired; and Jack Ribbner was of average height, with dark brown sideburns, beard, and long hair that fell to his shoulders. Leaving their homes along the Brazos River, these men had come all this way with Jim Bowie to pay their respects to his friend, John Cooper Baines, and to see the great Texas ranch that was already becoming legendary in the Southwest.

Jim Bowie continued to speak. "John Cooper's a whizbang when it comes to using a long rifle or a knife—I wish I had a hundred like him for my Rangers. Now, that would get us off to a good start."

"First we have to get the governor to approve the idea of having Texas Rangers, Jim," Dexter Melton reminded him.

"Hell, that's going to be easy. We'll be doing his work for him. There isn't any law and order here at all. And Texas is a huge country. Why there's four or five hundred acres per each settler. We're going to protect the settlers who came in on Moses and Stephen Austin's say-so. They're family people, and all they want is land and a chance to have their families and crops and live a good, simple life. Our Rangers, once we get them recognized, will see to it that the settlers aren't interfered with," Jim Bowie stoutly declared.

The four men came within sight of the vast settlement of the Double H Ranch. There was grazing land as far as the eye could see, with the *vaqueros* on horseback riding among herds of cattle. There were horses and sheep, and in the distance were all the ranch buildings, including the barns and stables, the workers' cottages and the large main house, as well as the fine-looking new church. One of the *vaqueros* rode up to the men and greeted them, then led them to the gateway that served as the main entrance to the ranch. Telling the men to dismount and wait, the *vaquero* went to fetch Miguel Sandarbal.

Miguel came out of the bunkhouse. Recognizing Bowie, he strode forward and offered his hand, grinning from ear to ear. *"Bienvenida,* Señor Bowie! It does my heart good to see you again. I've a note for you from the Señor Baines. He left for Argentina."

"What the devil—Argentina, of all places," the tall leader drawled, shrugging. "What for?"

"Business, señor," Miguel cheerfully explained.

"That's a shame; I was counting on saying hello to him again. Well, what can you do? Here are my friends Carl Yeend, Dexter Melton, and Jack Ribbner. Boys, this is Miguel Sandarbal, the best *capataz* in the Southwest."

"You do me too much honor, Señor Bowie," Miguel said, smiling at the compliment.

"Not a bit of it! I hope you'll show us around. We'd like to learn about how you run the ranch and your defenses here. You see, we want to help all the settlers coming into Texas. We're going to form a kind of military guard. We're going to call ourselves the Texas Rangers."

"An excellent idea, *amigo*."

"Miguel, you know that the Señor Baines told me all about Ramón Santoriaga, who used to be in the Mexican military service and had the same rank Santa Anna did. I understand he came here to the ranch to start a new life for himself and his family and is now in charge of the defense of this *hacienda*."

"That's true, Señor Bowie."

"Well, if it's not too much bother, during our little stop-over my men and I would like to meet him."

"He has a house over there to the northwest, Señor Bowie," Miguel said. "I know he'll be very glad to see you. So will the *patrón*, Don Diego." Then his face fell. "We've had some bad times around here. One of the reasons that Señor Baines isn't here to see you is that he lost his wife—"

"That's a damned shame! How did it happen? Fever?"

Miguel's face hardened. "No. She went out riding, and a *cobarde*, a man named Francisco López—may he burn in hell for all eternity—lay in ambush and shot her."

"I'm crushed by that news," Jim Bowie said, his face sobering. "I can understand why he'd want to go away from here and sort things out for himself. What about this López?"

"The Señor Baines tracked him down and killed him with his bare hands. I prayed he would," Miguel said with an angry grimace.

"That's another reason why I'm so anxious to form this group of mine. I know it's a lot of territory to cover, but I think we can smell out the scoundrels before they have a chance to do much harm. Now, with your permission, my men and I will go find the Señor Santoriaga."

"*Vaya con Dios, amigos,*" Miguel wished them.

Don Diego and Carlos welcomed Jim Bowie and his friends, and Ramón Santoriaga, as well as the latter's wife, Mercedes, dined with the visitors in the *hacienda*. Bowie affably turned to the handsome, former Mexican officer and said,

"You know, Señor Santoriaga, I think it's very important to have a good line of defense against possible attack in these unsettled times."

Ramón took a sip of wine and nodded. "Agreed, Señor Bowie, and you will find that our men here at the Double H Ranch are well trained to look after our families and property."

Bowie glanced at the Texans who had traveled with him. "The men here with me are just the beginning of our own defenses, I'm hoping. Texas is such a big country; I could easily recruit several hundred men. We want to do a thorough job of patrolling and protecting not only the settlers here now, but also those who are certain to be coming."

"I am afraid, Señor Bowie," Don Diego anxiously put in, "that there may be trouble with the Mexican authorities if too many settlers come to Texas. There is resentment against the *americanos*."

"It's bound to happen, Don Diego," Jim Bowie replied. "Differences in religion, differences in temperament, differences in living, you might say. That's at the heart of it."

"But do you think, Señor Bowie," Carlos asked, "that your Rangers will interfere with the Mexican patrols? If that happened, would it not create incidents that would make for unpleasant relations between México and los Estados Unidos?"

Bowie shook his head. "No, sir, what I've in mind is to patrol Texas. I won't go south of the Rio Grande. We'll have enough on our hands just looking after the territory. If we build Texas up so that it's strong, and we Rangers look after security and defense, I doubt that the Mexicans will pick a fight with us." He shrugged and glanced at his friends. "Of course, knowing how the Mexicans think—after all, I do have a Mexican wife—I wouldn't rule out the possibility. To annex Texas would be a mighty big advantage for them because they'd dominate the Southwest and close off trade to Santa Fe again, the way the Spaniards did some years back."

All the men nodded gloomily at this memory. Soon, however, the mood grew lighter and the evening ended with a round of toasts.

Early the next morning, Jim Bowie and his three friends went on a tour of inspection of the *Hacienda del Halcón*, with Carlos, Ramón, and Miguel accompanying them. When they rode back in time for lunch, which Tía Margarita and

Rosa Nuñez prepared, old Jeremy Gaige, who had remained at the ranch after Ernest Henson and Matthew Robisard had returned to St. Louis, left his room in the *hacienda* to take a stroll. Francesca and Diego, Carlos's son, who had become very fond of the old prospector, accompanied him.

They were intrigued by his stories of the many fabulous treasures for which he had prospected and never found, and were also amused by his fascinated interest in Don Diego who, in his opinion, as a former *hidalgo* of Spain, could document incredible hoards of gold and silver plate, bullion, and jewels.

Francesca took his hand as the trio walked slowly toward the Frio River. "Mr. Gaige," she asked, "what was the best treasure you ever looked for?"

"Well, honey, I'll tell you. Long before you wuz born, I was out by myself along the Missouri River. I'd heard tell of some river pirates who used to lie in wait in coves 'n then put out in boats and raid a flat boat, when they knew there wuz some wealthy passengers aboard. Anyhow, someone told me that one of these river pirates had stashed away a chest full of gold pieces 'n precious rings he'd taken off folks that he'd done in. His name wuz Ben Worthy. Seems like he'd never been caught and all of a sudden there wuz word that he'd up 'n died from a bout with river fever. Well, mind you, everybody in creation set out to find that chest. I did, too," he ruefully added with such a woebegone expression that both Francesca and Diego giggled. "Don't you laugh, now, missy, and you either, sonny," he admonished them, stiffly drawing himself up and glaring at them. Then his weather-beaten face creased into a winning smile, and he continued, "Well, the upshot of it wuz, I spent nigh onto two months lookin' in all the caves along the Missouri I could find, and all I did wuz stir up some bats 'n a passel of rattlesnakes. I tell you, I got out of that territory fast. What I heard last, nobody yet found that chest. If I had, I'd be a rich man."

"What if you got rich, Mr. Gaige?" Francesca asked with a look of wonder on her face.

"Well now, missy," he drawled, favoring her with a wink, "I'd have me a fine house, mebbe back in St. Looey, with an eiderdown quilt 'n a mattress stuffed full of goose feathers. I'd have me a nice, fat old housekeeper to cook my meals, so's I wouldn't have to do any work. I'd buy me a nice beaver hat 'n a suit 'n a cravat 'n go around in style 'n everybody'd say, 'There goes Mr. Jeremy Gaige, the richest prospector we ever done had in this here town.' That's exactly what I'd do, missy, sonny."

"But tell me, Mr. Gaige," Francesca pursued, "have you ever found a real treasure?"

Jeremy screwed up his face and scratched his head, lost in the rapid concoction of a yarn that would satisfy this young girl's curiosity. Finally, he drawled, "Well, missy, to be honest with you, if I hadn't been chased by a band of Delaware on the warpath, I'd have had a chance to dig deeper in a cave near the Missouri River where I jist knowed there wuz gold, 'cause one of my friends had found some in his pan a coupla miles downriver from there." He reminiscently touched his sparse white hair and chuckled, "As it is, I'm lucky to still have my scalp; I can tell you that for certain."

At that moment, Jim Bowie came out walking, wearing his buckskins and puffing at a pipe. To his delight, Don Diego had given him a pouch filled with strong, aromatic Havana tobacco, which had come in from New Orleans. He happened to overhear Jeremy Gaige's last comment and came forward with a genial grin on his handsome face. "So you two tadpoles have treasure on your mind, is that right?"

Francesca proudly drew herself up and, with a withering look, declared, "I'm not a tadpole, Mr. Bowie. I'm going on twelve."

"I beg your pardon," Jim Bowie said, doffing his leather cap and making her a low bow.

Primly, she responded, "I fully accept your apology, Mr. Bowie. Also, Diego's just about thirteen. You ought to know yourself, from all the stories I've heard about you, that a boy here on the frontier grows up really fast and becomes a man while he's still in his teens."

Jim Bowie grinned. "Beats me how smart you are. Now mind you, I'm not downgrading females. Where would I be without my sweet wife? But I will confess I wasn't expecting to find such a knowing young lady here on a Texas ranch."

"Thank you, Mr. Bowie." Francesca shot a glance at Diego and was rewarded by his amiable grin. Her defense of him before this famous scout and Indian fighter had cemented their bond of friendship.

"But the fact is, if you want to know about real treasure, I can tell you a tall tale that's got plenty of truth in it," Bowie went on, giving an affable nod to Jeremy, who pricked up his ears at the mention of treasure. "There's a lost gold mine in the San Saba Valley. I'm here to tell you. Lots of men have tried to find it, and nobody has, to date."

"I can't rightly place where you say it is, Mr. Bowie," Jeremy complained.

"Well, there's a little town which takes its name from the valley, and that's up by Brownwood. I'd place it about a hundred miles northwest of Austin, as they're starting to call one of the settlements founded by that great father-and-son team of Moses and Stephen."

"Is there really a gold mine, Mr. Bowie?" Diego piped up, and Jeremy nodded to indicate that he was even more interested than Carlos's young son.

"Tell us about it—did you ever find it, Mr. Bowie?" Francesca asked.

"No, I didn't find it. If I had, I mightn't be here right now," Jim Bowie humorously retorted. "But I talked to enough fellows who claimed to have gotten close to it. There was an old Indian scout, an Apache named Big Nose, whom I ran into a couple of years back. The way he told it to me, he and his braves were on the trail of some Comanche when they stopped to make camp late at night. They were near a big mesa, and there was a small series of hills along one side of it. All of a sudden, it started to thunder and lightning, so Big Nose and his friends got their horses into a couple of the caves, and then started making something to eat and waiting till the storm blew over."

"Go on, Mr. Bowie!" Francesca urged. Jeremy stood openmouthed, absorbing every syllable.

"Well, I'm telling you now what he told me, and he pretty much placed it. Just as he was getting ready to leave at dawn, he happened to look at the back of the cave, and sure as you're born, there was a dull yellow streak along a vein. He didn't have any time to stop and scratch up any of that gold, and in the first place, he wasn't that much interested in it. You see, the Indians of the southern Plains were mostly concerned about hunting and changing their strongholds so their enemies wouldn't wipe them out with a surprise attack. Anyway, Big Nose thought it was strange, and he had never seen anything like that before, so he remembered where the cave was. Now, what he told me was that it was a huge mesa, stretching for almost two miles, and then off to the left was a fertile valley, the San Saba, as we call it today."

"But didn't he ever go back to look for the gold, Mr. Bowie?" Diego wanted to know.

"Guess not, son. Problem was, he had fallen into disgrace with the chief over some ruckus or other, and they sort of sent him packing. That's why he became a scout for us, you see."

"But if you know where it is, why don't you take time off and go find it and stake a claim on it, Mr. Bowie?" Francesca asked.

"Well, I haven't had time off from my marriage and my work helping the settlers and laying in supplies and all to do much prospecting."

"Gosh!" Francesca exclaimed. "So the treasure is still there, then?"

"So far as I know."

Jeremy asked reflectively, "That San Saba Valley—it's a hundred miles northwest of Austin, you say, Mr. Bowie, sir?"

"Give or take a few miles, yes. Well, I've got to go round up my men now. We're going to meet with Ramón Santoriaga and learn some more about the ranch. We'll talk about treasure another time."

"Thank you for telling us about it, Mr. Bowie," Francesca politely responded.

"Thanks a heap, Mr. Bowie," Jeremy chimed in. "You jist gimme a real good idea. Maybe I jist might take out on my own after that lost gold mine. Jist one strike like that, 'n I could have me a fine, new house anywhere I please, St. Looey or mebbe New York—or again, down in Mexico, where there'd be lots of purty young girls to take care of an old man like me, cook my meals 'n wash my clothes 'n look after me in general. Yes, sir, thanks again, Mr. Bowie."

"Hello again, Señor Santoriaga," Jim Bowie said, holding out his hand, which the former Mexican officer warmly shook.

Ramón exclaimed, "My men are waiting for my signal to begin our military maneuvers. We are going to show you just how we defend in case of an attack. If you are ready . . ." At the nod of Bowie, who was joined by his three friends, Ramón reached into the pocket of his breeches, drew out a whistle, and blew three shrill blasts. Out of the bunkhouse, thirty armed *vaqueros* came running, and Miguel left his cottage to join them. Esteban Morales hurried to the corral and mounted his gelding, then rode out westward toward the older *trabajadores* who were tending sheep.

Since Francisco López's attack on the *Hacienda del Halcón* the previous December, even the sheepherders carried weapons with them. Some of these were old muskets, but others were new Belgian rifles and pistols that John Cooper had bought in New Orleans. Miguel, Esteban, and Ramón had rehearsed the riders and the workers twice a week, so that each man knew what was expected of him and just where to position himself. Some men ran to the paddocks to guard the horses, others crouched by the side of the *hacienda,* and still other men climbed onto the bunkhouse roof, where they lay flat, their rifles ready. In all, some fifty *trabajadores* and *vaqueros* had moved to their positions to cover every possible approach of attack.

Jim Bowie, Carl Yeend, Dexter Melton, and Jack Ribbner cheered the men who had shown their excellent training and readiness under a surprise attack. Bowie grinned as he came to Ramón to offer his hand. "I think that even if Santa Anna had had all his soldiers around you, you'd have given a fine account of yourselves. My congratulations! If any of your *vaqueros* have a hankering to join our Rangers, I'd be proud to sign them up!"

Ramón gave Jim Bowie a courteous bow, then smilingly shook his head. "Impossible, Señor Bowie! The men here are loyal to their *patrón,* Don Diego de Escobar. They would give their lives also for their beloved *capataz,* the Señor Miguel Sandarbal. Finally, they revere the Señor Baines, after whom this ranch is named, by his Indian title, the *Hacienda del Halcón.* I do not think you will find any recruits from here—but I admire your mission, and I wish you all success of it."

Thirteen

John Cooper and Andrew and the four *vaqueros* entered the outskirts of New Orleans a little more than two weeks after beginning their journey from the Double H Ranch. No incidents had marred this first stage, and the Texan found himself enjoying the time with his oldest son. The four *vaqueros* whom he and Miguel had selected were tactful and quiet during camp, sensing that their *patrón* wanted to be with his son as much as possible.

What particularly pleased John Cooper was that Andrew was able to bring in his own share of game with his long rifle. He had flushed a *jabalí* out of the bushes and had killed it with his very first shot from three hundred feet away.

When John Cooper had sent a courier bearing a letter to be taken to New Orleans and thence expedited to Raoul Maldones in Argentina, he had sent another note to Fabien Mallard, apprising the latter that he expected to be there within two or three weeks, and that he would welcome the chance to play host this time to the factor and his handsome wife.

John Cooper and the *vaqueros* drove the carts and the dozen long-horned steers toward Fabien Mallard's sprawling, one-story warehouse located on the levee of the Mississippi. Mallard's workers took the animals from the Texan, leading the cattle to a stall at one end of the building, and the palominos to the other end, with the stallion in a separate stall from the mare.

Fabien and Hortense Mallard accepted John Cooper's invitation to supper. While the *vaqueros* ate heartily at the restaurant in their hotel, the Texan and his son met the Mallards outside a charming little Creole restaurant in the French Quarter. Mallard was sympathetic but tactful, sensing that John Cooper had no desire to discuss his tragedy. His wife, Hortense, equally perceptive, did what she could to brighten

144

the evening by relating anecdotes concerning her own travels. John Cooper was interested to learn that she had been to Haiti, France, and Gibraltar, and had spent six months in England, before visiting relatives in the Pyrenees. "But I'm quite content to stay here in New Orleans, M'sieu Baines," she smilingly told him as she reached over to squeeze her husband's hand and exchange a loving look with him. Then she continued, "I'm told you speak Spanish fluently; it will serve you very well where you're going. I'm sure you'll have a most interesting time."

"My wife is right, as always," Fabien Mallard genially observed. "Actually, M'sieu Baines, you'll be arriving in Argentina at about the start of their winter. Their climate is just the opposite of ours. In fact, between June and October, the low temperature is as cool as you may find in the northwest, well beyond your ranch. Now, M'sieu Maldones is a most interesting correspondent; I've known him for several years and his letters are filled with details about the country, the weather, and, to be sure, the political situation. Indeed, I had still another letter from him expressing his eagerness to meet you. He's an enormously wealthy man, but he has a good deal of humility. He's a widower. His wife, a devout girl out of the convent and from a very fine old family in Buenos Aires, died about five years ago. She gave him four daughters, but he has always wanted a son. It's understandable, when you think of his holdings. On the *pampas* the land is almost limitless. Cattle is in overabundance, I'd say, though it's hardly of the quality that you're raising on your Double H Ranch. To begin with, they don't fatten their cattle. That means they're lean, and even scrawny—" he smiled "—especially by the standards of your giant longhorns. I went over to the warehouse to look at them, and I'm impressed. I shouldn't care to get into a bullring with any one of those steers of yours."

"I'm not sure I'd care to, either, M'sieu Mallard," John Cooper said, chuckling as he took a bite of the delicious swordfish he had been served. "By the way, I meant to ask you, how long do you think this journey will take?"

Fabien Mallard pondered a moment, then said, "It's about seventy-five hundred nautical miles from New Orleans to Buenos Aires. Mind you, M'sieu Maldones has his ranch somewhat inland and about twenty-five miles south of Buenos Aires. There isn't any port except Buenos Aires, and the ship will have to drop anchor well offshore. If the winds are favorable, your three-masted frigate, the *Miromar,* which sails tomorrow at high tide late in the afternoon, should reach there within four to five weeks, I should judge." He shrugged. "If there are slack winds, it might be a week or ten days longer. It's bound to be a long journey, and for a man of action like yourself, I daresay somewhat chafing."

"It will give Andrew and me time to think a bit about what's happened, as well as to get better acquainted," John Cooper remarked. "I'm grateful to you, M'sieu Mallard."

The Creole factor was touched and put his hand on John Cooper's shoulder. "My friend, Hortense and I wept when we heard. It is unjust, but then there is so much in life that is unjust that we perhaps do not concern ourselves with it, unless it touches us personally. Both of us pray that you will find peace and happiness. Perhaps it will be through meeting this very estimable gentleman."

"I am in need of meeting good, honest men, believe me, men like yourself, M'sieu Mallard." John Cooper said as the dishes were cleared away and coffee was served. Then, sipping the strong, rich chicory brew, he said, "You know, I don't know much about this country I'm going to. Is Argentina a democracy, a republic, or a monarchy?"

"That's an excellent question, M'sieu Baines. Argentina is a republic. Spain dominated Argentina until the time of Napoleon, but the native-born, who are called the *criollos,* and the *gauchos* who are equal in some ways to your *vaqueros* because they are horse-riding hunters and cowboys, oppose the rule of the Spanish-born. Then, of course, when Spain was occupied with the Napoleonic wars, there was no chance for trade with Buenos Aires. English and French ships blockaded the Spanish port and, in fact, twenty years ago an English warship attacked and took Buenos Aires."

"Wow!" Andrew responded with a wide-eyed look. "Will we see warships when we get there?"

"I don't think so, *mon ami,*" the factor told the boy. "Since then, an army of *gauchos* recaptured the city. When they learned that they could defend their country from a foreign power, these *criollos,* the native-born, remembered our example of the United States. A year later, when the English attacked them, they won again. Then Ferdinand VII treated them with much the same contempt that he did Mexico, and at last they were ready for their independence."

"How did it come about?" John Cooper asked.

"Well, M'sieu Baines, a provisional government was formed eleven years ago and offered Argentina to the English as a self-governing colony. A year later, Argentina declared its independence from Spain. Unfortunately, those who ruled in Buenos Aires and those who lived on the *pampas* and were resentful of any action that would limit their way of life, came into conflict. There was a series of revolutions with much bloodshed, and as a result of this, both Paraguay and Uruguay, which had been part of the great Argentinian peninsula, sought their freedom and became separate countries. There were many provinces fighting one another, and many types of governments were tried. But just last year, the first general Congress took place in Buenos Aires, and the last word I had from M'sieu Maldones was that, as its first constitutional president, the Congress has appointed Bernardino Rivadavia, a remarkable man who organized the police and the postal systems, even universities and schools. Happily, he knows something about law, and so he established the legal system of Argentina, and he has also been able to separate church from state, a most notable achievement."

"He sounds like a great man," John Cooper declared.

"He is. Last year, when he tried to establish a national unity, the bosses—who are called *caudillos* in Buenos Aires—tried to stop him and made him leave the country. But they soon discovered that, without him, and without any constitution, they got involved in a war with Brazil over Uruguay. To make a long story short, this year the Congress called Rivadavia back and made him President. He is about to end the war with Brazil and free Uruguay. But M'sieu Maldones tells me that he still does not have unified support behind him, and he may be forced out of office. It would be a pity to lose so brilliant and ethical a man."

"It seems that, just as in Mexico, there must be many people who are fighting to be *numero uno*," John Cooper quipped.

"You're absolutely right. But my guess is that when you're at M'sieu Maldones's ranch and you're on the *pampas*, you won't think about politics when you see the beauty of that country. And you'll find your host a fascinating man."

"Thanks for all the information, M'sieu Mallard. I'll write you once I get there and tell you how we get along together, this M'sieu Maldones and I." John Cooper smiled as he paid the bill for their meal, then the foursome left the little restaurant. They bid each other good-bye and bon voyage, and the factor and his wife took their carriage back to their *villa* while John Cooper and his son walked the short distance back to their hotel in silence, the tall Texan's arm around his son's shoulders, both deep in thought about the upcoming adventure.

John Cooper turned to his tall young son and gestured toward the frigate, with its three towering masts pointing toward the blue and nearly cloudless sky. "Well, Andy, that's the *Miromar*. Looks mighty big, but my guess is that by the time we land, you'll be aching to get your feet down on solid ground."

"Are we the only passengers on that ship, Pa?"

"No. There's an elderly Spanish couple getting off at Buenos Aires, the captain tells me. Then there are three men who he says are very important people in the government in Buenos Aires. And a husband and his young wife who got married here in New Orleans. Hey now," John Cooper exclaimed, "it looks like everyone's gone aboard. Let's get moving. Take a last look at this big levee and remember you're in the United States now, and that's where we're coming back to, God willing."

"Amen to that, Pa."

The *Miromar* had been built in New Bedford, Massachusetts. Both John Cooper and Andrew took an immediate liking to its captain, Silas Blake. A tall, grizzled, sparse-bearded man in his mid-fifties, he had been captain of the sturdy frigate for the past decade. He had run away from a fashionable Boston home at the age of fourteen, when he learned that his parents intended to apprentice him to a lawyer. He had a dry sense of humor, and an enormous store of anecdotes about his sailing experiences. Prior to his captaincy on the *Miromar*, he had commanded a whaler in the South Seas, spent several years with the Dutch East India Company, and also plied the Eastern Seaboard between the ports of New York and Charleston.

"I took the liberty, Mr. Baines," he announced at the first supper in the ship's saloon, having insisted that John Cooper and his son be seated at his table, "of going down to the hold and looking over those palominos of yours. Also, those Texas longhorns. I've never seen cattle like those before, not with such a wide horn spread."

"Actually, I've got more than I know what to do with," John Cooper smilingly responded.

"That's what you might say about the Argentinian cattle business, too," Captain Blake drily observed. "They've thousands of head of cattle on the *pampas*. Cattle are mighty cheap."

"I'm bringing Señor Maldones a pedigreed bull and heifer so that he can improve his stock," John Cooper explained.

"I know this Señor Maldones. Mr. Mallard has shipped him goods from New Orleans aboard the *Miromar,* and Señor Maldones sends back spices, grain, and herbs, and some hogsheads of native wine and rum he brews down there. By the way, Mr. Baines, you mustn't think I'm being rude in not inviting my other passengers to sup with me tonight. Fact is, those three men you see at the first mate's table work for the government in Buenos Aires, and they fancy themselves as being better than anybody else. The elderly couple are with them, as you see, and the young couple want to be at a table by themselves. I suppose you might excuse them, since they're newlyweds."

They ate their tasty chicken in silence for awhile, then John Cooper spoke up. "I've noticed that you've got cannon on your first deck, Captain Blake."

"I sure have. You know there's still a war going on against Brazil, and some of those South American countries are mighty tetchy. Just in case anybody decided they'd want to put out to sea and maybe sink an American ship, I got myself the best cannon money could buy and signed on some crackerjack gunners to handle them."

"That's good to know. Well," John Cooper said, raising a glass filled with Canary wine, "here's to a good and safe voyage."

"I'll drink to that," the captain replied, and sipped his wine.

Andrew now spoke up. "Pa, could I try a glass of that wine?"

John Cooper smiled. "Andy, this is probably as good a time as any for me to find out just how you handle wine, when you're alone with me on a long journey like this. Is it all right with you, Captain?"

"Of course!" Captain Blake replied. "Steward! A glass of wine for Mr. Baines's strapping young son!"

One of the stewards came forward with the decanter of Canary wine and filled Andrew's glass, after first refilling the captain's and then John Cooper's. Captain Blake raised his glass. "Gentlemen, now let us toast to our homeland, to the Yankees and the Union," he proposed.

John Cooper watched his son carefully sip at his wine and smiled to himself. Yes, now that he was aboard, and the animals were in the hold, he looked forward to this voyage. The best thing about it was that Andy and he would be close together. In that way, a father and a son could communicate.

Favorable winds directed the *Miromar* sixteen hundred miles from New Orleans to the port of San Juan in five days, cheering John Cooper, who hoped that the voyage would continue to be shortened by just such excellent weather. Pacing the deck of a ship gave him far too much time to reflect upon his life and, particularly, on the bleak anguish that Catarina's death had imposed upon his spirit. He was restless and stared helplessly at the blue horizon and the vast expanse of ocean on each side of the frigate, wishing that he might be again on land, astride Pingo or old Fuego, "Long Girl" in the saddle sheath beside him.

He spent long hours in the bright sunshine on the deck, practicing with the fine knife he had received from Jim Bowie before he left the Double H Ranch. The captain had set aside for his use an area about twenty-five feet long. Using a packing crate, he drew a series of circles to represent his targets. From a distance òf twenty-five feet he found he was easily able to hurl the knife into a target the size of a half-dollar, and Andrew, who joined him in these practice sessions, was astounded by his father's accuracy.

"It's quite a knife, this Bowie knife, Andy. It has a great feel to it, a terrific balance. Here, try it yourself."

Andrew, too, practiced with the knife, and following his father's instructions, learned how to hold it and throw it. After several afternoons, he was becoming proficient himself, frequently able to throw the knife into a circle with a six-inch radius.

"When we get back home," John Cooper promised his son, "I'll ask Jim Bowie for one of his knives for you. You've shown you really know how to use it."

The *Miromar* dropped anchor in the harbor of San Juan and remained there for half a day. Andrew begged his father to go ashore and to take him on a tour of the city. It was better, to be sure, to do that than to sit in the cabin and mope, his father concluded. He hired the driver of a calash near the dock at which the frigate was anchored to drive his son and himself to the famous, imposing Morro Castle, which stood defiantly at the entrance of the harbor, and which had been erected 237 years before. From there, after Andrew had insisted on walking around it and observing it in great detail, the obliging driver took them through the most colorful streets of the old city.

That evening, back on the ship, they enjoyed a profusion of exotic fruits, such as mangoes, papaya, and melons the like of which they had never before tasted, all of which had been taken on board before they set sail.

They were at Captain Blake's table, and he asked, "So what do you think of my ship, Mr. Baines?"

"It's a fine, strong vessel, from all I can tell, though you know that I'm a landlubber," John Cooper smilingly replied. "My son and I are quite comfortable, though, thank you."

"I'm glad to hear that, Mr. Baines. It's just too bad that the other passengers seem to want to keep to themselves. However, only this morning that elderly couple over there, the Señor and Señora Corte, expressed a desire to meet you. I told him that you were going to visit the Señor Maldones who runs a big cattle ranch on the *pampas* south of Buenos Aires. That seemed to interest him a good deal, and he asked me if you would sit with him some evening, you and your son, to be sure."

"Certainly. Please extend my appreciation for his thoughtfulness."

The next evening, at the captain's table, John Cooper Baines was presented to Señor Alberto Corte and his white-haired wife, the Señora María Corte. The elderly aristocrat, impeccably dressed in a flowery cravat, elegant waistcoat, and silk shirt with high collar, acknowledged the American's presence at the table with a cordial, *"Buenas noches, señor americano,"* to which John Cooper responded in Spanish, "And to you and your charming wife, I wish the same."

"You speak Spanish well for a *gringo.*" Old Corte faintly smiled, glancing at his wife, who nodded in agreement.

"Señor Corte, since I've lived in Taos and Texas about

fourteen years and been married to a Spanish girl, the daughter of a former *hidalgo* of Spain, it is not surprising that I should be fluent in your language," John Cooper replied in excellent Spanish. The elderly woman's eyebrows arched, and then she smiled and nodded, this time more enthusiastically.

"I understand you are traveling with us to Buenos Aires, Señor Baines, to visit Señor Raoul Maldones," her husband politely said. "Well, things have been quite unsettled in Buenos Aires. I must tell you that the man you are going to see has enemies in Buenos Aires."

"Señor Corte, there is no man living who does not make enemies; I have found this for myself in my own country," was John Cooper's response.

"This is your first trip to our lovely country?"

"Yes, Señor Corte. I look forward to it."

"I hope we shall have the privilege of meeting you in Buenos Aires. You will find our *villa* at the end of the calle Avenida. If you will send a message to us, we shall be most happy to receive you. But now, to continue with what I was saying before." Old Corte lowered his voice almost to a whisper and leaned toward the young American. "I don't wish to alarm you, Señor Baines, but there are important people in the city government who look with greed on the rich lands of the *pampas*. Of course, they have been underdeveloped all these years, and they have been the home first of the Indians, then the *gauchos*, who are the freest of all people in Argentina and accept no law except their own. As our nation progresses, and as we learn more from the Western world, the men in power in the city will want the land even more enviously, to turn a profit, and they will not care who stands in their way. Because your friend, this Señor Maldones, does not share their views, they hate him. I say this not to frighten you, but to warn you to be cautious."

"If by that you mean not talking politics, believe me, I'm not going to Argentina for that, Señor Corte," John Cooper boyishly grinned. "But I'll bear it in mind."

The three-masted frigate swung past the Leeward Islands, beyond Barbados, where the ship anchored briefly to take on more supplies, and thence sailed into the vast expanse of the Atlantic Ocean beyond Georgetown and Cayenne, which was one day to be the infamous French prison colony known as Devil's Island. Captain Blake was encouraged by the weather, for the winds had filled their sails to the fullest, and, as he told John Cooper, "We are at least four days ahead of schedule, Mr. Baines. Let's hope our luck continues."

They were nearing the equator, yet long weeks were still in store for John Cooper and his son before they would reach their destination. The Texan, whose nerves had begun to fray at being deprived of the feel of earth under his feet, saw that young Andrew's spirits were also beginning to flag. His oldest son was often seen at the rail of the vessel, staring out into the distant horizon, as if he were homesick for the Double H Ranch far away.

John Cooper was reminded with a full resurgence of all that he had lost, now seeing his oldest son so mournfully silent and contemplative. Moving toward him at the rail, he put an arm around Andrew's shoulders and softly said, "I know, Andy. I know just what you're thinking."

To his surprise, Andrew turned to face his father, and John Cooper could see tears in the youth's eyes. "I can't help it, Pa. Darn it all, I didn't mean to cry."

"Now, just a minute," John Cooper firmly interposed, gripping Andrew by the shoulders and staring steadfastly into his eyes, "there's nothing unmanly about crying, not when you've a reason—and you and I both have. It shows real feelings. Anybody who was as close to your mother as we were—and then to have her taken away so brutally and needlessly—wouldn't be a man if he didn't feel grief and show it. He'd be a walking skeleton."

"I—I think I understand what you mean, Pa," Andrew faltered.

John Cooper's voice grew more gentle as he relaxed his grip on the boy's shoulders. "I'm sure you do, son. Look, Andy, you're old enough by now to understand that everybody has to die, everything in this world. The flowers, the animals, the birds, the insects. Yes, even those we love. I'm going to die, one day. What you and I try to do, as men leading an outdoor life, active as we are, is to try to cope with these dangers—though, of course, it's God's will as to when the death day will be. But there again, Andy, we wouldn't feel much like men, unless we made an effort to taste life to the fullest, to live every day and to believe that the sun will rise for us tomorrow morning, so we can go on with our plans and be decent, God-fearing men."

Andrew put a fist to his eyes and began to knuckle away the tears, then straightened. "Thanks, Pa. I'll be all right."

"I know you will, son. But I'll tell you this; I miss your mother something fierce. She was a beautiful woman and we'll remember her as she was for the rest of our lives."

"Pa?"

"Yes, Andy?"

Andrew Baines turned to face his father, struggling to keep his features impassive. But his voice quavered as he said, "Pa, I love you. I mean it, Pa."

Now it was John Cooper's turn to fight off the tears that welled up in his eyes. There was a lump in his throat as he said, his voice hoarse and unsteady, "Thanks, Andy. I love you, too. Now, damn it all, this sea air has made me as hungry as a wolf. How about you?"

"You know, Pa, I could eat something, too."

"Then let's go see what the cook has in store for us." His arm around his son's shoulders, John Cooper strode off the deck toward the ship's saloon.

Fourteen

A week later, the weather pleasant and the winds gusty, the *Miromar* dropped anchor at Recife, in northeastern Brazil. The stevedores took on fruits, vegetables, flour, coffee, and sides of beef. John Cooper, watching from the rail, realized that the meat would be tough, since South American cattle were so scrawny. He thought to himself that the cook would need a special kind of culinary magic to make this beef palatable.

As he had hoped, the cook, a Portuguese, had skill enough to marinate the meat in spicy sauces and wine, so that it was at least edible. The tropical fruits, particularly mangoes and superbly sweet melons, more than compensated for the chewy, nearly tasteless beef.

A few hours after they had eaten, the *Miromar* sailed from Recife. Captain Blake joined John Cooper and Andrew on the quarterdeck where the wind was brisk and pleasantly cool. Captain Blake smilingly remarked to John Cooper, "If we hold to our course and the weather favors us, I hope to land you in the port of Buenos Aires by about the first of June, God willing."

"That will be fine with me, Captain Blake. I confess I've a longing to stretch my legs and to get on a horse and ride for miles the minute I do," John Cooper smilingly responded.

"Well, Mr. Baines, you'll be able to do plenty of that on the *pampas*. You know, it's a marvel to me, though I've seen it many times, how far it extends. If anyone should wish to farm there, he'd find black soil, rich and free of any stones or pebbles. The *gauchos* are a good deal like your frontiersmen back home, Mr. Baines, especially in your part of the country. They're free with hundreds of miles of wonderful tall grass around them, with no one to bother them."

"I certainly want to meet some of these *gauchos*."

"Meet them you will, because Señor Maldones has a good number of them attached to his *estancia*. That's the Spanish word for ranch used in Argentina."

"I'll remember that. If these *pampas* are such a distance from Buenos Aires, how can the city *políticos* bother the ranch owners?" John Cooper asked.

"Their power is enormous and extends very far." Captain Silas Blake snorted almost derisively. "It's good that our three taciturn friends from the city don't know you've asked this question. They would look upon you with most unfriendly eyes—they do already, but that's only natural. They wonder what business you can have in Argentina, and they resent you because you're an *americano*.

"I've nothing to hide, Captain Blake. I don't want to make any enemies, God knows. If something is troubling them, I'd be happy to talk to them."

"I shouldn't advise it. The trouble is, they know that you're going to see Señor Maldones."

"How did they find out?" John Cooper asked.

"On the first day when they boarded the ship, they asked to see the passenger list, and they went down to the hold and saw your horses and cattle. I was occupied with getting ready for the voyage, you understand, so they asked my second mate. He has a wagging tongue, so he gave them all the information they wanted."

"It can't be helped, and I'm not particularly worried. It's not as if I were committing a crime."

"That's true, but you see, now that the country itself has just gained independence and has a new president and all, there are bound to be ambitious men in Buenos Aires who will start to think of colonizing the *pampas*. They may try, and cause considerable bloodshed in the process."

"I try to keep out of trouble whenever I can. But if it's forced on me, I know how to protect myself," John Cooper declared.

The *Miromar* followed the coastline from Recife to Salvador, a distance of five hundred miles, and reached that port four mornings later. John Cooper and Andrew were glad to go ashore for an hour and walk around the colorful city; in one of the shops the Texan bought *ponchos* for Andrew and himself.

Meanwhile, Señor Corte and his gracious, self-effacing wife continued to befriend John Cooper and his son, and proved to be informative and pleasant conversationalists. Three days out of Salvador, old Corte glanced over his shoulder and, leaning forward toward John Cooper, murmured, "Those three *políticos* don't seem to like the fact that, as a *porteño*, I am fraternizing so freely with you, Señor Baines. They give me very black looks."

"*Porteño?*" John Cooper echoed.

"*Sí*, Señor Baines. That word denotes a citizen or native of Buenos Aires. Just as we call the man who was born in Madrid a *madrileño*."

"I see. *Gracias*."

"Understand, Señor Baines, my wife and I have nothing to fear from these *políticos*. To begin with, we're both quite old, and we do not interfere in politics. We were born in Buenos Aires, we love it, we have seen the struggle for independence against Spain, and we have survived. My philosophy is one of live and let live."

"Mine also, Señor Corte," John Cooper affably replied. "I only hope that my presence here in your company and my interest in your conversation and that of your charming wife will not create any difficulties for you, when you go back to your home."

"Absolutely not, Señor Baines." Old Corte vehemently shook his head. "We do not have a dictatorship, and we do not have sufficient military men at the head of our new government to make us fear oppression." He swiftly, stealthily crossed himself. "Let us hope that Argentina never has that. To be sure, it was necessary to employ a force of arms to break away from Spain, but that is over and done with."

John Cooper still chafed under his confinement and sought to distract himself by continuing to practice knife-throwing with Andrew. The Spanish dagger, which still hung in a sheath around his neck, was occasionally his weapon; but for the most part he used the long sharp knife that Jim Bowie had given him. This time the target was a short spar on the aft deck, and John Cooper increased the distance to thirty-five feet. Andrew proved to be adept at hitting this new target, though he could not match his father's ability to hit dead center of the mast.

A few days later, the *Miromar* dropped anchor at the port of Campos. "We'll not stop at Rio de Janeiro," Captain Blake explained to the Texan, "because I have orders from these three bigwigs aboard. However, I've friends in Campos, especially a trader who'll sell me food and other supplies at a very reasonable price. He has a fondness for American tobacco, so I always bring him a seaman's chest full of it."

John Cooper and Andrew went ashore with the captain and, near the wharf, found the shop of José Figueroa, fat and possessed of an enormous mustache, but with a warm kindly face and soft speech. Perceiving the American ranch owner, he exclaimed to Captain Blake, in a dialect that reflected his mixed Portuguese and Brazilian descent, "But here is a man who could be a *gaucho*, yet he is a *gringo!*"

John Cooper, amused by this description, spoke up in Spanish, saying, "In my country, the United States, one might call me a *vaquero*, which is like your *gaucho* on the *pampas*."

The delighted trader almost embraced John Cooper, so amazed was he that a *gringo* could speak such excellent Spanish. He insisted on making the American and his son presents of two small silver crucifixes on chains, and when John Cooper demurred because of their obvious cost, José Figueroa emphatically declared, "But, señor, Capitán Blake has brought me my favorite tobacco, enough almost for six months. I would give a chamber pot made of gold for such a treasure as that. Besides, you've given me great pleasure in speaking as you do, and you bring my little shop much honor. May they bring you good luck, you and your *hijo!*"

Suddenly John Cooper remembered that he had kept the eye of God in one of the pockets of his buckskin jacket; and, on an impulse, wishing to give a present for a present, withdrew it and handed it to the trader. He knew Tía Margarita would want her *patrón* to use it in this way. *"Es un ojo de Dios,* Señor Figueroa. Accept it from me, and may it bring you as much good luck as I'm sure these crucifixes will to my son and me."

When they had gone back aboard the frigate, Captain Blake turned to John Cooper and said genially, "That was a good thing you did, Mr. Baines. It'll stand me in very good stead when next I come to buy supplies."

"It was fortunate I had it in my pocket. Actually, it was embarrassing to take a present without giving something in return. Our Indians have a custom of exchanging gifts."

They again set sail, with the next stop scheduled at Porto Allegre. What pleased John Cooper during this part of the voyage was Andrew's eagerness for knowledge. Occasionally, he would see his tall son engaged in conversation with one of the stevedores, and since Andrew spoke fluent Spanish, he was able to make himself understood. One of the stevedores pointed out the huge dorsal fin of a giant shark, which had been following the *Miromar* for nearly a week, and said to Andrew, "That one is hungry, but the cook throws the garbage overboard to feed it. You would not want to go for a swim in these waters, señor."

Later that same day, Andrew exclaimed that he saw a school of flying fish, and an hour later, he saw playful dolphins gamboling about the stern of the ship. "Pa," he called, pointing toward the dolphins, "I've never seen fish like that!"

"My mother once told me they were a sign of good luck when they followed a ship, Andy," John Cooper said. Then remembering what else he had learned, he exclaimed, "Come to think of it, Andy, they're not really fish. They've got a body like a fish, but they're considered mammals. They eat fish, that's for certain. Look at that beaklike snout they've got for a head. They could gobble up a lot of little fish with that, and big ones, too, probably." At this moment, the stevedore approached. He was a short, wiry Portuguese who had been on every voyage with Captain Blake; his disposition was unfailingly cheerful. He carried a bucket with him and handed it to Andrew, saying with his enthusiastic smile, "I heard you speak about those *delfines*. *Sí*, they do eat fish. If you wish to throw them some, they will be your friends, and they will bring you luck, as they do all of us."

Andrew Baines spent a diverting half hour tossing fish from the stern of the frigate and exclaiming with delight as the nimble dolphins leaped from the water to snare the fish, gulp them down, and then disappear, only to reappear and to swim in playful circles.

"That was kind of you, Antonio," John Cooper gratefully told the Portuguese stevedore.

"*De nada*, Señor Baines." The stevedore saluted and then went down into the hold of the frigate, for he was one of the men assigned to the chore of feeding the palominos, the bull and heifer, and the long-horned steers.

John Cooper stared at the setting sun, which was an enormous orange ball on the rim of the ocean, turning the entire sky a flaming red. He exhaled a long sigh of contentment, for he was beginning, thanks to this friendly encounter with the humble worker, to come out of the brooding, taciturn mood that had fallen over him. These dolphins that were following the *Miromar* seemed to be a premonition that life awaited not only him, but Andrew as well.

On a morning in early June 1826, the *Miromar* moved into the inlet of the great Rio de la Plata, which separates Uruguay from Argentina, and dropped anchor in the harbor of Buenos Aires.

John Cooper and Andrew and the *vaqueros* stood at the rail to watch the cargo being unloaded and the passengers disembarking. Since Buenos Aires did not have a deep-water port, it was necessary for large vessels to anchor about three quarters of a mile out. Passengers were taken to shore in one of the ship's dinghies, while cargo was unloaded by hoists onto barges that were sent from the docks.

The shy young couple, hardly glancing at anyone and with their hands intertwined, were already sitting in the dinghy waiting to be lowered from the ship's deck into the water. As they were about to step into the little boat, the Cortes said good-bye to John Cooper and his son, who shook hands with them and wished them well. The old man repeated, "Don't forget, Señor Baines, if ever you come to this beautiful city, my wife and I insist that you be our guest, you and your fine son. Good luck to you—and don't forget what I've told you."

"Thanks again for your invitation, Señor Corte, Señora Corte," John Cooper replied in Spanish, "and I shall remember everything you've said. May God go with you both and give you a long life!"

"And to you the same." The old man hesitated a moment, sighed, then added almost wistfully, "I wish I were young enough to make an excursion into this Texas of yours, Señor Baines. I would like to see your *estancia*. It certainly must be a beautiful country. But then, as we heard you say once before. Man proposes; *el Señor Dios* disposes. ¡*Adios!*"

With this, they climbed up into the ship's dinghy and took their seats.

The three government men who had held themselves aloof from the others during the long voyage appeared. Captain Blake had told John Cooper their names: Gregorio Pordoña, Luis Toriano, and Geraldo Viseyama. All three of them, according to the captain, were employed in the *Oficina del Interior*, part of the provisional government that proposed to unify and centralize the various provinces. As they were about to leave the frigate, one of them, a fat man in his late forties, with a thick, drooping mustache surmounting a ripely sensual mouth, turned to whisper to his two associates, then turned and came forward toward John Cooper. "Señor Baines?" he said questioningly in a sneering tone.

"That's my name, señor," John Cooper pleasantly replied.

"You are the *americano* from Texas in los Estados Unidos, are you not?" the official persisted.

"Right again, señor. How may I be of service?"

"That is a joke, Señor Baines. You come here on a mission that we regard as a disservice to the nation."

"I don't understand, señor."

"I am Gregorio Pordoña, Señor Baines. I am a government official, and I have the honor to serve our good Presidente Rivadavia."

"That sounds as if you've an important job, Señor Pordoña."

The fat man's sneering face darkened and his eyes narrowed. "I detect sarcasm in the way you address me, Señor Baines. But then, I should not expect a *gringo* to respect our nation, now that we have won our independence. I say only this to you; you would do well not to become too friendly with a certain *estanciero* to whom you are bringing livestock from your country."

"You mean Señor Raoul Maldones, Señor Pordoña?"

"I do, indeed. We do not look favorably upon him in Buenos Aires."

"Understand me, Señor Pordoña, I know nothing of enmities or political factions. I am a citizen of the United States. I'm here to sell horses and cattle. I have no interest whatsoever in your political squabbles."

Pordoña's tone was dripping with venomous sarcasm. "Do not forget that this is Sudamérica. Our ways are different here, Señor Baines."

"I don't plan to do anything to hurt your country, Señor Pordoña. So far as I'm concerned, once I deliver the livestock to my customer, I shall turn around and go back home."

"You would be well advised to do exactly that and no more, Señor Baines. At any rate, I wish you and your son and your men a safe homeward journey. *Vaya con Dios.*" The government official stared at John Cooper; then his mouth twisted into a sinister grin as he briskly nodded and turned to follow his companions into the dinghy. Now two crewmen—who would row the craft to shore—clambered aboard, and the dinghy was slowly lowered into the water.

John Cooper, Andrew, and the *vaqueros* were going to stay on board the *Miromar* until the cargo was unloaded and the crew went on shore leave. Then the cattle and horses would exit by a hatch in the hold, enter the calm waters, and swim to shore.

As they continued to watch all the activity of the unloading, Captain Blake came up to John Cooper and said, "I've news for you. Antonio, who has just returned from a trip to shore in the dinghy, tells me that there was a mounted courier from your client, waiting beyond the dock. When he saw that the *Miromar* had come into port, he rode to the south. So you may be sure of a warm welcome, for the *gaucho* will tell Señor Maldones of your arrival; he will no doubt be on hand himself to greet you when you disembark in the morning."

"Now that we're so close, Captain Blake, I think I can hold back my impatience to get ashore," John Cooper said.

"Perhaps I shall see you on your return to the States,

Mr. Baines," the captain said. "At any rate, my cook has promised a good supper tonight, and you and your son and your workmen will be my guests."

"I look forward to it, Captain Blake."

The last evening aboard the *Miromar* was made exceptionally pleasant for John Cooper and Andrew, as well as for the four homesick *vaqueros* who had accompanied them, since Captain Blake had thoughtfully arranged for musical entertainment to accompany one of the cook's most imaginative meals. It consisted of crayfish and a superb flounder, cooked with wine and shallots, and, for dessert, a magnificent *flan* with a carmelized sauce that made Andrew smack his lips and ask for a second portion.

Three of the stevedores, talented musicians, played the guitar, the violin, and the flute. While the men ate, they played native Argentinian dances—rhythmic music that alternated languorous melodies with swiftly syncopated passages. It was a fitting way to celebrate a safe, speedy journey.

It was a few hours after dawn when Captain Blake directed his seamen to prepare the dinghy in which John Cooper, Andrew, and the four *vaqueros* would be rowed to shore, not to where the loading docks were, but to a cove about a quarter of a mile to the south, where the livestock could easily get on land. Meanwhile the crewmen who had stayed on shipboard would then direct the unloading of the livestock.

"I hope that the courier reached Señor Maldones," John Cooper said to the captain as he and the others were about to board the dinghy. "If so, he'll have some of his cowboys on hand to catch the stallion and the mare when they reach the shore. I've no desire to mate them in advance before they become his property."

"Look! That will answer your question, Mr. Baines." Captain Blake pointed toward the distant shore. John Cooper saw, on the edge of the shore, twelve mounted men in *ponchos* and *sombreros,* and at their head, mounted on a fine black gelding, was a tall, stately figure of a man.

"The rider on the black horse is Señor Raoul Maldones, Mr. Baines. The other men are his *gauchos.* They'll handle your stallion and mare, as well as your cattle, have no fear. I know that we've heard about the Comanche and the Apache being great riders, and of course your Texas *vaqueros* are well

known to us, even in the East. But these *gauchos* are horsemen such as you've never seen before, Mr. Baines."

"I look forward to meeting them," John Cooper said.
"Maybe my *vaqueros* can learn something from them." Then
he added, "Well, now, Captain Blake, I want to thank you
again for your gracious hospitality." John Cooper smiled and
shook hands with the captain, as did Andrew and the *vaqueros*.

Andrew followed his father into the dinghy, his eyes
bright with excitement as he studied the shore. The four *vaqueros*, whispering among themselves, deferentially waited for
their *patrón* and his son to enter the dinghy before clamber-
ing in themselves, staring into the distance at the *gauchos*.
The stevedores opened the door of the hold and began to
drive out the long-horned steers. Bellowing their displeasure,
they splashed heavily into the blue-green water and then began to swim, their horns bobbing like corkscrews on the
placid water of the inlet cove. The bull, then the heifer, followed, for the stevedores had been warned that both stallion
and mare and bull and heifer, if released too closely to one
another, might be distracted by proximity and do themselves
an injury or even drown.

Finally, after a lengthier pause, the young palomino stallion was urged into the water and began at once to swim, its
head held high, tossing its thick mane. Behind it, a few
minutes later, came the mare, whinnying upon making contact with the water.

Four stevedores rowed the dinghy toward the shore, and
as John Cooper leaned forward, shielding his eyes from the
rising sun, he saw that the *gauchos* had brought ox-drawn
carretas for the bull, the heifer, the palomino, and the mare,
and he smiled with relief. He said to Andrew, "That courier
must have ridden hard to reach Señor Maldones in time to
give us such a welcome."

As the dinghy neared the shore, he saw six of the
gauchos dismount and hurry toward the animals. They had
lariats, made of rawhide, heavier than those used in Texas,
but efficient. As the animals came onto shore, two of the men
roped the necks of the mare and her stallion mate, two others
did the same for the bull and heifer and, shouting to them in
a dialect that John Cooper could not fully understand, led
them toward the waiting *carretas*. The two other *gauchos*
helped pull them in, then drew up the rear gates of the *carre-*

tas and made them fast. The half-dozen other *gauchos* had already followed the swimming longhorns, and as soon as they had reached shore and begun to clamber out, shaking themselves and tossing their huge, wide horns, had taken their lariats and flourished them like whips, urging them forward.

John Cooper leaped from the dinghy onto the sandy bank and stepped at once into the thick grass that grew almost to the water's edge. Andrew and the *vaqueros* followed. John Cooper and Andrew waited as the bearded, gray-haired man rode toward them. He was tall, his face austere and stern, but his eyes were brown and soft and friendly. His face was weather-beaten and bronzed from the sun, and his smile was genuine. "¡*Bienvenida a* Argentina, Señor Baines! This fine, tall young man is your son, ¿*no es verdad?*"

"Yes, this is my son Andrew, and you must be Señor Raoul Maldones?"

The bearded man on horseback nodded, his smile deepening, then reached down to extend his hand to John Cooper, who warmly shook it. The grip was firm and the two men eyed each other for a long moment. At last Maldones released the American's hand and said, "My *gaucho* rode like the wind, though he tells me that he never again wishes to go through that accursed city of Buenos Aires. You see, *hombre*, out here on the *pampas*, we have little love for the *porteños.*" He shrugged. "But of that, no matter. Do not let me shadow your first moment on Argentinian soil by dwelling on the unsettled condition of our country. From what I have seen, the livestock you bring me is magnificent. I am very pleased."

"I'm glad. But you have so many cattle here. I was curious that you wanted steers from Texas," John Cooper remarked.

"That is merely to satisfy my old eyes, Señor Baines. Señor Mallard has often written to me about the enormous *cuernos* of these *ganado*, so I wished to see for myself. My men will brand them and we will observe how they adapt to *pampas* grass and to the climate. But now, I am forgetting my manners. Coribos, bring the horses for the Señor Baines and his son. And you, Jorge, the horses for these good *trabajadores* who have come such a long way to see what *gauchos* look like!"

Two stocky, *poncho*-clad *gauchos*, both with thick, curling black mustaches, rode up. They were wearing spurs on their short leather boots, and their two-edged knives that resembled huge daggers were thrust into wide, metal-studded belts. Leading a string of six sturdy colts by the reins, they puffed out their chests with pride to show off their skill in the way the horses obeyed them before their *patrón*.

"Drive the *carretas* on to the *estancia*," Raoul Maldones said, turning to a tall, haughty *gaucho*, with a hawklike nose and a bushy black beard. "I pray you, Oudobras, remember that these oxen that pull the *carretas* do not have the brains of your horses, so you must use all your skill and cunning." Turning to John Cooper, who had mounted a sturdy brown colt that had been equipped with a small saddle with a large pommel, Maldones smilingly added, "Oudobras is my *capataz*. That does not mean he is my servant. The *gaucho* knows no master, but he is loyal if he is befriended. When I came here many years ago, I made friends with the *gauchos*. It was that friendship that saved me from the raids by the Guarani and other tribes who were hostile to the first settlers. Once you have made friends with them, they will lay down their lives for you."

John Cooper glanced around and saw that the mounted *gauchos* were studying his buckskin costume with considerable interest, turning to whisper among themselves. "They look like proud, strong men."

"We have a long journey ahead of us," his gray-haired host apologized. "My *estancia* is inland, some twenty-five miles from here. It is northwest of the town of Lobos." Raoul Maldones smiled warmly at John Cooper. "I warn you, I shall ask you many questions about los Estados Unidos, and particularly about your *estancia*. I have always promised myself one day to go there, but somehow I have never been able to take time away from my family and the building of my *estancia* and those things that are necessary to survive here on the *pampas*."

"I'll answer all your questions, Señor Maldones. In turn, you must tell me all about your country. I've never seen grass like this before, stretching so far. Your men seem to have cut a trail."

"That is done with the knives, sometimes even with the *bolas*—those lariats with two stones attached you see on their saddles—tearing up great clumps of grass. Of course the constant riding of horses back and forth along the same pathway makes for a good trail. Also, sometimes friendly Indians who live not far from the *estancia* take their *machetes* and cut a trail for us. You see, that one was done at my orders in anticipation of your arrival here with your livestock."

As they rode along, John Cooper observed the expert horsemanship of the *gauchos,* who handled their sturdy colts with a nonchalance and ease that even one of his oldest *vaqueros* would have envied.

Raoul Maldones turned in his saddle to look back at the oxen-drawn carts, beside which the *gauchos* rode, shouting encouragements to the beasts of burden who docilely plodded along. Then, turning back to John Cooper, he amiably declared, "My men will see to the livestock, Señor Baines. I suggest we ride ahead, for I want you to be able to enjoy a short *siesta* before we honor you with our *charcutería.* To use your English word, it will be a barbecue, with good meat cooked on turning spits over a fire in a stone oven. There will be dancing and singing, for we wish to show you how pleasant life can be on an *estancia.* Come now, let us see what you think of my horses. They do not have the wonderful pedigree of your palominos, but they are quite durable, all the same. Oudobras, you ride with us. *¡Vámanos pronto!"*

Fifteen

It was late afternoon when John Cooper, Andrew, and the four *vaqueros* rode through the forests on the edge of the vast *pampas* into a clearing dominated by a sprawling, rectangular house made of the sturdy, hard wood of the *quebracho* tree. To one side was a wide porch over which a colorful cloth canopy had been stretched, and under it was a French chaise longue, as well as an upholstered couch, singular marks of civilized luxury in so primitive a country.

West of it by some three hundred yards was a large stable, built of the same kind of wood, sturdily beamed and with heavy doors. Across from the stable, to form a courtyard, were several small adobe houses, painted white. Raoul

Maldones drew on the reins of his horse and leaned toward John Cooper, saying, "One of the little houses you see belongs to my *capataz* Oudobras; that is, when he chooses to live with an *estanciero* like me. Most of my *gauchos* love the *pampas* so much they make their homes there, and only briefly return to their houses on my ranch, if they have wives or sweethearts or children. There are times when they even take their families out into the *pampas* and make temporary shelters wherever night finds them. Truly, these men are born to the saddle, and their women understand it and are patient with them."

"I suppose the additional huts belong to some of your household staff, Señor Maldones?"

"Exactly. Since we plan to have a great feast in your honor tonight, you will meet most of my workers. Oudobras has told me that the *gauchos* plan to stay over during your visit here, for they are curious to see how a *gringo* like you rides a horse and perhaps even has contests with them in the throwing of the *bola*."

"That's a test I'll be glad to accept, Señor Maldones."

"Then we shall have good sport! They will respect you for meeting them out in the open. The only way to impress these men is to be a man among them and to equal them at the feats they perform. Happily, despite my being almost fifty, I have been fortunate enough to enjoy good health and to be able to give a good accounting of myself before these powerful rascals." From his indulgent smile, it was evident that he was on the best of terms with his *gauchos*.

Señor Maldones dismounted, and from the entrance of the ranch house, there came a kindly faced, gray-haired man in a white *camisa* and black trousers, who, seeing him and his guests, called out. Two young men, similarly clad, hurried from the barns to take the horses.

The *hacendado* said to John Cooper, "Your *vaqueros* are proud men; I can see that already. They ride very well. They will take their horses to the stable. Let them see what kind of—I believe you use the word *remuda*—I possess."

"An excellent idea, Señor Maldones," John Cooper said. "These men are not *gauchos*?"

"No, indeed. The elderly man is Fernando, my majordomo. He is actually seven years older than I am, and in the old country, he served my father and looked after me when I was a boy. The two others are his sons. We do not use the

word *servant* here. I am called the *caudillo,* which means, to
use another term with which you may be more familiar, *jefe.*
But it is on suffrance only. My *gauchos* are, in a sense, my
protective army. They are the best scouts one could find, as
good as the Indians. And, of course, they protect my family
from enemies."

"Enemies?" John Cooper asked, remembering his earlier
conversation with Señor Corte.

Raoul, a congenial arm around his guest's shoulders,
urged him toward the ranch house. "Ah, yes. Not only in the
city, among the insolent *porteños* who covet my land, but
also neighbors who are allied with those in the city. But do
not let me spoil this evening with recriminations or com-
plaints." He turned to look at the setting sun and drew in a
deep breath. "The air is pure; the sky is good; the land is
rich. There can be happiness and freedom for everyone, if
only we had the ability to understand what *el Señor Dios* has
given us."

John Cooper had already warmed to his host. This last
remark, which so exactly ran parallel to his own concepts of
a free life on the open range, cemented the bond between
them. He looked at Raoul, smiled, and nodded. "We have the
same philosophy in Texas, Señor Maldones. I am very glad I
came here. Already I like your *estancia.* You have, I see,
comforts that I did not expect to find here in what might be
called the wilderness."

"Ah, yes, wilderness. I and the *trabajadores* have carved
our home out of rugged land. We have held it against Indian
attacks, we have held it against *bandidos,* even from as far as
Uruguay, and now we must hold it against the inroads of the
porteños who think that because they sit in council in a government that is new and that presumes to help all the people,
they may give orders of life and death. There I go again, and
I had promised not to say anything gloomy. But come in; I
will show you and your son to your rooms, and your *vaqueros* may occupy rooms here, too."

As John Cooper took in all the new sights, the *hacendado* humorously remarked, "I see you have already observed
the furniture on my porch. Those pieces came from New Orleans, and your very own factor, the Señor Mallard, was kind
enough to purchase them for me. He has sent me many arti-
cles that help remind me of my father's origin in Madrid.
Then, too, when one has women in one's life, it is necessary

to provide them with dainties and luxuries to make up for living in isolation, as we do."

"I was told that you lost your wife, Señor Maldones. I was sorry to hear that."

"Yes, it is true," Raoul said in a low voice, crossing himself. "My beautiful wife, Carlotta, died five years ago. But she gave me four lovely daughters, and they remind me of her constantly. But come in; I am neglecting my duties as a host. You shall meet them directly."

Fernando returned from his errand and ushered John Cooper and Andrew into the house, through the wide foyer that narrowed into a hallway along which the Texans could see several doors. At the other side of the rectangular ranch house there was a similar passageway. The hardwood floor was strewn with thick Oriental rugs and runners, and John Cooper marveled at the contrast of this luxurious interior with the isolated setting of the ranch itself.

Observing John Cooper's scrutiny, his host softly explained, "It was for my wife's sake, you see, Señor Baines. I confess I myself enjoy the comforts, and I can afford them, but I do not count on material possessions as an aim in life. I enjoy giving, and because my beautiful wife gave me these wonderful girls, I acquired things that would please them and make their lives easier here, in the midst of nowhere."

As he spoke, a tall, somber-faced woman emerged from a room at the end of the passageway, wearing a *mantilla* with a comb and a black dress with a high neckline and puffed sleeves, looking the very picture of a formidable elderly aunt or chaperone.

Raoul beckoned to her and turned to John Cooper. "This is Señora Josefa, my daughters' *dueña*, Señor Baines."

"It is a pleasure to make your acquaintance, Señor Baines," Señora Josefa said with formal diction and an icy air. She eyed him suspiciously, observing his buckskins, and then turned to her employer. "*Con su permiso*, Señor Maldones, I have told the young ladies that we shall eat outdoors this evening."

"Just so, Señora Josefa. I have invited Señor Baines and his son Andrew, whom you see before you, to partake of our celebration. If you will be kind enough to assemble my daughters here in the foyer, we may proceed with introductions."

"At once, Señor Maldones," the *dueña* said, inclining her

head and disappearing. A few moments later, from a room directly opposite hers, four girls emerged, elegantly dressed, even to the youngest, who could not have been more than six years old.

"Ah, *mis lindas,* you are just in time to meet our guests," their father exuberantly exclaimed, turning to John Cooper and Andrew and beckoning them to approach. "I have the honor to introduce to you the Señor John Cooper Baines from Texas, and his son Andrew."

The four girls curtsied, and John Cooper could not help noting that the oldest, as she bent her head, regarded him with a charmingly coquettish smile, while her dark eyes rested on his for an instant, before her thick eyelashes lowered and her face took on a demure and expressionless mask.

"This is my oldest, Dorotéa. Here is Adriana," Raoul proceeded, as with a wave of his hand he designated a slim, curly-dark-brown-haired girl with a heart-shaped face and a roguish expression, accentuated by two dimples in her cheeks and one at the cleft of her chin. Andrew stared at her, wide-eyed, for it seemed to him that her smile had been particularly directed at him.

"This is Paquita," their host continued, designating a ten-year-old, rather chubby girl, with a charmingly ingenuous face and long black hair that fell nearly to her hips. She wore crinolines under a white dress with ruffles at the hems and sleeves, and a ribbon in her hair. "And this is María," he concluded, pointing to the youngest, who giggled and then clapped a hand over her mouth, aware of her father's disapproving glare. "You must forgive her, Señor Baines; she is not used to visitors from los Estados Unidos, like you and your tall, fine son."

"But there is nothing to forgive," John Cooper smilingly replied, as he made a cavalierlike bow toward the four girls. "They are charming and very lovely, and they surely do you credit, Señor Maldones."

Dorotéa eyed him again as she straightened. Her lips twitched in the semblance of a smile, and their eyes met. He was startled at the sudden interest that leaped in him at her almost bold and inviting gaze.

At this moment, the four *vaqueros* entered the ranch house, accompanied by Fernando. Raoul Maldones turned to welcome them. *"Hombres,* Fernando will show you to your rooms. Then, with my warmest invitation, you will join us at the feast." He turned to John Cooper. "Now, Señor Baines, before we go out to enjoy our repast, may I show you the rest of my house?"

Polite and friendly *mestiza* maids brought bowls filled with hot water to Andrew and his father, as well as to the four *vaqueros*, who had been ushered to their rooms.

After Andrew had washed, he came out into the passageway and waited for his father to join him, then said in wonderment, "Pa, my room has things in it very much like what we've got back at home."

"I know, Andy. As Señor Maldones said, he imported a great many fine things from New Orleans to please his wife and also to make things comfortable for his daughters. They're certainly very good-looking young ladies, aren't they? Or hadn't you noticed?"

At this quip, the tall youth turned crimson and, uneasily shuffling his feet, stammered, "Sure I have, Pa. I'm all ready to go eat now, if you are."

"I am, indeed, and I'm just as hungry as Yankee would be after a long day on the trail. I hear music. There's going to be quite a feast. It's a fine way to end our first day in Argentina." He turned to look down the passageway and, seeing his four men coming to follow him, genially encouraged them, *"Adelante, muchachos,* are you comfortable in your rooms?"

"Sí, patrón," stocky Bartoloméo Mendoza said, energetically bobbing his head. "I almost feel like a *patrón* myself, for it's certainly better than our bunkhouse—not that I'm complaining, you understand, *patrón."* He glanced uneasily at John Cooper, who burst out laughing and clapped him on the back.

"Speak your mind, Bartoloméo. I'll tell you what, when we get back—and with the profits I should have from the sale of the palominos and the bull, the heifer, and the steers—I'll see to it that a few little comforts are added to the bunkhouse. Perhaps you'd like a lace-embroidered pillow and some sachet, so you can think of a *novia?"*

His three companions burst out laughing at this and jibed the young *vaquero*, while he grumbled and tried to make light of the matter by assuring them, as well as John Cooper, that he required neither pillow nor sachet, particularly since he had no *novia*. Enrique Saltanda, tall and rangy and with a long mustache of which he was proud, winked at him and said, "Perhaps you'll find one from among these *criadas*. The one who brought us the bowl of water is *muy linda, no es verdad*?"

"A pox on you, *hombre*," the discomfitted *vaquero* grumbled. "Speak for yourself. I'm here to serve the *patrón*, and that's what you should be thinking of, not *criadas*!" Laughing, they came out into the *patio* and toward the clearing where the feast was being held.

The servants had made torches of handfuls of thick plaintain grass dipped in palm oil, and they thrust the sticky sheaves into the openings of tall brass stanchions, hollowed out at the top to a depth of about two feet. These uprights were placed all around the clearing and cast a bright, flickering light that cut through the inky darkness that had already settled over the *pampas*. Four middle-aged women were busy turning the spits and basting the sides of beef and mutton that turned over the fires in the stone ovens. Long rectangular hardwood tables, covered with fine linen tablecloths, had been set up in the middle of the clearing, with benches placed before them, these covered with blankets made from llama wool.

The *gauchos* who had gone with Raoul Maldones to drive the oxcarts had not yet returned to the ranch, but many other *gauchos*—those who lived on the *pampas* with their families but who worked for Raoul—were now in attendance for the great feast.

On a short bench at right angles to the guests, five *gauchos* sat, playing a violin, a mandolin, a drum, a cornet, and a curious kind of flute, something like a recorder. As John Cooper and his son approached the bench toward which Raoul Maldones smilingly beckoned them, the *gaucho* with the flute began to play "Yankee Doodle Dandy" in honor of the *gringo americano*.

John Cooper turned to the *gaucho* musicians and inclined his head, then clapped his hands and called out, "*¡Gracias, es muy bueno!* Now, *hombres*, let me hear music from your own native land, from the *pampas*."

"It will be sad and also gay, *señor americano*," the man with the flute-recorder called, grinning and winking, then bent to confer with his fellows. A moment later, the five musicians began to play a languorous tune, which spoke of love amid the thick grass of the *pampas* in the shade of the *ombú* tree, which protected the lovers through the hot, sunny afternoon. Then the tempo changed, and the music became faster; the song was now about an attack by outlaws who wished to take the lover's *querida* away from him, and how he killed them and was reunited with his beloved. When the music ended, Raoul, seated next to John Cooper, explained, "You see, Señor Baines, the *ombú* is native to our *pampas*, and about it naturally many superstitions have evolved. You saw several of these trees on our way to my *estancia*, and there is one to the north of here that has a girth of fifty feet. The wood is so soft and spongy you can cut into it with a *cuchillo*, a knife."

"At least it protects one in the sun," John Cooper said.

"That it does, Señor Baines. But the leaves, which are very large and glossy and something like the laurel, contain a deadly poison. There is a superstition that no one should remain at night under its branches, lest he be poisoned. That is why the song my men just played tells of how the young lovers enjoyed themselves during the sun of daylight, and then sought refuge away from the *ombú* when night fell, only to be accosted by the *bandidos*."

"This is such a vast country, and it must have so many legends," John Cooper smilingly replied.

His host affably nodded. "By the way, there will be another guest, a neighbor of mine who owns an *estancia* to the northwest of here."

"I shall be happy to meet him, Señor Maldones."

"He is the *novio* of my oldest daughter, Dorotéa. He has known Dorotéa since she was a little girl. Ah, here he comes now!" His host rose from the table and went to greet a man of medium height, with thick black hair with faint streaks of gray at the temples, and a thin mustache that gave his indolent features a supercilious look.

"Rodrigo, what a pleasure to have you here!" Raoul genially exclaimed as the two men shook hands. Then, turning to the tall American at his right, he completed the introduction, "Rodrigo, this is the *americano* I was telling you about, Señor John Cooper Baines, and next to him is his son Andrew."

"A pleasure to meet you, Señor Baines." The mature, black-haired man gave John Cooper a lazy nod of his head, then took his place at Raoul's left.

"Señor Baines, Rodrigo Baltenar is an *estanciero* like myself, and like myself, his antecedents began in Madrid."

"In the good days of the monarchy, long before that usurper Napoleon," Rodrigo Baltenar said in a diffident tone. He turned away from John Cooper and looked across the table at Dorotéa.

Dorotéa's *dueña*, Señora Josefa, was seated beside her. She leaned over to whisper to her charge, who dutifully nodded, her eyes downcast, for she had not yet acknowledged her fiancé by any gesture or sign. Since Don Diego had often regaled his son-in-law with stories of the Spanish court and of how families kept close surveillance over their marriageable daughters, John Cooper understood the presence of the *dueña*. Yet, strangely enough, though he had only been here a few hours, he found himself regretting that Dorotéa was to be married to so colorless and stodgy a man who was more than twice her age.

Now the maids began to bring the side dishes of food and the wines from the kitchen. Seeing that the meat turning on the spits was done and the men had begun to cut it into portions, Raoul rose and lifted his glass of wine. "*Hombres*, you who are my *gauchos* have been told this is a night of celebration to pay honor to this *gringo* who has brought me such wonderful horses, the pedigreed bull and heifer, and the dozen steers with the giant horns. It is his first visit to our beloved *pampas*. Also, tonight, we welcome our dear friend, the Señor Rodrigo Baltenar, who as all of you know is betrothed to my daughter Dorotéa. Now, since I see that the meat is ready, let the feast begin. My *criadas* will pass about the tables filling your glasses with the red wine of the provinces. It is strong, as you *gauchos* are, and it is the color of your valiant blood, which makes the *pampas* free. Drink now to the health of our guests and to your own prosperity and freedom!" He raised his glass, and John Cooper imitated him, as did Andrew.

John Cooper winked at his son and smiled, as if to say he approved of Andrew's conduct and was enjoying sharing this experience with him.

As Andrew lifted his glass, Adriana, who at twelve already showed the promise of becoming a real beauty, shyly raised her eyes and looked at him. Andrew's face colored, and then, as John Cooper watched in secret amusement, the youth lifted the glass to his lips and nodded his head slightly, as if to indicate that he was drinking to Adriana. Now it was her turn to color and instantly to lower her eyes as Señora Josefa, preening herself like a nervous bird to make certain that all her charges were behaving themselves, glanced sharply around the table.

The women began to serve the guests. Besides beef and mutton, liberally basted with a spicy sauce, there were yams, sweet peppers stuffed with ground bits of meat, and loaves of chewy bread. To finish the meal, there were melons and berries, a tasty *flan* with a sauce made from brown sugar and a liqueur that John Cooper could not identify, and the strongest coffee he had ever imbibed.

As he sipped his coffee, John Cooper saw the *capataz*, Oudobras, rise from the large table where he was seated with the *gauchos* and with John Cooper's *vaqueros*. The *capataz* came toward his host, respectfully inclined his head, and waited for permission to speak. Raoul smiled and gestured to encourage his foreman, who said, "The men are asking, *señor caudillo*, if the *gringo americano* would show them tomorrow how he uses his long gun."

John Cooper leaned toward the foreman, broadly smiling. "I'd be happy to do that. Since we're on the subject, I'd like to see how you *gauchos* use the *bolas* I see tied to your saddles."

The foreman grinned and eyed his *caudillo*. "If you have no objections, *patrón*, perhaps tomorrow we might show the *americano* what we do with the *bolas*."

"Of course!" Raoul turned to John Cooper. "I wager you have nothing like this in Texas, Señor Baines. These men have great skill. They can fight a duel to the death with the *bolas;* they can trip a runaway steer or horse, but without injuring its legs."

"That I'd really like to see," John Cooper said.

"You shall, tomorrow, after we have had breakfast and made sure that you have had sufficient sleep. This long voyage must surely have exhausted you."

"On the contrary, Señor Maldones," John Cooper smilingly replied. "Andy and I found it very pleasant. We had time to talk a good deal, as a father and his son should always do."

A shadow crossed the handsome face of the gray-haired *estanciero*. "You do not know how I envy you that, Señor Baines. My dear wife, who is now in heaven—" he crossed himself "—always wished to give me a son. But *el Señor Dios* wished otherwise. Nonetheless, I am proud of my daughters, and although we have no schools out here on the *pampas*, I have tried to give them an appreciation of books, of music, and of the arts like sewing and cooking, which are expected of women—especially when they marry."

John Cooper smiled understandingly, then asked, "What was that silver tube I saw in your foreman's hand, Señor Maldones?"

"Oh, yes, that is a *bombilla* through which the *gauchos* drink their *yerba maté*. This is a tea made from wild herbs, and that drink, along with meat, comprises the principal diet of my men. And now"—this with a smile and an almost imperceptible wink—"I see that my oldest daughter is desirous of addressing a question to you. Very well, Dorotéa."

"*Gracias, Papá.*" The enchanting young woman slowly raised her eyes to John Cooper's face, while her *dueña* watched, frowning, and she glanced also at John Cooper, as if wishing to observe with what manner of respect he addressed the most eligible daughter of her *patrón*. "You wear a most unusual costume. I have never seen anything like it before."

"Señorita Dorotéa," the *dueña* reproved in a sibilant whisper, shaking her head and putting a pudgy forefinger to her disapproving mouth.

"It is not rudeness; it is curiosity," Dorotéa's father diplomatically interposed. "Just as our guest has come here to learn about us, so must we learn about him. If you wish to answer, Señor Baines, my daughter and I should be very grateful."

"Well, you see, Señorita Dorotéa," John Cooper said slowly, trying to phrase his reply in the purest Spanish he could muster, "before I came to Texas, I lived with Indian tribes on the Plains. We killed deer; we tanned the hides and made them into these garments. They are comfortable, they allow freedom of movement, and they often act as camouflage when one is hunting or, sometimes, alas, trying not to be shot at by an enemy."

"*¡Madre de Dios!*" Dorotéa gasped, then clapped a hand over her mouth and blushed furiously. "*Los indios* in your country are savage? They attack the *gringo*?"

"Yes, in many parts of the United States the Indians resent the coming of the white man who takes away their land and their hunting grounds, and drives away the buffalo so that they starve."

"Here in Argentina, Señor Baines," Raoul observed, "we are troubled from time to time by hostile Indians from the southwest. We have made friends with the Guarani, but deeper into the *pampas*, there are still the fearsome Araucanian who sometimes raid *estancias* that are not too well protected and are isolated. Also, there are the fierce Abipón and Charrúa of the north. So far, praise be to *el Señor Dios,* we have not suffered from these attacks this close to Buenos Aires. Yet, there are other dangers in that closeness."

Once again, John Cooper detected an ominous foreboding in his host. As quickly as he had become serious, however, Raoul brightened and added, "To be sure, when my daughter is married to Rodrigo, our lands and our *gauchos* will be merged, and we will be very well protected against any kind of attack. Now then, I see that our musicians are waiting for us to finish the feast so that we may dance. My dear Dorotéa, would it please you to lead the dance? You, Rodrigo, shall of course be her partner. Adriana, would you do me the honor of dancing with me?"

The twelve-year-old girl, whom young Andrew had been admiring, rose, curtsied to her father, and accompanied him into the clearing. The musicians struck up a languorous, waltzlike melody. It was a formal dance, in which both the man and the woman remained at a distance from each other, only their fingertips touching the other's shoulder or elbow, and it demanded considerable coordination from the male partner to indicate to the female in which direction he wished to turn, advance, or retreat.

After the first measures had been played, Raoul Maldones called to his *gauchos,* "Next, *amigos,* you will dance the dance of the *pampas* for our distinguished guests."

One of the *gauchos,* a raw-boned, thickly bearded man in his early thirties, called out with a loud guffaw, *"Señor caudillo,* it is a pity we did not bring our wives or sweethearts so that we could show the *gringo americano* how dancing is really done under the stars."

"Hush, Cornado," Raoul called back, "remember the modesty of my daughters. It is not yet time for them to be acquainted with the ways of the *gaucho* in such matters."

The *gaucho*'s neighbor at the table, a portly, squat man with a face lined with wrinkles that deepened when he grinned, which was often, spoke out. "The *caudillo* is right, Cornado. Drink your *yerba maté* and do not forget that tonight you are a guest, also!"

After the two couples had gone back to the table, John Cooper observed that Dorotéa's mature fiancé led her to her place, bowed to her, then thanked her *dueña* and her father for the privilege of this dance. The musicians now began to play a spirited, fiery tune, with many stops and flourishes. A dozen of the *gauchos* in their calf-length boots, *ponchos*, and short-brimmed hats moved to the center of the clearing and began to execute a dance that involved much kicking, squatting, and twirling. They were dexterous and nimble. They cried out and their eyes glittered with animation as they imitated the fighting of enemies or the hunting down of a rhea or a wild horse. Taking their *bolas*, they twirled them in the air with such expert balance and skill that none of the hard balls at the end clashed together.

John Cooper leaned toward his son and muttered, "Tomorrow, we'll find out how those *bolas* are used, Andy. I can see how they could be used as weapons. If you cast those thongs out with a snap and they curl around someone's face, they could break his nose or his jaw, even put out his eye."

It was midnight when Raoul Maldones cocked his head, put up his hand, and exclaimed, "I hear the oxcarts! Well, Señor Baines, the *gauchos* have brought back the livestock. They will drive the steers into a special corral I have had constructed for them, and we have stalls in our barns for the bull and the heifer, as well as for the stallion and the mare. There is still plenty of good meat and wine left for the feast, and the men will enjoy that. The musicians will go on playing for them. But for us it may be time to think of retiring. Certainly it is time for my daughters to say good night."

Pretty, vivacious Paquita, having overheard, petulantly spoke out, "Oh, please, *Papá*, can't we stay up a little longer? We would like to see the *gauchos* dance some more!"

"No, my dear, it is certainly past your bedtime. Now be an angel and go with Señora Josefa, after you have bidden good night to the Señor Baines and his *hijo*," her father smilingly directed.

Paquita made a tiny *moue* but docilely rose from the table, curtsied low before John Cooper and Andrew, and in a sweet, childish voice, bade them good night. Little María, being six, had very nearly fallen asleep, and Raoul turned to

John Cooper and murmured, "Sometimes a father is too indulgent when he has only girls." He smiled and shook his head. "If you are not too tired, we might take a little stroll about the grounds before going to bed. And, in my study, I have a superb old brandy that will certainly help you to sleep."

John Cooper knew that his host was perturbed. Remembering what he had learned from Señor Corte on shipboard, John Cooper thought it best to learn exactly what the problem was. With that in mind, he accepted the invitation.

As he and his host rose from the table, John Cooper glanced back at the other tables. The *gauchos* who had brought the bull and heifer, the palominos and the steers, were now enjoying themselves, eating with gusto and drinking the good red wine. The musicians played with renewed enthusiasm some of the wild, exciting dances of the *pampas*. Two of the *gauchos* rose and began to dance in their short boots, twirling their *sombreros* in the air, and one man drew off his *poncho* and waved it about, dancing with a kind of pantomimic daintiness in setting down the toes of his boots as he followed the music's rhythm.

Raoul put a hand on John Cooper's shoulder and directed him around the sprawling ranch house and toward a small copse of flowering trees. The night air was pleasantly cool, and John Cooper remembered that seasons were just the reverse below the equator, and this was winter in Argentina.

When they had gone a little distance beyond the ranch house, Raoul stopped. "Señor Baines, I have the feeling that this will not be the only time you visit me to sell me livestock. I wish to do more business with you, and not only because I like you."

"Thank you, Señor Maldones."

"I think you should know something about our country, since I hope we will see you here often. The history of your country is perhaps fifty years old, since you declared your independence from the British. With us, it is a different matter. Centuries ago, the *conquistadores* came to South America, and they dominated and tyrannized. Sixteen years ago, a handful of Creoles conceived the idea of separating from Spain. Our Independence Day is July ninth, for that is our anniversary; ten years ago a few delegates from a few provinces of what we now call Argentina and Bolivia met in Tucumán to break with Spain and to declare the independence of the 'United Provinces of South America.' Nonetheless, many groups in that area, which included all of the viceroyalty of La Plata, refused to accept the leadership of Buenos Aires."

"Those must have been unsettling times," the American commented.

"Yes, and we cannot yet speak of them in the past because they still exist. If anything, they increase in danger and even in violence. You see, between 1810 and 1816, we had one *junta*, two triumverates, and four men who called themselves supreme director, and each of these ruled briefly. Some of them remained faithful to Ferdinand VII, some wanted a king that they themselves could nominate and support, while the others wanted a free republic, which we now have. But it is not yet entirely free, Señor Baines."

John Cooper nodded, then said, "When I was on the *Miromar*, the captain pointed out three men who disembarked at Buenos Aires. He told me their names, and one of them came up to me and said that it would not be a good idea for me to continue any long friendship with you."

"I feared as much. Well then, I must explain. Understand, there is no danger in your coming here; you are an American citizen and I have engaged your services to sell me livestock. Nonetheless, I am not popular in Buenos Aires with the present government. Neither are many of my neighbors. Conversely, there are other neighbors who openly side with the government and who would be happy to force me into exile. This I will not permit, for I carved out this ranch, I built the house, and I enlisted the sympathies of the *gauchos*."

"I can understand that very well, Señor Maldones. In some ways, it is not unlike what we ourselves are facing in the next few years. We have settlers constantly coming into Texas, but the Mexicans are not fond of this, and since we have no law courts or police to guard our possessions and our land, we have to rely on ourselves."

"Precisely. Now today we have a president who, though he is a cultured and enlightened man, cares nothing for the provinces. The *porteños*, the citizens of Buenos Aires, do not recognize our rights. For this reason, we have grown as strong as we can. They would take over the land themselves, and they are more interested in foreign trade and in drawing new settlers to their prosperous region. But they know nothing of the *pampas,* never visit them, and they have nothing but contempt for us provincials, especially for the *gauchos,* whom they regard as savages."

John Cooper's host smiled sadly. "I myself, to gain strength against what I fear will be the corruption of the *porteño* rule seek to increase my own holdings. I will admit with not a little shame that this was one of the reasons why I permitted Rodrigo Baltenar to seek my oldest daughter's hand in marriage. Although she does care for him a good deal and he is a civilized and cultured man."

John Cooper had listened with growing interest to his host's description of the situation in Argentina. The encounter with those three officials aboard the *Miromar* had given him some misgivings. Now he understood the reason for his curious presentiment.

Raoul shrugged, put a hand to his forehead, and apologetically declared, "I am ashamed of myself that I have taken such unfair advantage of you, Señor Baines. I have made you listen to me, though I am sure that you are dying for sleep. I apologize for this long and overly political lecture."

John Cooper gave his host a steadfast, smiling look. "On the contrary, Señor Maldones, I found it extremely helpful. It has given me a better understanding of your country. I'm a pretty fair judge of character, and my instincts in the past have helpd me survive a good many dangers. My instinct now is that you're a man of honor and imagination, and I want to be your friend. I hope to be of some small service if difficulties are forced upon you."

"You are far too kind. Well now, shall we have that old brandy as a nightcap and then to bed?"

"Nothing would suit me better."

Sixteen

It was noon of the next day when John Cooper was wakened by a discreet knocking on his door. When he called out, *"Adelante, venga,"* a timorous young *criada*, with eyes modestly downcast, brought in his breakfast of chocolate, melon, and a native bread that had the texture of a doughy cake. Bowing to him as she set the tray on the hardwood taboret, she deferentially informed him that her *patrón* had asked if he and his son still wished to go out in the afternoon with the *gauchos* who would show their skill with the *bolas.* He enthusiastically replied, "Tell your *patrón* I look forward to it. Tell him also that I shall bring my long rifle, and we shall have a contest."

The shy *mestiza* again bowed and withdrew. John Cooper was ravenously hungry and hurriedly downed his breakfast, then washed his hands and face in a bowl of water, dried himself with a fine linen towel, which had been imported from Belgium, and, donning his buckskins over his underdrawers, went out into the hallway. His son Andrew was just emerging, and John Cooper smiled and said, "Feel ready for some action today, Andy? We're going to get a lesson in how they use those *bolas.*"

"I'd like that a lot, Pa. Are you going to show them how 'Long Girl' works?"

"I aim to, Andy, and I'll also bring my Bowie knife. You bring your rifle, too. Now let's go say *buenos días* to Señor Maldones. He's a fine man."

"Yes, he is, Pa," was all Andrew said as they strolled down the hall. John Cooper noticed that his son looked somewhat haggard, as though he had gotten little sleep, perhaps because of the long, exciting journey or perhaps because he was homesick or thinking about his mother. John Cooper did not want to pry, so he put his arm around Andrew's shoulders and merely asked, "You all right, son?"

"Sure, Pa, sure," Andrew replied, looking up and attempting a smile. John Cooper, aware that Andrew was making an effort to be cheerful in his host's home, was proud of his son and gripped his shoulder a little tighter.

A few minutes later Raoul Maldones joined them in the *patio*. Six of his *gauchos* stood around, holding the reins of their horses. One of them, a man of about thirty-two, nearly as tall as John Cooper himself with high-set cheekbones, a sharply aquiline nose, and an enormous mustache, doffed his short-brimmed hat and exclaimed, "*Buenos días, señor americano.*"

"To you also, *amigo,*" John Cooper genially answered.

"This is Felipe Mintras, Señor Baines," Raoul proffered. "He was unable to be present at last night's feast, but when he arrived at my ranch today, I asked him if he could stay for this afternoon's contest. He is exceptionally talented with the *bola,* and he is equally gifted with the *facón*—once he killed a puma with it."

"I am pleased to know you, Felipe." John Cooper and the *gaucho* shook hands, taking each other's measure and liking one another from the outset. "A man who will go after a mountain lion with just a knife is truly *hombre macho.*"

Felipe Mintras grinned, pleased by this praise, as he replied, "I would like the *señor americano* to know that it was not courage, but because I didn't want to die, that I had to kill it. My Luz and my two little boys would never have forgiven me otherwise."

His fellow *gauchos* burst into laughter and John Cooper joined in, then said, "Well, *amigo,* I once had to kill a mountain lion to save the life of a man whom *el Señor Dios* destined to be my brother-in-law. But you are braver than I, since I used my rifle."

"Looking at you, *señor americano,*" Felipe at once riposted, "I do not think any man would question your bravery."

John Cooper warmed even further to this friendly *gaucho.* "Wait until I prove myself."

Felipe grinned from ear to ear. "You almost think like a *gaucho, señor americano.* It will be a pleasure to show you how we use the *bolas.*"

They mounted their horses, while two men brought out

sorrel geldings for John Cooper and Andrew. Raoul mounted his new palomino stallion.

"He is wonderfully gentle," the Argentinian said, "and he already likes me. I made friends with him in the stable directly before I came here. I shall give Dorotéa the mare as an engagement present. She has named it Belleza, for beauty. You have made her very happy, Señor Baines."

"She is such a lovely young woman that I wish her every happiness." John Cooper spoke in formal Castilian to indicate his respect for the Maldones family.

His host was pleased and remarked, "Truly, Señor Baines, you would make an excellent diplomat, if ever you cared to go into politics. But I do not advise you to try it in this country, for there is too much turmoil. Come now, let us have some sport!"

Raoul led the way, beaming as the young palomino stallion stretched its long legs and effortlessly covered the terrain at a gallop. John Cooper smiled, proud of his horse. Now that he was outdoors, with men of action and integrity, his shadowy anguish could be put aside—at least by day. He glanced over at Andrew and saw that his son's face was still tense. The boy's eyes were fixed on the riders ahead of him, and his lips were tightened. He thought to himself, *Andy isn't over Catarina's death, yet. I have to keep him busy, so he won't dwell on it.*

They rode out for about six miles until they reached a huge clearing and several hardwood trees, as well as an *ombú*. Raoul reined in his palomino and turned to John Cooper. "Sometimes rheas come out of the grass in this place, Señor Baines," he explained. "Usually, we find wild rabbits. They are somewhat gamy, but with sauces they are quite edible. Now I shall have Felipe show you how he uses his *bola*."

John Cooper reined in his gelding and waited beside his host, while Andrew remained slightly behind his father.

Felipe uncoiled his *bola*, and John Cooper observed that it was a plaited rawhide rope about eight or nine feet long, ending in two round, heavy, ball-like stones, from which the weapon derived its name. Eyes narrowed, taut in his saddle, the *gaucho* awaited the flushing out of whatever game was hidden in the tall grass just beyond the clearing.

Raoul turned to John Cooper and said, "About a quarter of a mile beyond, there's a small creek. Perhaps we shall flush out a capybara. It is something I'll wager you don't have in your Estados Unidos."

"I've never heard of it. What is it?"

"It stands about two feet high at the shoulder, and it can be from three to four feet long. Sometimes, it weighs up to a hundred pounds. It is a species of rodent found only in our country. Sometimes they come in herds, and they are a nuisance. There's one now!"

A gigantic ratlike animal darted out of the grass into the clearing, halted, and then turned back to flee. But Felipe, who had already uncoiled his *bola* and was holding it at waist level, swiftly whirled it around his head and sent it flying. The two balls wrapped around the rodent, which emitted a squeal, thrashed and kicked, then lay still. The leather-encased stone had smashed its skull. The *gauchos* sent up a cheer, and Felipe dismounted, bent, and unwrapped his *bola*, making a grimace as he kicked the huge rodent. "It is not a pleasant sight, *señor americano*," he said, turning to address John Cooper, "but it was a good target. Perhaps we shall have better sport. I have seen a rhea not far from this creek. This is where Pablo Cincharta and I once came upon two rheas who ran at us, and we brought them both down with our *bolas*."

The men had ridden around the edge of the clearing, waving their hats in the air and calling out, trying to force the creatures hiding in the tall grass to emerge in the hope of saving themselves. Suddenly, there was a booming sound, much like a foghorn, and Raoul Maldones stiffened in his saddle, his eyes bright as he turned to John Cooper. "That is the mating call of the rhea. By next month, you will hear that all over the *pampas*. This bird is very fast, and it can outrun horses—though I should think my new stallion would be a match for it. Wait now—ah, just as I thought, here it comes!"

Suddenly, out of the tall grass came running a singular bird, the likes of which John Cooper and his son had never before seen. It was a little more than four feet tall and quite as long, with a thin, scrawny neck and a sharp beak, darting bright eyes, and three toes on each foot. It had an ungainly, wingless body, and to John Cooper it seemed to be a doomed target.

But as it scrambled out of the tall grass, it spied the *gauchos*, and with a squawk and a shake of its long neck, it turned and began to run. A *gaucho*, a stout, jovial-featured

man with a bulbous nose and incongruously slim hands and
wiry wrists, took after it. Kicking the horse's belly, he reached
for his *bola* and whirled it in the air. Suddenly he cast it out,
but at that same moment the rhea swerved and disappeared
into the grass.

There were jeers from his companions, and one of them
shouted, *"Estúpido,* you could not catch a virgin if she were
brought to your very bed in the *jacal!"*

John Cooper hid his smile at this sally, and Andrew felt
somewhat embarrassed at the *gaucho's* ribald joke. The discomfitted *gaucho* reined in his horse, leaped down, retrieved
his *bola,* then doggedly remounted and rode after the fleeing
bird.

The *gauchos* shouted mingled encouragements and jibes
as they watched him gallop toward the rhea, which suddenly
swerved, turned, and raced back toward all of them. Its long
neck bobbed as it moved its head this way and that, seeking
an avenue of escape. Once again, the *gaucho* swung his *bola*
in the air and let it fly, wrapping it around the bird's legs.
The rhea fell heavily and began to squawk and thrash about.
Smiling triumphantly, the *gaucho* rode up to it, leaped off his
horse, and drawing his *facón* and avoiding its kicks, swiftly
slit its throat. Then he cut off a sheaf of feathers and, flourishing them in the air, cried out, "With these my wife will
make a quilt on which we'll lie when it's dark and make ourselves another *niño* who will be an even better *hombre de bo-
lear* than I am!" As he rode back to his compatriots, they
sarcastically cheered him and there were many lewd remarks.
Andrew shook his head. "Pa, that was really something! I'd
like to try my hand at that."

"Sure, son. Wait until we're invited, though."

"There are quail in this vicinity, Señor Baines," Raoul
called to him, "so let us see how you use that long rifle of
yours. My *gauchos* will flush out the birds. You and your son
be ready."

John Cooper said in a low voice, "All right, Andy, let's
show them what we can do."

"I'm ready," Andrew said as he drew his rifle from the
saddle sheath, while his father slid out "Long Girl" from his,
inspected it, and waited.

The *gauchos,* particularly Felipe Mintras, watched the
two visitors with keen interest. Catching a sign from his
patrón, Felipe rode toward the thicket of grass, shouting and

waving his short-brimmed hat. Suddenly, a dozen quail lifted from the ground and soared into the icy blue sky. John Cooper swung up "Long Girl," fixing a bead through the sights, then pulled the trigger. Almost simultaneously, his son pulled the trigger of his rifle, and two quail plummeted down from the sky and thudded into the grass, which concealed them.

The *gauchos* cheered, and Felipe declared, "Señor *americano*, I think that you and your son could defeat an enemy army single-handed!"

"Felipe, *amigo*, you're making me feel right at home," John Cooper humorously called as he swiftly primed and reloaded, eyeing his son while the latter emulated him. "You're doing very well, son; I'm proud of you."

The tall youth glanced at his father, his face flushing, then lowered his eyes and mumbled, "Thanks, Pa."

Damn, John Cooper thought to himself, *I can see the boy's moping. I hope we'll meet someone who can understand what Andy's going through and maybe make him feel a lot easier inside.*

As Felipe doffed his hat to the American, his horse suddenly became skittish, pacing the ground and tossing its mane. To his right, from out of the *pampas* grass, had crawled a snake with jet-black markings on its green skin. Andrew quickly shouldered his rifle, squinted along the sights, and pulled the trigger. The snake's head was blown away by the ball.

"*Gracias, mi compañero*," the affable *gaucho* called. "But I was in no danger from that one. It's a colubrid; it has no venom. Indeed, one could be put to sleep by its hissing. Truly, *señor joven*, it is a snake that speaks to you. All the same, that was a very fine shot!"

"Back in Texas," John Cooper interposed, "we're taught to shoot first and ask questions afterward, especially when it's a matter of snakes. Most of ours are poisonous, like the *cascabel*." Then with a wink at the friendly *gaucho*, he whimsically added, "You see, my son is concerned about your beautiful wife and your two sons, Felipe, and we wish nothing to separate you from them."

The other *gauchos* laughed, and John Cooper felt a warm glow of camaraderie. He glanced at Andrew and found that his son was smiling. But it was a wan smile, without any joy.

Raoul, astride his horse, smiled at John Cooper. "Do

you know, Señor Baines, I am envious of your rifle. We have nothing like this here in Argentina."

"Mine was made in Pennsylvania many years ago, Señor Maldones," John Cooper answered. "It was my father's, and he wouldn't let me shoot it until I had become a crack shot with the musket."

"I am thinking that the next time you come here, Señor Baines," his host thoughtfully pursued, "you might bring me a consignment of these rifles. Undoubtedly, our factor, Señor Mallard, could procure them for us."

"I'm sure he could. But to speak honestly, I'm concerned that with the political situation in Argentina such as it is, bringing in weapons might be forbidden."

"Your point is well taken. It would be a pity to purchase these fine rifles, only to have them confiscated by the authorities in Buenos Aires. At any rate, I and the *gauchos* are eager to see this famous knife of yours."

"It's longer than those which your *gauchos* wear," John Cooper explained, "and it has a single edge to their double. If your men will flush more game out of the grass, I'll show you what it can do."

Raoul made a sign, and Felipe walked his horse about the edge of the tall grass and waved his hat and shouted taunting challenges at those birds and animals that refused to show themselves. *"Cobardes,* have we frightened all of you? Now be polite, for there is a *gringo americano* who is here and wants to see you. If you don't come out, you will embarrass me a good deal. *¡Caramba, venga aquí!"*

Even as he uttered the last words, a jackrabbit burst through the edge of the grass, halted a moment, its eyes wide with terror, then tried to dart back. John Cooper, who had dismounted, had already drawn out the Bowie knife, holding it by the tip. Stepping forward, he sent it flying through the air to imbed itself into the rabbit's side. Without a sound, the hare flopped over, lifeless, and the *gauchos* cheered.

"I've never seen a better throw, *señor americano,"* Felipe admiringly called out. "If you stay here long enough, we'll make a *gaucho* out of you; isn't that so, *patrón?"*

Raoul laughed and nodded. "You would not have to teach him much, Felipe, except perhaps how to use the *bola."*

"My son and I would like to learn how to use the *bola,* if you'd like to teach us, Felipe," John Cooper called.

The *gaucho* grinned, then tipped his hat, and made a

mocking little bow. "I'll be glad to show you what I know, *señor americano,*" Felipe volunteered. "But let's ride a bit more. See that big *ombú* tree? From there, due west for about a mile or two, there's a herd of wild guanacos—an animal related to the llama. My Luz has been asking for a warm coat for this winter, and the guanaco has soft, thick fleece!" Wheeling his horse, the *gaucho* rode off at a gallop, and John Cooper quickly mounted his horse and at once followed, Andrew alongside him.

John Cooper studied the beauty of the *pampas.* In this section there was a vast field of thistles and clover and rich, dark green grass. The cool wind stirred the tops, making it look as if invisible men or animals were moving about, camouflaged in its lush verdure. He turned to Raoul, who had caught up with him, and asked, "I'm sure this grass is good for grazing cattle, Señor Maldones, but you've told me there are so many herds that there's an overabundance of beef. How is it sold?"

"Well, Señor Baines, apart from the salted beef that I told you is a small part of our commerce, we sell mainly the hides and the tallow. The only problem is the transportation. If, for example, we were to ship as far northwest as Salta, it would take several months. A huge cart carrying almost a ton of hides and drawn by a team of powerful oxen makes very slow progress. Then there are tariffs throughout the provinces, which take away almost all the profits. As for meat, the *gauchos* have a free hand with it, and they kill the cattle as they need them. Sometimes their women strip the hides off the carcasses and then tan and cure them in the sun. Off to the western side of my holdings, I have a flock of sheep that I bred from merinos, whose wool is superior. I have in my household skillful maids who know how to weave this wool into shawls, coats, jackets, and even linings for the insides of winter boots. This will one day, I hope, become a major industry in our nation—if we get over the unsettled times through which we are now going."

Felipe led the party away from the *ombú,* for nearly two miles, till they came upon the fringe of a clearing marked by clumps of hardwood trees. There were patches of brambles and wildflowers, and beyond that stretched more *pampas* grass. Felipe turned to the others, a finger to his lips. "See there?" he whispered. "About fifty guanacos. Now then, *señor americano*, I'll show you how the *bola* works. Then you and your son can try it for yourselves."

Uncoiling his *bola* and holding it in his right hand, Felipe bent low over his horse's neck, his left hand gathered in its thick mane, and shouted, *"Adelante, mi caballo."* The wiry horse charged into the herd, scattering the animals, and the *gaucho* whirled the *bola* over his head and then let it fly. The leather-clad balls wrapped around the forelegs of the leader, felling it to the ground, stunned. Dismounting and taking his *facón*, the *gaucho* gripped the guanaco by the ears and deftly slit its throat. "Now I'll skin it, *señor americano,*" he called out to John Cooper, "and I'll leave the skin here by this *ombú* to dry. In about two days, it'll be ready to be worked on, and Luz will be warm."

"Hombre, do you mean to say that the guanaco will keep your *esposa* warm where you can't?" one of his companions ribaldly shouted at him. Felipe looked up, grimaced, then grinned and drew his knife from left to right, just beyond his own throat, and pointed his left forefinger at the offender.

Another *gaucho*, squat and short and with grizzled beard, swiftly dismounted and, with his own *facón*, helped Felipe strip the hide from the fallen animal. The other animals had run off. John Cooper and Andrew studied the fallen beast. It was about seven feet long and five feet high, and John Cooper estimated that it weighed about two hundred pounds. It was a young animal, and its coat was soft, russet-colored, and thick.

Raoul Maldones, who sat his mount beside John Cooper, said, "It is related to the llama, Señor Baines, but it is wild, and it has never become a beast of burden as the llama is."

"It looks as if it might be from the camel family," the American observed.

"That is true. I am no historian, but it is possible that when the *conquistadores* came, they might have brought a camel or two, especially from the southernmost end of Spain. Maybe there was interbreeding—who knows? Of a certainty, it is a very useful animal, when our *gauchos* and, for that matter, my family, want woolen quilts or jackets."

In less than ten minutes, Felipe and his companion had stripped the guanaco. The *gaucho* sprang into the saddle and galloped off toward the *ombú* tree, over whose lowest branch he draped the bloodied hide, then rode back to the others.

"Now, *señor americano*," he cheerily declared as he leaped down from his horse, "try your hand at the *bola*."

John Cooper dismounted, took the *bola* from the *gaucho*, grasped the end of the rawhide rope, and experimentally whirled the balls around his head.

"That's the way. You have to judge for distance, the wind, and the speed of the animal you're chasing. It takes practice, *amigo*," Felipe genially remarked as he stood beside the tall American. "But we've scared off the guanacos. Wait a bit. I spoke too soon. Here come a pair of them! Hush now, all of you, and let's see what the *señor americano* can do!"

The others had dismounted and crouched low, while John Cooper stood waiting, his eyes bright with anticipation, swinging the *bola* in the air and getting the feel of it.

One of the animals came about a hundred feet away, quizzically watching them with its brown eyes, and at that moment John Cooper sent the *bola* flying. The guanaco turned to bolt, but the first leather-wrapped ball caught it around the neck and the other hit it in the legs, felling it. The *gauchos* yelled their approval. "*Bueno*, very good; the *gringo* is *muy hombre!*"

"That was wonderful, Pa," Andrew admiringly said.

John Cooper smiled, while Felipe ran up to the fallen guanaco, unwound his *bola*, and let the frightened animal stagger to its feet, then bolt off.

"Let your *hijo* try his hand now," the friendly *gaucho* volunteered as he came back to Andrew and handed him the *bola*.

Andrew took the *bola*, balanced it, swung it experimentally, and lifted it above his head, keeping his arm off to the right, as he had seen Felipe do. His father watched him, critically intent, as Andrew swung the weapon, then let it fly at the branch of an *ombú* tree. Both balls wrapped around the limb.

Father and son spent another half hour throwing the *bola* at the branches of *ombú* trees, till both John Cooper and Andrew were satisfied that they had grasped the basic skill. Then, exhilarated, they rode back to the *hacienda*.

As they rode into the courtyard, Fernando hurried out to inform his master that Padre Emilcar Rancorda had just arrived, that his horse had been put into the stable, watered, and fed, and that he awaited Raoul Maldones in the study.

"We shall have lunch served shortly, Señor Baines," the Argentinian *estanciero* told John Cooper. "Dear old Padre Rancorda married me to my beloved Carlotta and performed her last rites. It will be he who will unite my daughter Dorotéa with Rodrigo Baltenar the first week of October on my daughter's nineteenth birthday."

John Cooper mulled over this news. Quickly, in a low voice so that Andrew could not hear, he said, "If you have no objection, Señor Maldones, I should like to meet this priest and to have him visit a little with my son."

A look of understanding passed between the two men. The handsome, gray-haired rancher nodded. "I shall see to it."

Servants took away their horses, and John Cooper stood beside Andrew as the *gauchos* called encouragingly to both of them and then rode back to the *pampas*.

John Cooper and his son entered the *hacienda* and made for their rooms to wash and change for lunch. Fernando met them in the hallway with a *criada* who carried a tray on which there were two glasses filled to the brim with a yellowish liquid.

"It is the juice of melon, señores, to which rum has been added. Not too much rum, but just enough to sharpen the appetite," the majordomo politely explained. Then, with a bow to John Cooper, he went back to his post, while the *criada* entered John Cooper's room and set the tray down on a table near the shuttered window.

Andrew went into his father's room, took a glass, and tentatively sipped it. Then he grinned. "It's great, Pa!"

John Cooper considered his glass, sipped thoughtfully, then added, "It is indeed." Studying his son, he waited until Andy had taken another sip from his glass, then said, "Do you feel you want to get home in a hurry, son?"

"I don't know, Pa. That's up to you, you know."

"Yes. Only I thought—well, maybe being away from Texas a spell wouldn't hurt either of us. There's a good deal we can learn from these *gauchos*, and maybe our *vaqueros* will get some ideas we can put to use back in Texas."

"Sure, Pa." Andrew stared at his glass, took another sip, set the glass down on the tray, and walked toward the shuttered window and stood staring at it. John Cooper sighed silently and shook his head. Finally he said, "Andy, what's wrong?"

The boy turned to look at his father. His eyes were filling with tears. "Pa—it's just that—I don't know if I'm homesick or not, but it's just that I wonder what's going to happen to all of us," Andrew tried to explain.

John Cooper walked over to his son and put his arm around his shoulders. "Andy, there's a time in everybody's life when he feels low. Look, I'll tell you something. When I came back to the ranch and found out what had happened, I almost took off Esteban's and Miguel's heads, when they tried to be kind to me. Nothing in the world seemed to matter then, except what was in my heart about your mother. I can tell you're not over it yet, either. I'll tell you whom I'm going to have you meet, Andy. Señor Maldones told me, as we rode in, that there's an old priest who's going to marry Dorotéa to that fellow we met at the *fiesta*, that Rodrigo Baltenar. Well now, I want you to have a talk with him. Maybe he can tell you something that will make it easier for you to bear what you and I both have to live with for the rest of our lives."

Unexpectedly, Andrew Baines buried his face in his father's chest and sobbed.

John Cooper patted Andrew's head, muttering, "That's right, son, let it all out. Don't hold it back; it's good to get it out of your system. All right, now. What do you say we go see what they're going to serve us for lunch?"

Padre Emilcar Rancorda was a plump, nearly bald little man, in his sixtieth year, wearing the white robe of a Dominican friar. Although ordained in Buenos Aires by no less a personage than the bishop of Madrid himself, he was determined to seek parishioners among the provinces, particularly the *gauchos* and the servants of the *estancieros*. For, as he had told the bishop, "The poor have no voice, except their own to *el Señor Dios*. I wish to intercede for them; I wish to give them comfort."

For nearly thirty years he had traveled hundreds of miles throughout the provinces, all the way to the Andes and back. Many times he lived with the *gauchos* in their huts, sharing their simple meals of beef and *yerba maté*. Baptizing, confirming, even aiding with the birth of children whom he then blessed, Padre Emilcar Rancorda did not seek to convert in the manner of those who followed the swords of the *con-*

quistadores with the crucifix, but rather to comfort and to assure the poor that God had not forgotten them.

After a simple luncheon, John Cooper took the priest aside for a moment and quickly explained the tragedy that had left Andrew without a mother and himself without a wife. "Perhaps you can comfort him, *padre*," he asked. "I've tried to find my own peace, but the boy is still anguished. Then there's his homesickness. Whatever you can do for him, I'll deeply appreciate."

Padre Rancorda, a kindly, compassionate smile on his wrinkled, sun-bronzed face, approached Andrew and suggested that they talk in the *hacienda*'s little chapel. Andrew nodded his agreement and followed the priest down the hall and into the chapel, which was paneled with dark wood and contained a dozen or so wooden chairs and an altar.

"I speak some English, my son," the old priest said in a gentle voice as they sat before the altar. "But your father tells me that you speak our language very well. Whatever comes easier to you, my son, share your feelings with me."

Andrew's face was taut and bleak as he looked at the priest and said slowly, "Then my father told you about how my mother died?"

"Yes, my son. It was an evil deed. We should not be ashamed of our truest feelings. You mourn your mother; I know you do."

"Yes, *mi padre*." Andrew's voice was hoarse and wavered slightly, as he dug his nails into his palms.

"But your love is strong, as are your memories. You will remember her for her kindness and goodness to you, as well as to your father. Our dear Lord granted her the time with your father to express her love for him and for you and your brothers and sisters. Her spirit will be present always in your thoughts, my son."

"Do you really think so, *mi padre*?" the youth asked as he fought back the tears.

"Assuredly, my son. Because you love her so deeply and you mourn her so greatly, you help keep her spirit evergreen in your heart and soul. She will pray for you to our dear Lord that you be given a good life, the chance to have a family of your own to cherish, to work for, and to do good upon this earth, as she herself did. Death, my son, comes to all of us, and all of us owe *el Señor Dios* this time by which to end our mortal days upon His earth. What we do with those days, He leaves to us. When your time has come to render your accounting to our dear Lord, my son, you will find your mother there, before His throne, to welcome you to paradise."

Andrew wept, his head bowed and his face in his hands, and the kindly old priest touched his shoulders and murmured, "These are tears of love, and you are not less of a man because of them, but more so. I will pray for her, and for you also, my son. Do not torture yourself over her passing. She is with our dear Lord. In the name of the Father, the Son, and the Holy Ghost, I ask God's blessing upon you and your father, your brothers, and your sisters. Go in peace, my son."

Andrew Baines slowly rose, tears staining his cheeks, and he nodded. The old priest's words had been a healing balm, and he felt less troubled.

Seventeen

On the second day after his arrival, John Cooper woke at dawn. The air was cool and the sky was blue and almost cloudless, so he decided to take a stroll around the *estancia*, to familiarize himself with it. The thought idly came to him that it was strange that Raoul Maldones had not remarried, since he loved life so much and was so devoted to his daughters. In five years, he thought, a man like the Argentinian *estanciero* could certainly have found a sympathetic woman who would be surrogate mother to his daughters and a comfort to him. With a sigh, he shook his head: He was a fine one to think such things, himself so recently a widower and the memory still so fresh and burningly vivid. He squeezed his eyes shut impatiently, trying to banish the ghoulish image of Francisco López's livid, twisted face.

He wanted to shake this mood, which was so brooding and dour. It was strange that, at the very outbreak of this

beautiful day, he should have such gloomy thoughts. He
thought his long sea voyage would have banished all that.
Was it an instinct deep within him that made him so sensitive, so volatile to the imminence of some danger? This
thought led to the remembrance of what that sneering
porteño had said to him before disembarking at Buenos
Aires.

No, there must be happier thoughts to pursue. Then he
brightened, and his eyes widened with delight. Coming out of
the stable, clad in a riding skirt, jacket, and a dainty soft hat
creased down the middle and with a short brim, was Dorotéa
Maldones, riding the palomino mare. What an enchanting
sight she was, and how well she sat. Strange that at this very
moment, he should think of Catarina, and how, before they
were married, she had ridden off on her mare, disregarding
his advice, till she had been captured by the renegade Mescalero from whom he had had to save her.

Dorotéa saw him and wheeled the mare with a soft
touch at the reins. John Cooper admired her handling of the
sensitive horse.

"You are up early, Señor Baines," she said to him in a
soft voice with a touch of huskiness to it.

"I might say the same of you, Señorita Maldones," he
courteously parried. "But it's my habit, back in Texas, to rise
early and to see what the day holds. I hunt a good deal, and
I also go for long rides with my wolf-dog."

"How savage a wolf-dog must be! Isn't it difficult to
train?" she exclaimed.

She was gazing down at him from her horse with interest, and he observed that she was an extremely beautiful
grown woman, despite her eighteen years. Her black hair was
drawn at the back of her neck into a tight bun, her forehead
was high-arching, and her eyes were large, widely spaced, and
of a limpid brown. Her mouth was full and ripe, yet with no
petulant sensuality; rather, there was candor and sweetness to
it. Her nose was dainty, a touch aquiline, the nostrils sensitive
and thin. She was, he judged, perhaps a trifle taller than Catarina. Suddenly he wondered why he was making compari-
sons.

To her question, he replied, after a moment's thought,
"It's true that the breeding has its dangers. The wolf is a
predator. Yet, if it's trained from puppyhood, it's quite pos-

sible to tame it, to make it a loyal watchdog who still can fight against enemies."

"I must thank you, Señor Baines, for this beautiful *caballo*. I will tell you a secret. When I first saw this beauty—and Beauty is what I have named her—I prayed that my father would make me a present of her. How gentle she is. Already we seem to be good friends."

"That's because, Señorita Maldones, you do not use a harsh bit, and you rely on her intelligence. Sometimes, I think, animals are friendlier with humans than humans with each other. But then, since I lived so many years with the Indians and had only my wolfhound Lije as my truest friend, it might well be that my experiences have influenced me."

"You have had such a fascinating life, Señor Baines." She hesitated. "Before you came, my father told me that you were married and had children, and then I was so sorry to hear about the tragedy that befell you. But I am being very ungracious to remind you, Señor Baines, and I pray you will forgive me."

"There is nothing to forgive, Señorita Maldones." Then, to change the subject, he hazarded, "I wonder that a girl who is under the protection of a *dueña* is allowed to rise at dawn and go out riding by herself."

She flushed, stiffened in her saddle, and looked almost hostile. "Señor Baines, my father knows that I have been well educated, that I do nothing to disgrace his name, and that I love the outdoors, especially horseback riding. I am, as I am sure you must have heard the other evening, betrothed to Señor Rodrigo Baltenar. I think that if I am ready for marriage, I may be permitted a ride when there is no one else around."

"I beg your pardon, Señorita Maldones. I did not mean to offend you."

As quickly as she had frowned, she smiled, and it was tender and warm. She said softly, with that exquisite huskiness that reminded him of Catarina, "It is I who have offended you. Mine is the worse sin, since you are our guest. Perhaps, before you go, we can ride together."

"I should like that very much, Señorita Maldones."

"Till then. You must tell me all about your *estancia* back in Texas, Señor Baines. There is much I would like to know about your country. Now, if you will excuse me, I shall have my ride and return for breakfast before Señora Josefa is scandalized." She flashed him a dazzling smile, wheeled the palomino toward the north, and rode off at a gallop.

John Cooper stared after her. There was a touch of imperiousness to her, but that was only natural: As the eldest of four daughters it would not be unusual that she should be spoiled. He wondered if she went along with her father's belief that a liaison between himself and Rodrigo Baltenar would strengthen them against the political maneuvering of the greedy *porteños*. Then he wondered again whether it would be a marriage in which there would be any love. Baltenar was in his early forties, and he seemed something of a foppish prig who was undoubtedly well experienced with women. A man like that, he thought, would surely have a mistress, perhaps many *criadas* who would service his carnal needs. How could a sensitive, refined young woman acquiesce to such a union? Then again, he reasoned, the *mores* of this country assuredly must differ from those with which he had been brought up. He knew that a Spanish girl docilely accepted her father's wishes and that many marriages were arranged, even against the brides' preferences. Besides, when it came down to it, it was truly no concern of his.

All the same, he could not help feeling a little annoyed with himself because, as he went along on his walk, he found himself thinking of Dorotéa Maldones.

An excellent lunch was served to John Cooper and his son. His four *vaqueros*, who had no tasks, were taking full advantage by making their own tour of inspection of the *estancia* and befriending the *gauchos*. They took their food out on one of the long tables where the *fiesta* had been held two nights before, and afterward, they experimented with the *bola*.

John Cooper observed that Andrew seemed far more composed and was grateful that he had had the opportunity to meet kindly Padre Emilcar Rancorda. He said as much to Raoul while they were enjoying fine Havana cigars and cups of strong, bittersweet chocolate, a Peruvian delicacy that, in the American's opinion, surpassed the sweet variety he was familiar with in Texas. Andrew, meanwhile, had gone off to watch the *gauchos* and the *vaqueros* compete with the *bola*.

Now Raoul suggested that they have a look at his horses. "Of course, they pall into insignificance, compared with those wonderful palominos of yours. My Dorotéa is enchanted with her mare."

"I know. She told me so," John Cooper blurted, then wished he had not said anything, in the event that he had committed an impropriety. However, Raoul did not question him, but remarked, "My *gauchos* have been able to tame many fine wild horses. They have been kind enough to make me a present of a dozen."

They went to the stable, and there John Cooper studied the horses. He remarked to his host that he found the colts wiry and strong, similar in many ways to the herds of wild mustangs that roamed throughout Texas. Suddenly, as they were leaving the stable, Raoul looked up and frowned, for the elderly majordomo, Fernando, was hurrying toward them, his face taut with concern. "*¿Qué pasa*, Fernando?"

"*Señor patrón*, it is the Señor Ramos. He rode in a few minutes ago and demanded to see you."

"Very well, Fernando. I will not receive him in my house. Tell him that if he wishes to see me, he must come here to the stable."

Fernando bowed low, his eyes warm with comprehension. "*Muy bueno, señor patrón.* I will tell him exactly that."

"*Gracias*, Fernando." Now Raoul explained to John Cooper, "Back in Spain, the families of Maldones and Ramos were rivals and enemies, and had been, for generations. The first Ramos in the court of *El Rey* bore false witness against my great-grandfather. There was a duel, and the first Ramos was wounded. He swore an oath of vengeance to which he bound all his future descendants. In Madrid, this man, this Porfirio Ramos, was my enemy at the court of Carlos the Fourth, and whenever he had the opportunity, he sought to malign me in the king's eyes."

How strange the ways of fate, John Cooper thought to himself. For what Raoul Maldones had just told him paralleled the destiny of his father-in-law Don Diego de Escobar. Because a false friend, who was truly an enemy, had maligned him to the king, Don Diego had been exiled from his beloved Madrid and sent in disgrace as *intendente* of Taos. He said softly, "I understand, Señor Maldones."

"I do not ask you to take sides. To go on: I determined to put an end to this feud between my family and that of Ramos. I came to Argentina, for I had a good friend in the Spanish navy who had taken a ship there and who had told me of the rich land of the *pampas*. Ramos followed me. He established his own *estancia* some thirty miles south of mine, though much farther inland. He is a friend of the *porteños*, and the man who spoke to you on shipboard is his chief ally. He has plagued me in the past by using his political influence to acquire hectares of land, which were rightfully mine by prior settlement. He has incited his *gauchos* to fight with mine, and he has succeeded in driving many of my men away. Here he comes, fuming, pompous mountebank of a man that he is."

As he spoke the last words, Fernando returned, following a stout, gray-haired man with a waxed mustache, wearing a linen suit with a ruffled shirt and cravat, exactly as if he had been a Creole dandy of New Orleans. He had heavy jowls and a bulbous nose, and his narrowly spaced, squinting eyes were slitted in a look of insolent distaste. "Señor Maldones, I have here an order from the office of the *presidente* himself that many of your *ganado* must be destroyed, for they have acquired a contagious disease."

"A contagious disease? Señor Ramos, my *gauchos* have told me nothing of this," Raoul stiffly replied.

"Oh, to be sure they would not," the fat man sneered, "for they ride along the eastern coast and nowhere near the Arroyo del Ombú, which is near my own holdings. I tell you, Señor Maldones, my *capataz*, Hermán Salcedo, came to me this morning and told me that he had found some of your *ganado* dead near the *arroyo*, and some of mine as well. Yours drank from that water and they were sick, and when mine drank, they were poisoned. This is not the first time this has happened. For the past month, I have found dead steers and cows as well, and most of them have your brand."

"That is a damnable lie, Señor Ramos!" Raoul bristled, straightening and glaring at his fat neighbor. "I should not be surprised if you had that scoundrel of a *capataz* of yours contaminate the water of the *arroyo*, so that you could concoct this falsehood and send the news to your important friends in Buenos Aires."

"Take care, Señor Maldones, how you talk! It will not be long before such a remark will be considered treasonable."

"I warn you, Señor Ramos," John Cooper's host replied in a low, shaking voice, "that, if you do not mount your horse and go back to your *estancia*, I will not be responsible for the consequences. As for your order from the office of *el presidente*, that, too, is a lie, for he has no time for such petty concerns."

Porfirio Ramos drew himself up, his sneer deepening. Then he turned to the tall Texan in his buckskins and drawled, "I am told that you are an *americano*, a *gringo* from los Estados Unidos, that you have brought livestock to this man. In your own interest, *señor americano*, I would tell you that you would be best advised to go back to your own country as quickly as you can. For if you stay, I can only conclude that you are a friend of this man who is already suspect—"

"¡*Bastante, Ramos!*" Raoul interrupted, livid with fury and clenching his fists. "If you do not leave my land this instant, I will have my *gauchos* wrap their *bolas* around your fat neck and drag you off to drown you in that creek."

Porfirio Ramos uttered a gasp of fury, made as if to speak, then stomped off toward the courtyard of the house where one of the *servidores* was holding the reins of his piebald stallion. He tore the reins from the man's hands, swore at him, hoisted himself with some difficulty into his saddle, savagely wheeled the horse around as the sharp bit drew an agonized squeal from the animal, and rode off at a gallop.

"Forgive me, Señor Baines," Raoul said as he turned to John Cooper, trembling with anger.

"Señor Maldones," the American responded, "I don't like being intimidated or threatened. Besides which, I've a great respect and liking for you, for your family, and for your *gauchos*. Finally, I just don't like men who wax their mustaches."

Raoul looked blank for a moment, then burst into laughter and gripped John Cooper's hand. "What a pity," he said after he had stopped laughing, "that you could not have said those very words to that fat popinjay who struts about, sanctified by his own importance. Come to my study now; we'll have a glass of old brandy and forget this unpleasantness."

Two days after the encounter with Porfirio Ramos, Gasparo Lobán, a twenty-two-year-old *gaucho* whose parents had been murdered by Indians from the north and who had been adopted by the men attached to Raoul Maldones, rode his colt out toward the creek that bordered the boundaries of the two ranches. Felipe Mintras had told him of Ramos's accusation that the *patrón*'s cattle were contaminated with a contagious disease. Like his *patrón*, he knew this to be a lie, and he believed that the *capataz*, Hermán Salcedo, had been put up to poisoning the water himself, so as to blame it on the Señor Maldones.

The plan was for Gasparo to take his canteen and fill it with some of the water from the creek. He would bring it back, and they would give it to a capybara rodent that Felipe would catch and bring back to the shed near the corral.

Now young Gasparo slipped out of the saddle and hid behind a thick bush of flowering jacaranda, making a sign to his wiry colt to remain still. The young *gaucho*, squatting down and carefully parting the bush with his fingers, caught his breath as he saw, coming from the northwest, a group of four *gauchos* and a fifth man, whom he recognized as Hermán Salcedo. Salcedo was a heavy man in his early forties, brawny without corpulence; his sun-bronzed face was marked by ugly, purplish knife scars on both cheeks, and his nose had been split with a knife in a fight a decade ago. His hair was thick, coarse, and matted, and he wore a short, pointed beard. To designate his position among Ramos's *gauchos*, he wore a red jacket and black-cloth trousers, which flared widely and descended just below the knees. He also wore bright, red calfskin boots, which rose as high as the ends of the trousers.

Gasparo watched as the four *gauchos* dismounted and Salcedo impatiently gestured to one of them to approach. When the man had done so, Salcedo reached into the pouch of his jacket and took out a small leather pouch with drawstrings. Grinning wickedly, he ordered, "Pour it into the water. The mixture of *ombú* and the shredded flesh of that guanaco that died of a virulent fever will make Maldones's cattle sicken to death."

Gasparo was horrified. In his haste to return to Felipe and tell him of Salcedo's monstrous crime, he rose too quickly and stumbled, making a noise.

"*Momentito, hombres,*" Salcedo murmured as his eyes narrowed to glistening slits and he stealthily reached for his rifle. "We have spies to deal with."

Gasparo seized the reins of his colt and mounted, wheeled it toward the east, and in a hoarse whisper, bade it gallop. But Salcedo had seen the movement through the bushes and, training his rifle, pulled the trigger. The young *gaucho* stiffened, his eyes rolling in their sockets, then slid lifelessly from the saddle and sprawled on the ground, as the frightened colt galloped on.

"One less spy to deal with, *hombres*," Salcedo gloatingly announced. "Now empty the sack into the creek. Remember not to use it for a time. There's water enough to the west and to the south of us. *¡Pronto!*"

Felipe Mintras had caught a capybara in a trap that had been set some weeks before, and very carefully, using a fishnet whose sides were sewn to a piece of hardwood by rawhide cords after he had first bored holes into the wood, he had put it into the shed to await Gasparo's return with the canteen.

Felipe was shocked when the *gaucho*'s colt returned to the ranch without its rider, and he immediately decided to ride out to see what had happened to Gasparo.

When he reached the creek, he looked around and called out softly, "*Hola, Gasparo, ¿dónde estás?*" Receiving no answer, he dismounted and walked toward the jacaranda bush, only to utter a cry of horror as he nearly stumbled upon the young *gaucho*'s corpse.

Kneeling down, he gently rolled Gasparo over and saw the bloody hole in the young man's back. "Murdering swine!" he swore under his breath, suspecting that the killer was Salcedo. Then, gently, lifting the inert body, he draped it over his horse just ahead of the saddle, mounted, and, gripping Gasparo's sash with his left hand, galloped back to the *estancia*.

Felipe rode into the courtyard and dismounted. Old Fernando, who had seen him coming, hurried out at the sight of the dead body draped over Felipe's horse's neck. "*¡Qué lástima! ¿Quién es, Felipe?*"

"Gasparo, the *joven*," the *gaucho* somberly responded. "Will you tell the *señor patrón* that I have come back from the creek? He will want to know this, *por cierto.*"

"*Sí, pronto,*" the majordomo replied, then turned and ran back into the *hacienda*. A few moments later, Raoul Maldones came out and strode directly to the *gaucho*. "Fernando tells me that Gasparo has died—how did it happen, Felipe?"

Felipe explained to his *patrón* the plan he and Gasparo had to determine if the water was poisoned, and he also told of his suspicions regarding the murderer. "What this man

Ramos, and Salcedo, do, they do to us, as much as to you, *señor patrón*."

Raoul crossed himself as he looked at the dead *gaucho*, and said in a solemn voice, "May God rest his young soul." He bit his lips, pondering a moment, then said, "Ramos would like it very much if I would have you and your men pay him back for Gasparo. But we will not do this. That would be playing into his hands. If he wants to steal my land, he will have to do better than this. We will bury Gasparo. Padre Rancorda will perform the ceremony."

"May I say something, *patrón?*"

"But, of course. Speak your mind freely, Felipe."

"Gasparo once said to me that if he should die before his time, he would like to be buried next to the *ombú* tree that is near the coast. You know, where you and the rest of us waited for the *gringo americano*."

"It will be done." Raoul clenched his fists, his face bitter with anguish and hate. "That devil Ramos! He wants a war with us." He pondered a moment, then sighed deeply. "I will talk to the *padre* now about burying Gasparo. Poor soul, snuffed out so young, and so uselessly! But, if there is justice in heaven, and I know there is, Felipe, Ramos and Salcedo will pay for this. So, now we know who poisoned the creek. Killing Gasparo was an admission of guilt, and that bullying Ramos thought he could charge me with it!"

"I knew he lied, *patrón*. From now on, I will have the men water the cattle and the sheep and the horses, too, at the Salado River. It will be a little farther to go, but it will be safe. Ramos will not dare have his men poison that water, for it runs through the lands of neighbors with whom he is friendly and who would make trouble if they found out that he was doing such a thing."

"*Bueno*. That is good thinking, Felipe. Now, I'll go find the *padre* and ask him to be ready to give poor young Gasparo the last service we can perform for him on this earth." Again, Raoul crossed himself.

Eighteen

Andrew Baines had finally reconciled himself to the loss of his mother. The kindly old priest had treated him like a grown man, reasoned with him, and made him understand that death did not mean obliteration. Important, too, was his father's recognition of him as an equal, in discussing his thoughts, his plans, and aspirations.

Now Andrew's youth, his energy, and resilience came to the fore, as he decided to go for a ride by himself before lunch. The *capataz*, Oudobras, had taken him aside the previous afternoon and told him that he had himself caught and started to train a roan horse, who had more stamina than any yearling he had seen on the *pampas* over the past several years. He had taken Andrew to the stable and shown him a high-strung and prancing horse fighting the tether rope that kept it in its stall.

Oudobras had taken the colt out, saddled it, and urged Andrew to try it. No sooner had the boy mounted into the saddle than the horse had begun to buck and rear, whinny and snort, turning its head back, its eyes wild and rolling. Andrew had remained with it, his legs tightly clamped around the colt's belly, both hands gripping the reins, exultant in this fierce conflict between man and steed. After twenty minutes, the colt had resigned itself to being ridden by its young master.

Andrew had given it the name of Frenesí, or Fury. Almost overnight, they were friends, and so he went to the stable with a handful of sugar, which Frenesí gobbled, then rubbed its muzzle against the youth's hand. Andrew laughed in sheer exhilaration over his new friend, and then he saddled Frenesí, led the horse out, mounted it, and rode off toward the east.

He had gone three or four miles when he saw another

rider ahead of him, struggling with a balky mare. Urging Frenesí to gallop, he shortened the distance between himself and the unknown rider and discovered that it was Adriana, in a pretty, green riding skirt and a white blouse, with the hat of a *gaucho* atop her lovely head. She uttered a cry of fright as her mare tried to nip at her, and Andrew leaned forward, grasped the reins out of Adriana's hand, and jerking them up short, scolded the mare.

"*Gracias,* Señor Baines. I don't know what's come over Condesa. She's never acted like this before."

"Every time you move, Señorita Maldones," Andrew blurted, "it seems to hurt her. Let me help you down. Maybe there's a burr under the saddle."

"I hadn't thought of that. *Gracias.*" Slowly, she got down from the saddle, and Andrew found himself lifting his arms to catch her and ease her to the ground. She leaned a little on his encircling arm, and her soft brown eyes were warm with gratitude.

Andrew could not help blushing at this intimate contact, but he efficiently uncinched the girl's saddle and lifted it up.

"That's what I thought—see that?" He pointed at a thistle that had inserted itself under the saddle and had cruelly pricked the young mare. "Whoa now, Condesa," he urged the restive mare as he deftly plucked it out, then began to stroke the injured spot on the glossy hide.

"I can't begin to thank you enough, Señor Baines. It was very kind of you."

"I'm glad I could help, Señorita Maldones."

"My gracious, you speak to me in such formal Spanish that it was as if I'm already grown up—but I'm not. Please, call me Adriana."

"If you like, then, Adriana," he assented.

"You mustn't tell Señora Josefa that you found me out here riding all by myself," Adriana pouted, giving him a long, sultry look that set the blood racing in his veins. Innocent as he was of any experience with a female, he stammered, flushing self-consciously, "Of course I wouldn't tell her!"

"That is very nice of you, Señor Baines."

"If I'm to call you Adriana, you should call me Andrew," he countered.

Now it was Adriana's turn to blush and avert her eyes. Softly, she said, "I have tried to tell her many times that I am twelve, and that it will not be too long before I am married. But she still treats me like a child, as if I were Paquita or María. But I can ride just as well as Dorotéa, and I'm only six years younger than she is, after all."

"I'm sure you're right, señorita—I mean, Adriana," he blurted, while she continued to eye him, a little smile playing about her soft red lips.

"I think the mare is all right now, Adriana," he said. "Maybe we should go back now. It's almost time for lunch."

"Oh, very well, if you want me to. Do you want to race back to the *estancia?*"

"Why, yes, I'd like that a lot," he said.

"*¡Bueno!* I will count one, two, three, and then we will start to race, *¿comprendes?*" Adriana cheerfully proposed.

"Yes, I'll be ready when you are, Adriana. Do you want—shall I—you ought to be helped into your saddle."

"That would be very nice of you, Andrew."

He grew suddenly more confident. "Here, put your foot in my hands, and I'll lift you up."

She gave him a dazzling smile and deftly mounted astride the mare. Now that the thistle burr no longer pained the horse, she remained quiet, whinnying softly.

"Now, I'll race you," Adriana proclaimed.

Andrew mounted his colt and saw that Adriana was again looking at him with that tantalizing little smile. He was conscious, too, of the dimples in her olive-sheened cheeks and the cleft of her chin. Her curly hair was formed into ringlets, and Andrew, bewitched by the proximity of this coquettish young girl, found himself smitten for the first time in his life.

"Are you ready now, Andrew?" she asked in a soft, sweet voice.

He found his throat so congested that he could hardly speak. Instead, he nodded. He was staring at her, as if he had never before seen a girl, and Adriana could not help blushing, though she was playing a teasing little game with him. He was really such a handsome *gringo*, she told herself. So very gallant, not at all what she had expected from an *americano*.

"All right, then, one—two—three, and go!" she suddenly called out, kicked her heels against the mare's belly, and darted off.

Andrew found that he had been taken by surprise but lost no time in catching up with her.

Hunched over the neck of his wiry young horse, he lost himself in the sheer exultance of being outdoors, with the cool air and the almost cloudless blue sky above. The scenery of the *pampas* that fringed their trail back to the *estancia* was lush, with mingled shades of green. Galloping swiftly, he far outdistanced Adriana, but then slackened the pace a little, so as to look back to see where she was.

He saw her charming, saucy face frowning with concentration and not a little petulance, and he understood that it was important to her to equal him, if not to best him. He resumed the galloping, but this time without the energy he had shown from the outset. More relaxed, leaning back a little in the saddle, he pretended not to notice that Adriana was catching up with him, and he heard her imploring her mare, "¡Pronto, Condesa, por favor! Quiero qanar, lo quiero mucho!"

The mare responded beautifully, stretching out her long legs, her mane flying, and for a moment Adriana passed Andrew. She turned back to glance at him, and there was a mockingly triumphant smile on her face. Andrew flushed, conscious of the magnetism of the opposite sex.

For a few moments, he let her stay ahead by two lengths, and then, kicking his heels against his horse's belly, urging it on with coaxing words, he forged ahead by half a length. As they neared the buildings of the *estancia*, he drew in on the reins just enough to let Adriana come up equal with him and then called to her, "It's a tie, Adriana; we've finished at the same time! You're a wonderful rider, ¡es verdad!"

Breathless, her cheeks flushed, a radiant smile on her soft, sweet mouth, she leaned forward to pat the mare's neck and to murmur words of endearment and gratitude for Condesa's speed and obedience. Then, drawing the panting mare to a halt, she waited for Andrew to come abreast of her. She looked at him, and her thick lashes fluttered a little as she smiled. "¡fue maravilloso, Andrew! Tell the truth now; isn't Condesa just as fast as the horse *mi padre* let you ride? Be truthful now with me!"

"Oh, yes, she's just as fast, Adriana." Andrew told a white lie, but his conscience did not at all prick him. Even if it had, he was instantly rewarded with the most dazzling smile from that roguishly lovely face, and he felt his heart beating faster, a reaction not entirely due to the energy he had expended in the long race back to the *estancia*.

"Now I must go in, for Señora Josefa will scold me for being out so late," Adriana said. "Perhaps you would like to race again?"

"Very much, Adriana. Thank you for riding with me."

"*De nada*, Andrew." Now, her tone was playfully formal, but the ardent look in her eyes told him that he had made a friend. Quickly wheeling the mare's head, she rode off to the stable. Andrew, bemused, watched her and uttered the same sigh that a young poet might have emitted after a tryst with his beloved.

Two days after young Gasparo's death, Rodrigo Baltenar rode into the courtyard of the *estancia*, accompanied by his foreman, Luis García. The latter was stocky, with a huge, leonine head accentuated by a thick spade beard and heavy sideburns, and an equally thick mustache emphasizing the sensual fullness of his mouth. He wore a black, short-brimmed hat, typical of the *gauchos*, except that his was trimmed with a silver braid around the rim, and he bore himself astride his gelding with an air of arrogant self-importance.

John Cooper and Andrew had, a few moments before Dorotéa's fiancé arrived, gone riding toward the coast. John Cooper had borrowed two *bolas* from Felipe Mintras, and proposed to his son that they practice with them.

Fernando hurriedly announced the arrival of Dorotéa's future husband, and Raoul Maldones emerged at once from the *hacienda* to greet his prospective son-in-law.

"A great pity, Raoul," Rodrigo Baltenar drawled. "One of my *gauchos* told Luis here of your misfortune the other day by the creek."

"It was not so much misfortune—though, of course, it was an injustice for poor young Gasparo to die as he did— but, rather, vicious behavior on Ramos's part," the *estanciero* heatedly replied. "Will you and your *capataz* join me for *el almuerzo?*" He added, with a knowing smile, "I shall ask Señora Josefa to accompany Dorotéa to our table, and Adriana as well. You see, I wish a serious discussion with you, Rodrigo."

"I will dine with you," the latter said. "Will you have one of your servants take our horses? *Gracias*. Come along, Luis."

"*Sí, patrón.*" The heavyset *capataz* disdainfully dismounted and instantly tossed the reins to a young *mestizo* who had come out of the stable to quarter the guests' two horses.

Raoul ushered both men into the dining room, bade them be seated, and filled their glasses with Madeira from a cut-glass decanter. "To your health, Rodrigo. To the closeness between our houses, and to our alliance against that greedy, ambitious representative of the *porteños*, who has the misfortune to dwell so close to me."

"I will drink to that," Rodrigo responded as he slowly lifted his glass, eyed the wine, then took a tentative sip. "Not a bad wine. Perhaps a trifle too young, but it will suffice."

Going straight to the point, Raoul said with an anxious tone in his voice, "I consider it extremely important that we meet now and plan some course of action to anticipate what Ramos will do next. I tell you, Rodrigo, if he is successful through his connections in Buenos Aires in getting the land away from me, you will be the next, since it is well known that you are not only a friend, but also Dorotéa's intended."

"I do not think that anything impetuous should be done, Raoul." Rodrigo addressed him without deference, almost as if he were an inferior. He glanced over at Luis García, who pursed his lips, then sipped his wine and made a smacking sound to signify that he found it satisfactory.

At this moment, Señora Josefa entered, followed by Adriana and Dorotéa. Raoul smiled and waved his hand. "Señora Josefa, we are honored this noon with a visit from Dorotéa's husband-to-be and his *capataz*, the Señor Luis García."

"A good day to you, señores," Señora Josefa said, glancing at her two young charges to make certain that they remained demure and silent in this company of lordly men.

"My compliments to you, Señorita Dorotéa," Rodrigo declared as he took up his linen napkin, held in a silver ring, and unfolded it, placing it in his portly lap.

"Gracias, Señor Baltenar," Dorotéa properly replied, with a slight inclination of her head. The *dueña* smiled proudly, eyeing her employer as if to intimate that the conduct of his young daughters was proper and entirely due to her precepts.

A maid brought in a large covered dish and set it down in the center of the table, then served first the three men, then Señora Josefa, and finally Dorotéa and Adriana. It was a mutton stew, delicately blended with herbs and spices, and there were side dishes of okra, cabbage, and a special kind of snap beans indigenous to the region. Another maid brought a bottle of red Bordeaux, which Fernando had selected from the cellar of the *hacienda*, and filled the men's glasses, as well as that of Señora Josefa, but only half a glass for each of Raoul's daughters.

"You are blessed with a superb cook, Raoul," Rodrigo spoke up, after he had finished nearly all of his portion of stew and longingly eyed the covered dish in the center of the table.

"*Gracias*, Rodrigo. Yes, she is a treasure. One could eat beef or mutton every day of the week and still find them different each time she prepares them." Raoul was making small talk, but the frown on his face indicated that he wished to get to the subject of Gasparo's death as soon as feasible.

As Carolina, the young *mestiza* who had brought in the food, reappeared from the kitchen, the *estanciero* motioned to her to serve his future son-in-law more of the stew, and Baltenar's face brightened. He licked his lips as his plate was filled with the savory food. The other maid, Elena, hurried in to serve Baltenar and the others more of the vegetables, and also to pour more wine for the men and another glass for Señora Josefa.

Finally, a *flan* with slices of ripe melon was served for dessert, and strong black coffee. Carolina replaced the goblets that had contained the Madeira with other glasses into which she now poured a fine port for the men and a glass for Señora Josefa, but again only half a glass each for Dorotéa and Adriana.

As Dorotéa's fiancé fastidiously took a sip of his port, Raoul came at once to the point he had wanted to make ever since the visit began. "Rodrigo, let us have an end to platitudes and generalizations. It must surely be obvious to you that one of Ramos's men killed my poor young *gaucho*, Gasparo. And why? Because Ramos himself, a few days ago, dared to come here to inform me that he had a letter from the office of the president himself insisting that I destroy many heads of cattle that, according to Ramos, had become diseased, and therefore threatened his own herd. Now, your *capataz*," nodding to García, "has a reasonably large herd that mingles with mine. Will you, *señor capataz*, tell me whether you have had any sick animals?"

"No, Señor Maldones, there has been nothing wrong with our cattle."

"So you see, Rodrigo," Raoul said, looking intently at his guest, "if my cattle were truly diseased, as Ramos claims, then your cattle would be infected. No, my cattle have been poisoned. That is a further proof that this man continues his vendetta against me. His purpose is to put me into bad repute with my *gauchos,* to tell his *porteño* friends that I defy the government, and to ultimately petition that my lands be confiscated. Undoubtedly he will be the one to whom they would be awarded, if such a thing came about."

Rodrigo shrugged and spread his hands in a gesture of bewilderment. "But what do you wish me to do, Raoul?"

"You have as many *gauchos* attached to your *estancia* as I do, Rodrigo. I ask only that you inform your men what Ramos is trying to do, and tell them that he may well move against you in his turn, when he deems it profitable to do so. If your men and my men stand together, are cautious, and prepare for treacherous attacks, then Ramos will understand that the two of us are united against him."

"But, my dear friend, I do not wish to involve my *gauchos* in violence. Heaven knows they quarrel enough among themselves. I am more concerned with having my *gauchos* look after the horses and the sheep and the cattle. This is why I have my own brand, just as you do yours. No, Raoul, in all conscience I cannot ask my men to fight beside yours against Ramos. I do not recall a single instance in which he has shown any enmity toward me, or to my *gauchos.*"

"That is your last word, Rodrigo?" Raoul asked, leaning forward to emphasize his question.

Again his guest shrugged and spread his hands out, then reached for his glass of port and downed it before replying. "Come now, Raoul, you exaggerate. It's true that perhaps because of this family feud, he seeks to harass you. But there is a limit to what a reasonable man will do."

"Ah, yes, but Porfirio Ramos is not a reasonable man!" Raoul countered in a tone of exasperation. "When one deals with an unprincipled man who is at heart a scoundrel and who goes so far as to invoke the name of the president as his authority for ordering me to destroy my cattle, then this is a man against whom both of us must defend ourselves. The stronger we are, by united aim and action, the less danger he can be to us."

Dorotéa had listened intently to this dialogue between her father and her fiancé. She was frowning, though she kept her eyes demurely fixed on her plate and tried to seem indifferent. Her father quickly glanced at her, nodded to himself as if confirming a thought that had just entered his mind, and then said, in a more casual tone, "Let me ask you this, Rodrigo. When you marry my daughter Dorotéa and she goes to live in your *estancia*, are you prepared to defend her against Porfirio Ramos?"

"Why, to be sure, that goes without saying, Raoul. Come now, you are seeing ghosts everywhere. All of them seem to have the features of this Ramos. Your charming daughter and I will lead the happy life of a loving couple, and as her husband I shall protect her when it is necessary."

At this bland remark, Dorotéa turned to stare at her fiancé, and her lips curled with contempt. To her, this entire discussion revealed an undeniable fact: Her intended husband was slothful, self-centered, and preferred his own comforts to any loyalty to her father. What he had said about defending her was not even the impassioned declaration one would expect a *novio* to utter concerning the woman he was going to marry.

She glanced quickly away before he could intercept her look, but her father had noticed it. He leaned back in his chair, silent for a moment, as he pondered his next words. Finally, he said, "Dorotéa is very dear to me, as you can understand. It is my hope that the man she marries will care deeply for her, and will be concerned about her welfare, her happiness, and her safety. These are troubled times, Rodrigo."

"You are too dramatic, Raoul," Rodrigo chuckled, then turned to Carolina, who was hovering about the table, and gestured to her to bring more port.

"I have always believed that to be forewarned is to be forearmed. Assuredly Porfirio Ramos has warned me very bluntly about his intentions. But if your men will not join mine against him, then I must pursue the fight by myself with all the strength I can muster. I am sorry if my remarks have disturbed you, Rodrigo. I know that you would like to pay your respects to Dorotéa. Señora Josefa, if you will remain with my daughter, Adriana and I will take Señor García on a little tour of the *estancia,* so that he may see our *gauchos* at work."

García turned to his master, his eyes questioning, and Rodrigo nodded and again waved his hand by way of dismissal, saying, "By all means, Luis, go with my good friend. Indeed, I wish to pay my respects to my lovely *novia.*"

Adriana and her father went out to the stable, where the servants had saddled horses for both of them, while Luis García mounted his and joined them. He was disgruntled that he had not been allowed to remain at the table, for he would have enjoyed more port and coffee. Still in all, he understood that his master wished to be as much alone with that *muchachita linda* as propriety allowed. What was more, his private opinion was that his master was absolutely right; there was no need to involve the *gauchos.* Let Ramos and Maldones settle their differences man to man; that was how he saw it.

Raoul politely pointed out some of the work that was going on at the *estancia.* In a shed about a quarter of a mile from the *hacienda* itself, several of his men were occupied in the preparation of a strong native rum. Occasionally, several of his *gauchos* rode into the town of Lobos to sell jugs of this rum to the storekeeper in exchange for tobacco, flour, and other staples. In another, much larger shed, Raoul told the *capataz,* at springtime and in the fall, several of his men who were sheepherders and who had come from the Basque country some years before, sheared the sheep and sold the wool, retaining some for their wives to use in making garments.

García was bored nearly to the point of rudeness, though he realized that he dare not show it. He wanted nothing better than to return to the *estancia* of his *patrón,* for there was a pretty *mestiza* girl, Miranda, who had caught his fancy and with whom he wished to ingratiate himself. It would be very simple: He had only to tell her that the *patrón* was displeased with her work and might well discharge her, and he was certain that she would be most docile to his demands. His thoughts in this direction helped relieve the glum expression that had settled on his face after about half an hour of the tour.

When they rode back into the courtyard, he mumbled an expression of thanks and pleaded that it was essential for him to return to his *patrón*, while Adriana and her father went back to the stable with their horses.

As they were leaving the stable, Adriana turned to him. "Are you really going to let Dorotéa marry that dreadful man?"

"Adriana, that is not your concern!" her father sharply rebuked her. "You know that it is arranged."

"Yes, I know, *mi padre,* but if I were Dorotéa, I would not like at all the way he acted at *el almuerzo* today. Why, he did not even want to help you, and what he said about protecting Dorotéa—"

"That will do, Adriana! I wish to hear no more on the subject. You must remember that the Señor Baltenar is a mature man, and I do not expect a girl of your age to be able to comprehend him. Dorotéa, six years older than you, is a woman already, and she understands the importance of such an alliance. Now then, we will go back to the *hacienda,* and you will be pleasant to the Señor Baltenar."

"Very well, *mi padre,*" Adriana said meekly. But she was thinking, *I'm glad I'm not Dorotéa, because I'd run away rather than marry that milksop of a Rodrigo Baltenar!*

Nineteen

Dorotéa had been unable to sleep for the past two nights, ever since the luncheon with her fiancé and father. Up till now, she had been indifferent to Rodrigo Baltenar, reconciling herself to her father's wish that she marry him. It was her belief that she owed this much to her father, to assure the comfort and the peace of his later years. In this isolated area of Argentina, with their only neighbors miles away, Dorotéa had had little opportunity to learn about men. When her father had carefully explained over a year earlier the dangers that threatened their peaceful *estancia*, she agreed with him that their only salvation was for her to marry his neighboring *estanciero* to provide a strong bulwark against the *porteños*. It was, after all, a woman's destiny to marry and to submit to her husband; and in this era a daughter, particularly that of a bereaved widower, did not oppose her father's aspirations.

He was not repulsive to her, and she could accept his maturity. She had been educated by her father, her *dueña*, and her nurse, and they had inculcated within her a deep sense of humility, which had served till now to exorcise the latent rebellious independence of her nature. Where Adriana, six years younger, would express with direct and even brutal candor her feelings on the matter, Dorotéa much preferred a diplomatic course of passive acceptance. Since she was a virgin and had not been courted until now—relatively late in life for an Argentinian female—she ingenuously believed that, once she was married, she would learn to love her intended husband.

When he had come to lunch with them, however, and had objected to her father's proposal that he permit his *gauchos* to aid in the defense of their estates, she had begun to see him as an aging man, pompous and importunate, callously selfish and unfeeling. From that point, she had lost all respect for him.

That was why she had been unable to sleep, and that was also why, early this morning after a hasty breakfast of hot chocolate and biscuits in the kitchen, she went to the stable to take out her palomino mare, harness her by herself, and ride off toward the Salado River. Perhaps the exercise would calm her restless, agitated mind.

John Cooper had also awakened early, as was his wont. Though it was the beginning of July, the Argentinian winter proved so invigorating that he was eager to enjoy the pleasant air and drink in the magnificent scenery. Moreover, he was anxious to try his skill alone with the *bola*, and he had even gone so far as to wonder if he could not persuade Felipe Mintras, with whom he had struck up a friendship, to manufacture a dozen or more of these ingenious lasso-weapons to take back with him to Texas. The *vaqueros* might use them in rounding up rambunctious strays on a drive to New Orleans or San Antonio.

By this time the cook and her young helpers had taken a fancy to the *gringo americano*. His geniality, his tall good looks, but above all else, his ability to speak Spanish so fluently and to pay them compliments that they had not expected from a *gringo*, had endeared him to them. A few minutes after Dorotéa had finished her hasty breakfast and gone to the stable, he came into the kitchen and, with an apologetic smile, asked the cook if he might have something to eat, assuring her that he wished her to go to no trouble in preparing it.

Since there was plenty of chocolate and biscuits, John Cooper had a satisfactory breakfast. Then, as he was about to leave the *hacienda* and go out toward the stable in search of Felipe, who was usually near the *hacienda* at dawn to plan his work for the day and to direct his companions, one of the *criadas*, a somewhat addlepated, teenage *mestiza* named Soledad, giggled and, before the cook could admonish her, blurted out, "If the *señor americano* wishes to see the young mistress, she has gone to the stable and saddled her horse. She is very fond of the mare that you brought her."

"Hush, Soledad, you wicked girl," the cook scolded, shaking her ladle at the culprit, who backed away. "This is a gentleman, Soledad; he does not follow señoritas, unless they wish it. Now go do your work and let me hear no more of you, or I will let you feel this ladle across that fat backside of yours!"

The maid promptly began to cut up a melon so that Raoul Maldones and his other three daughters might enjoy it when they wakened and came down for breakfast.

John Cooper gave the discomfitted young *mestiza* a covert smile and wink and touched his forefinger to his head in token of gratitude at this piece of unexpected information. It occurred to him that he could exercise with the *bola* later in the day, at which time he could seriously confer with Felipe. A canter on the wiry colt that he had been riding ever since he had arrived in Argentina—and perhaps even a chance meeting with Señorita Maldones—would be more exhilarating.

He hurried out to the stable and saddled the colt, who whinnied and nickered at his approach but who gratefully accepted the piece of sugar that John Cooper held out atop his palm. Mounting swiftly, John Cooper rode out and headed in the same direction as Dorotéa, seeing that the tracks of her horse led inland, away from the coast.

Even though his host had assured him that within the immediate terrain of this *estancia* there were no real dangers from snakes or wild animals, John Cooper's years with the Indians had taught him that the most sensible plan was to carry weapons just to be prepared. Thus, he had brought along "Long Girl" in its sheath and thrust the Bowie knife through a special loop in the belt of his buckskin breeches.

Dorotéa had gone about a quarter of a mile ahead of him, and for an instant, he had a glimpse of her in her riding skirt and jacket mounted on the mare, only to see her vanish in the distance along a winding trail amid a clump of flowering trees.

He was in no hurry. The air was marvelous, and there was a moist, almost intoxicating smell to the earth with all the fertile flowers and trees and grass. The sun had risen, but it was not yet too warm; nor would it be. The pleasant, temperate weather was a welcome contrast to the oppressive heat he would have encountered back in Texas at this moment.

As he rode along at a leisurely gait, he wondered about his growing involvement with the Maldones family, which had gone beyond that of a business relationship. His business was concluded; he had received the draft on the factor at New Orleans that would pay him handsomely for the time and trouble he had taken to bring the steers, the bull and heifer, and the two horses to Argentina. Yet he had not even thought of inquiring when he might board the next sailing vessel for New Orleans.

Dorotéa Maldones was still delighted with Belleza, for she had never had a more docile yet understanding mount that responded so quickly to the slightest touch of the reins or to a word. How good it was to be alive, to ride like a man, to have the freedom of the *gauchos*.

Then she frowned, for she remembered that in a few short months she would become Señora Baltenar. The way her fiancé had talked to her father at *el almuerzo* the other day had made her see him as she had never before seen him. There was something else, too, of which she had said nothing to her father. A year earlier, Señora Josefa, just after Dorotéa's father had told her that he would permit Rodrigo Baltenar to court her with a view toward eventual marriage, had told her that an *estanciero* is a law unto himself and that out here on the *pampas*, he does not live by the code of the *porteños*. When Dorotéa pursued this, the *dueña* unexpectedly confided in her ward. Señora Josefa explained that a man like Dorotéa's *novio*, until he took himself a wife, was permitted to enjoy the companionship of *criadas* or *mestizas*.

Although she was a virgin, Dorotéa had seen enough of the mating of horses and cattle on her father's *estancia* to comprehend the sexual roles of male and female. And she knew about the conjugal duties that would be expected of her as a wife. Just before Dorotéa's mother had died, when she herself had been only thirteen, Carlotta Maldones had closeted herself with the girl and sympathetically explained such matters as the lunar tides of the female and her God-given gift to bring children into this world. Because Carlotta was emancipated for that early era, she had instilled in Dorotéa a calm and logical understanding of these basic differences between the sexes.

Now, irked by her fiancé's refusal to defend the *estancieros* against the attacks of the *porteños*, and particularly against a man who, though himself an *estanciero*, sided with the *porteños*, Dorotéa thought to herself that she would have to submit to her wifely duties with a man who had thus far shown her no romantic courtship and who, worst of all, impressed her as being something of a coward.

The previous night, without telling her *dueña*, she had asked Padre Rancorda to hear her confession. In the chapel there was a little statue of the *Cristo*, a superb *bulto* made by one of the *gauchos* who had a talent for working in wood and clay and using paints made from herbs and berries. Kneeling beneath the *Cristo*, she had asked the priest to advise her on the duties of a proper daughter who had been pledged by her father to a man she found she did not love and, what was worse, was not certain she could respect.

"*Mi hija*," he had gently responded, "the Holy Church admonishes children to respect their elders. You have been brought up properly, and I myself baptized you and confirmed you. When your mother died, I told myself that your father would have a most difficult task in being both parents to you. Yet he has done splendidly. You are educated, you have high moral integrity, and now you feel a filial obligation to your father to aid him. But remember, you also have an obligation to God, Dorotéa, and you must look to Him for your answer. I think He would tell you that if you do not love this man, and your heart tells you so as well as your mind, you must tell your father. You must be honest with him. He is a kind and compassionate man. He would not sacrifice you simply for his own personal gain."

"I know that also, *mi padre*. Yet it would hurt him if I went against his wishes."

"But your life, young as you are, is a treasure that must be guarded. Besides"—the priest gave a knowing smile—"the banns have not yet been announced, and the wedding is still some months off. Much can change in that time, if our dear Lord wills it. Pray, my daughter, and He will hear your prayers."

She had left the chapel, not quite satisfied and yet realizing that she must tell her father what was in her heart.

As she rode, mulling over what had taken place the last few days, she thought back to the time when Rodrigo Baltenar had sat with her *dueña* and pursued his courtship of her. All had been done according to the accepted mode, and there was no impropriety. Señora Josefa had beamed, her hands folded in her portly lap, as she listened to the two exchange polite remarks and heard Dorotéa's fiancé avow his love for her and his plans to bring her happiness and give her all the luxuries she could desire. "You will be mistress of the *estancia*, my Dorotéa," Rodrigo had assured the beautiful young woman. "You will not have to lift a finger, and there will be servants to anticipate your every need. I ask only— and this is because of what I feel in my heart for you—that one day we may be blessed with an heir to carry on my name, which is of one of the oldest families of Madrid. You will bring it honor and distinction, my beautiful one."

Señora Josefa had coughed and put a hand to her mouth, glancing sharply at the *estanciero* for having dared to interpolate so daring a comment, which was not proper for the ears of a tender young virgin. Yet, inwardly, she was telling herself that here was a kind, good man who would make Dorotéa a proper *esposo*. He would be firm with her, give her children, and satisfy all her desires. What else, after all, could any well-brought-up girl expect in this life?

But even from that time something had been nagging at Dorotéa's mind: It was the plaguing notion that her fiancé was being inordinately selfish in thinking only of his ancestral line and furthering it, using her as the vessel.

Logically, she said to herself, *My father has already told me that, when I marry Rodrigo Baltenar, I shall have saved my father's estancia. Very well, I accepted this—but now, if this man who is to marry me refuses to come to my father's aid, am I not justified in telling my father that there are two sides to a bargain, and, if one is not kept, it is no bargain at all?*

She thought of all this as she rode, and there were tears in her eyes. Yes, she would tell her father. She would await the proper occasion.

She had ridden for nearly two hours, and she knew that the young palomino mare wanted to rest and drink. They had come to the river, where there were many hardwood trees and the earth was moist. There was thick shrubbery all around, dark and mottled green, and the river was sluggish and narrow. She leaned over and patted Belleza's neck and crooned to the mare, telling her how pleased she was with her performance, her ability, and her instant response to her directives.

So preoccupied was she over her sudden change of heart concerning the man to whom she had been promised that she scarcely noticed what looked to be a greenish log with dark black blotches interspersed along the surface. It was a young anaconda, ten feet long, nearly two feet in girth, weighing over a hundred pounds. It lay in wait near the edge of the bank, with just its eyes and nostrils above water, ready to capture any bird or mammal that would come down to drink its fill. It had not eaten for some time, and it was hungry.

The palomino mare did not see it either, for she had been bred in Texas where there was no such lush foliage with intermediate shades of green merging so subtly that one could hardly make out the difference. Thus, trustingly, the mare stood on the riverbank only a few feet from the anaconda's head.

Dorotéa slid down from the saddle with a sigh of exhaustion. She had ridden farther than she had intended to, but she had been so preoccupied that she had lost track of time. Now, realizing that Belleza was breathing hard and that there was some slight lather about her mare's muzzle, she ruefully apologized to the beautiful palomino. "Forgive me, *querida*. It was all my fault. Perhaps yours a little, too, since you're so beautiful and you move so wonderfully that I couldn't even think of how long we've been out together. We'll be great friends. I'll take better care of you, I promise it. Now drink, but not too much, *querida*."

Holding the reins lightly in her left hand, she led the mare to the water. As the palomino dipped her muzzle, the anaconda suddenly swirled toward her, striking and missing, for instinctively the mare had withdrawn her head. But the unexpected, violent retreat of the horse jostled Dorotéa, who uttered a cry and stumbled, falling into the shallow water. Immediately the anaconda was upon her.

She saw the hideous head, the mouth yawning to bare the terrible large, backward-pointing teeth. With a terrified scream, she caught it by the neck, keeping the fangs away from her. For the anaconda—or water boa—attacks the vertebrae of its prey, paralyzing it, then coils around it, suffocates it to death, and devours it.

Belleza reared, whinnying wildly, then turned tail and galloped back along the path whence she had come. Dorotéa, trying to clamber to her feet in the sluggish water, was seizing the neck of the anaconda with both hands, forcing it away from her face. She was cringing with horror, and then suddenly she felt its coils around her thighs. Again she uttered a piercing scream: *"¡Ayúdame, por el amor de Dios!"*

John Cooper had been following at a leisurely gait, not wanting Dorotéa to catch sight of him and come to the conclusion that he was trying to force himself upon her. He could no longer see her, but then the trail wound and turned this way and that, and there was so much foliage and so many sturdy hardwood trees, glossy and moist with moss and lichen, that he saw very little.

Hearing her scream, he galloped toward the riverbank. He saw Dorotéa's mare run by him, the eyes rolling in their sockets, foaming at the mouth in her terror. Swiftly, he flung himself off the colt and saw Dorotéa falling backward, with the head of the hideous green and black boa constrictor perilously close to her contorted face. He saw also the sinuous coils, thick and pulsating, wrapped around her thighs and waist.

He drew his Bowie knife and plunged into the river, his left hand seeking the neck of the anaconda. It turned its head, seeing him with its hideously cold, glassy eyes. He struck with all his might, just below the neck. Dorotéa cried out again, nearly fainting. The coils had tightened around her so torturingly that her breath had been cut off, and now she fell back and submerged under the water as John Cooper followed the anaconda's coils. His left hand gripping the snake's neck, he struck again and again, making certain that he did not wound the woman caught in its twisted body.

Suddenly, the anaconda released its hold, for one of his

thrusts had found a vital spot. The giant reptile writhed and twisted convulsively in the water, then released the hysterical young woman. John Cooper lifted her up from the muddy bottom of the river and held her. She was trembling violently. He had never before seen so large a snake, and he held the knife in his hand, gripping it like a dagger, ready to strike again, if need be.

"There, there now, it's dead; it won't harm you anymore, Señorita Dorotéa," he panted, his voice hoarse and trembling.

She sank back, half-fainting in her fright. His left arm was around her waist, supporting her.

John Cooper sheathed the Bowie knife, used both arms to lift Dorotéa out of the water, and stepped back onto the bank and then lay her down on the grass, just beyond it.

He took off his buckskin jacket and covered her with it, then knelt down, staring at her, worried that perhaps the boa constrictor had hurt her badly. But when he saw the steady rise and fall of her bosom, he breathed a sigh of relief. "Señorita Dorotéa, it's all right now, you're safe. I'm here with you, and the snake is dead," he hoarsely repeated.

Her eyes slowly opened, and she uttered a sobbing little cry, then burst into tears. "Oh, thank God, Señor Baines, thank God you came! I was so afraid. I'd forgotten that there were *culebras* like these in the water. Oh, you've saved me, *gracias, gracias por mi vida!*"

Unexpectedly, stunning him with her change of mood, she lifted herself a little and clasped her arms around his neck and kissed him, sobbing, "Oh, Señor Baines, I owe you my life, I do, I do! Oh, Señor Baines, I love you!"

"*Querida,* you can't mean that! Dorotéa—I mean, Señorita Dorotéa—you were just frightened and I saved you and you're grateful—" He tried to soothe her, but her words had been so ardent and the hold around his neck of her soft arms was such sheer enchantment that he was tempted to kiss her. Yet he fought this temptation, for it would be all too easy to succumb. "Rest there a little, and then we'll go back," he gently told her. "Are you warm? You must not get chilled."

"Yes, I'm warm, thank you, with your jacket around me." She was calmer now and said softly, "I thank God that you came here to be with my father, Señor Baines. And I really do love you."

John Cooper was trembling. He remembered Carlos's words and wondered if perhaps this was destined. Just as the cloud had resembled a horse to direct him to come to Argentina, perhaps this was the love to which Catarina, as she lay dying, had directed him.

"You are very beautiful, *mi dulce*," he said tenderly. He stroked her cheek, his other arm around her shoulders. "Yes, it would be so easy to love you, Dorotéa. But what you feel is out of gratitude because I saved your life. Both of us must know each other longer, in the days ahead when there's no danger for either of us; then we can see each other and then decide what is best for us."

"You're right, Señor Baines. *Dios, must* I go on calling you this? Your name is John Cooper Baines." She pronounced it so deliciously that again he wanted to kiss her but held himself back only with the greatest effort. "You will be my John Cooper, and I will be your Dorotéa."

"We'll see, my dear one. Now, do you think you can stand up?" he asked.

"Yes, I—I think so." He helped her to her feet, and again she clung to him. This time, with a sweet little sigh, closing her eyes, she put her mouth to his and gave him a long and tender kiss. John Cooper was shaken by the tumult of feelings that it aroused within him, and he gently pulled himself away.

"*Querida,*" he told her softly, "your mare has gone back to the *estancia.* You will have to ride up behind me with your arms around me. We'd best be getting back, or they'll be worried."

"Yes, John Cooper, *mi amor,* I want to go back. I want to tell my father what you did, and what I feel for you."

He helped her up onto the colt; then he mounted and galloped back to the *estancia.* She rested her chin on his back as her arms clung tightly to him.

For John Cooper Baines, it was like a dream, and yet he knew it was no dream. Perhaps, indeed, it was the fulfillment of a prophesy.

Twenty

It was the Fourth of July 1826, the fiftieth anniversary of the Declaration of Independence. On this day, two great former presidents of the young United States died: John Adams and Thomas Jefferson.

For Carlos de Escobar, life had begun all over again. Teresa, whom he had longed for since their first meeting over two years earlier, had shown him in many ways that she had no further doubts about remarriage. There was a rapture of concord between them. His love for her was fully returned, and his delight in her grew with each new day. He had put to rest the gentle ghost of lovely young Weesayo, though he knew that her spirit would always be with him like a protective and benevolent aura.

There would be a *fiesta* to celebrate Independence Day, and it would be more than a patriotic celebration: It would also be a celebration of the Double H Ranch itself, and the individuals and families who had helped it grow and prosper. Though Don Diego's health had not been the best during the past several years—what with the tragedies of losing first his daughter-in-law Weesayo, and then his own beloved daughter Catarina—he was looking forward to this evening with new zest. For now he saw Carlos happy again, and he thoroughly approved of the beautiful, courageous young woman who had agreed to share his son's life.

Miguel Sandarbal, a father once again, for Bess had given birth to a baby boy, was eager to take an active part in this *fiesta*. His assistant, Esteban Morales, had been busy since morning preparing for the outdoor feast. In the kitchen, old Tía Margarita was bustling about, her round, plump face aglow with the excitement of the work in preparing tasty viands. In her old age, she basked in the praise of Rosa Nuñez, the girl whom John Cooper Baines had brought away from the village of Acuña. Rosa worked with such enthusiasm and humility that Tía Margarita often found herself with little to do. Rosa was constantly smiling and saying, "Tía Margarita, you should rest more. I know what to do; I will follow your recipe to the letter; you'll see. Now let me bring you a nice cool drink before I start the tortillas."

There was a special reason for Rosa's happiness. The young *vaquero*, Antonio Lorcas, had asked her to be his wife. He had been courting her for the last few months, playing his guitar and serenading her from the steps of the bunkhouse, or whenever he saw her leave the kitchen and go out to the well to draw water. Blushingly, her eyes downcast, she had pretended not to notice. Then the previous week, when she had had a particularly heavy bucket to carry back, he had put down the guitar and hurried to her and stammeringly asked if he might not carry it for her. She had pretended to be reluctant, but her blushes gave her away, and finally the young *vaquero* gently took the bucket away from her and insisted that he bring it to the kitchen. On the way, he began to tell her that he had a bright future at the *Hacienda del Halcón* and that he wanted nothing more in the world than to find a sweet wife with whom he could share his life. By the time they had reached the kitchen, Antonio had proposed to Rosa, and she had accepted him. She found him handsome, gentle, considerate, and kind.

As for the children of the Double H Ranch, they could hardly wait till evening to taste the fine foods that would be set before them, to hear the music, and to be allowed to stay up late because it was such an important holiday. In particular, Charles Baines felt almost as if the Fourth of July were his birthday. Without Andrew's presence, he could not help feeling that he was growing almost into manhood as he eagerly did the chores that either Miguel or Carlos had assigned him: caring for the horses, cleaning up the shearing houses after the sheep had been clipped, even riding out with the *vaqueros* when they rounded up the cattle. Charles had the respect of all the workmen, and already he had begun to act with almost an avuncular patronage toward Ruth and Carmen, rather than as a brother, lecturing them on what they should do to keep out of mischief, warning them not to go too far beyond the creek, lest they come across a snake or a wild boar.

There was one other young member of the Double H

Ranch community who had also experienced a number of changes. Young Bernardo Morales, now sixteen and quite sturdy for his age, had become altar boy for Padre Jorge Pastronaz, and his mother, Concepción, and father, Esteban, were very proud of him. Bernardo was torn between his love for the Church and his eagerness to become a *vaquero* like Miguel Sandarbal, whom he idolized. Thanks to the school that Doña Inez, Bess, and Catarina had organized, Bernardo, together with the children of the other *vaqueros* and *trabajadores*, had learned to read and write in both English and Spanish. This was why his mother argued with Esteban, "It is more important if he has a calling from *el Señor Dios* to become a deacon or a priest, than to be a *vaquero*. I do not say this to make you lose face, my dearest husband, but consider what you yourself might have become if you had had the same advantages of education."

"What you say is true, *mi corazón*," Esteban admitted. "I will let Bernardo make up his mind. Padre Pastronaz will know if he has a calling. Meanwhile, it does him no harm to be a complete man. Was not Peter, on whom our dear Lord built his church, the rock of stability, a fisherman? *Jesú Cristo* Himself was a carpenter. So if Bernardo is good with his hands and able to lasso cattle and to round up horses and train them, and still he has this calling. he will be, as I say, a complete man and, thus, more compassionate toward the poor and the needy."

"I agree," Concepción had smilingly assented. "We are indeed fortunate in such a son."

Carlos had spent at least two hours each day with Yankee, remembering John Cooper's exhortation to continue the young wolf-dog's training. Because of the savage strain in him from the timber wolf with which his sire, an Irish wolfhound, had mated, there was always the danger that like his predecessor Lobo, the young, fierce, and strong animal might misunderstand the sudden impulsive gesture or movement of a child and turn on him. Carlos had worked diligently, and Teresa herself had taken an interest in his training. Already, Yankee was fond enough of her to come up, bow his head, and slink on his belly toward her, while she ran her knuckles over his head and made him emit a contented growl.

On the morning of July fourth, Carlos decided he would go hunting with Yankee. He procured his Belgian rifle, and slung over his shoulder a pouch of ball and powder. Calling Yankee from the shed in which he slept at night, Carlos squatted and greeted the wolf-dog by stroking Yankee's muzzle. Nearby was another small building—the kennel—in which Yankee's littermate, Luna, as well as the Irish wolfhounds Hosea and Jude, were quartered. These dogs were also trained by two *trabajadores* who had bred dogs back in the province of Durango where they had worked on farms before being engaged by Miguel. Luna was nearing her season and could soon be mated with one of the wolfhounds. Miguel hoped she would have her litter in a few months.

Carlos set out on horseback, with Yankee loping along and glancing up now and again at the handsome Spaniard, alert and tense. As Carlos glanced down at him with an encouraging smile, the wolf-dog emitted a short bark, and Carlos laughed aloud in sheer delight at the beauty of the day and the pleasure of going hunting with this intelligent animal. *"Amigo,"* he called down to Yankee, "I swear you're almost human, because you can tell how happy I am."

The wolf-dog seemed to nod his head and again uttered a joyous, yapping bark, wagging his tail. Carlos, his face serene, laughed again, savoring life to the fullest.

Yankee loped along, glancing back at Carlos from time to time to make certain that the young Spaniard was keeping up with him. His eyes blazed with eagerness, and his ears were flattened against the sides of his vulpine head.

Suddenly a small deer broke out of a clump of mesquite and, seeing Yankee, turned tail and raced furiously toward the north. Yankee easily overcame the distance and leaped at the deer's throat, just as Carlos, sighting along his rifle, triggered a shot, which dropped the deer dead in its tracks. It was done out of mercy, for he did not wish Yankee to kill the deer with his sharp fangs.

The wolf-dog stopped dead in his tracks, his hair bristling, glancing back at Carlos and glowering at him, as if disappointed that he had been denied a chance to make the kill.

Dismounting, Carlos strode toward the fallen deer, which was just a yearling and weighed no more than a hundred pounds, lifted it up in his arms, and draped it over the horse's neck. The venison would be a welcome addition to the feast this Fourth of July.

"That'll do for now, Yankee boy," he told the wolf-dog.

"Your master will be proud of you when I tell him the way you went after that deer. Come along, boy!"

Wheeling his horse back toward the *hacienda*, Carlos rode easily. But his thoughts were on John Cooper, and he wondered how his brother-in-law was adapting himself to that far-off country which, like Mexico, had once been a Spanish possession.

At four in the afternoon the oppressive heat was dispersed by a pleasant gust of wind from the northwest, some two hours before the scheduled *fiesta*. Pretty little Dawn, now seven years old, the last child born to Carlos and Weesayo, had been playing with the wooden toy that Esteban Morales had made for her, a miniature Spanish galleon. She proposed to Inez, nearly three years her senior, "Inez, why don't we go to the creek before supper? I want to sail my boat, and Esteban made a boat for you, you know, last month."

"Yes, he did. You mean, we can sail our boats in the creek?" Inez, a slim, oval-faced, spirited black-haired girl, asked.

"Yes! We can pretend the creek's a giant river and that our ships are making a voyage. It will be lots of fun! We'll take Dolores with us." In their twilight years, Doña Inez and Don Diego had adopted two orphaned children whose parents had been killed by raiders: Juan, now five, and his sister Dolores, near her seventh birthday.

Dawn and Inez went off to look for Dolores and swiftly induced her to accompany them to a little creek south of the *Hacienda del Halcón.*

Because of the many preparations for the *fiesta* this evening, neither Don Diego nor Doña Inez, nor, for that matter, Carlos himself, noticed that the three little girls had left the *hacienda* and walked past the bunkhouse and the church, heading toward the Frio River. The creek was a quarter of a mile southeast of the placid river, and there were nut trees growing along its banks.

As the three girls made their way toward the creek, Julia Sandarbal, now nine, and with her mother's blond hair and sweet face, hailed them. "Come along, Julia," Inez called, "we're going to play down by the creek before it's time for supper. We'll have lots of fun!"

Julia nodded, and hurried to catch up with the trio.

Yankee, back from his outing with Carlos, recognized

the children by their voices, and when he heard Julia calling out for the other three girls to wait, he bounded away from the kitchen door—where he was hoping for some hand-outs—and went to join the children, whose company he enjoyed and who often spoiled him with treats. At the front of the *hacienda* and at the side, the *trabajadores* were setting up the tables, preparing a low platform with chairs on which the musicians would sit, and they paid no heed to the wolf-dog. Yankee bounded off after the girls, his tongue lolling out of his mouth, his eyes bright with the anticipation of another romp.

Julia turned to see Yankee loping up toward her and giggled, "You want to play with us, Yankee?"

The wolf-dog wagged his tail, looking up at Julia, who smilingly rubbed his head, then scratched the back of his neck. Yankee closed his eyes, blissfully receptive to this sort of petting, and the three other girls, turning to see why Julia had not caught up with them, uttered squeals of joy to see their playmate joining them.

"Let's make him fetch sticks! We can throw them and see how fast he can bring them back to us," Inez proposed.

"Oh, yes, I'd like that," Dawn agreed. "There are some trees down by the creek, and we can break off the branches and throw them for him to bring back."

This seemed like a capital idea, and forgetting for the moment the idea of playing with their boats, the four girls hastened toward the little creek, with Yankee following them as they walked in a row, then swiftly advancing ahead of all four. He constantly looked up to solicit more caresses, and the girls were only too happy to pet him and encourage him with praise.

The ground near the creek was moist, and to the left, as the quartet of children approached, there was a huge semicircular patch of thick grass. Dawn, on the right of the quartet, was petting Yankee with one hand and holding on to her wooden boat with the other, when she stumbled and, trying to catch her balance, took several hasty steps, only to find herself in the thick grass. Suddenly, the ground seemed to give way beneath her.

"Oh, I'm sinking; I'm going down! Help me!" she cried.

Inez, Dolores, and Julia uttered shrieks of fright, running this way and that in confusion. Dawn had dropped her boat and began to sob that she had lost it; but by now the bog had sucked her down as far as her knees.

"Oh, please, I can't get out; go get somebody; have them pull me out," Dawn cried.

Dolores and Julia were too frightened to move, and only Inez, the oldest, had presence of mind to call out, "Don't move around so much; you'll go down faster! Try to stay still; I'll run for one of the *trabajadores!*"

Yankee growled and carefully and gingerly put one paw ahead of the other, till he was at the very edge of the patch of thick grass. Seeing him, Dawn, who was crying in her fright, sobbingly called, "Yankee, help me get out; please help me!"

The wolf-dog seemed to understand the little girl's predicament. He uttered an angry growl and then edged forward even more gingerly. Secure of his footing, he made a lunge and caught the hem of Dawn's cotton skirt and then began to back up, trying to drag her out by her clothes. But the material was soft, and his fangs were strong, and as he gave a vigorous jerk backward, the skirt ripped, and Dawn uttered a scream of terror. "Oh no, not like that; you tore my dress, oh, Yankee! Help! I'm going down; I can feel it, the sticky mud! Oh, please help me!"

With another growl, the wolf-dog backed away and looked about. There was a fallen branch from a live-oak tree a few yards away, and he ran toward it, gripped one end in his fierce jaws, and came back to the little girl struggling in the bog.

Again setting one paw down after the other and moving very slowly, the wolf-dog nudged the other end of the branch toward Dawn. She reached out and gripped it with both hands. "I've got it, Yankee. Pull me hard; pull me out of this, pull me—"

Yankee gave a low growl as he kept his strong fangs clenched onto the end of the branch. Then he began to back up, his body taut with strength, and slowly, as Dawn held on, desperately aware of the peril she faced, she felt herself drawn out of the bog inch by slow inch.

Inez had found her father, who was conferring with Miguel on the plans for the *fiesta* that evening. With a cry of horror, Carlos turned and raced out to the creek and came upon the scene. Dolores and Julia were crying, jumping up and down, and shouting encouragements to Yankee.

"*¡Dios!*" Carlos called out, and then cautiously moved alongside Yankee.

"Hold on to the branch with one hand, *querida*, and reach your other hand out to meet me!" he shouted.

Dawn nodded, her face twisted with mingled fear and concentration, as she tried to obey her father. Her left hand holding tightly to the other end of the branch that Yankee continued to drag backward, she reached out her right hand and her fingers just brushed her father's hand. Heedless of the danger, Carlos leaned forward a little more and just managed to catch Dawn's hand and to take good hold of it. "Now hold on tight; I'm going to pull you out," he hoarsely exclaimed. Using all his strength, he dragged the sobbing little girl out of the bog. Yankee dropped the branch and wagged his tail, uttering that peculiar growl that was characteristic of him when he was pleased with something.

"Poor darling, you're all right now," Carlos said soothingly to his daughter as he held her in his arms and kissed her. There were tears in his eyes as he turned to Yankee, who was wagging his tail. "That was very brave, *muy inteligente, mi amigo!*"

Then, turning to Inez, he said with pride, "You helped save your sister's life, Inez, by running for me. But we all owe a debt of gratitude to Yankee."

"I lost my little boat that Esteban gave me, *Papá*," Dawn sniffled as she clung to her father's neck with both arms.

"He'll make you another one, an even better one. I never knew there was a bog there. Tomorrow, I'll have the *trabajadores* fill it up and make it safe, maybe build a little fence around it, so that nobody else will fall in. Oh, Dawn, my heart was in my mouth when your sister came for me and I saw you there—"

He hugged her and then walked slowly back to the *hacienda*. "Now you'll have to have a bath, young lady, and of course a new dress, so you can be very beautiful at the *fiesta* tonight!"

"Yankee should get a reward, *Papá*," Inez proffered.

"He will; he'll have all the beef or mutton he wants to eat, as well as the venison he helped me get this morning, and that's a promise," Carlos said. He kissed Dawn's tears and whispered something to her. She began to giggle. Yankee, walking along, glanced up at Carlos and the little girl; his tongue was lolling out of his mouth and he looked happy.

The July Fourth *fiesta* was a great success. Yankee's heroic rescue of little Dawn made it a celebration for thanksgiving, as well as an observance of the founding of the young United States, with its falling frontiers and its countless miles of unexplored territory awaiting the courageous pioneer. As yet, of course, there was no word from John Cooper. Carlos, after conferring with Miguel who had met the New Orleans factor and learned something of the time it took sailing vessels to arrive at distant ports, had figured that it would still be a few weeks before there might be a letter from *el Halcón*.

Everything at the ranch was going along without a hitch. The children were enjoying the summer, and the *trabajadores* had completed the rebuilding and remodeling so that the construction was once again solid and secure.

This being so, Carlos determined to take his honeymoon with Teresa by journeying back to Taos. He had discussed this with her on the evening of the *fiesta*, and she had welcomed the idea. She looked forward to seeing her majordomo and some of the loyal old servants who had accompanied her from Havana after her elderly husband's death. Also, remembering the gracious hospitality of Don Sancho de Pladero and his wife, Doña Elena, she was eager to pay a courtesy call. The prospect of a long journey on horseback delighted her, for she had always been a good horsewoman.

Carlos asked Doña Inez and Bess Sandarbal to look after Inez and Dawn. Diego, who was a month older than Andrew Baines, could look after himself, and at the moment he was engaged in a deepening friendship with Francesca. Each respected the other, and both of them had a communal interest, secret treasure, hidden away, just as Jim Bowie had told them, when he had made his visit shortly after John Cooper's departure for Argentina. They shared this interest with old Jeremy Gaige, who was formulating in his own mind plans to go out and find the treasure Bowie had told him about.

To make Carlos's joy complete, on the evening of the *fiesta*, Teresa had whispered to him, "I am with child. So far as I can tell, it will be born by the end of next January or by early February." Carlos had taken her hand and kissed it and said, "I am the luckiest of men, and I pray to *el Señor Dios* always to be worthy of you, *mi corazón*." He had, with a typical husband's concern, hesitated a moment after both of them had discussed the prospect of going to Taos. Teresa, who understood his sudden hesitation after both of them had been so eager, had come to him, put her arms around him, then whispered into his ear, teasingly, *"Mi esposo,* you have not married a Dresden doll. There are Indian women who bear their children in the fields, and an hour later are picking corn, or curing the hide of a buffalo. It is a long way off before I shall be discommoded. Meanwhile, we are young and in love with each other, so let us be by ourselves along the trail back to Taos."

So, ten days after the *fiesta,* Carlos and Teresa rode off to Taos with an escort of two *trabajadores,* Manuel Mircante and José Yradier. In their late twenties, Manuel and José were expert marksmen and had helped defend the ranch when Francisco López had launched the savage nocturnal attack the previous year. They drove a supply wagon containing provisions, including food; presents for the Jicarilla Apache, whom they would visit; and even fencing equipment, for Carlos and Teresa expected to have plenty of time to practice with foils, as they loved to do. Carlos and Teresa also looked forward to having the time to go hunting and to kill enough game along the way to augment their provender.

There was also a secret reason that motivated Carlos to leave the complacent luxury of the *hacienda* for the open trail. John Cooper had told him of Kinotatay's gloomy forecast that he, Kinotatay, would not live much longer, and the handsome young Spaniard was anxious to visit the Jicarilla Apache chief before he died, and to introduce him to his new wife.

More than ever, Carlos felt a mystic tie between himself and his blood brothers, the Jicarilla Apache. So much had happened in his life because of his association with the Indians of the stronghold. Through John Cooper, he had been taken to them and met Weesayo. Then, when Santa Anna's two spies had shot him down and left him for dead, he had been nursed back to health by them. This time, he would go there with Teresa, and she would show the Apache how she respected their customs and their way of life. Yes, it would be a wonderful augury for their future life together.

They set out at early dawn. Teresa leaned over from her horse and quickly kissed Carlos on the mouth. "I am so content, Carlos," she said, shifting back and drawing her horse away from his. "I am so content with my life. I must apologize that I made you wait so long for my hand in marriage, but it did not hurt you in the least."

"Oh, is that so?" he countered, and made a wry face at her that set her off into peals of laughter. Suddenly she galloped forward, looking back and calling out, "Come race me!"

Behind them in the wagon, Manuel and José smiled to see their young *patrón* and his *esposa* in such good humor. They themselves were still bachelors, but already each of them had come to some kind of understanding with a lovely *criada*. In due time they would be married and know what it was to be a householder.

Twenty-one

Neither Carlos nor Teresa knew that their visit to Taos would come at a time of chaos. Doña Elena de Pladero had debated several times on the wisdom of sending a letter to the *Hacienda del Halcón* to acquaint Don Diego with the turbulent state of affairs that she had found upon her sorrowful return the previous year. Mourning her husband Don Sancho, who had died the year before, she had sought consolation back in Taos with her grandchildren and her son, Tomás, and his Conchita.

But the new *alcalde mayor*, Alonzo Cienguarda, who had married his former mistress, Luisita Delago, had undertaken to turn his post into a dictatorship, making life miserable for everyone except his cronies and favorites. He could flout public opinion in Taos because he basked in the favor of *el gubernador* of Nuevo México at Santa Fe, Antonio Narbona, because he was able to send larger tithes to the governor's coffers than any previous *alcalde mayor* before him. There had been petitions from a few of the *hacendados* near Taos, complaining over the high-handedness of the new *alcalde mayor;* Governor Narbona had simply tabled these and ordered his secretary to dispatch a brief, almost rebuking answer: "Your *alcalde mayor* has my complete confidence and trust, for he has proved himself. After all, you are one of the *ricos,* and you should not, therefore, whine over paying a few more *pesos* to maintain your high-ranking position in the province. Be content, and remember that in the Scriptures it says, 'The Lord loveth a cheerful giver.' "

To compound matters, Governor Narbona had actually had his secretary send copies of these letters and his replies to Cienguarda, who could show them to any malcontent and intimate that continued protestation against his policies was tantamount to treason. That would give him the pretext, if he needed one, to punish those who spoke out against him, or who opposed his edicts.

The year before, Cienguarda had levied a tax of a *peso* per month on every male and female inhabitant of the pueblo village who sold wares or services. In addition, anticipating that the Pueblo Indians might be driven to revolt by this onerous tax, he had decreed that it was necessary to establish a local militia to protect the citizens of Taos. His argument was that, since the capital was in Mexico City many hundreds of miles away, Taos could expect neither civil nor military support.

He had sent for an old friend of his from San Luis Potosí, Ferdinand Mondago. He had appointed Mondago as *jefe de policía* and inscribed his name on the city payroll at a salary of two thousand *pesos* per annum. Mondago would be his legal enforcer, with autocratic powers coming from Cienguarda himself. To meet this huge expenditure, as well as to build revenue that would provide for his militia, he ordered that each *hacendado* in Taos was to pay a hundred *pesos* semiannually.

Finally, and it was the straw that broke the back of the Pueblo Indians, Cienguarda reasoned that, since the *indios* would also benefit from the protection that his new chief of police would provide, every pueblo dweller, including children, was to pay an additional tax of fifty *centavos* per month. If an *indio* household was comprised of a husband, wife, and six children, the husband would be obliged to pay four *pesos* a month to the collector of tithes. To make certain that there was no lapse in collections, Cienguarda had appointed his own majordomo to the post of collector.

Armando Díaz, a fat, lazy man of forty-six, had worked on Cienguarda's estate during the fatal illness of the former's first wife. He was a man who took the path of least resistance and had never questioned the death of his employer's first wife, whom Cienguarda had poisoned. Finding him so trustworthy, his master had doubled his wages. Now, he had received another reward by being named collector of tithes. His master cynically commented, "Armando, so long as you see to it that my coffers are filled, I do not care what happens to the rest." This carte blanche was exactly the sort of bribe that had cemented Díaz's loyalty to his master, though at the cost of infuriating the poor, helpless, Pueblo Indians.

Not content with all this, Alonzo Cienguarda and his unscrupulous, beautiful new wife had increased the tariffs, which, though allowing American traders like Matthew Robisard and Ernest Henson to legally enter Santa Fe and Taos to sell their wares, imposed so stringent a tax upon them that this opportunity become prohibitive. For instance, Jeremiah Calder, an intrepid divinity student from Boston who had turned his back on the ministry and come to St. Louis to live with a distantly related cousin, had become a trader like his cousin. Two months earlier, he had traveled along the Santa Fe Trail with five men and a dozen burros loaded with trade goods. As he and his company had neared Taos and ridden along on the mountain road beneath the Sangre de Cristo, they had halted at the angry order of the *jefe de policía* himself.

Ferdinand Mondago, resplendent in his uniform—a white shako with green plumes, black breeches, and shiny new leather riding boots with vicious spurs—had held up his hand and, with an imperious gesture, beckoned to his men to examine the load of goods strapped to the backs of the burros. "Now then, señores," he arrogantly addressed the traders, "explain your purpose in coming to our peaceful Taos!"

Jeremiah Calder turned to his men and muttered, "Just take it easy, boys; we don't want any trouble. Let's see what this fancy dressed galoot has got in mind. Damn it all, after this long trek out here, we've got to sell our goods, or we'll really be in debt!"

Cordially, the American trader had smiled at Mondago and answered, "We're bringing trade goods to Taos and Santa Fe, señor. We mean no harm. We had heard that trading is open now, since you've broken away from the Mexican government."

"How dare you, *gringo* dog, tell me what the laws are here?" Mondago sneered. "You must have a permit from His Excellency, the *alcalde mayor* of Taos, before my men and I will allow you to pass."

"All right, then. I don't mind getting a license."

Mondago ordered his men to open the bales of trade goods strapped to the burros' backs, while Calder fumed and forced himself to be silent, lest he offend this garishly dressed official. After the inspection was completed, Mondago turned to him and sneeringly said, "I will save you some time, *señor gringo*. I have the authority from the *alcalde mayor* himself to issue a temporary license. But you will have to pay for it. My men tell me that the goods you have here demand a levy of two hundred dollars. You may pay this to me, and I myself will give you a permit. Unless you do it, my men and I will confiscate your goods and turn you back."

"Like I thought, boys, it's a shakedown," the trader muttered to his companions. "But we've got to go along with it because, otherwise, we'd be in real trouble." In Spanish, he said to Mondago, "I'll buy a license from you."

"Now that is being sensible, *señor gringo*," the *jefe de policía* mockingly responded as he lifted his hat and then replaced it on his head. "Let me see the color of your money, and you shall have your permit."

Glumly, the trader paid over the bribe, after which Mondago cynically remarked, "*Gracias, señor americano.* Pedro, you can read and write, so be kind enough to write out the *gringo* a pass, and I will sign it." Then, to the trader, he smirkingly added, "This will take you through Taos and Santa Fe. But when you return, señor, you must report to my office in the town square and declare the amount received from the sale of your goods. Then you will pay an additional tax for the privilege of leaving and not going to our *cárcel* with your men for breaking our law. Is that understood, *gringo?*"

Grudgingly, the Missourian nodded, accepted from the grinning corporal of police, Pedro Dismarda, the sheet of paper with a few scrawled words in Spanish that Mondago had signed. "Now be on your way, *gringo*," Mondago told him.

The trader and his men, greatly relieved, drove their burros along the trail, and Mondago looked over to his troop and chuckled. "That was very well done, Pedro. We shall watch the roads when the *gringo* returns, and we shall levy an even greater tax on him. He will have money to pay the tax after his sales, and he will want no trouble with us."

Out of the two hundred dollars that the Missourian had paid to the scheming *jefe de policía*, Ferdinand Mondago returned a hundred dollars to Alonzo Cienguarda, who was highly satisfied with the vigilant work of his subordinate. This was but one example of the ruthless power that Governor Narbona's friend wielded since being appointed to the post of *alcalde mayor* of Taos.

Like the *alcalde mayor*, his beautiful, amoral wife lost no opportunity to flaunt her wealth and torment the poor Indians of the pueblo. When she rode into the public square, she was invariably dressed in all her finery of silk and satin gowns, or elegantly embroidered riding jackets and skirts, lavishly decorated with jewelry. There was a sneer on her lovely face whenever she saw an elderly *indio* hobbling to a shop to attempt to sell his wife's woven blankets or beaded trinkets, in order to have a few more *pesos* with which to buy food and clothing, as well as to pay the exorbitant tax which her husband had levied upon Indians of the pueblo.

Aware that her husband was the favorite of *el gubernador*, Luisita Cienguarda felt that the people existed only to satisfy her needs and those of her husband. Now that Ferdinand Mondago had asserted himself in his new post as chief of police of Taos, Cienguarda's wife had only to indicate this or that *peón* or *indio* who had been insolent to her, and the unfortunate culprit was jailed and forced to stand trial before a hostile court. As an example, Rocaldi, a stout, pleasant-natured *indio* in his mid-forties, had irked Luisita the previous June. He was in the plaza and saw her reprimand an old woman who had sought to sell her a bunch of mountain flowers so that she might buy medicine for her ailing daughter. Luisita had taken the flowers from the woman and had flung them into the dust, telling her coachman to drive on and not to stop for beggars again or her husband would have the man whipped. Rocaldi had uttered a cry of horror at this indignity to poor old Marsida and could not restrain himself from exclaiming, "Have you no heart, woman? Do you not see the aged and the crippled and how unfortunate they are, as compared with you?"

Luisita Cienguarda had not had the Indian punished for this insolence because when she got home, her husband presented her with a new emerald necklace, making her forget, at least temporarily, Rocaldi's insult. But then this same *indio* crossed her path again, this time just a few days earlier. She was once again in the plaza, shopping for some fine silk with which to make an attractive *mantilla*, when, coming out of the shop and heading for her carriage, Rocaldi rode by on his scrawny burro. The animal had defecated on the street just a few yards from where Luisita was crossing, and she saw this as a deliberate and supreme affront. When she returned to her *villa*, she described this incident to her husband, reminding him also of Rocaldi's behavior the previous year. "Can you imagine, Alonzo, *querido*! First that Indian dared to threaten me, all because I would not be importuned by a beggar woman with her miserable flowers; then he has the temerity to allow his filthy animal to pollute the streets. Decidedly, you must protect your wife in public; you must punish that *indio!*"

Cienguarda weighed the balance scale between pleasing his wife and antagonizing the lowly *indios;* his lust for Luisita won over all other considerations. That was why, at about the time when Teresa and Carlos were nearing the Jicarilla stronghold, Ferdinand Mondago, with two privates belonging to Cienguarda's militia, entered the Pueblo Indian village with a warrant for the arrest of Rocaldi. His wife, eight years his senior, was ill, and his twenty-year-old daughter Epanone, betrothed to a young brave two years older than herself, was in the yard of their *jacal*, weaving blankets, when the pompous, burly *jefe de policía* swaggeringly pushed his way past the little rickety wooden gate and entered the *jacal*. Aghast, the young woman rose and uttered a stifled cry as she saw her father being dragged out by the two militia privates. "But what has my father done?" Epanone plaintively demanded.

"Quiet, *mujer*, it is not your concern. I arrest him on the charge of treason. He has dared to insult the wife of our *alcalde mayor*," Mondago declared. "Pay no attention to her, *hombres;* take the man to the *palacio* of the *alcalde mayor!*"

Epanone uttered an anguished cry as the two soldiers dragged out her father, gripping his elbows and pulling them behind his back to make him march almost on tiptoe. When she tried to intervene, Mondago brutally struck her across the

— side of the face and knocked her to the ground. "Let that be a lesson to you, *puta!* Do not interfere with the justice of Alonzo Cienguarda! If you say another word, I shall have my men take you next, and perhaps a touch of the whip will teach you better manners, Indian slut!"

Epanone lay weeping, watching the soldiers force her father out and toward the center of the town, where he would be taken to the *palacio* of the *alcalde mayor* to await sentence.

Staggering to her feet and weeping while rubbing the flaming mark on her cheek where Mondago's brutal blow had bruised her, she made her way into the hut of her parents, to check on her ailing mother and relate what had been done to her father.

There was worse to come. Two hours later, the same two soldiers dragged the stout, mild-mannered *indio* out into the street and toward a platform, where Alonzo Cienguarda had had erected a pillory and a whipping post. Rocaldi was to suffer this humiliation as a warning to the other Indians not to revolt against their *alcalde mayor.*

This represented Cienguarda's authority over the villagers of Taos. He wanted to show the lowly *indios* that he meant to rule without mercy or consideration. By doing this, he ignored the law passed several years before that gave the Indians rights as citizens. Who, after all, would be the spokesman for these worthless dogs who did not deserve to be on an equal with the *ricos?* With his militia gaining power and strength, he knew that no one would dare complain to Governor Narbona; even if it were done, the *gubernador* would sustain him over the complaint of an insignificant nobody.

So Rocaldi found himself locked in the pillory all the long sweltering afternoon, till he nearly fainted with thirst. At sundown, Mondago himself appeared on the platform and released the victim, turning to the dozen *indios* who had gathered in silent protest. "I warn you," he declared, "that there is to be no rebellion. What you see here was an act of justice, punishment for an offense. It would have been the same had the man been a *rico.*"

One of the young braves muttered to his companion, "That is a lie. What are we to do?"

His friend whispered back, "Someone must tell Ticumbe what this *alcalde mayor* does to our people. It will grow worse. This man and his wife have no love for us, and they will grind us into the dust."

The Pueblo Indians who, in compassionate, angry silence, had watched the pillorying of Rocaldi, went back to their village and sent old Maguay as their spokesman to the hut of Ticumbe. No elder in the village was more respected than Ticumbe, who had once been a member of the Comanche tribe, the Wanderers. He had married a Mexican girl, whom he had captured in a village across the Rio Grande, and had two sons by her, only to have a fellow tribesman kill her and the children when she had refused to yield to him and thus betray Ticumbe.

The powerful Comanche had pursued the murderer and killed him with his bare hands, and it was said that Padre Juan Moraga—who had been the priest in Taos when John Cooper first arrived there so many years earlier—had witnessed it and fearlessly demanded that Ticumbe explain so brutal an act. The two men had spoken for a long while, and Padre Moraga had begged Ticumbe to return to Taos and become a Christian. He had done this, and ever since that day many years before, he had lived in the village of the Pueblo Indians, learned their language, and become a faithful *católico*. He had pursued the trade of blacksmith, at which he was expert. Because of his great courage and his conversion, and because the name of Comanche was still the most feared in all of the Southwest, he had won the respect of every villager. His wisdom, born out of the tragedy of his life and his conversion to the Christian faith, had made everyone turn to him for advice and counsel.

He was working now at his forge, in the extension of his hut, which he had built with his own hands. As he had done with the martyred Padre Moraga, Ticumbe visited his successor, Padre Madura, and each week gave a small portion of the money he had earned that past week as a contribution to the little church.

He was tall, lean, and dark brown from the sun that had beaten down upon him during the many years when he had ridden with the Wanderers. His hair was white, and the week before, he had celebrated his fifty-third birthday. Many of the villagers said among themselves that a man so proud should have a woman to cook for him, if no more; but Ticumbe had refused to grant himself this indulgence. Indeed, even some

of the attractive younger girls of the village had told their
parents that they would deem it an honor to be wed to such a
valiant elder. He had been approached by those parents, but
calmly and gently he had refused, using words that would not
demean them or make them lose face. "It was not meant by
el Señor Dios for me to have anyone to replace my Jiralda.
No other woman ever gave me such joy, and with her death I
took a vow of celibacy. Now that I am *católico*, I endure by
myself, and I pay tribute to Him who brought me to salvation in His name and to this village, where you are all my
friends."

There were some eighty braves who clustered in front of
Ticumbe's huge *jacal* and watched feeble old Maguay go
toward the door and call out, in his wavering, cracked voice,
"Ticumbe, heed us! We have need of your wisdom! Come
speak to us, my brother!"

From the *jacal* they could hear the clanking of metal on
metal, and they could smell the smoke of the forge. The noise
ceased, and Ticumbe came to the entrance of the *jacal* and
faced his audience. "Maguay, I know you. Why do you call
on me as your brother?" he demanded.

"Because there is evil in Taos, *hombre*," old Maguay
told him. "The *alcalde mayor* has done a terrible thing. He
has put Rocaldi into the pillory so that all might mock him.
All because the *mujer* of our *alcalde* says he insulted her.
Now, the *alcalde mayor* has used Rocaldi as an example to
us, to show us all how little he thinks of us. We are dogs who
should be driven from the campfire, and we are not even
worthy of a bone that he would toss to us. What are we to
do, Ticumbe?"

The blacksmith stood there, still holding his hammer
from the forge. He looked out at the eager, questioning faces,
and there was a long silence. Suddenly it was broken as
Epanone, the young daughter of Rocaldi, came shoving her
way through the villagers, sobbing hysterically, "My father
has killed himself! It was too much shame! He died by his
own hand, and the *alcalde mayor* is his murderer! And my
mother, seeing it done, closed her eyes and followed my father in death!"

There was a gasp of horror as the crowd made way for
her. She stood, her fists clenched, tears running down her
cheeks, facing Ticumbe. Epanone had been Christianized,
too, and Padre Madura himself had given her lessons in the

faith and rehearsed her catechism. That, perhaps, was why she showed such public grief, for it was not the way of the Pueblo Indian, any more than that of the Comanche, the Apache, or all the strong tribes of the southern Plains. They bore their sorrows and torments in impassive silence.

"My daughter," Ticumbe spoke at last, "I can say no words to comfort you. But we know what he did for us and the dignity and honor he preserved for all of us. It will be remembered."

"How? When he is dust in the grave, a suicide, not even buried by the Church in which he believed?" the young woman hysterically retorted, striking her bosom with her fists. "You will do nothing! You will remember him and never again speak his name, and that will be his memorial. It is not enough! Do you not see what this *alcalde* and his *puta* are doing to all of you? He will not be content, nor will she, till all of us are dust, and this village forgotten."

Old Maguay, who had stood facing Ticumbe during the young woman's bitter denunciation, now tried to intervene. "Epanone, it is not right to speak to Ticumbe so. What would you have us do?"

"Be men, not fawning dogs who lick the hand that cuffs you," Epanone scornfully retorted as the tears still streamed down her face. Then she turned and flung out her arms to all of them, sobbing, "Avenge him! Oh, if I were a man, I would lead you with any weapon I could find, be it bow or lance or knife!"

"Epanone," Ticumbe at last spoke in his deep voice, "I share your sorrow. But this is not the way to avenge your father. Instead, we will go to the *casa* of the *alcalde mayor*. We shall tell him that his taxes are unjust, and that we are men, not slaves. This is what we will say to Alonzo Cienguarda."

"He will spit on you," Epanone sobbed. She covered her face with her hands and ran blindly through the crowd, which separated to let her pass, back to the hut of her father, where he lay on his pallet, his knife driven into his heart.

The villagers muttered among themselves, but Ticumbe held up his hand and addressed them. "Epanone is a woman, not a warrior. We who are still warriors and who have learned to live in peace among the *wasichus* are sometimes, as now, driven to desperate means. The *alcalde mayor* wishes for this. If we rise against him, he will have all the excuse he needs to kill us and call us rebellious mongrels who must be

exterminated. The only course is to go to his house and speak
to him. If we are strong and speak with one voice, perhaps he
will understand that we will not live in fear like slaves who
grovel before a tyrant."

Old Maguay turned to the villagers. "Ticumbe is right.
This is what we must do. Let us all march together to the
house of the *alcalde mayor*."

There were whisperings and murmurings here and there
before the villagers called out their agreement.

They left their village, some sixty of them, marching
slowly in rows of twos, toward the sumptuous *casa* of Alonzo
Cienguarda on the outskirts of Taos.

Although Alonzo Cienguarda had told Governor Narbona that he would be content with a modest little house, and
did not care to take over the *casa* of Don Sancho de Pladero,
he had built for himself a magnificent mansion with several
wings, a sumptuous courtyard ornate with flowers, shrubs,
and trees, a stable, and a bunkhouse for his newly appointed
militia. Some fifty men resided in the bunkhouse. At least
half of them had been imported from the provinces of Durango and Chihuahua, ne'er-do-wells who would do anything
for *dinero*.

On the evening of Rocaldi's humiliation and subsequent
suicide, Cienguarda was dining in his elegantly furnished dining room, attended by half a dozen lovely young *criadas*,
with his voluptuous young wife, Luisita, his *jefe de policía*,
Ferdinand Mondago, and his majordomo, Armando Díaz.
The *jefe* had served, in this instance, as both judge and jury,
and he was there to report that Rocaldi had seemed a broken
man when released from the pillory. "I tell you, Your Excellency, we shall have no more trouble with these Indian dogs.
When they saw Rocaldi skulking away, dripping with sweat
from the hot sun, I am sure they learned a lesson. No, Your
Excellency, you may be quite sure that there will be no further rebellion from these despicable curs."

"Thank you, Ferdinand," Cienguarda replied. He was
nearly forty-nine, tall and haughty, with a military bearing,
slim waist, straight shoulders, and the face of an intellectual
ascetic. He lifted his glass and made an impatient gesture to
the nearest *criada* to fill it again with a fine French Bur-
gundy. Frowning, he drawled, "Luisita, *mi amada*, you must
be more severe with the servants. They are getting into

slovenly habits, like that Pía there, who neglects filling her master's glass with wine."

"I will have Díaz give her a good whipping in the morning, *mi corazón*," his voluptuous wife propitiatingly declared.

"High time, too."

The young girl, who was not more than eighteen, began to tremble and then sob, stifling the sounds with the palm of her hand as she hurried out of the refectory. Armando Díaz, stroking his beard, looked after her with a lustful glint in his eyes. It would be a joy to lay the whip on so charming a *muchachita*, he thought to himself. He was certain that, in view of her terror—for she had been whipped once before by him and had sworn that she could not bear such torment— she would be willing to exchange her favors for his leniency in applying the stripes to her satiny olive skin.

"Well now, my good friends," Cienguarda smiled at his *jefe* and majordomo, "I have entrusted you with special powers. Ferdinand, you have served me well as *jefe de policía*. Tonight, I appoint you to a higher status. Of course there will be compensation for your extra work."

"Your Excellency is far too kind to a humble servant," Ferdinand Mondago floridly answered, inclining his head.

"From this moment on, Ferdinand, you are not just *jefe de policía* but also *capitán* of my militia. Remember, these soldiers must be ready to quell any uprising within a moment's notice."

"You can trust me, Your Excellency," Mondago said, beaming and rubbing his hands in anticipation. Lecherous as he was, the thought of having even more power over the Indians excited him. There were many attractive young women in the village, and it would be child's play to coerce anyone who struck his fancy into submitting to him, in order to save her father or brother or *novio* from being imprisoned or publicly shamed as that stupid fool of a Rocaldi had been.

"Now you, Armando," Cienguarda said, turning to his majordomo, who was glowering at this mark of favor being extended to Mondago, "do not look so sour. You will, of course, retain your function as steward of my household, and you will still represent me as the collector of taxes that I have levied against the *ricos* as well as the *indios*. I suspect already, knowing your efficiency, that you have pocketed a few *pesos* out of the money you have obtained."

At this remark, Díaz flushed and looked uncomfortable,

but Cienguarda reassuringly laughed and added, "I am not vexed with you, Armando. You are entitled to a commission, shall we call it, for your efforts."

"Thank you, Your Excellency," Díaz said, looking less disgruntled.

"Now then, Ferdinand," Cienguarda said, turning again to his *jefe*, "you will conduct military drills at least three times a week. I want these men proficient in the art of weapons, in the event that *los indios* decide to cause trouble."

"I shall take charge of my responsibilities with an eager heart, *excelencia*." Mondago was radiant with pride at this elevation of his status and the augmentation of the power that he could use so unscrupulously on his own behalf.

Luisita turned to her husband. *"Mi esposo,* do you think that fifty soldiers are enough to keep these Indian beggars in their place?" she asked.

"Come now, my dove," Cienguarda said as he reached out to stroke the back of her neck while, at the same time, eyeing his guests as much as to say, *how delicious she is, and she's all mine.* "The fact is that my fifty are armed, and *los indios* have at most some lances and bows and arrows. I doubt that there are many guns or *pistolas* in their village. Incidentally, Ferdinand, that is something for you to see to, in the future. You and your militia should search those *jacales* from time to time, to make certain that no weapons are being collected that might be used against the authority of Taos."

"Consider it done, Excellency," the *jefe* staunchly retorted and reached for his glass of wine, which he drained with a gulp. Luisita made a covert grimace, for she did not like his manners, and for that matter, she did not care very much, either, for Armando Díaz, the majordomo.

"Now then," Cienguarda exclaimed, "shall we enjoy some good coffee and brandy? For you, Luisita, my dove, I have an especially fine cordial, which I think you will enjoy."

He rang the little silver bell at his right hand several times, his eyebrows arching in a supercilious frown of impatience.

Before the kitchen door could be opened for one of the servants to enter and take his order, a tall, short-bearded servant in his mid-thirties, dressed in red and black livery, hurried into the dining room, visibly frightened and almost breathless. "Forgive me for intruding, *señor alcalde mayor,* but there is a group of many *indios* outside in the courtyard, and they demand to see you."

"Ten thousand devils out of hell!" Alonzo Cienguarda swore as he sprang from his chair, his eyes narrowed and angry. "Ferdinand, go out the kitchen door and to the bunkhouse. Assemble your militia at once; have them prime and load their rifles and *pistolas*. Order the men in a flanking movement around the side of the *casa*, to make certain that you have these beggars under control."

"At once, *excelencia*," Mondago hastily agreed as he got up from his chair and hurried out to the kitchen.

Led by Ticumbe and venerable old Maguay, the aggrieved villagers had marched to the sumptuous house of the *alcalde mayor*. Epanone had insisted on going with them. She had tearfully told Ticumbe, "I shall go mad if I stay in that *jacal* with my father's and mother's dead bodies. I beg you, Ticumbe, let me come with you and, when we go back, help me get a Christian burial for my parents and find a *jacal* for me where I can perhaps forget the horrors that I have seen this day!"

Old Maguay murmured to Ticumbe, "See how the *alcalde mayor* lives. This is a house that would shelter a hundred of our villagers. This he enjoys at the expense of our poverty and wretchedness. Surely the Great Spirit turned His face away from us on the day when Don Diego de Escobar left Taos and then his good friend, Don Sancho de Pladero, was called before Him. Since then, we have no one but you, Ticumbe, to speak for us."

"But do not forget Padre Madura," the white-haired former Comanche murmured. "Did you not know that he has become one of *Los Hermanos Penitentes*—the order of Penitent Brothers? He and his brothers have done much to offset the cruelties and injustices in Taos. You well know how the *sangrador* of the *Penitentes* has punished with his whip the servants of the *ricos* for the evils they have done against our people and how even the *ricos* themselves have been forced to pay tithes. Padre Madura is stronger than you think. And his faith, a faith that all of us have in Him who created us, makes us stronger than if we had weapons."

"Yes, Ticumbe, I know. But even *Los Penitentes* have been unable to drive fear into the heart of our evil *alcalde*. He has forbidden them to meet now, and his police chief keeps an eye out for them so that they can no longer make their nocturnal visits to unscrupulous *hacendados* and bring them to justice in the name of *Jesú Cristo*."

"Yes, all this is true, Maguay, but like Padre Madura we must be strong in our faith. We must also remember the blood that runs in our veins. You know that long years before even you or I were born, Popé led the *indios* of the pueblo against their cruel taskmasters, the *conquistadores*. I do not say that violence is the way, but we must be able to fight back. Wait, the servant who saw us comes back to the door now. Perhaps he has brought the *alcalde mayor* out to speak with us, as we requested."

The door opened, and Alonzo Cienguarda stared with widened eyes at the group of Pueblo Indians who waited in front of his enormous *casa*.

"Why have so many of you left your village at night to come to disturb me when I am entertaining guests?" Cienguarda demanded.

"It was not our wish to disturb anyone, *excelencia*," Ticumbe spoke placatingly, "only to ask you to ease the burden of the taxes that you have placed upon us. The trade is not good this year, and many *americanos* no longer come to Taos because of the tariff that you have restored, and that we had thought would be removed once Nuevo México gained its independence from Nueva España."

"Do you dare to question my authority as *alcalde mayor* of Taos?" Cienguarda demanded.

"No, *excelencia*. I ask only that you understand what difficulties we face. Is it not better to take some revenue that we can afford and that still gives us the chance to survive in peace, than to oppress us, so that we starve and see our children without hope, our old people without food or shelter?" Ticumbe parried.

"I know your name, Ticumbe. Take care that you do not offend me, for I have the power to clap you into the pillory, as I had done with Rocaldi this very day."

"That is true, *excelencia*. What you may not know is that, in his shame, Rocaldi took his own life," Ticumbe responded.

"That is no concern of mine. He should have thought of the consequences before he dared insult my *esposa*. It was necessary to make an example. You have never had the power over a province as I have, Ticumbe, and so you cannot understand what must be done if there is rebellion and dissension."

"But this rebellion and dissension of which you speak, *excelencia,* comes from your actions against us."

"Take care, Ticumbe, you are dangerously close to speaking treason. You would be better advised to go back to your village and hold your tongue."

During this dialogue, Ferdinand Mondago had assembled the militia. Some thirty of them, in their uniforms and carrying their rifles, bayonets, and pistols, hurried out of the bunkhouse behind him and around the left side of the great house.

Ticumbe, exerting all his patience and with a weary smile on his thin lips, once again tried to reason with the *alcalde.* "*Excelencia,* we are not here to speak of treason. Our people were here centuries before yours came. But that is not the issue. Surely your people and mine can live together in peace. All we ask is a lessening of these taxes."

"If this is all you have to say to me," Cienguarda snapped, "I order you to go back to your village. All of you, or I shall have you dispersed, and those who oppose me will find themselves wishing they had not been so brash. Know that, so long as I am *alcalde mayor* of Taos, you, as well as the *ricos,* will obey my orders. To make certain that you do not yield to the temptation of doing battle with me, I shall have my *jefe* search your huts. If he finds any weapons, he will confiscate them. Those of you who cannot explain why you have loaded weapons will find that your punishment will be much worse than Rocaldi got. That is all I have to say to you."

He turned as if to go back into the *hacienda,* but Epanone suddenly cried out, "You call yourself a Christian? You take what little bread we have and you do not even show sympathy for me, who now has neither father nor mother! May your days be filled with the remembrance of the evil things you have done to us, and your nights filled with nightmares that will make you sweat in terror!"

At this moment, around the side of the house, the uniformed militia came, led by Ferdinand Mondago. His voice, high-pitched with excitement, broke out: "Form in ranks of four; aim your rifles and *pistolas* at these insolent dogs!"

Old Maguay saw the militia and began to tremble as he murmured to Ticumbe, "We have been betrayed. There is no hope for us. They would shoot us down like mad dogs, and they will not even listen to what little we ask."

Mondago, aware that his employer's eyes were on him, now came forward, drawing a pistol from its holster and aiming it at Ticumbe's heart. "Go back to your village, all of you! I will give the order to fire on you, if you stay here to make trouble, Indian dogs!" he growled.

"We are men, not dogs," Ticumbe protested. "You, *alcalde mayor* of Taos, will not listen to us because we are Indians."

"I have no more to say to you, Ticumbe," Cienguarda snapped, drawing himself up and going back into the *hacienda*. Mondago moved forward till the muzzle of his pistol was pressed against the white-haired Indian's heart. "You heard His Excellency," he muttered. "I'll kill you; I swear I will, *por los cojones del diablo*! I will count to five. If, by then, you do not tell your followers to go back where they belong, I will pull the trigger, *¿comprendes?*"

Ticumbe drew himself up, his eyes calm, his face serene. "You may kill me. I am only a tool in the hands of the Great Spirit. But if you kill me, you will have all of the others to reckon with."

"I don't fear your pack of dirty dogs!" Mondago blustered. "One . . . two . . . three . . ."

"In the name of mercy, he's an old man. How can you shoot him down in cold blood?" Epanone cried.

Mondago glanced at her, remembering her from earlier in the day, when he had her father arrested. His eyes glittered with lust. To one of the tall, thickly bearded militia soldiers nearest him, he muttered, "Don't shoot her, *amigo*. Capture her for me and take her to my quarters next to the bunkhouse."

"*Sí, mi capitán*," the soldier sniggered.

Now Mondago turned back to stare at Ticumbe, who had not budged an inch. The muzzle of the pistol was pressed against his heart, but he did not waver or withdraw. He continued to look steadfastly into Mondago's dilated, glassy eyes and saw the livid, contorted face of his murderer. Silently, he said a prayer to the Great Spirit that his death would not be in vain. "Four! Your last chance, Ticumbe. All right, then, you Indian dog, five! Die, as you deserve!" Mondago pulled the trigger.

There was a cry of horror. Ticumbe stiffened, his eyes

rolling in their sockets, then he toppled and lay inert. Epanone flung herself upon the dead Indian's body, wailing in her grief.

Two of the younger Pueblo Indians nearest Ticumbe rushed forward now, brandishing knives that had been hidden in their blankets. Three of the militia men fired point-blank, and the two young Indians fell dead near Ticumbe.

The others turned to flee, and the soldiers fired shots over their heads as Mondago bawled, "That's it; run to your kennels, you cowardly dogs! Don't try this again, or we'll come to your village and burn you out, ¿comprenden?"

The sergeant now advanced and bent over the still sobbing, prostrated Epanone. He seized her in his arms and dragged her around the *hacienda* and to the hut that Mondago had commandeered.

In the distance, far to the northwest, there was a low rumble of thunder. It was an ominous omen. The man whom Governor Narbona had appointed—out of friendship and in the belief that the former shared his own convictions toward a just peace and an equality for the Pueblo Indians—had defied all moral and written laws to set himself up as the reigning tyrant. This was only the beginning of the violence that would fall upon Taos.

After the crowd had dispersed, Ferdinand Mondago went to his master. "The worst troublemaker, that fool of a Ticumbe, defied me, *excelencia*," he boasted. "I gave him every chance to save himself. He defied me, and I killed him. Then two of those dogs tried to attack me and my men, but my brave soldiers shot them down. We fired into the air, and the rest fled back to their village. You will have nothing more to fear from the Pueblo Indians, I swear to you, *excelencia!*"

Alonzo Cienguarda had put on his red silk dressing gown and belted it. He stood outside his bedroom door, while in the great four-postered, canopied bed, his seductive wife awaited him, perfumed and ardent, ready to reward him for having avenged her honor by the punishment of Rocaldi.

"You are to be commended, *mi capitán*," he told the beaming Mondago. "Now listen carefully, and absorb it the first time, for I am weary. Doubtless one of those fools will take it into his head to go to Padre Madura, perhaps even to ride to Santa Fe to tell Governor Narbona what has been done tonight. Therefore, we must have a sufficient refutation of any lies they would convey to my good friend Antonio."

"I understand perfectly, *excelencia!*"

"Also, there is always the danger of revolt. Now that their leader is dead, they will be angry, and they may, like the mad dogs they are, strike without warning. Thus you must put down, once and for all, these rebels."

"I am all ears, *excelencia!*"

"Listen, yes, but use what brains *el Señor Dios* gave you also, *estúpido!*" Cienguarda irritatedly declared. "You will give extra wages to some of the best men in your army. Here is how they will serve you—and me into the bargain. You will have them dress like *los indios*. They will commit crimes. I do not wish to know what they will be, whether they steal women or horses or *dinero*. Let it be sufficient that they commit enough crimes so that the soldiers under your command will be justified to arrest the malefactors who, of course, will be the *indios del pueblo*. There will be a trial, and I myself will be the judge. Then these malefactors will be shot, or perhaps we may even restore the *garrote*. It is a very picturesque way of killing a man, Ferdinand, and it is a terrifying example to those who do not have the stomach for a slow, lingering death. You are familiar with it, I trust?"

Mondago gulped uneasily and put his hand to his throat.

"A man is placed in a chair, bound hand and foot and around the waist, so that he cannot budge. The executioner stands behind him with a rawhide thong and a length of solid metal. The thong is circled around the neck, and the executioner inserts the piece of metal between the flesh and the thong and twists. He may prolong death for hours that way, if he so chooses. In Madrid, I once saw a *puta* put to death like that because she had killed her lover, and he was a member of the nobility. She was very beautiful, and so the executioner prolonged it. What a spectacle it was!"

"I understand you fully. Your orders will be carried out."

"*Bueno.* Now, tomorrow morning, talk to the men who will play the role of Pueblo Indians, Ferdinand. *Buenas noches.* Do not disturb me for the rest of the night, or I'll demote you and cut your wages in half." With this, Cienguarda entered his bedroom where Luisita waited. He closed the door and locked it.

* * *

Before Ferdinand Mondago went into his hut, he dismissed the grinning sergeant, handing him a few silver *pesos*. "Do not disturb me till morning, Jaime," he ordered. "Directly after I have risen, I will select some of the men to go on an errand for the *alcalde mayor*. They will be paid additional wages for dressing like the Indians and committing crimes, so that we may take retribution on the stupid Indians of the pueblo. In the meantime, you will take temporary charge of the rest of the militia. You might have killed more *indios* tonight and rid us of a few more troublemakers."

"My apologies, *señor capitán*." The sergeant grinned and winked. "But the girl was in the way, and I knew that you did not wish to have her harmed—not that way, at least."

"Go to the devil with you! Get back to the barracks."

He watched until the sergeant had gone back to the bunkhouse and then, licking his lips in sensual anticipation, entered the hut and slammed the door shut.

Epanone lay on the bed, stripped naked, gagged and blindfolded, her wrists tied behind her back.

"Well now, *querida*," he chuckled as he began to disrobe, "I expect you to be very grateful to me. You could have been shot down like that fool of a Ticumbe and those other *indios* who wanted to show that they were heroes. If you are a very good girl, *muchachita*, I will keep you here as my *puta*. You will be well fed, better than the scraps they give you in the village. I may even buy you some pretty clothes. But now let us see how obliging you can be to your *capitán* who saved your life."

Epanone stiffened and murmured a silent prayer as he flung himself upon her, brutally ravishing her. For several hours he used her, till at last he was exhausted. Then, staggering over to the table where there was a half-filled bottle of tequila, he drank most of it down. He sprawled upon the bed and lay fast asleep and snoring, in a drunken stupor.

Epanone fought her bonds, as she had done throughout the prolonged rape. Finally, she freed her wrists, and took out the gag and removed the blindfold. She clambered out of bed, a hand against the wall, her eyes closed, steadying herself as waves of nausea swept through her.

When she had regained some of her strength, she made her way to the pile of his discarded garments and donned his uniform breeches and jacket and the shako. She looked for a weapon, but he had come unarmed, assured of her capitulation because she had been trussed up like an animal for the slaughter.

She had been a virgin until now. In one horrible day she had lost both parents and honor. Where could she turn for help? Now that Ticumbe had been murdered, who would lead the *indios* of the village against this butcher, this assassin?

Her eyes widened as she remembered. There was a tribe of Indians whose names were feared as men of courage who did not hesitate to give battle, even against hopeless odds, for their freedom. They were the Jicarilla Apache, and Kinotatay was their chief.

She would find a horse. It was not far to the stable, and she had heard Mondago tell the *sargente* about what he was going to have his men do. Somehow, she must get to Kinotatay and tell him what was being planned in Taos.

Very carefully, she opened the door and looked out. She could see the light of an oil lamp from the shuttered window of the bunkhouse, and she could hear jeering laughter, but there was no one on guard. The night was still.

She tiptoed toward the stable, glancing fearfully around her, and made her way to one of the stalls. There was a strong, black mare, and she whinnied. She put out her hand to stroke her muzzle, and the mare nuzzled her and whinnied again.

She did not need to saddle her; she knew how to ride bareback, and the horse was strong. It would be a long ride to the Jicarilla stronghold, but she must get there at all costs.

She could forget the violation of her body, her body that was marked with blotches and scratches and bruises from the lecherous embraces of Mondago. She could even forget what had been done to her father, for a greater evil loomed! Her people were going to be blamed for crimes they did not commit!

She mounted the mare and rode out into the night, lifting her eyes to the starless sky and saying a prayer to the Christian God and, for good measure, to the Great Spirit who had, through these many centuries, protected the Indians of the pueblo of Taos.

Twenty-two

Carlos and Teresa had taken a leisurely pace from the outset of their journey. From time to time, they had raced, and every afternoon, just before sundown, they practiced with the buttoned foils. Fencing was a reminder to Carlos of how he had first seen Teresa in those early days when she had come to the *hacienda* of Don Sancho de Pladero as a widow. In her riding costume, her eyes sparkling, her lovely face animated, she parried his lunges and thrusts, and the clash of steel that brought them face-to-face, smiling at each other in this mock rivalry, served to bind them even more closely together.

There was also Carlos's unspeakable happiness in knowing that Teresa would bear him a child, a child born of their love.

The trip was a lovely honeymoon, a leisurely journey to the stronghold where Carlos had met Weesayo and been taught that the brotherhood of man does not depend on the color of one's skin or one's habits. Yet there was also sadness as Carlos, his wife, and the two *vaqueros* approached the stronghold, for Carlos knew that Kinotatay had been ailing and had predicted that his own death would occur before many more moons. At least he would have one more opportunity to be reunited with his blood brother, the valiant *jefe* of the Jicarilla.

Their supplies from the wagon lasted longer than they had hoped, since Carlos and Teresa, both expert marksmen, rarely saw a day go by when they did not bring down game with their rifles. There were quail, partridges, fat ducks, and occasionally a small deer or rabbit. The *vaqueros* welcomed the meat, for both men were excellent cooks, causing Carlos to remark jokingly, "You will have no trouble finding wives, particularly if they learn that you are better in the kitchen than they are, *amigos*."

The first ominous note of the journey was struck just a week before they reached the stronghold. Along this route, they had seen few travelers. Then one day they saw, about a mile and a half to the north, six riders, behind whom were three heavy wagons driven by oxen. "They must be traders," Carlos remarked to Teresa. "I might ride up to them and see if they have any news from the United States, or can tell me anything about Santa Fe and Taos."

"Do that, *querido*. Since we shot two deer this morning, invite them to be our guests for supper this evening," his wife suggested.

Carlos smiled and leaned forward from his saddle to kiss her cheek. Teresa, on her horse beside him, impatiently cupped his face and turned his mouth so that their lips met. "I do not like being kissed on the cheek, *mi corazón*," she murmured, and there was a mischievous glint in her beautiful eyes. "It suggests a dutiful conjugal kiss, and it is far too early in our marriage for you to act so indifferently toward me." With this she gave him another long kiss on the mouth and whispered huskily, "I will say only that if these traders turn down our invitation for supper, I shall not be too disappointed. Then I can have you to myself, and you can persuade me in better ways than words how much you still love me. Go now!"

He tilted back his head and laughed, hearty ringing laughter. Then he galloped off toward the riders and soon caught up with them, waving his *sombrero* and calling out to them. As he drew abreast of them, the leader, a tall, lanky man with a long, red beard, called out affably, "Well now, stranger, good to see someone to talk to in this godforsaken country. Where are you bound for?"

"First an Indian stronghold in the mountains to meet my friends who live there, and then I'm off to Taos, *amigo*," Carlos explained. "I am Carlos de Escobar, and I used to live in Taos. I've come from the Double H Ranch near the Frio River."

"Tarnation, I know where that is. That's not too far from the Brazos, where old Eugene Fair's new settlement is," the red-bearded man said with a big, gap-toothed grin. "My name's Jeff Thorman, all the way from St. Looey. I'm a trader, and these others are my friends and partners. Meet

Davey Jessup, Cal Hennessey, Ed Farmington, George Kenzie, and Phil Oliver."

Carlos smilingly nodded toward each. "A pleasure to know you, *amigos*. You've plenty of trade goods bound for Taos and Santa Fe, I've no doubt?"

"That we have, Mr. de Escobar," Jeff Thorman agreed with a scowl as he glanced back at the wagons. These were driven by three half-breeds, whose Indian background served them both as scouts and fighters. "But don't go counting on the profits we'll make this trip from the size of our wagons. Fact is, this is our second trip, and we've already been pretty well told what's expected of us. They've got a high muckety-muck in Taos, 'pears like, and he's got a fellow he calls the *jefe de policía*—never could speak Spanish worth a damn; you'll excuse me for it—and he comes around with his hand out, or you don't pass through his town and on to Sante Fe."

Carlos was puzzled. "High tariffs? But I thought that went out when the Spanish gave up México and Nuevo México, as well."

"Seems like you haven't been around there for a spell, Mr. de Escobar," the St. Louis trader glumly countered. "Well, whatever the case, they got a bad 'un sitting on top of things there now, so an honest trader can hardly make a good dollar anymore. Yes, sir, if we don't make out this trip, I doubt we'll be back. I tell you, Mr. de Escobar, this fellow in Taos thinks he's a cut above everybody else, and he lets you know it. What was his name there, Ed?"

"Something like Ciengard, near as I can recollect," the thin, black-bearded trader proffered.

"Alonzo Cienguarda," Carlos said in a low voice. "Yes, the man Governor Narbona appointed when Don Sancho retired. My father's good friend was *alcalde mayor* before this man, Señor Thorman. He, any more than my own father, would never have charged you a *centavo* to bring your goods to Taos and on to Santa Fe for the fair. But I came here to see if you and your men would have supper with us. We're camped to the south of here. My wife and I shot two deer, and there is venison to eat."

"That's mighty friendly of you, Mr. de Escobar. Thanks a heap. You hear that, fellas?" Thorman was grinning from ear to ear. "You sure we won't be putting you to any trouble?"

"Not at all, señores. My wife and I have seen almost no one since we started from our ranch the third week of July."

"We'll be there with bells on. Maybe we can bring along something out of our supply wagons as our share," Jeff Thorman told him.

Carlos saluted the trader, then wheeled his horse and rode back to Teresa. He quickly explained about his meeting and, with a downcast look, added, *"Mi corazón,* since they're coming to dinner, we won't have that time alone together."

He looked so woebegone that she burst into laughter. "Never fear, *querido,"* she declared. "They will not stay all night. When we are quite alone and in the dark, there will be ample opportunity for me to prove my love for you."

Toward the end of July Carlos and Teresa reached the mountain of the Jicarilla stronghold. The stories the traders from St. Louis had told Carlos had filled him with a troubling presentiment. What Don Diego and Don Sancho de Pladero had feared had happened. Since governmental authority had been decentralized from Mexico City, and since the far-outlying provinces of Mexico itself were being left to shift for themselves, a tyrant had grasped the reins of government in Taos. Yet Carlos was now an outsider. He and his father had moved away from Taos to Texas, and his own opinions would count for nothing before a man like Alonzo Cienguarda. Such thoughts weighed on him as he approached the stronghold.

The Indian sentries, high above on ledges of the towering mountain, saw the little group come along the plain. With hands over their eyes to shield them from the blazing sun, they stared down to make out the tiny figures. They saw the wagon drawn by horses with the two *vaqueros* driving it, and the tall young man erect in his saddle and the woman beside him.

One of the sentries quickly mounted his horse and rode back up the narrow trail to the top of the mountain, where the Jicarilla stronghold was located. He told his chief what he had seen, and Kinotatay's first thought was that it might be *el Halcón,* who had found himself a new mate. It would be a helpful thing, a blessing for so active a man as his blood brother, to care for someone and to forget the cruelty of that unjust death dealt Catarina by the Mexican traitor.

Kinotatay turned to the young brave and said, "Dimargo, there will be visitors. The wagon they have brought with them will have to remain down on the plain, for harnessed to the wagon, the horses would find this climb up the mountain too arduous. Go now and see to them and bring the wagon to a place of safety for the night, which will soon be upon us."

"I hear and obey, *mi jefe*." The young brave saluted, hurried to his mustang, swung himself into the saddle, and rode swiftly down the trail and out of sight in a few moments.

A short time later, Carlos and Teresa rode up onto the level of the village, with the two *vaqueros* at a respectful distance behind them, riding on the workhorses. Kinotatay and Pastanari awaited them. Quickly dismounting, Carlos helped Teresa down and, taking her hand, led her to the ailing chief of the Jicarilla. "My blood brother, I have the honor to present *mi esposa querida*, Teresa, to you."

"It is an honor for me to meet you at last, Kinotatay," Teresa said. She did not offer her hand, knowing the Apache customs, for Carlos had briefed her during their journey to the stronghold. The tall Apache inclined his head and smilingly responded, "You are more than welcome, Señora de Escobar. I can tell by the way you look at my blood brother that the two of you are happy together."

"Oh, yes, Kinotatay!" Teresa smiled radiantly.

"That is good." Kinotatay turned to Carlos, and together they made one of the signs of blood brotherhood, a clasping together of their arms.

Kinotatay at last presented the former Chief Descontarti's son, now a man, married and with two sons and a daughter. "Here is Pastanari. It will be he who takes my place as *jefe* of the Jicarilla."

"It is good to see you again, Pastanari," Carlos greeted him. "You know my wife, who is now Señora Teresa de Escobar."

"I thought it would happen, *mi amigo*," Pastanari smilingly responded, "when you rode back with the treasure, and I saw how courageous she was and fought beside you."

"I bring you greetings from *el Halcón*," Carlos told the two Apache. "He is in Argentina, but I have had no letter from him yet. After his grief, it was a good thing for him to change his surroundings."

"Yes," Kinotatay gravely agreed. "Now, let me take you

to your wickiup. We shall have a feast tonight to welcome your return to your blood brother."

"I am concerned, Kinotatay, about what is taking place in Taos," Carlos earnestly interposed. "As we came to the mountain, we met a group of traders from St. Louis. Their leader told me that they had been there last year, and that the *alcalde mayor* had treated them very badly. He has, it seems, imposed high tariffs, expecting bribes for the privilege of trading in Taos and Santa Fe."

"It is worse even than that, my blood brother," Kinotatay said, shaking his head. "But of this we will talk after we have welcomed both of you and your men to our stronghold. Now then, Lonitay," he said to a young Apache girl of seventeen, who had shyly approached from a wickiup across the way, "take my blood brother and his *esposa* to the wickiup that is reserved for our honored guests. Find another for these brave *vaqueros* who have accompanied them all this long way from Texas."

The girl inclined her head respectfully, then signaled the four to follow her.

The newcomers walked through the stronghold, the villagers greeting the handsome young Spaniard as the blood brother of Kinotatay and their loyal friend. As they were led to their wickiup, Teresa looked around in wonder. She was entranced with the friendliness of the hard-working people caring for their livestock, curing skins, or tending campfires for the evening meal. Then she noticed that it was mostly squaws and children doing all the work, and she asked Carlos about this when they were alone in their little wickiup, where fresh pine boughs had been laid on top of the earthen floor.

"Yes, my dear one," Carlos explained to Teresa after he held her face in his hands and gave her a kiss, "the Indian women, as well as both the male and female children, do the work in the village. The women also make the wonderful straw baskets you see here in our wickiup; they are renowned for their handiwork, and they sell their baskets at the annual fair in Taos. It is the responsibility of the men to hunt, to guard the stronghold, and to go to war, though the Jicarilla have been at peace for many years now, even with their old enemies, the Mescalero Apache. But now come, let's visit with Kinotatay and Pastanari before the feast."

Carlos had brought many gifts, including Spanish knives, bolts of cloth, and good tobacco. He presented these to the chief, and then he and Teresa, as well as the two *vaqueros*, were led to a place of honor around the cooking fires. Then the feast began.

There were venison and antelope, turning on spits over the fire, and there were cornmeal cakes and vegetable dishes. Serving Carlos and Teresa was Colnara, the young daughter of the Jicarilla shaman.

"Colnara, I have often thought of you," Carlos exclaimed, delighted to see her. He turned to his wife. "Teresa, this is the girl who helped me regain my health after I was shot by Santa Anna's henchman."

Colnara smiled and murmured, "I am happy for you both. My husband and I will always wish you well."

"Your husband has a treasure in you, Colnara," Carlos said.

As the meal was concluded and the men lit pipes and the women tended to the fires and cleaned up, Kinotatay turned to Carlos. He said gravely, "Now we must talk of what is taking place in Taos, my blood brother. You come at a distressing time. This *alcalde mayor* who was appointed by *el gubernador* has levied taxes on the poorest dwellers in the pueblo village, and higher ones still on the *hacendados*. Thus, he has made enemies of everyone. He has a *jefe de policía* and his own private army. I tell you, *mi amigo*, the people in the pueblo may revolt, and it will be the kind of revolt that we have not seen in our time, and like one that happened many long years ago, when Popé led *los indios* against the Spanish tyrants."

"Is it truly as bad as that, Kinotatay?" Carlos anxiously demanded.

"I will tell you what I know. A few days ago, a young girl from the pueblo village, Epanone, rode into our stronghold. She asked us for refuge, and we willingly gave it to her. She told us that her father, highly respected in Taos, had supposedly offended the wife of the *alcalde mayor* and was severely punished, which shamed the man so that he took his own life. Ticumbe, who spoke for the Indians of the pueblo, went to the *alcalde* to protest, and he was shot down by the *alcalde's jefe*."

"What an abomination!" Carlos gasped, shaking his head in distressed compassion.

"Epanone is still with us, and we told her she may make her home with us for as long as she likes. Now, right after she came here, one of my braves, who had gone to Taos to buy supplies for us, met one of the young men of the pueblo. My brave was told that only the night before, men dressed like the Indians of the pueblo rode out of Taos toward a small ranch, and there, after binding the *esposo* and his young son, took their lustful pleasure with the mother. Not content with this, they robbed the *hacienda* of all they could take away—silver, the jewels of the woman, bottles of wine, and the like. One of them told the *esposo*, 'I am from the pueblo, and I do this to show you that we have had enough of the rule of the *hacendados*.' "

"You think—"

Kinotatay interrupted with a fierce nod. "The villager who told my brave what had happened said that these men who attacked the ranch were men employed in the private army of the *alcalde mayor*. This is just as Epanone has told us. You can understand, my blood brother, that if Cienguarda wishes to suppress and crush the villagers in Taos, he arranges to have crimes committed in their name, so that the citizens blame these peaceful *indios*."

"But that's incredible, Kinotatay!"

"For many years, my blood brother, the men of the pueblo have walked the road of peace. Now they are treated like curs, punished at every turn, and taxed beyond their means; even the most patient of them wishes no more of it. I feel that they will rise against the *alcalde mayor*."

"If that is the case, Kinotatay, I will do all I can to help them and to ally myself with you and your braves. I know that you will go to the aid of the Pueblo Indians."

"Yes, my blood brother. Because in treating those gentle people as he has, Cienguarda shows that he hates all Indians. It will not be long before he turns his attention to our stronghold and tries to seize it, to drive us away, to exterminate us. This will not happen in my lifetime, nor that of Pastanari. I have taken an oath to the Great Spirit on this. But here is my plan. Now that you have arrived, why do you not first go into Taos to see the situation for yourself? Then send for me and my braves."

"I agree to do as you say, Kinotatay," Carlos said.

Since Kinotatay and her husband had spoken in Spanish, Teresa had followed the dialogue between them with growing concern. She now intervened. "Forgive me, if I speak on this matter, Kinotatay, for Carlos has told me that women do not enter into the councils of men and tribal elders. But you see, I lived for some time in Taos, before I married Carlos, and I love the Pueblo Indians. If I can be of any help in stopping this unscrupulous *alcalde mayor*, I want to offer my aid. I still own property in Taos, and my old majordomo can give me information about this grave situation. I can then give you news that will help prepare you for your resistance against the tyrant."

Kinotatay listened politely. "It is quite possible that you can indeed send back information that will strengthen our defense against the Señor Cienguarda. I thank you for this."

It was nearly midnight, and the campfires were flickering out. The women, children, and old men had gone to their wickiups, and even many braves had begun to depart from the clearing in which the reunion between Carlos and his blood brother had taken place. Kinotatay suddenly winced, and the muscles of his cheeks and jaws tightened and flexed, as a sudden spasm of pain wrenched him. He turned away, but Carlos had seen it, and he murmured, "Kinotatay, you drive yourself too hard. You must rest."

"My blood brother, I have within me the poison that saps my strength and will soon send my spirit to Him who is the Giver of Breath. I hope only that before He summons me to the accounting of my life, I may have strength left to direct my people on the side of the Pueblo Indians. It may be we once again shall paint ourselves with the colors of war and take up the lance and the bow and stand beside our brothers of the pueblo. It will not be against the whites of Taos, I promise you that. It will be only against the *alcalde mayor* and his soldiers."

"Here is my hand, Kinotatay. I am your ally, as much as I am your blood brother and your friend. It is a debt I owe you for the life that you helped me regain." He paused and turned to look tenderly at his wife, and then smilingly added, "A life that is now more precious to me than I could have dreamed, when I left your stronghold cured again and strong. Because now this *mujer* of great courage and wisdom shares that life, and she has told me that she will give me a child at the beginning of the year to come."

Teresa reached for his hand and squeezed it, giving him a long, silent look. Kinotatay smiled wanly, for the pain that tortured him daily had begun to grow more and more onerous. By sheer force of will, he controlled the grimace caused by the burning pangs deep within him. When it had passed, his face was again calm and impassive, and his voice gentle as he bade his guests good night.

In Taos, other plans were being made to put an end to Cienguarda's reign of terror. Noracia, the beautiful *mestiza* who had so cleverly risen from the lowly status of slave and concubine to wealthy, beautiful matron and the wife of the *caballero* Alejandro Cabeza, had come to the conclusion that the regime of Alonzo Cienguardá could prove perilous to her own thriving enterprises. Her shops and her importing business had made her rich, and Cienguarda's tax against the *hacendados* of Taos included her. On the day when Carlos and Teresa came to the Jicarilla stronghold, she had received a note from Cienguarda brusquely declaring that he had personally assessed her affairs in trading of goods and commissioning imported merchandise from the United States and Mexico on order by the *ricos*. He decided to set a tax of two hundred *pesos* a month against her, so long as she continued to operate her shops in Taos.

When John Cooper had killed Noracia's former master, Luis Saltareno, in a duel to answer the *hacendado*'s slanderous accusation that his father-in-law, Don Diego de Escobar, was a traitor, Noracia, a household slave, had seen a chance to gain her freedom. She proposed to the men and the *criadas* of the household that she would employ them at good wages as free citizens of Taos if they would back her. She had won their loyalty.

After receiving the note from Cienguarda, she found her husband in the salon of their *hacienda*, reading a book. By now, Alejandro Cabeza was reconciled to his role of subordinate to his strong-willed, imperious wife, enjoying as he was all the luxuries of the pampered lover. Leaning over the back of his chair, putting her arms around her husband's neck, Noracia said, "This man, Cienguarda, has his own army now, and he decks them out in uniforms that dazzle the people. But we have our own little army, too, Alejandro. The *trabajadores* who are loyal to me do not willingly see this man mistreat *los indios*, since so many of them are in my household now. They know that if Cienguarda continues to raise his taxes and his tariffs against the goods that I import, and that if I am forced to leave Taos or end my business here, they will have no work, no *dinero*. When it comes to loyalty,

Alejandro, I think my *trabajadores* will fight for me and against Cienguarda."

"My darling one, you are right," he said, chuckling as he drew her around the chair and to him.

He released her, hugely pleased by her affection. At first he had snubbed Noracia, thinking her beneath him. At that time he had been courting none other than Teresa de Rojado. Alejandro was only after the young widow's money, and it was Noracia who had put an end to the affair by telling Teresa of Alejandro's intentions. Then, wanting the handsome *caballero* for herself, she actually had her men kidnap him, making him a prisoner in her *hacienda* and compelling him to give her pleasure. Alejandro had hated her then, but now all of that had changed. For Noracia was as passionate as she was clever, and she was also intensely loyal, if loyalty was offered her in return. Philosophically, this jaded *caballero* had learned that, as her accepted husband, he was better off than he had ever been before in all his life. That was why he said, "Yes, Noracia, I can be of help. You're forgetting that I am an expert with the sword, the rifle, and the *pistola*. I'll train the *trabajadores;* I'll make them better *soldados* than any of that fancily dressed militia that Cienguarda parades around Taos. We'll fight on the side of the Pueblo Indians. Who knows—you and I may one day replace him and rule Taos in his stead!"

Twenty-three

Teresa and Carlos rode into Taos with their *vaqueros* and went at once to the *hacienda* of the late Don Sancho de Pladero. The estate was still prospering under the management of his son, Tomás, who continued to raise sheep, now numbering well over five thousand head.

In the parlor of the *hacienda,* Carlos and Teresa were tearfully welcomed by the widow Doña Elena, as well as

Tomás and his wife, Conchita. Wiping away her tears of happiness, Doña Elena said, "You travel together. Am I to hope that my secret prayers have been answered, and you are now *esposa* and *esposo?*"

"It's true, Doña Elena. Teresa has done me the great honor and joy of accepting me. More than that, she will bear me a son next year."

"Not so fast, *querido,*" Teresa laughingly interposed. "It is for God to say whether it will be a son or a daughter. I hope you do not mean that if it is a daughter, you will reject me?"

"Even in jest, even to think such a thing distresses me." Carlos gave her such a mockingly reproachful look that Teresa burst into laughter.

"Praises be to *el Señor Dios!*" Doña Elena exclaimed. "I cannot imagine a happier pairing in all this world. I shall be delighted to have you here as my guests for as long as you wish to stay."

"We are grateful for your invitation, Doña Elena," Teresa said. "We have come partly on a most important matter, which concerns the *indios* of the pueblo."

"Ah, yes, I can guess," Doña Elena said with a sad expression. "It is our *alcalde,* Cienguarda. Not only does he raise taxes, but he has his own army."

"Kinotatay told us some of the things that he has done. The worst is that he has dressed his soldiers like the Pueblo Indians and ordered them to rape and plunder so that the Indians would be blamed. This would allow Cienguarda to take ruthless measures against the supposed offenders," Carlos explained.

"I wish I could be of help, but I am only an old woman. Tomás has spoken with the other *hacendados* to see what they can do to put a stop to this man, but I have begged my son not to become involved. Our family has found peace and happiness, and I want nothing to happen that will upset this."

"Tomás will not need to do anything, Doña Elena," Carlos politely responded. "Kinotatay has promised aid to the Pueblo Indians, once we send word to him. One of his braves journeyed with us to Taos. Once we know what is taking place, he will send for his *jefe* and the Jicarilla warriors. They are strong enough to overcome this private army of Cienguarda's; never fear."

"I am greatly relieved to hear this, Carlos," Doña Elena

said. "Here I am forgetting my duties as a hostess. Please do come with me, both of you. You shall have the finest room in my house."

The next morning after breakfast, Teresa mounted her horse and rode to her *villa*, which her majordomo, Novarra, maintained for her. Although she had authorized him to sell it in her name, he had not yet done so, for there were no buyers for it in Taos. Tall, impassive, nearly forty-five, Novarra, a Pueblo Indian, had been Christianized. Teresa knew that he could inform her about Cienguarda's crimes against the people of Taos.

He was overjoyed to see her, as were the other servants whom she had employed during her stay in Taos. "Señora de Rojado, it is a joyous day for me to welcome you back to your *casa*," he exclaimed.

"It is equally joyous for me to see you again, Novarra. But I am no longer the Señora de Rojado, but, rather, the Señora de Escobar."

"Ah, then it was that fine *hombre*, Carlos de Escobar, whom you accepted at last," Novarra smilingly replied.

"The very same. I think you always approved of him," Teresa said sweetly as she shook hands. "Now if I may have a few moments with you, I am eager to know what has been happening in Taos since I left."

Novarra's face was gloomy as he led his former mistress into the exquisitely maintained *villa*. "The very worst that could possibly happen, señora," he told her. "The *alcalde* detests my people, as does his wife. Just last night, señora, at least five of his men, dressed like *los indios pueblos*, entered the village, forced their way into two of the *jacales*, killed Tamarna and his wife, Lupe, as well as Jomanda, and carried away the two daughters of the couple to be their *putas*. They left headbands and a quiver of arrows marked with our tribal sign."

"So that Cienguarda can say that it was your people who committed these atrocities," Teresa broke in. "What an abomination! Who is the spokesman of your village now that Ticumbe is dead?"

"The elders of the village, two nights ago, appointed Palvarde to take Ticumbe's place. He is my age, señora. His wife weaves blankets and he is a shoemaker. They have two young sons who were baptized in the faith. He is a good man, and even now he is preparing a petition to *el gobernador* to come here to Taos to learn what the *alcalde* he appointed has done to us."

"I do not think that will succeed. Governor Narbona is a friend of Alonzo Cienguarda. You can expect nothing from Santa Fe. Well, I must go now, for I wish to tell Carlos what you have just told me about this last infamy. First, one last question. You say that Cienguarda sent five of his men dressed like the Indians of the pueblo. Is it known whether they went back to his *hacienda?*"

"Not yet. After they left our village, they rode toward the Sangre de Cristo Mountains, and young Caldones, who is a scout, followed them. He has watched ever since, hoping that our new spokesman, Palvarde, will send our braves into the mountains to find and punish them."

"You must not do this. Let it be done by Kinotatay and by my husband. Then there can never be any accusation that the Indians of the pueblo turned to violence. If Cienguarda should somehow escape the justice of your people, he would take cruel reprisals. Heed my words, Novarra."

"I will, señora. I will get word to Palvarde at once. *Vaya con Dios, señora.*"

"And you also, Novarra."

While Teresa was conferring with her former major-domo, Carlos de Escobar rode to the *villa* of Noracia. Carlos had come to know this woman while he was courting Teresa. Noracia had unabashedly invited him to her *hacienda* on a few occasions, though he had politely declined, explaining that he was in love with Teresa. It was at this point that Noracia took it upon herself to seek out Teresa and speak to her in Carlos's behalf. For that the young Spaniard was grateful, and it was because of this that he believed she was an ally.

Upon arriving at her *hacienda*, Carlos was greeted by one of Noracia's *trabajadores*, Feliciano Servilas, over six feet tall, with long arms, powerful wrists, and a firm chin adorned by a crisply pointed black beard. Servilas had been appointed *capitán* of Noracia and Alejandro's private army, which comprised some thirty *trabajadores* who had once been in bondage to Luis Saltareno.

Noracia received him in the salon and uttered a cry of delighted surprise at the sight of the tall, handsome Spaniard.

"What an unexpected pleasure, Señor de Escobar! My house is honored by your presence."

"I thank you for your courteous reception, Señora Noracia. And I must tell you right away that Teresa has accepted me as her *esposo*."

"You have married her, then? I'm happy for you." Noracia smiled as she came toward him, put a hand upon his shoulder, and looked deep into his eyes. "I myself have married Alejandro. So things have worked out well for each of us, *¿no es verdad?* I'm glad we are friends, Carlos. You know that I've always admired you and, yes, wanted you."

Carlos flushed and lowered his eyes. "You are a beautiful woman, Noracia. Your interest flattered me."

"Will you lunch with Alejandro and me?" Noracia asked.

"Yes, for I need your help. Kinotatay, *jefe* of the Jicarilla, promised his support of the Indians of the Pueblo. You yourself have Indian blood in your veins, Noracia."

She straightened, her eyes flashing. "I am proud of it. Alejandro and I have had our own army organized because Cienguarda has one. Let me assure you that my men will work with the chief of the Jicarilla and his braves."

"Splendid! I will send word to Kinotatay. We can bring about the downfall of this corrupt *alcalde*."

"You speak words that gladden my heart, Carlos. Now that we have agreed on an alliance for the good of Taos, will you not come with me to say hello to my husband?"

Alonzo Cienguarda himself had ordered Mondago to carry out the latest raid, of course. He had said to Mondago, "After you've done it, keep the *putas* with you in the woods, high along the range, and wait at least a week before you come back to my *hacienda*. I do not want anyone to see you, or they will suspect what is being done, *¿comprendes?*"

The five men, together with Mondago, had made a camp halfway up one of the snowcapped peaks of the Sangre de Cristo range. They had bound and gagged the two young daughters of the couple they had killed, and ridden by a circuitous route through a difficult trail up to a plateau fringed by spruce and fir trees and thick shrubbery. It camouflaged them from the winding road below, and was ideal for concealment and lecherous indulgence.

Mondago's five men had brought along provisions for a

stay of at least a week, after the pompous *jefe* had informed
them of their master's order to keep away from his *hacienda*
until the hue and cry over the disappearance of the two
Pueblo Indian girls had died down. Then, as Cienguarda had
intimated, his *jefe* could take more of the private soldiers into
the village and arrest the alleged culprits, who would be accused of the kidnapping and murder of the two Indian girls.
The Indians whom they would frame would, of course, be
those ringleaders whom Cienguarda believed to be the chief
troublemakers. Already, Ticumbe's successor, Palvarde, had
been one of the names mentioned to the *alcalde*.

Mondago chuckled now as he licked his lips and stared
down at the two trembling, helpless captives. One of them,
not quite sixteen, was Lita, and her older sister, almost nineteen, was Wikima. The older girl had fought her captors with
tooth and nail and had inflicted scratches and bites on two of
Mondago's men, as well as on Mondago himself.

To punish her, they had tied her to a tree, her wrists
drawn around the trunk and bound with rawhide thongs, with
another around her waist. Then, before her eyes, despite the
frantic moans and sobs of the gagged younger girl, they had
stripped the latter naked, flung her down in front of her sister, and each of the six men had ravished her.

Then Lita had been bound to a tree in the same way
and it had been Wikima's turn. She looked at them with
loathing and courageously suppressed any cry or sign of supplication for mercy.

Since her nails had left a bleeding scratch on Mondago's
fat jowls, he insisted that he punish her first, before enjoying
her. So his men had stripped her naked to the waist and had
handed him a thin, pliant switch, with which he had lashed
her across her breasts till she nearly fainted with agony.

Then he had taken her virginity, and after that his men
had enjoyed her as they had Lita.

It was the fourth day of the girls' captivity, and both of
them remained naked, flung down on the ground, with their
wrists tied behind their backs. They were bruised and marked
with welts from frequent switchings. Wikima, though pale
and haggard, had not once shown a sign of weakening. When
her ravishers had coupled with her, she had closed her eyes
and tried to obliterate them from her mind and silently
prayed to the Great Spirit to avenge her and to punish the
men who had bismirched her younger sister.

No man would wed either of them now; of that she was certain. She prayed that since their lives were over, they might somehow be granted the opportunity to wrest a weapon away from their captors and, before taking their own lives, kill these odious *wasichu*.

"When should we go back, *mi capitán?*" Jaime Tresmanza indolently asked as he took the coffeepot from the coals of the fire and poured himself half a cup, then swigged it down almost at a gulp. "Ah, *mi capitán*, there's nothing like strong, hot coffee to give an *hombre* new energy—and we'll need it for these *putas indias* here!"

"We'll go back when I say, not before. At least another three or four days."

"We'll take the girls?" a nearly bald, scar-faced man in his early forties eagerly asked.

"The *patrón* doesn't care. There are plenty of prettier ones in the village, *soldados*," Mondago chuckled, as he reached out his hand and squeezed one of Wikima's swelling breasts. The young woman sucked in her breath and tensed herself, closing her eyes tightly to shut out his leering face. "Much prettier than these and much less fight in them. Besides, we've marked them a little too much to please the *patrón*. No, after we've had our fill, we'll kill them, and we'll use arrows marked with tribal feathers."

Kinotatay and twenty of his braves, as well as a dozen men from the private army of Noracia and Alejandro, reined in their horses and waited for Carlos to join them on the mountain road. Carlos had sent word by the courier who had accompanied Teresa and him back to Taos, after their visit to the stronghold. The ailing chief of the Jicarilla, foregoing sleep and food, had led his warriors down from the stronghold in two days and nights.

"We are here, my blood brother," Kinotatay exclaimed. "You say that the men of the *alcalde* are up there somewhere along this range?"

"That's what I've been told. The young *indio* from the pueblo who has been watching every night, hidden along the only trail they could take back to the *hacienda* of the *alcalde*, told me only an hour ago that he still has not seen them return. No, they are keeping those girls up there in their hidden camp, waiting to go into the village and arrest some of the

Indians as murderers and kidnappers. I am beginning to fear that before they leave their camp, they will kill the girls."

Towanka, a brave of Pastanari's age, excitedly pointed upward with his lance. "Look there! I see a campfire!"

"That is where they are!" Kinotatay agreed. "Men, leave your horses here. We shall take these *cobardes* by surprise. Then we shall take them to the home of the *alcalde* and confront him with them."

Even as he spoke, a spasm of pain made him wince and tighten his lips against an outcry. Carlos saw that grimace, and his heart was heavy. Death was upon Kinotatay, but the valiant *jefe* of the Jicarilla would not yield to it till this deed was done.

The Jicarilla and the dozen *trabajadores* began to climb the mountain, and Carlos followed them. As they neared the plateau of the sheltered camp, Kinotatay held up his hand for silence, and the braves and other men waited, as they heard the distant sound of bawdy laughter, oaths, and the gasps and groans of the two young women.

"We have caught them, and now the *alcalde* will not be able to dispute the proof of his own evildoing," Kinotatay murmured to Carlos. They raised themselves onto the plateau and, crouching low, parted the thickets to see the knoll where the captors' camp was. Kinotatay ground his teeth in silent rage at the sight of the two bound naked young Indian girls lying beneath two of Mondago's men, who were violently raping them. Mondago himself, smoking a *cigarillo*, watched, his eyes glistening with lust.

Carlos cupped his hands to his mouth and called, "If you don't want your men to die, tell them to let the girls alone. Quickly now, you filthy pig!"

"Who speaks to me like that, I, the *capitán* of the army of the *alcalde* of Taos?" Mondago blustered, turning around in dismay at the sound of Carlos's voice.

"We have thirty-five men here, *cobarde*," Carlos yelled. "Call off your men!"

"Do what he says, quickly. We're in a trap!" Mondago panted, looking wildly around for his gun, which he had laid down on his military jacket.

Carlos came through the thicket with a pair of pistols cocked and ready. The two men who were violating the Indian girls turned to look up and saw the muzzles of the pistols aimed at their foreheads. With a simultaneous cry of fright, they rolled off and staggered to their feet.

The other three men raised their hands in the air, and one of them babbled, "Don't shoot, *amigos!* I surrender; I didn't do anything. It was his order; it was the *jefe*'s order, I swear it!"

"Untie those girls. Give them your jackets. Yes, your trousers too, two of you. Hurry, or I'll blow off your vile *cojones!*" Carlos angrily threatened as he gestured with his pistols.

Two of the men hurried forward to cut the rawhide thongs binding the wrists of Lita and Wikima, helping them to their feet, whispering promises of many *pesos* if they would only tell *los indios* that they were not the ones who had harmed them.

As Carlos came forward and prodded them with his pistols, they hastily removed their jackets and then their military trousers, and stood shivering in their *calzoncillos*.

"Señoritas, can you ride horseback, do you think?" Carlos politely asked the two trembling sisters.

Wikima spoke up, her voice listless and without emotion. "I can, *gringo.*"

"Good. I wish you and the other girl to come with us back to your village. Then we are going to take these men to the *alcalde* and make him confess what he has done to your people," Carlos said in Spanish.

Hope flickered in Wikima's eyes. Turning to her younger sister, she embraced Lita, and both young women burst into tears.

Carlos compelled two of Mondago's men to give up their horses to the Indian girls. They were forced to walk, as were the others, including Mondago and the two who wore only their drawers and boots. Two of Kinotatay's braves took their horses, tethering them in back of their mustangs. Carlos led the Indian girls back to their village and, from his pouch, gave them each a handful of *pesos,* saying, "Go to Palvarde, who speaks for your people. He will see that the old women nurse your hurts. You have not lost face, nor have you committed a sin, remember that. One day, all this will be forgotten, and you will be happy with an *esposo* and the children you will give him." He watched them go back into the village, and then he turned to Kinotatay and said in a harsh voice, "Let us make these *cobardes* trot a little. They have had things much too easy. When I think of what they did to those brave girls, I would as soon shoot them here and leave them dead for the buzzards in the road."

"Oh no, señor, have mercy," Mondago whined, clasping his pudgy hands in supplication.

"I don't want to look upon your greasy face, you slimy whelp of a coyote," Carlos growled at him, then gestured with his pistol. "Keep marching and trot now, as fast as you can, or I'll put a bullet in your heels!"

The braves emulated Carlos by pricking the men with the sharp points of their lances, as Mondago and his five *soldados* stumbled and fell, hastily picking themselves up and, with wails of apprehension as they saw the Jicarilla bearing down upon them with their lances, tried to run as best they could.

They arrived at the *hacienda* of Alonzo Cienguarda, and Carlos, dismounting, strode to the door and beat upon it with his fist, calling, "Come out, *alcalde!* We summon you for reckoning!"

The door was opened by a sleepy servant. He saw the mounted Jicarilla, the fierce-looking *trabajadores* of Noracia and Alejandro, and Carlos with two pistols in his hands. Then catching a glimpse of Mondago and his five companions who had sunk down on all fours, exhausted and panting for breath, the servant fled back into the house.

A few moments later, Alonzo Cienguarda, in his dressing gown and slippers, came angrily to the door. "By what right do you disturb the *alcalde* of Taos?" he began. Then, catching sight of his *jefe*, he uttered a strangled cry. "By all the saints, what idiocy is this?"

"Your own, *señor alcalde*," Carlos coldly said. "Kinotatay, his warriors, these *trabajadores*, and I came upon your man here and the soldiers of your private army. They were abusing two young Indian girls. They have already confessed to us that they wore the garments of the *indios* of the pueblo when they attacked innocent people, and that they left them behind, as well as bows and arrows marked with the tribal insignia. Your plot has been found out, *señor alcalde*."

Blustering, Cienguarda turned to Mondago. "I dismiss you from my service. You are stupid; you have involved me in a scandal." Then to Carlos he said, "I wash my hands of it all, señor."

Coldly, Carlos looked a long moment at the pompous *al-*

calde, then turned to Mondago. "I order you to leave Taos forever. If you do not, I will talk to Padre Madura, and *Los Penitentes* will come for you and deal out severe punishment."

"Oh, no, I'll leave, yes, yes; don't send them to me. In the name of merciful God in heaven!" Mondago wailed.

"See that you do, and before sundown tomorrow," Carlos said. Then, contemptuously looking at the *alcalde,* he said, "You, *señor alcalde mayor,* are no better than he is. Indeed, you are worse because you have total power and abuse it to your own ends. How easy it would be for these oppressed Pueblo Indians to kill you and to blame it on your own men, like that fat Mondago, for instance."

"No, please, don't hurt me. I—I'll do whatever you want. Perhaps I've been a little too harsh on the Indians. I'll remit their taxes. I'll promise whatever you want," Cienguarda stammered, losing all poise in the face of the menacing scowls of the mounted Indians and white men.

"That may well be," Carlos avowed. "Nevertheless, before I return to my home, I intend to ride to Santa Fe to speak with Governor Narbona. I will not leave his office until I am satisfied that he fully understands the gross injustices that have taken place in Taos under your administration. How Governor Narbona will deal with you is for him to decide, but I am certain no one in Taos will miss you if he insists upon getting your resignation. However, maybe it is best that you stay on. We have you in a good position now, and you will certainly be less of an evil than whoever might replace you."

Carlos continued, "Palvarde, the new spokesman of the pueblo village, will report to Kinotatay. If you continue your tyranny, *señor alcalde mayor,* if you continue to tax the Indians and impose high tariffs on American traders, word will be sent to the Jicarilla and to me at my ranch. We shall be back with many armed men to punish you. Think well on it, before you again try to persecute the Indians of Taos or attempt to harass the Americans who come here!"

"Yes! I promise I—I'll treat both the Indians and the traders better. But I assure you, it was Mondago who—"

"You are lying, *señor alcalde mayor.* You have saved your skin, at least for a time. You are on probation, shall we say. *Los Penitentes* will watch you from afar, and they will know when you lie. I bid you a good night." With this, Carlos wheeled his horse, and the Jicarilla followed him.

The *trabajadores* returned to the *hacienda* of Noracia and Alejandro, while Carlos and the Jicarilla headed for the *hacienda* of the late Don Sancho de Pladero. They halted on the outskirts of the property, and Kinotatay turned to Carlos. "My blood brother, it has done my heart good this night to go with you to punish evil. I shall see that my men watch what the *alcalde mayor* does. My men will know how to punish him, if he has lied to us."

"Kinotatay, I cannot say what is in my heart. I pray for you."

Kinotatay closed his eyes as a spasm seized him, and he swayed in his saddle. Carlos almost put out a hand to aid him but remembered in time that it would be an insult for the proud *jefe* of the Jicarilla. Carlos said gently, "You know that Teresa and I are going to Santa Fe to see the governor, then directly back to the ranch in Texas. But we will visit you again at the stronghold the next time we come to Taos."

"No, my blood brother," Kinotatay said softly, moving closer on his horse to Carlos so that his warriors could not overhear him. "I shall not be there when you come. The Great Spirit is calling me. I go back to the stronghold, and I pray to Him to grant me a little more time before I go out and sing my death song alone and under the blue sky, which smiles down upon the Jicarilla. The air will carry my song to Him who gave me breath, as He did to all men. This is farewell, my blood brother. To you and to your señora, and to my other blood brother, the brave *Halcón*, I wish many moons of happiness and peace."

"Kinotatay, I salute you. You are the bravest of the Jicarilla."

"No, my blood brother, for I fear death as any man does. But I can go to it with greater courage tonight because a *wasichu*, a white man who has exchanged blood with me, has ridden side by side with me against a tyrant who would exterminate the Indians. Tell *el Halcón*, when you see him, that I wish we might once again have sat by the campfire and smoked the peace pipe and talked of the days that have gone by. It will be Pastanari whom you will see when next you come to the stronghold, my blood brother."

With this, Kinotatay wheeled his horse and, raising his

lance, called out in a guttural voice the command to his braves to ride swiftly after him, he who was still *jefe* of the proud Jicarilla Apache.

Carlos watched until they turned around the bend in the road, but even before then he could not see them, for his eyes were wet with tears.

Twenty-four

Sister Eufemia had prayed that she and her eleven Dominican nuns would reach the ranch of Don Diego de Escobar by the end of June, or certainly by mid-July. The town of Parras, where she and her sister nuns had lived in the abbey until the *alcalde* had threateningly bade them leave, was some five hundred miles from the sanctuary of which Padre Madura had written her. Though they went on foot—with a burro drawing the cart containing supplies, possessions, and the hidden silver crucifix from the old church of Parras—Sister Eufemia had reasoned that if they walked only five miles a day, she and her companions could make the journey in a hundred days. That would be three months at the very worst, and since they had started in April, they must assuredly reach their destination by mid-July.

But here it was late July, and they still had a long way to go. From the very outset, everything had gone wrong. The burro had been an ill-natured, balky sort, with a dour obstinacy that enabled it to stand stolidly, even when Sister Eufemia used a switch on its hindquarters to move it. It would shake its head, its long ears flopping, and then bray derisively, immobile in the center of a dusty path, with the sun beating down. Some days they could travel just one or two miles, due to the weather or road conditions or the bad health of one of the nuns. They frequently had to stop in little villages to rest for a few days before resuming their slow journey northward.

As Sister Eufemia told Sister Caridad, who was very nearly her own age, these things were indeed a demonstration of the parable of Job. "Our dear Lord," she said, as she crossed herself and glanced up at the cloudless blue sky, "has posed these obstacles in our path to test our faith."

"I have no doubt you are right, Sister Eufemia," said Sister Caridad, who was nearly sixty, stout, and inclined at times to be morose. She had become a nun at the age of twenty, in the Church of the Angels at San Luis Potosí, and she had blamed herself all these long years for the unintentional death of her brother. He had been ill with fever, and the old priest who had visited him had a brother who was an apothecary. The latter had given Sister Caridad a vial of medicine and instructed her to give him a small portion of it after every evening meal. One night, he had been so wracked by the pain of his illness that he had pleaded with her to give him more of the good medicine that would cure him. She had done so. In the morning, when she had come to his bedside, she had found him dead. This was her sin, and her expiation had been a life of exemplary piety. Yet, for all that, she had not been able to rid herself of this terrible feeling that if she had not yielded to his plea, he might still be alive.

"I know what you are thinking, Sister Caridad," Sister Eufemia smilingly intervened before the portly nun could continue. "You saw in the behavior of that wicked *alcalde* but another step along the path of your own suffering. No, let me speak. I have known your anguish all these years, Sister Caridad. In my view, you were no more guilty of your brother's death than that burro."

"Sister Eufemia—Mother Superior—I cannot let you speak like that to me!" the nun gasped, her face reddening, as she fingered her rosary and murmured silent prayers.

"But it is high time that I did. It was God who ordained that your brother would pass into the next life. No, Sister Caridad, make peace within yourself and pray to Him to grant you more compassion for yourself. That is not vanity, believe me."

"I understand you, Sister Eufemia. Yet—"

"No," Sister Eufemia said, shaking her head with a benign smile as she put her arm around the other's shoulders, "it is not too late to begin a new life of joyous humility. We go now to a place that will be our sanctuary. Of this I am certain because I trust Padre Madura. We must expect hardships, because our Lord wishes to test us, to see if we are worthy of that sanctuary."

"Yes, I understand you. All the same, I do wish we might have had burros for all of us," Sister Caridad sighed.

"It has done us good to walk. We have not had enough exercise in that town we have left behind us. It has been beneficial to us. Also—and what is most important—by observing how the poor people of this country survive and continue in their faith, we have had good examples to hearten us along our way," Sister Eufemia smilingly went on.

During this last week on the road, they had come only a dozen miles. The unruly burro, resenting a flick of the switch from Sister Eufemia, kicked backward so violently that the animal overturned the cart and broke its traces. Finding itself free, harnessed though it was with the straps dangling in the dust, the burro took to its heels, braying lustily. Sister Eufemia watched the animal trot with a greater celerity than she could have ever imagined. She philosophically shrugged. "It is not worth the effort, sisters," she said with a wry smile. "Fortunately, we have the means whereby to purchase another burro, who, let us all pray, will be more docile."

Sister Caridad compressed her thin lips with vexation. She foresaw endless walking under the hot sun toward their haven in Texas, and although her spirit was willing, she did not think that her overly abundant flesh could endure.

"Oh, dear, Sister Eufemia," she groaned, "how are we to draw this cart now, when we have no burro?"

The mother superior indulgently replied, "Until we can find another burro in the next village that a kindhearted man will sell to us at not too dear a price, we must draw it ourselves."

"How dreadful!" the elderly, plump nun gasped.

"Why, not at all. There are all together twelve of us. Fortunately, since the dear Lord provides all things even when we humble mortals do not always think of them in advance, I was given the foresight to bring along some good, sturdy lengths of rope. You will find them in a flour sack, where I have also hidden the crucifix."

"You do think of everything, Sister Eufemia," the plump nun sighed, glancing up at the sky and crossing herself.

The younger nuns, with rare good humor, followed their mother superior's suggestion and soon had tied half a dozen lengths of the strong cord to the narrow crossbeams at the front of the cart and, gripping the other ends in both hands, marched forward. They went slowly, and there were many pauses while they stopped to get their breath, or to stretch and ease aching muscles hitherto not used for such arduous labor. Sister Eufemia, who herself took hold of one of the ropes and pulled with energy surprising for one her age, exhorted them to be of good cheer and to pray for strength, while Sister Caridad, at the rear of the cart, walking along and fingering her rosary, muttered almost rebellious prayers.

By the time the sun had set, they reached a tiny hamlet several hundred yards east of this dusty, well-traveled road. There were perhaps a dozen adobe huts in all, a rickety barn, a trough half filled with stagnant water, and near one of the largest huts was a plot of cultivated ground. Vegetables, particularly corn and sweet red peppers, could be seen.

"I shall go ask if we may spend the night in the stable." Sister Eufemia let go of the rope she had been drawing and straightened, trying to hide the grimace of pain that an unpleasant crick in her back impelled. "There, in that first large hut, I see a light. Perhaps it belongs to the *jefe* of this little village."

"Do you think they would have a burro they could sell us, there in that stable, Sister Eufemia?" Sister Rosalie eagerly spoke up.

"My dear child, I shall find out. Now then, rest yourselves. I will go and do what must be done."

As she spoke, an elderly Mexican, holding a heavy wooden bucket, came out of the doorway of the large *jacal*. He saw the sisters and, with a gasp of surprise, dropped the bucket. He crossed himself and knelt down, saying in a hoarse voice, *"el Señor Dios* Himself has sent you! Truly, I believed this place to be accursed!"

"Why do you say that?" Sister Eufemia gently asked.

"We have called this village Santa Fuente, because, you see, Sister, we dug a well when we came to live here five years ago. Then came the fever, and then the bandits— though there was not much for them to take. Then, the few young men here tired of this forsaken place and went to work in the silver mines to the south."

"But I see other *jacales*," Sister Eufemia interposed.

The elderly man, still kneeling, uttered a bitter laugh and crossed himself. "Oh, yes, Sister, they are still there, it is true. But now the only people left here in Santa Fuente are myself and my shameless daughter, whose wickedness has damned her for all eternity!" He glanced over his shoulder toward the other *jacales,* closed his eyes, and uttered a groan of anguish.

"How can you say such a thing?" Sister Eufemia exclaimed.

"Wait, Sister, I have not told you all that has happened to us. I said that bandits came to us a year ago and took what they could, but my daughter, Juana, was attracted to the *jefe* of the *bandidos,* and she went with him of her own accord. What wickedness, to be a *puta!* It would have been far better if she had died at birth! My poor wife, in trying to plead with her—though, of course, the bandits would have taken her by force with them, if she had not gone willingly—was struck by one of them who had a rifle and swung the butt against her. She died then and there."

"My poor man, you have truly suffered," said Sister Eufemia. "I will pray for you and for your daughter, too. But you must not judge her as a *puta;* perhaps the *bandido* married her."

"No, Sister, he did not. Three days ago, he brought my Juana back, and he said to me that he was tired of her. She is bearing his child in that last hut there, and I can do little for her. I know nothing of such things, how to deliver a child, Sister. Those others who remained, when Juana was brought back and abandoned, they came to me and they said, 'We will live here no longer, not with a *puta* who takes her pleasure with a *bandido* who has robbed us and who killed your wife. We shall go to the southeast, to the village of Dalacorda, and there we shall begin again.' Yes, Sister, and that is why you see no one except myself here." He burst into tears and covered his face with his hands.

"The poor soul," Sister Caridad suddenly exclaimed, "left all by herself with a child to be born, and no one to help her. I will help her!"

The other nuns turned with surprise toward the old nun who had complained so much during this journey. "You, Sister Caridad?" Sister Eufemia wonderingly asked.

"Yes! My poor brother was married, and his wife had a child, and he was away in the fields when she gave birth. I was there, and I helped. I have not forgotten. Take me to her, *hombre!*" Sister Caridad stepped forward and stared down at the kneeling, sobbing old man.

"Oh, may *el Señor Dios* forgive me, Sister, but I cannot. I do not ever want to see her again. When I think that, because of her, my sweet Madalena died, all I will do is pray!"

Already Sister Caridad had turned to the other nuns and, in an authoritative voice entirely new to her, ordered, "Sister Rosalie, Sister Mercedes, see if you can find some water and heat it. Go to the other huts and see if there are any blankets you can bring and some cloths for the birthing."

With this, she walked toward the last hut, while the two younger nuns, after a moment of hesitation, hurried off to enter some of the nearer *jacales* to find what they could to help the unfortunate Juana.

Sister Eufemia put her hand on the old man's shoulder and said in a low voice, full of compassion, "It is wrong to have hate in your heart. You are setting yourself up as judge, and only He who watches over all of us has that right."

"Ya lo sé, ya lo sé, Sister!" the old man sobbed, wringing his hands and bowing his head before the mother superior. "I tell you, I have prayed, and yet I do not have the heart to do anything. I think only of the shame she has brought upon us, of how my Madalena died because Juana had eyes for the *jefe* of the *bandidos.* How all the rest of the people who lived here and who were our neighbors and friends scorned me and left. I have nothing. My life is over, and yet I cannot forgive her. Pray for me, Sister!"

"I will, my son. And pray yourself also, that this hatred may be lifted from your heart, for in the days ahead it will give you no peace to remember that you cast her out."

He sobbed while she put her hand upon his shoulder and her lips silently moved in prayer.

Sister Caridad and the two young nuns had entered the last hut and found a young woman of about nineteen, lying on a straw pallet, about to deliver a child. She was gasping for breath, groaning and writhing. Quickly Sister Caridad knelt down and, swiftly explaining to the half-conscious young woman that she was here to help and that she was a nun, went to work at once.

Her pudgy fingers were gentle as they drew the infant out of the mother's womb, and she quickly bade the young nuns to remove the afterbirth, telling them what they must do. Inwardly, they marveled at her transformation and her knowledge, and they obeyed.

The young woman was wan and exhausted, and she had

eaten almost nothing for two days. This information she
whispered to Sister Caridad, who gently questioned her. It
was evident that her mind was wandering, and her strength
was rapidly failing.

"Rejoice, it is a fine son, a son, Juana," Sister Caridad
exclaimed. She had wrapped the newly born child in a small,
clean blanket from their wagon and held it up before the
young woman's glazing eyes. "My poor child, I will pray for
you. God will receive you in His bounteous mercy and
love—"

Already the young woman's eyes had closed; her body
gave a last convulsive shudder and was then motionless.

The two young nuns crossed themselves and began to
pray.

"We must bury her, Sisters," Sister Caridad said as she
rose, holding the infant in her arms. "And we must find milk
for this child. I do not know how, but the Lord will provide.
It is a miracle that we came here, and now I begin to know
the meaning of His redemption."

They stared at her, not comprehending. It was as if she
were alone, not seeing or hearing them. She stared at the
child, and tears ran down her plump cheeks as she murmured, "A life for a life. My brother died because of me, but
the dear God has heard my prayers and has let me bring
forth the life of a man! Oh, blessed be He who forgives a sin-
ner!"

In that squalid little hut, the old nun knelt and wept,
purged after all these long years of the guilt she had harbored
deep within her.

At last she rose and walked back to the others, Sisters
Rosalie and Mercedes following her, their eyes wide with
wonder.

"It is a boy," she told Sister Eufemia. "But the mother
died. She was too weak. She had eaten almost nothing. We
must bury her."

"It is best that way," the old man muttered, crossing
himself.

"It is your grandson," Sister Eufemia softly reminded
him.

"Oh, no, I am alone; I am old and sick. I cannot look
after a child—and that child would always remind me of my
daughter's wickedness and of my wife's death through it. I

implore you; take the child; give it to some family; I never wish to see it again!" he hoarsely exclaimed.

The other nuns gasped at this renunciation, and Sister Eufemia frowned. But when she turned, she saw the transfigured face of Sister Caridad, the eyes shining, tears running down the nun's plump cheeks. Sister Caridad murmured, "Let me care for him. Somewhere, I'll find a goat; it will give milk. I beg of you, Sister Eufemia; let me care for the child, at least until we can do something better with him."

"It is with your consent, then, my son?" Sister Eufemia bent down to the sobbing old man. He could not speak, but he nodded.

"So be it. We shall give the child a Christian baptism, and we shall see that he is given to a family who will care for him and love him. We will pray for you, my son. Now we shall bury your daughter. Will you not come and make your peace with her? Now she is with God, and He will judge her, and He will pardon her transgressions."

The old man shook his head, continuing to sob, and Sister Eufemia sighed and also shook her head. Looking up at the dark, cloudless sky, in which a half-moon shone with brilliant, luminous clarity, she clasped her hands and prayed silently. Then, taking a deep breath, she became again the practical realist that this tragic situation demanded. "My son, we shall take the child and care for him; have no fear of it. Shall we baptize him in your family name? We shall give him the first name of Innocente, for surely this child in the eyes of God is without sin and has no reckoning of what preceded his birth."

The old man raised his face, contorted with anguish and hate, toward the mother superior. Hoarsely, he cried, "I never wish to see it again. No, it shall not have my name, for it was an honorable one and I wish no tie with it. I have renounced my daughter; I renounce her child as well. Nor need you know my name. I shall leave this damned village and go to a cousin of mine in Sonora."

"My son, it grieves me to hear you speak so harshly. Yet I understand your grief. I shall pray to Him to grant you peace and greater compassion in the years to come. But now, since we are taking this child, it will be necessary to give him milk. Do you have a goat, perhaps? Also a burro?"

He stared at her uncomprehendingly for a moment, still absorbed with his bitterness. Then, with a humorless laugh, he replied, *"Pero sí,* I do have a goat, and it gives milk. I have a burro also—two, in fact, since my neighbor Luis Belardán made me a gift of them, when he left last week to go to work in the silver mine."

"Would you sell these to me? I will give you—" she thought swiftly "—I will give you thirty *pesos.*"

"Bueno. I can use the *dinero;* it will give me a stake in my new life—if there is any left me," the old man morosely answered.

The transaction was completed. Sister Eufemia went to the cart, opened the sack in which the crucifix and the ropes had been concealed, and drew out a little pouch that contained some of the silver that Padre Madura had sent her. She counted out thirty silver *pesos* into the old man's bony hand. Suddenly, remembering how Judas had betrayed the Son of God for exactly thirty pieces of silver, she added three more, saying, "If you have no objection, my son, we should like to stay here overnight, until we set forth in the morning. Let these three *pesos* be the payment for our lodging in the deserted *jacales.*"

Twenty-five

The little town of Lobos was some two hundred miles southwest of Buenos Aires and on the fringe of the *pampas.* A number of wealthy *estancieros* lived around the environs, and all of them were friends of Raoul Maldones, sharing his views that they must unite to defend themselves against possible legal, as well as military, infiltrations by the power-seeking *porteños.*

Like John Cooper's host, all of these *estancieros* had come from Spain, where the tradition of the bullfight had already been established. In order to retain the illusion of still continuing the link with their homeland, they had had their *trabajadores* build an open arena in the town. It was circular, with rows of comfortable seats, in which they staged, twice a week during this pleasant winter season, a classical *corrida de toros*.

Soon after John Cooper had saved Dorotéa from the anaconda, a courier arrived from Lobos and the *estancia* of Heitor Duvaldo, who, like Maldones himself, was a widower, but with two sons. He had been a friend of Raoul's family back in Madrid, and his wife, Amelita, had died from a lung disease.

The courier brought with him an invitation for John Cooper's host to attend a series of bullfights, which would begin on the following Friday. Raoul pursed his lips in thought, while the courier waited in the former's study. He turned to his majordomo, Fernando, and said, "Be kind enough, Fernando, to bring the Señor Baines to me at once." Then, to the courier, he added, "I shall not keep you overly long, *amigo*, but I have a guest from los Estados Unidos here, and if he accompanies me, as I mean to invite him to do, I shall then have a more specific message to send back by you to your master."

"I'm at your service, Señor Maldones," the stocky, pleasant-featured young Argentinian replied.

A moment later, Fernando returned with the tall American.

"I have something to ask you, my friend," Raoul spoke up. "Will you accept an invitation to go with me to the town of Lobos for a *corrida de toros*, a bullfight? Have you ever seen one?"

"No, to tell the truth, I haven't," John Cooper replied. "I've heard of them. Yes, I certainly would like to go with you. May I bring Andrew?"

"To be sure." Raoul turned to the courier. "Will you convey to the Señor Duvaldo the message that I'm overjoyed at his invitation. Tell him that I will have two guests, and that I will bring my two oldest daughters. Tell him also I look forward to having the chance to talk to him about several problems that have just arisen here."

"It shall be done, Señor Maldones. *¡Vaya con Dios!*" Ostentatiously bowing, the courier turned and left the study.

Now John Cooper and his host were left alone. Hesitating a moment, Raoul leaned forward and said earnestly, "Señor Baines, you have put me very heavily in your debt."

"I don't quite understand—" the American began, non-plussed.

"I refer to my daughter Dorotéa, Señor Baines," the *estanciero* gravely replied. "You know how much my eldest daughter means to me, Señor Baines, and she told me, when she came back to the house, all about the hideous incident with the anaconda. I can't thank you enough, Señor Baines."

"I want no thanks, Señor Maldones," John Cooper said.

The gray-haired *estanciero* put a hand out to touch John Cooper's wrist, his eyes steadfastly fixed on the other man's flushed face. "There is something else I must tell you. As I said, Dorotéa told me how you saved her life. Something more. She says that she is in love with you. More than that, she asked me to release her from the pledge by which I betrothed her to the Señor Baltenar."

"I—Señor Maldones—believe me, I didn't seek her out—I told her that what she felt was gratitude because it was very dangerous for her—that snake could have killed her—and I think she might have said that to anyone who had rescued her—"

"No, *amigo*." Raoul shook his head, a wise, compassionate smile on his handsome face. "She spoke from the heart. She told me also that she thinks Señor Baltenar is a *cobarde*. She saw the *padre*, and she told him all this. She asked him for advice. He said to her, 'Tell your father what you have told me; he is a wise and understanding man.' Yes, *amigo*, I am such. When I heard Rodrigo Baltenar speak to me as he did, I told myself that I had made a grievous error in letting him have my daughter. I sought an alliance, and now I know how wrong I was. Dorotéa is not the usual type of young woman who is subservient to her father, and I am glad that she is not. Otherwise, she would have married him without a word of objection. She would have been miserable, and he would have been of no service to my *estancia* and still less to her. So I told her that I released her from that pledge. I told her, also, that I would leave her to make the choice. She has made her choice, *mi amigo*."

John Cooper turned half away, unable to control his emotions and thoughts. His face flushed, he dug his nails into his palms as he strove to find the right words. At last, he faced his host and said, with a forthright, candid air, "You know something of my situation, Señor Maldones. You know that my wife was murdered by an assassin, and that I avenged her. Before she died, my Catarina said to me that she wished me to remarry. Yet, as I told your daughter, it is much too soon. We hardly know each other. In my case it is mourning and loneliness, and in hers it is gratitude and the contrast between myself and this Señor Baltenar."

"You are a very wise man, *mi amigo*. But I'll tell you this; I think that you care for my daughter, that you would love and protect her. I do not ask you to help me in my situation. I would not bargain and use her as an inducement to win your support to my cause—"

"Señor Maldones," John Cooper interrupted, "in my years with the Indians, I learned to judge people quickly. I had to, to survive. I don't like this man, Baltenar, and I like still less the men I met aboard the *Miromar*. I don't know too much about your politics, but if someone wants to steal your land, that I would not allow. That's all I'll say. But I ask you, since you've spoken so freely to me, to let me stay a few more weeks, let me talk to your daughter—with, of course, Señora Josefa there as chaperone—and let us see what happens. If it's meant to be, it will be."

"Again I say, you are a very wise man, Señor Baines. Well then, now that we've come to an understanding, let us look forward to our visit to the *corrida de toros*. Dorotéa will accompany us, and so will Adriana."

The *capataz*, Oudobras, was put in charge of the *estancia* the next morning, when Raoul Maldones, his two daughters and the Señora Josefa, and John Cooper and his son Andrew set out for the town of Lobos. Out of deference to Señora Josefa, who never learned to ride horseback, the women rode in a carriage drawn by two bay mares and driven by a young *gaucho*.

For part of the journey, John Cooper and Andrew rode a short distance behind the others, so that they could talk. John Cooper wanted to find out how his son would feel if his father courted Dorotéa Maldones.

"I don't know if she and I are right for each other, Andrew, and I can't say we'll actually get married, but if we did, what would you think?"

Andrew spoke without hesitation. Looking up at his father, his eyes shining, he said, "Pa, I think that would be just great. She's a wonderful person—her whole family's wonderful. I'd be happy if you married her."

"You understand, of course, that your mother will always be in my heart?"

"Of course, Pa. And I'll never forget Ma, either. I'll always love her. And I'll always love you, too, Pa."

John Cooper smiled and looked away from his son. But Andrew, watching his father, could see the strong emotions on his face.

The small party arrived in Lobos at sundown and rode into the courtyard of the *hacienda* of Heitor Duvaldo. He and his two sons emerged from the spacious ranch house to welcome his guests, and he hurried forward to offer his hand to Raoul as soon as the latter dismounted. Heitor Duvaldo was several years older than Raoul, portly and dignified, with a high-arching forehead and large, expressive, dark brown eyes. His black hair was streaked with gray, as was his pointed, short beard.

"*Por todos los santos,* Raoul, I bid you welcome! How good it is to see you here for our little *fiesta!*" he exclaimed. Then, coming forward gallantly, he hurried over to the carriage to open the door and hand down the flustered Señora Josefa, as well as her charges, Dorotéa and Adriana.

Dorotéa looked beautiful in a black skirt decorated with lace, a short-sleeved blouse, and a black *mantilla* made of llama wool. As he watched her being handed down from the carriage, John Cooper, still mounted on horseback, felt a thrill, and he told himself, "Easy now, take your time. What will be will be."

"Heitor, it is my pleasure to bring two very dear friends of mine from los Estados Unidos," Raoul told him. "This is Señor John Cooper Baines and his *hijo* Andrew."

"*Mi casa es su casa, señores,*" the *estanciero* beamed, shaking the hands of John Cooper and his son as they dismounted. "My majordomo, Antonio, will show you all to your quarters. You do my *estancia* great honor by coming here."

"And you honor us by making us your guests," John Cooper replied. His eyes again wandered to lovely young Dorotéa, who stood beside her sister Adriana, with Señora Josefa already officiously haranguing them in surreptitious whispers as to what behavior was expected of them. Nonetheless, Dorotéa managed to turn her head and send him a warm, intense look and an enchanting smile, which made his heart beat faster.

Andrew gawked at Adriana, who fluttered her eyelashes and sent him a dazzling look, which made him blush and turn away to see to his horse.

The majordomo, Antonio, a slim, dapper man in his late forties, hurried out as, bowing and with effusive gestures and flattering words, he took charge of the three women from Raoul Maldones's household, showing them to their rooms. Meanwhile, John Cooper's host told Heitor how he and the American had come to know of each other, and about the wonderful pure-blooded palomino stallion and mare, as well as the fine Texas cattle.

"Señor Baines, we must talk this evening because I, too, am interested in the strengthening of the breed of my cattle. I have the feeling, as does Raoul, that one day our young nation, like that of los Estados Unidos, will be a great beef-producing country—unless the *porteños* make it impossible for us to develop the resources of the *pampas*."

During the course of their stay, Heitor Duvaldo showed himself to be a highly sympathetic, well-read, and intelligent man who did not have the usual prejudice against a foreign *gringo*. When Raoul Maldones told him that John Cooper had shown himself to be proficient in the use of the *bola*, as well as his own "Long Girl" and the Bowie knife, the *estanciero* urged the American to compete with some of his most skillful *gauchos*. Like his friend Raoul, Heitor had earned the respect and loyalty of the *gauchos* of the *pampas*, and they had taken his two sons, Benito and Enrique, fourteen and sixteen respectively, under their wing and turned them into expert horsemen and marksmen.

At noon on the second day of their stay, Heitor held an outdoor feast for his friend and the latter's two guests and, when the food and wine had been consumed, rose from his seat at the table to proclaim that there would be a contest between his boys and Andrew Baines.

This was a new test, the likes of which young Andrew had never before experienced. At the end of the courtyard, a tall wooden stake had been erected with a crossarm. Fixed to a hook at the end of the crossarm was a chain with a gold ring. Andrew was given a lance with an arrow-headed spearpoint at its long wooden end, and told to watch how Heitor's sons comported themselves at this tourney.

The younger son galloped toward the dangling, narrow

ring, the point of his lance bearing upon it. At the last moment, when his horse swerved, he missed the target and, disgruntled, flung himself off the horse and began to scold it for its antics. Enrique, calmer and more dignified, waited his chance, gauging the distance, then slowly mounted his horse and rode it forward at a canter, till he was about twenty feet away from the ring. Then, quickening the gait of his mount, he leveled his lance and thrust the tip through the ring, breaking it off amid the huzzahs of the watching *gauchos*.

Then it was Andrew's turn. Dorotéa and Adriana were seated at a nearby table, and as Andrew mounted his horse, he was aware that young Adriana was looking at him with an intense smile on her lovely face. Stiffening, he caught his father's eye and noticed the twinkle of amusement, which made him blush. Accepting the lance from one of the *gauchos*, he slowly mounted, fixed his eyes on the tiny target, and then leveled the lance till it was at the height of the dangling ring. He rode forward at a gallop and, as he neared it, thrust with an unwavering gaze. The tip of his lance passed through the ring and tore it from the crossarm, and the *gauchos* cheered the young *gringo* who had proved himself the equal of their *patrón*'s older son.

"Well done, *muchachos!*" Heitor rose and lifted his glass of Madeira wine to toast the two youths. "Enrique, I will give you a prize myself; I am proud of you. As for you, Señor Andrew, you are a worthy contestant, and I proclaim you an equal victor. Tomorrow, I shall award your prize." Then, turning to John Cooper, he smilingly added, "Would you allow me to present your son with one of my best horses? It is a young colt, which we found wild among the herd and which my *gauchos* trained. It is fast as the wind, it has great courage, and it does not shy at the sound of gunfire."

"It's a very generous gift, Señor Duvaldo, and I accept on behalf of my son, with *muchas gracias,*" John Cooper smilingly declared.

But Andrew's reward was not the anticipation of the fine young colt but rather catching a glimpse of Adriana's piquantly provocative, lovely face, as she favored him with a deepening smile and sparkling eyes.

Later that afternoon, Heitor Duvaldo, two of his *gauchos*, his two sons, and his guests rode into the town of Lobos some three miles to the northwest to attend the bullfight.

The dirt floor of the arena was shaped in an oval, with an adobe wall enclosing it. The top of the wall was eight feet high, and there were ten stalls of hardwood. Heitor and his two sons took their places in one of these stalls and seated themselves on the red velvet-covered benches, while Raoul sat at the right of his *estanciero* friend.

At the opposite side of the stalls there was a pen with adobe walls, into which the bulls were led by several *trabajadores*. The door from the outside was then closed and instantly a vertically sliding hardwood door leading into the arena was opened.

Near this pen was a similar enclosure, also made of adobe. From this enclosure, there would come the *picadores* mounted on horseback and the *matador*.

Several other families occupied the other stalls, and John Cooper perceived handsome, beautifully dressed women with their spouses and children, though none was under twelve, so far as he could estimate. There were altogether some thirty people in the comfortable stalls.

John Cooper and Andrew, who were seated at the right of Maldones and his two daughters, watched several *trabajadores* tugging a recalcitrant short-horned, bulky black bull into the arena.

At the same time, the door of the enclosure on the left was opened, and in rode two men on horseback, carrying *banderillas*. These were the *picadores,* whose task it would be to drive the bull around and around the arena, while placing the pointed short spearlike darts into the animal's sides and flanks in order to make it angry and fierce.

The man who was to fight the bull, John Cooper observed, stood to the left of the stalls, with a *matador*'s hat, a white ruffled shirt with an open collar and embroidered cuffs, black cloth breeches, and knee-high boots. In his right hand was a sharp, short sword, with a cross-hilt of metal, and, as John Cooper watched, the *matador* lifted the sword and kissed the hilt, his lips murmuring a silent prayer.

Raoul leaned toward his guest and remarked, "My friend Heitor is very proud of his *matador,* Roberto Avila. He has bested at least a dozen bulls in the past month, many of them very fierce and dangerous. But to be sure, Señor Baines, our bulls in Argentina do not have horns with the tremendous width and sharpness of your Texas steers."

Heitor now rose from his velvet-covered seat and, cupping his hands, called out to the *trabajadores,* "Gonzales, untie the bull."

"*Sí patrón,*" one of the younger *trabajadores* answered. Then, swearing at the bull, he and his companion dragged the balky animal forward. As the two workers deftly slipped off their ropes, the black bull lunged into the arena.

The two horsemen rode after the bull, who charged each in turn, then retreated, stomping one front hoof and bobbing its head. One *picador* planted a sharp dart, shaped somewhat like a javelin, into the bull's left shoulder, but very nearly lost his horse as the wounded bull bellowed its pain and anger and, lowering its head, began blindly to charge.

Outside the left-hand entrance, where the *matador* waited, several of the workers stood by, ready to open the door if the *picadores* should be forced to ride away from the charging bull, while at the same time taking pains to prevent the raging animal's escape. Suddenly, the bull charged, its sharp horns nearly hooking the belly of one *picador*'s horse. The frightened animal reared, nearly throwing its rider, but the *picador,* with expert horsemanship, retained his seat and raced the animal around to the other side of the arena, talking to it and lightly jerking at the bit, till at last the horse quieted. The black bull abruptly turned and made for the other mounted horseman, who barely escaped, though he was able to thrust down one of the *banderillas* into the haunches of the snorting, bellowing bull.

John Cooper turned to watch the *matador,* who was examining his sword. As he did so, he caught the eye of Dorotéa, who was staring at him, her soft lips curved in a tremulous smile. As their eyes met, she blushed and looked away.

The first *picador* galloped his horse around the bull, waving a red scarf to entice the animal to charge. When it finally did so, the rider reined in his horse, wheeled it around, and thrust a *banderilla* into the animal's left flank.

Now the rider raced for the safety of the exit, and the bull took after him. The rider rode through, and the door slammed just as the bull reached it. There was a heavy thud, and another bellow of pain, as the spectators were shaken by the fury of the impact.

The other *picador* tried to emulate his companion, but the bull anticipated it, lowered its head, and charged. Only by

a skillful, wheeling maneuver was the *picador* able to escape
and to gallop toward the exit.

The door was slid down, and the angry bull crashed into
it again, its horns stuck for a moment, till, backing, snorting,
and bellowing, it freed itself. Then it began to lope around
the arena, lifting its head, its bloodshot eyes fixed on the
spectators.

Now the *matador*, Roberto Avila, approached, the sword
behind his back, and shaking a red cape held in his left hand,
attracted the bull's attention. The bull paused at the far end
of the arena, then came charging. Nimbly, Avila bent his
body just enough to let the bull pass under his cape without
goring him. The spectators applauded Avila's expertise.

Raoul sat on the slightly higher bench, while just below
him was the bench on which his two daughters and Señora
Josefa were seated. For the sake of propriety, the *dueña* had
posed herself at the right of Dorotéa and Adriana, and once,
as Andrew glanced over at Adriana, Señora Josefa intercepted his look and stiffened, trying to block his view with her
bulky form.

Avila extended the cape, thrusting the sword through his
sash, confident of his ability to outwit the charging black bull.
It lowered its head, snorted, pawed the ground, then charged.
Nimbly, the *matador* whirled and flicked the cape up his
body, only a few inches away from the horns. John Cooper
admired this gallant rivalry of agility and cunning against
savagery. Yet he saw the *banderillas* still sticking in the bull's
flesh, saw the splotches of blood on the earth of the arena,
and he grimaced with distaste. With the *matador* against the
bull, that was sport, true enough; but the men on horseback
who had tormented the animal and drawn blood from it
made a mockery of that sport.

Even as he thought this, there was a gasp of horror from
the spectators. Avila had come too close to the bull and had
turned swiftly away, only to trip and lose his footing and to
sprawl helpless in the sand. His sword, for which he had
reached even as he had moved to one side, was brushed aside
from his grasp by the grazing flank of the bull, which had almost gored him. It lay a few feet away from him. Stunned,
he stared helplessly as the infuriated animal completed its
headlong charge to the other side of the arena, and then
came back toward him.

John Cooper sprang from the bench on which he was

seated and vaulted over the adobe wall into the arena. He reached the sword before the bull was upon him and the fallen *matador*, and in almost the same movement seized the cape with his left hand and flung it over the bull's short but deadly, sharp horns, momentarily blinding it.

He held out his hand to Avila, saying in Spanish, "Get out of here. Climb over the wall. I'll handle the bull!"

"*Gracias, señor*, a thousand thanks!" Avila panted, his voice hoarse with terror. Regaining his footing, he ran toward the nearest wall, in which there were hollowed-out, vertical steps, to be used to climb the wall and get into the seats. He hoisted himself up and flung himself down on the nearest bench, still trembling and panting over his narrow escape. Though Avila had trained for several months with young bulls and had managed to kill a dozen in the arena during the past three weeks, this time his nerve had failed him, and he had counted himself as dead.

Dorotéa had risen with a cry of mingled horror and admiration as she saw John Cooper spring down into the arena. Her eyes fixed on him as he stood there with the sword in hand, watching the bull, which shook the cape from it and now, seeing him, snorted, pawed the ground, and then slowly came toward him.

John Cooper remembered how he had hunted buffalo with the Ayuhwa, and how many of his Indian companions had used their lances to thrust down behind the buffalo's neck to inflict the death wound. He gripped the cross-hilted sword firmly in both hands, using it as a dagger, warily watching the oncoming animal.

Just before it was upon him, he lunged to one side and, lifting the short, sharp sword high in the air, plunged it down with all his strength into the beast's neck. There was a shrill bellow, and the bull tottered, went down on one knee, then slumped over onto its side, kicked violently, lifted its head, then fell back dead. The spectators were on their feet, shouting, "¡Olé, olé! ¡Gran matador!"

John Cooper turned, moved toward the wall, and clambered up the hollowed-out steps, then swung himself back onto the floor of the pavilion. Andrew had hurried to him, his eyes shining. "Pa, that was great! I was scared! I thought you were a goner there!"

"Come to think of it, I did, too, Andy!" John Cooper said, out of breath.

Heitor had hurried over, his eyes glowing as he held out both hands, expostulating, "I have never seen anything like it before, Señor Baines! You, a *gringo,* to kill a bull your very first time! You have honored my *estancia* with your presence. You saved the life of Roberto Avila, one of my most loyal *trabajadores,* who I fancied was a *gran matador."*

Others in the audience had come over to congratulate John Cooper and to shake his hand. But he could not take his eyes off Dorotéa, who stood beside Adriana, hands clasped at her rapidly heaving bosom, staring ardently at him, her lips open in a dazzling smile.

Twenty-six

Heitor Duvaldo and his two sons were hosts on the evening following the bullfight to Raoul Maldones and his two daughters, John Cooper and his son Andrew, and five other couples and their children, in what the wealthy widower called *homenaje a mujeres muertas.*

John Cooper started when he heard the *estanciero* rise from the table, lift his glass, and propose the toast—homage to dead women—in memory of the wives of both Duvaldo and Maldones. It reminded him not only of Catarina, but also of beautiful Weesayo.

This somber mood was swiftly dissipated when Duvaldo turned after the first toast had been drunk to face him, lift his glass, and say, "To a *gran matador gringo,* who has adapted himself to our ways more amicably and graciously than anyone we have ever met before from his distant country."

"You do me too much honor, Señor Duvaldo." John Cooper rose to acknowledge the toast, his glass in hand. He saw Dorotéa's eyes steadfastly fixed on his face, without wavering or the coy fluttering of lashes. Clearing his throat, he responded to the toast by saying, "I honor your first toast, Señor Duvaldo, because, by proposing it, you have drawn me, a stranger, into your intimate circle. My own wife, Catarina, died a few months ago. Now, may I, a stranger, grateful for your acceptance, propose my own toast: to the beautiful women of Argentina, courageous, chaste, loyal, and truthful in all things."

There was vociferous applause from the men, and the women looked fondly at the tall, buckskin-clad *gringo*. Many of them, though happily married, secretly wondered what it would be like to make love with so virile, stalwart, and handsome an *americano*.

"Indeed, Señor Baines, you acclimate yourself magnificently," Heitor chuckled. "You have made a friend of every woman under my roof."

Raoul now rose, glass in hand, and turned to his neighbor. "Heitor, *amigo*, you know that I betrothed Dorotéa, my oldest daughter, to Rodrigo Baltenar. Yet, not long ago, outside the hearing of my *americano* friend, when I proposed to him that we needed an alliance to strengthen our defenses against the attacks of men like Porfirio Ramos, he wished no part of such involvement."

"I could have told you that," Heitor cynically responded. "He likes his comfort. The fact is, Raoul, I suspect him of being a turncoat. If Ramos came to full power, Baltenar would side with him. If you or I took the upper hand, then he would profess the utmost friendship and admiration for us both. That is the way it is, *amigo*."

"I know this, and that is why I take this occasion to announce that before I left my ranch, I sent one of my *trabajadores* to Rodrigo Baltenar to inform him that I revoke the agreement we made earlier concerning my daughter. My daughter is again eligible for marriage."

He turned to stare at John Cooper, then at his daughter. Dorotéa, with a happy little cry, clasped her hands against her swelling bosom and sent John Cooper the most poignantly yearning look that a woman who desires a man can proffer.

John Cooper was truly shaken. It seemed to be expected of him to make a public announcement of his intention to court Dorotéa.

Hardly believing that he would act this way in public, he rose from the table and, lifting his glass, declared, "Then, Señor Maldones, here and before witnesses, let it be known that I wish to be considered as a suitor for the hand of your daughter Dorotéa in marriage."

The weekend was halcyon, and John Cooper, on the morning after the banquet, went to the chapel in the *hacienda* of Heitor Duvaldo a little after dawn. He had been unable to sleep, thinking of what had been and what would be. He had critically examined his own conscience to make certain that it was not simply his loneliness and grief that had drawn him to this fascinating young woman who, at eighteen, was more sophisticated and candid than most women. He wished that he might be back in Taos to consult with Padre Madura about the alternate flights of fancy and pangs of guilt that surged through him.

He prayed, and when he emerged from the chapel, it was to see Raoul Maldones coming out of his room and toward him. "I'm very glad to see you this morning, Señor Maldones."

"And I you, *amigo*. I want to let you know most emphatically that I would be pleased to accept you as my *yerno*, John Cooper Baines," Raoul solemnly said as he held out his hand to the American. "And from now on you must call me Raoul."

"That I will do. And I promise you, Raoul, that I will cherish your daughter, defend her with my life, and that, in no way, will my memory of the past come between us."

"You are an honorable, brave man. I already knew this from the letters your factor sent me. I have seen it for myself now." He paused, then put his hand on John Cooper's shoulder. "You are of the same faith as our family. You would be a devoted husband to my Dorotéa. So, *mi amigo*, I give you my blessing."

"I don't know what to say, Raoul—"

"There is something else, though it is perhaps too early to speak of it. John Cooper, I have prayed so many times to *el Señor Dios* to give me a son, and Carlotta, my dear wife, wanted so badly to give me one. If you stay here with my Dorotéa, perhaps I shall have a son after all. If you wed my daughter, will you remain here in Argentina?"

"No, I must be honest with you," John Cooper replied. "Dorotéa will go with me to Texas. But we will return to you, and if we do have a son, you have my promise that I shall bring him here for christening."

"I can ask for no more than that." Raoul put his arms around John Cooper's shoulders and kissed him on both cheeks. There was moisture in his eyes as he contemplated his future son-in-law. "If things were normal, you may be sure I would not be so concerned to find my Dorotéa a husband so swiftly," he resumed. "But these are abnormal times. I think that Heaven sent you here to us. At least, if you take her to Texas, she will be safe there. Here, I cannot answer for it, because the *porteños* grow stronger daily. When they have an ally like Porfirio Ramos, you may be sure they are plotting ways and means of humbling all of us and bringing us toppling down, stripping the land from us and making us out to be traitors."

"I am distressed that you are confronted by such problems, Raoul." John Cooper said this in formal Castilian, which, with its flowery phrasing, was the language of diplomacy.

Again, Raoul put out his hand, and John Cooper shook it, as the older man said, "Well, what is to be, will be. I will tell Señora Josefa of the arrangement between us. She will be shocked, but I know you to be so honorable that I do not think there is any impropriety in letting you be alone with my daughter. I shall keep Señora Josefa occupied with Adriana and the other two girls." He chuckled and smiled reflectively. "It is almost like playing a charade, only of course I know the outcome of the game, before it even starts. So, John Cooper, when we return to my *estancia,* spend next week with my daughter. You will learn about each other, and I am confident that the love each of you professes for the other will only grow and become deeper."

During the remainder of the weekend at the *estancia* of Heitor Duvaldo, John Cooper Baines began his formal courtship of beautiful Dorotéa Maldones. Her father had told her, "Dorotéa, you are dearest to me because you are my firstborn. It would have been a great blunder to have gone ahead with the marriage plans between you and Rodrigo. In the *gringo,* whom I am now proud to call friend, I see a man of honor and integrity, of great courage and steadfastness. I have told Señora Josefa to let the two of you be together, on horseback, or practicing with the *bola,* or riding with the *gauchos.* In this way, you will learn what he thinks, and he will learn your feelings."

"Mi padre," Dorotéa had murmured as she kissed him, "I'm very grateful to you. I do love the *gringo*."

"It will not change your mind if, as he told me only yesterday, he intends to go back to his *estancia* in Texas?" Raoul anxiously asked.

"No, *mi padre.* I am sure that he will bring me to visit you and my little sisters." Then, with a flash of impudence, her eyes sparkling and her lips curved in a mischievous smile, Dorotéa added, "Do you know, *mi padre,* I think his son Andrew is in love with Adriana. Perhaps one day our families will be even more closely united."

"It would be a wonderful link, Dorotéa. But your own happiness is paramount to me. I know that John Cooper will stand by us if the *porteños* try to appropriate our land. Not only is he quick and resourceful, but also I believe him to have influence in los Estados Unidos."

Dorotéa embraced him again and then asked, "Do you really think that Ramos will try to harm you, *Papá?"*

"I do, *mi hija.* But I will tell you this, I am more heartened now than I was last week. My good friend, Heitor, and some of our other neighbors feel as I do; we have pledged to band together, and our *gauchos* will defend us as well. At the moment, since the government is still in a state of chaos, I do not see any immediate danger. We shall grow strong through these alliances. Now, my sweet child, go find John Cooper and ride out over the *pampas* with him and exchange those delightful secrets that will be part of your life henceforth."

"Yes, oh, yes, *Papá!"* Dorotéa said. She embraced him again, and then hurried off. Raoul Maldones stood watching her and sighed happily.

Heitor Duvaldo had a stable of fine horses. He had, just a year after Andrew Jackson had defeated the British at the Battle of New Orleans, visited a former neighbor who had left Argentina to settle in Virginia and maintain a cotton plantation where he bred horses as he had done in Argentina. He had sold Heitor an exceptionally fine stallion and two mares.

A young *gaucho* named Feliciano was in charge of the stable and saw to it that John Cooper and Dorotéa were provided with two piebald geldings, sleek, fast, and docile.

As soon as they had gone a distance beyond the *hacienda,* Dorotéa turned to John Cooper, her eyes bright and eager, and called, "Let's have a race! Tell me, *querido*, will you give me my very own horse when you marry me?"

Startled by her directness, he flushed as if he were a schoolboy. "Of course I will," he answered.

"I know that you will take me back to your Texas, won't you, John Cooper?" The way she pronounced his name with her exquisite Spanish accent, in that sweet, clear voice of hers, made him look at her as if he wished to memorize her lovely face. Her eyes were so luminous and her lips so warm and moist and eager that he forgot his resolve not to go too far or too fast in this formal period of courtship. Suddenly he leaned forward to kiss her.

The horses were docile as the riders embraced. Dorotéa, with a happy little sigh, linked her arms around his neck and, closing her eyes, surrendered herself totally in a warm and loving kiss.

He was shaken by its profundity and by its impact upon him. There was no doubt that she loved him. It was incredible that it should happen so soon.

"Now, I will race you, John Cooper," she declared as she pulled away from him. Swiftly, before he could recover from the dazzling candid sensuality of that kiss, she galloped off.

He tilted back his head and laughed. The sheer joy of living took hold of him. Now he knew what he had been foretold on the mountain where he had gone to make peace with his soul.

He had never really been freed from the emptiness and despair that he had experienced when he had seen his family murdered before his eyes while he had hidden in the cornfield with Lije that fateful September. Ever since then, until the time in Taos when he had been introduced to Catarina, he had erected defenses against that terrible isolation that only an orphan can know. It had been Catarina who had responded to him, loved him for himself, and altered her own pampered way of life to give him such happiness as he had not thought he would ever have.

Now, by the grace of God, Dorotéa Maldones offered him that same gift of love.

That afternoon, Heitor Duvaldo and his guests rode out to an area where, as he explained, an occasional puma had been seen. John Cooper had put "Long Girl" in the saddle sheath, and his Bowie knife was thrust through the belt of his buckskin breeches.

Four of Heitor's *gauchos* rode ahead as trail blazers to flush out the wily puma. Besides the *bolas,* they carried a sharp knife in the shape of a half-moon, attached to a long lance of hardwood. This weapon, as Raoul explained to John Cooper, was used by the *gauchos* during their cattle hunts, when they would ride into herds to hamstring bulls till they had all the animals they needed. After the hides were removed and meat was carved from the carcasses for the evening meal, the hides would be tanned and sold.

The day before, Heitor explained to his guests, his *gauchos* had killed about a dozen cattle and left their carcasses for the vultures and the pumas. It was his hope that this bait would attract the ferocious beast that had already killed one of his *criadas* and fatally wounded a *gaucho* who had tried to hunt it down by himself.

They rode by a lagoon, and John Cooper saw herons and flamingos on the banks, and a flock of wild ducks swimming in the placid water. There was a giant *ombú* tree on each side of the lagoon with long, gnarled roots and a monstrously large dome of green foliage.

They rode through an area covered with tall grass, which rustled and bent and turned in each direction, as gusts of wind swept over it. The air was pleasantly cool, and its purity and clarity allowed one to see the broad extent of this stretch of *pampas* for miles beyond.

"Sometimes the puma climbs to the top of the *ombú* tree, Señor Baines," the *estanciero* remarked as he drew abreast of John Cooper's horse. "It sees its prey from afar, and springs onto its back. Often, we have found the skeletons of dead guanacos, their necks dislocated from the blow of the puma's paw. They run in pairs, as a rule, just like the lion of Africa, of which I have read."

"They sound like our mountain lion in los Estados Unidos, Señor Duvaldo," John Cooper replied. "If they're as agile, one must be a crack shot to bring them down."

They turned westward, leaving the strip of *pampas* behind them and entering a desolate forest, whose trees were spaced twenty to thirty feet apart. Most of these were scrub trees, and there were small, wild beds of cardoons, with their silvery, bluish-green, many-lobed leaves. Heitor, who held his rifle by the barrel in his right hand, used it as a pointer to indicate these growths to John Cooper. "Here is a most useful plant, Señor Baines. You know it as the artichoke; we use its buds as food. So you see, the *pampas* and its surroundings furnish food and drink enough for a man to live on, if he so chooses. . . ." He was interrupted by a sudden snarl about two hundred feet due west.

John Cooper swiftly unsheathed "Long Girl." Dropping the reins of his horse and guiding it by the pressure of his knees, he brought the rifle into firing position, attentively squinting along the sights.

"The *gauchos* have flushed out one of those brutes," Raoul cried, as he spurred his horse onward.

"Be careful; be careful, Raoul," Heitor called in some alarm. "It may be hiding at the top of one of those trees waiting to—oh, *Dios!* It is as I feared!"

Suddenly, with an angry roar, a fawn-colored, two-hundred-pound puma leaped from the heavy branch of a tall live-oak tree.

John Cooper, already squinting down the sights, saw it and instantly pulled the trigger. There was a wild screech, and the great cat thudded to the ground, rolled over, clawed the earth a moment or two, and then lay still, only a few feet away from the mounted Raoul Maldones, whose horse was already rearing and pawing at the air with its front hooves, whinnying in terror.

Heitor turned to his American guest and said, *"Gran Dios,* it is like a miracle! Never have I seen a man shoot so swiftly and with such accuracy at such a distance! You have saved the life of my dearest friend!"

John Cooper was busy reloading "Long Girl." The *gauchos* circled back, and one of the bravest leaned forward from his saddle to prod the inert puma with the sharp tip of his half-moon lance. The animal did not move, for John Cooper's shot had pierced its heart.

"I am sure this is the one that killed the *criada, patrón,"* the *gaucho* called to Heitor. "It is the largest I have ever seen. *Dios,* what a shot!"

As John Cooper sheathed the rifle, Raoul rode up to him, his face pale. "You have saved my life, *amigo.* You are truly the man whom I would wish to be my *yerno."*

"That I will be, Raoul, for Dorotéa and I know we want each other, and all we need now is a date for our marriage."

"Then what say you to my asking Padre Rancorda to

marry you to my daughter a week from the day we return to my *estancia*? Does that please you?"

"Yes, Raoul, with all my heart and soul."

As they rode back to the *estancia* of Heitor Duvaldo, John Cooper thought to himself that he had won Catarina by saving the life of her brother, Carlos, from the springing cougar in the mountains of the Jicarilla Apache; and now, by a strange pattern of fate, he had also saved the life of his future father-in-law.

Rodrigo Baltenar scowled when he unfolded the letter from his prospective father-in-law. Curtly, hardly glancing at the *trabajador* who had brought it, he dismissed him. "Tell your *patrón* that I have received his message."

"Do you wish to send a reply, Señor Baltenar?" the man respectfully asked.

"Tell your *patrón* that I accept his decision."

After the man had left the *estanciero*'s chamber, Rodrigo Baltenar went to his desk and vigorously rang a silver handbell. A few moments later, his *capataz*, Luis García, entered, with an obsequious smile. "Luis, didn't we hire a pretty little *mestiza* a month or so ago to work in the kitchen?" Baltenar demanded.

"*Sí, patrón*. Her name is Evita Peshtigar, and she is sixteen."

"Very good. She has no *novio* here?"

"None at all, *señor patrón*. Do you wish me to bring her to you?"

"Luis, you are an incomparable *capataz*, and you know how to anticipate my wishes. Bring her at once. Then see that we are not disturbed."

The *capataz* withdrew with a knowing smirk. Baltenar, who wore a silk dressing gown over his *calzoncillos*, his feet encased in soft wool-lined leather slippers, turned to the little taboret beside his huge, four-poster, canopied bed and, opening a humidor, took out a Havana cigar. He chewed off the end and spat it out, then lifted a lighted candle till the flame touched the other end. For a moment, he amused himself with blowing clouds of redolent smoke rings and then musingly said, half aloud, "Well, it's no great loss. Dorotéa Maldones is much too willful for a man of my nature. She's forever riding horseback and doing other things that the *esposa* of an *estanciero* like me should not be doing. Hmm.

Now there's Adriana, nearly thirteen, and in some ways prettier— Let us see what happens in the next few years. If Señor Maldones finds himself in difficulties with Ramos, why, it well may be that he will seek me out again and, this time, I'll ask for Adriana."

He chuckled aloud at this fantasy and blew another series of smoke rings. There was a knock at the door, and he called out, "¡Entrate, pronto!"

The door was opened by Luis García, who pushed in a frightened, pretty black-haired girl whose father had been of Indian blood and whose mother was a *criada* from a neighboring *estancia*. At the sight of her master in so intimate a costume, she turned scarlet and, swiftly wheeling, found herself confronted by the grinning *capataz*, who shook his head and wagged a remonstrative finger at her. "*Pero no, muchachita.* You are to obey the *patrón*. Remember, if you do not do all that he desires, he will order me to give you a good thrashing. You would not like that, *querida*. Now be a good girl and remember, above all else, to do what you are told. It will come out well for you, if you do." With this, he left the room and closed the door behind him.

The middle-aged *estanciero* seated himself on the edge of the bed, puffing at his cigar as he deliberately studied the trembling young girl from head to toe. Evita, not knowing what attitude to take, clasped her hands in front of her, her fingers frantically twisting this way and that as she lowered her eyes to avoid his carnally appraising look. Finally, unable to bear the suspense any longer, she stammeringly pleaded, "Oh, please, *señor patrón*, I'm a good girl; I've never had a man; I just want to work and earn my keep here in your *estancia*—"

Before she could finish, he interrupted her with a lordly gesture. "Silence! You are going to do precisely what I tell you to, or, just as Luis says, I'll turn you over to him for a whipping. Take off your clothes."

"Oh, I beg of you, *señor patrón*, don't make me do it; please don't!" The girl fell to her knees, wringing her clasped hands as she imploringly stared at him. But Rodrigo Baltenar, usually so indolent and slothful, was unyielding, seeking as he was immediate assuagement from his disappointment over the loss of beautiful Dorotéa and her dowry.

"Shall I call Luis?" he asked snidely. "Because if I do, he will give you the whip, and he will be sure to take off all your clothes. Now be sensible, my little dove. If you are kind to me, I will be kind to you. It's as simple as that."

Sobbing, her head bowed, her trembling fingers reluctantly rising to the buttons at the bodice of her blouse, Evita Peshtigar began to undress.

Twenty-seven

John Cooper had already sent two letters back to the Double H Ranch. He had described to Don Diego and Doña Inez the pleasure he had experienced in visiting such a beautiful, strange country and the friendships he had made with Raoul Maldones and his *gauchos*. He had not touched on Dorotéa, save to comment that his host had four lovely, well-bred daughters, though he had somewhat wryly mentioned that young Andrew seemed to be smitten with Adriana.

He had let the aging *hidalgo* know that he had regained his peace of mind, and he gently urged Don Diego to rest assured that the memory of Catarina would always be in his heart; indeed, he had even felt her presence here in Argentina, guiding Andrew and himself in this new adventure.

He did not, however, write a third letter in which he would have related the betrothal of himself to Dorotéa and the subsequent marriage. He reasoned that he and his bride would arrive at the *Hacienda del Halcón* before the letter could be delivered. It was his intention to take Dorotéa back with him a few days after the wedding. John Cooper sensed that Don Diego's health, already having begun to fail, was waning fast, and it was his desire to have the old man meet and know the lovely girl who would take Catarina's place.

In the week of preparations that followed, the *trabajadores* as well as the *gauchos* were busy at the *estancia* decorating the courtyard, the chapel, and the house, bringing flowers and hunting game for the great feast and riding with invitations to Raoul Maldones's neighbors.

John Cooper went out with Felipe Mintras on the afternoon before his wedding. The two men had become fast friends, and although John Cooper had asked that the *gaucho* accompany him on a hunt using the *bola*, with Andrew riding along to test his own budding skill, the American's real purpose was to invite the friendly, homely, loyal *gaucho* to go back with him to the States. He had already asked his future father-in-law what he thought of the plan, and Raoul had endorsed it.

The afternoon was cool and beautiful, and their luck with the *bolas* was phenomenal. John Cooper brought down three quail, while Andrew caught a huge jackrabbit and a small deer, which he then dispatched with a shot from his rifle. Felipe accounted for a deer and two quail.

As they rode back to the *estancia*, John Cooper turned to the *gaucho* and said, "Felipe, tomorrow I shall marry the daughter of the *patrón*. Then we shall return to los Estados Unidos. I would like very much for you to accompany me, you and your wife, Luz, and your two sons. And your *patrón* thinks it would be a fine idea, too. You see, Felipe, I think that you could teach my *vaqueros* many useful ways to round up cattle, as well as to hunt."

"*Hombre,* I like you very much," Felipe said, beaming, "and your fine *hijo* there, who is almost a man himself. Yes, I would like this."

John Cooper clapped him on the back and laughed. "You had best tell Luz and the boys to pack. Within a week from tomorrow we shall all go back to the great *estancia* in Texas, which will be our home—yours, Felipe, as well as mine and Andrew's. I will give you land on which to settle, to have your own little house, which my *trabajadores* will help you build for you and your family. Yet you shall have the same freedom there that you know here on the *pampas*."

Felipe smiled and nodded. He halted his horse and reached over to John Cooper. The two men shook hands and exchanged a look of respectful admiration.

On the evening of the same day, Andrew went out for a stroll around the *estancia*. He was happy for his father. And after supper he went to the chapel to talk to old Padre Rancorda and to tell the priest how grateful he had been for the warm, compassionate advice that had eased his troubled mind over the death of his mother.

The priest smiled, made the sign of the cross over his head, and said, "My son, when you and your father came here for the first time, neither of you knew what *el Señor Dios* had willed for you both. Now, as you see, your father is about to take unto himself a fine, sweet, virtuous woman who will be a second mother to you. Perhaps He has already decreed whether you will return, and has ordained what will await you, when you do. I am glad, my son, that my humble words eased the hurt within you. Until tomorrow, then, when you will stand behind your father at the little altar that we have built out in the courtyard and where I shall unite your father to Dorotéa Maldones."

Andrew sighed happily. Yet there was a tinge of sadness to him, for he knew that within a week, he and his father would go back home. He would regret, he knew, not being alone with his father and sharing the latter's adventures and experiences, as he had done for all this time up to now. He could not quite explain why, but the sadness that had come over him made him wish that they could stay here for a few more weeks.

Perhaps a ride before going to bed would change this mood, he thought. He headed toward the stable, where he would saddle the fine colt Heitor Duvaldo had given him in Lobos. As he walked, he heard his name called, and when he turned, he saw Adriana.

"Adriana! It's dark and late! I didn't expect to see you—" he stammered, taken by surprise.

She put her finger to her lips, glancing warily back at the *hacienda,* as if afraid that someone would come out and take her back, then said, in a whisper, "Hush, or you will have Señora Josefa looking for me. She thinks I've gone to the chapel to say my prayers. Well, I did, but I saw you leave the *hacienda,* and I wanted to talk to you before tomorrow."

"That—that was very kind of you, Adriana. I—I wanted to talk to you, too," he said, his voice unsteady. She approached, and he thought that he had never seen a lovelier girl when she smiled at him.

"Señora Josefa will think I should have a good whipping for being so bold. But you will be going back to los Estados Unidos with your *papá* very soon, and then I shan't see you again."

"I—I told Padre Rancorda just this evening that I hoped I could come back one day soon, Adriana," he blurted.

"Oh? Why?"

"Well—because—well, Adriana, it's—well, your father is so kind, and I've had lots of fun learning how to use the *bola* and riding the horses here and meeting all the *gauchos*—and—and—"

"And what else, Andrew?" She put her hand on his and stood looking at him, scarcely a foot away.

Now it was Andrew's turn to glance around nervously. They were completely alone in the shadows of the evening, which darkened the stable off to one side of the *hacienda*.

He could no longer resist the impulse. For the first time, all his adolescent longing coalesced in the presence of this charming, saucy, spirited girl who had shown him such interest. He grasped her by the elbows, half afraid that she might slap him for his audacity, and before he knew it, found himself kissing her on the mouth. Then, still holding her, his face red as a beet, he gasped, "And—and I want to come back to you one day, Adriana! I—I like you so much—I think you're beautiful—please don't be angry with me—"

"Hush, hush, *querido*." Her words came in a soft, husky whisper, and he thought it was the most beautiful thing he had ever heard. "I'm not angry at all. *Te quiero mucho, mi* Andrew. I *do* want you to come back one day soon, *sí, es verdad!*"

"Will you—will you wait for me, Adriana? Like you, I—I'm not yet thirteen, and it's much too young to think about—you know—but—but I'm in love with you, Adriana—"

"And I with you, *mi corazón*," she whispered back. He let go of her elbows, and at once she flung her arms around his neck, squeezing him so tightly that he could scarcely breathe, as she kissed him again, then hastily whispered, "Now I must go back, for Señora Josefa will really give me a good whipping. I'm so glad you feel this way about me, Andrew. You'll write me, won't you, when you get back with your father and my sister?"

"Every day, if you want, Adriana," he promised.

She thought she heard someone calling her from the *hacienda*, gasped, then turned and fled. At the door, she turned back and blew him a kiss.

Andrew exhaled a sigh of ecstasy. He looked up at the

moon, and it was full. It had come out from behind a cloud, and its rays shone down on him. Maybe, he thought to himself, that was a good sign. He was much too excited to ride a horse. He wanted to go back and sleep and dream of Adriana. His *novia*. He didn't think he would tell his father just yet, because the latter had poked fun at him a little about Adriana. But maybe on the return journey, when they were alone, he would tell him that he hoped he could come back one day when he was old enough to marry her.

Porfirio Ramos paid a visit to the *hacienda* of Rodrigo Baltenar, for the outward purpose of congratulating him upon his forthcoming marriage; in reality he wanted to learn whether the wealthy landholder definitely stood on the side of Raoul Maldones and the other *estancieros* who continued to defy the *porteño* government in Buenos Aires.

The foppish Baltenar was pleasantly surprised as well as flattered by this visit, and had an excellent supper served to his guest. Then, as Evita, the lovely young *mestiza* whom he had made his concubine, served the two men brandy and coffee and lit their cigars, Baltenar told Ramos, "Señor, the betrothal between myself and the Señorita Maldones has been dissolved at the wish of her father."

Ramos was scarcely paying attention to his host as his eyes rested on the trembling, blushing young serving girl, clad in a sleeveless red silk blouse and a thin black silk skirt cinched at the waist with a silver belt.

At last Ramos answered his companion, "What a shame, Rodrigo—allow me to call you that, for I feel drawn toward you, *amigo*. Do you have any suspicions as to the reason behind this sudden and unexpected reversal of plans? Why, all the *pampas* believed that you would soon be the husband of that exquisite creature."

"Well, I will be frank with you, Porfirio—if I may return the compliment, for you were certainly never my enemy. Before the proclamation of the banns, I visited his *estancia* to pay court to my betrothed. He demanded of me that I swear to protect him with my *gauchos* and my *trabajadores* against the possibility of your attacks, or those of your *porteño* friends in Buenos Aires."

Ramos's eyebrows arched as he feigned a look of astonishment. "Incredible! But that is sheer nonsense; Señor Maldones must be seeing ghosts under the bed! I, attack him?

When it is well known that he has one of the largest *estancias* on the *pampas* and an army of *gauchos* fiercely loyal to him? He has neighbors, as well, who would be his allies. Why would I be such a fool to risk my own holdings? Oh, no, that is a total misunderstanding."

"That is what I thought, Porfirio, and that is why I refused to become involved. I have no desire for violence. I live here comfortably, as you can see." He beckoned to the trembling young girl to fill his goblet with more brandy and, as she did so, slyly ran his palm over the jutting curves of her resilient buttocks, so unnerving her that she very nearly dropped the decanter. "Careful, *mi corazón*. If you ruin that cut-glass decanter from Belgium, I shall have to turn you over to Luis García for a whipping. It would be a pity to mar such warm, satiny skin with the weals of the whip." He watched her back away, trembling, biting her lips in confusion, then abruptly dismissed her. Turning to his guest, he went on in a tone of self-pity. "It was evident that Señorita Dorotéa had no love for me, that she was simply being used by her father as a pawn in his little game to entrap me into hostilities that would be unjust and unfounded. That is why I refused. A man has his honor."

"Of a certainty, and one can tell how honorable you are, my dear Rodrigo," Ramos said with a sly note of sarcasm in his voice, which his host did not detect. "I shall not forget this integrity of yours, Rodrigo. I tell you this: If it is ever necessary to take action against the Señor Maldones because of his arrogance and his defiance of the welfare of the *pampas* and the land that he holds through the good graces of our *presidente*, I shall count upon you as a man of steadfast principle. My powerful friends at Buenos Aires will not forget that Rodrigo Baltenar stood against treachery and wrongdoing, even though it cost him the hand in marriage of one of the most beautiful young women in all Argentina."

"I am heartened by your words. I promise you that my *gauchos* will never take any action against yours, or, indeed, defend the land of Raoul Maldones. If he has a war with you, it is doubtless of his own making. I have no part in it, rest assured."

"I am happy to hear you speak so, my dear Rodrigo. What excellent brandy!"

"Let me call Evita back to fill your goblet, dear friend,"

the middle-aged *estanciero* fawningly proffered. "You will spend the night here as my guest, of course—"

"Yes, it would be most comfortable for me, for I rode a long way to come to see you."

"To be sure, to be sure! Well then, let me, as a token of our newly cemented friendship, Porfirio, offer you the attentions of the charming *criada* who will serve you brandy . . . and all your other needs this night."

"Oh, come, I would not for the world deprive you of the tender charms of that lovely creature," Ramos sniggered as he stealthily licked his lips and eyed his host.

"I insist!" Baltenar reached for the silver bell beside him and imperiously shook it. Evita hurried back into the dining room.

"Pour my good friend Porfirio more brandy. I am going to bed, Evita. You will attend my guest, and you will not leave him until he has no further need of you. Do you understand me?"

The girl uttered a choking sob, then bowed her head before her master's glaring look, and, in a tiny voice, responded, *"Sí, patrón."*

The next morning, greatly pleased with himself and the alliance he had made with Rodrigo Baltenar, Porfirio Ramos returned to his ranch and summoned his *capataz.*

"Listen to me carefully, Hermán," Ramos said. "Did you not once tell me a cousin of yours had joined the fierce Charrúa, who live in the grasslands north of the Rio de la Plata?"

"Yes, *mi patrón.* It is Alfredo Gómez I told you of. He killed a man in Mendoza and took flight lest he suffer the *garrote.* By good luck, he came upon a band of Charrúa hunting, and a wild *jabalí* attacked the chief. My cousin, who was hiding in a thicket because he knew the Charrúa to be hostile to *gringos,* drew his *pistola* and killed the brute with the first shot. For this, he was taken into the tribe."

"He is still there?" Ramos demanded.

"Sí, patrón. He married one of their women and has had three brats by her. I know him to be near Campana, about a hundred miles from Lobos. The main band is farther to the northwest, but Alfredo and some hundred of those *indios* live just beyond the town, in the high grasslands."

"Do you yourself know the Charrúa, Hermán?" Ramos pursued.

"*Pero sí, patrón.*" Hermán Salcedo's lips curved in a cunning smile. "I have met some of them, when I visited my cousin. I sell them the rum my *trabajadores* make, and they do favors for me. Do you not remember Itarda, the *mestiza* whom I brought to you last year for your pleasure?"

"I do, indeed." Ramos grinned and winked. "A real *puta,* that one."

"Well, *patrón,* when I knew that you sought a *muchacha linda* for your bed, one who would especially please you, I asked my cousin Alfredo to do me this favor. Some of his Charrúa braves kidnapped the slut from her master's *estancia,* which was not far from Campana. He believes her dead."

"So she must be by now," Ramos cynically retorted with a sardonic chuckle. "When I tired of her, I gave her to one of my *porteño* friends who owns a bordello on the outskirts of Buenos Aires."

"Yes, I'd almost forgotten. Now how exactly may I serve you, *patrón?*"

"In this way, and listen attentively, Hermán. I have learned that this *americano* dog and the Señorita Dorotéa are to be married a week from this very day. You will tell your cousin that you wish twenty-five of his *indios* to attack the Maldones *estancia.* From all I have heard, they are fierce fighters, those Charrúa."

"*Seguramente, patrón.* They use the skulls of their enemies as drinking cups. They are marksmen with the bow and arrow, for they can kill a rhea at a hundred yards. They are well versed in the use of the *bola,* the sling, and the spear. Oh, yes, even against any rifles and *pistolas* that the Señor Maldones and his men may have, the Charrúa could quite likely defeat them," the *capataz* boasted.

"I am not concerned whether they can defeat Maldones or not, Hermán," the *estanciero* countered. "Let these *indios* of yours kill a few *gauchos* and, if they are able, carry off a few of the *criadas.* That will be their prize. Take care, however, that they do no harm to Maldones's daughters, particularly the Señoritas Dorotéa and Adriana. I myself have plans for them, one day."

"But you told me, *patrón,* that the Señorita Dorotéa is to marry this *americano,*" Salcedo protested.

"If he is killed, it is a certainty that she will not leave

for los Estados Unidos once she is a widow. You take my meaning?"

"Only too well, *patrón*," Salcedo grinned.

"Then go at once to meet with your cousin Hermán. Take jugs of rum and some bottles of whiskey from my cellar as presents for the Charrúa. Promise them more, as well as the *criadas*. That will win their loyalty. See to it that the braves attack just at sunset. It will be, as I estimate, the height of the festivities celebrating the marriage of the *americano* to the Señorita Dorotéa. No one will be expecting it. Accomplish this for me, Hermán, and I will see to it that you are given part of the Señor Maldones's land, and you may have your choice of four of his loveliest *criadas*."

The *capataz* grinned again, baring yellow teeth in an ugly smile. "For such a reward, *mi patrón*, I would sell my soul to *el diablo* himself!"

Twenty-eight

John Cooper knelt before old Padre Emilcar Rancorda, with Dorotéa beside him at the ceremony that would make them one. The American had changed from his buckskins to a white linen coat and breeches given to him by his father-in-law, while Dorotéa was angelically garbed in a long white gown with puffed sleeves and bodice, and a train held up by her two sisters, Paquita and María. Adriana served as flower girl; she, too, wore white and carried an enormous bouquet of yellow roses. Andrew, uncomfortable in a silk shirt with a high collar and black cotton breeches, stood opposite Adriana.

Three of the couples who had been at the Duvaldo *estancia* ten days before, as well as Heitor Duvaldo and his two sons, were in attendance at the wedding. Raoul Maldones, elegantly dressed in a waistcoat, cravat, and breeches, had given the bride away, and stood at Dorotéa's right.

Señora Josefa was the matron of honor, and she was surreptitiously mopping her tear-filled eyes with a lace-trimmed handkerchief. Beside her stood old Stancia, who was Dorotéa's nurse. A woman in her early sixties, she had been a devoted *criada* to Raoul's dead wife, Carlotta, and won a place of honor in the household. Raoul had insisted that she do no work save to counsel and befriend his oldest daughter, for of course Señora Josefa had the role of *dueña* to all four girls when it was a question of social amenities.

Dorotéa and John Cooper rose as the kindly priest gestured to them and then began to read the service of holy matrimony. For John Cooper, it was a magical moment. It seemed to him, as Padre Rancorda intoned the first lines of the ceremony, that all his life was passing before him in review . . . he saw himself and Lije hiding in the cornfield and watching with horror the massacre of his family . . . the flight westward with its perilous encounter with the bushwhackers who had tried to kill him and take his bearskin and "Long Girl" . . . the sanctuary among the friendly Ayuhwa and his initiation into manhood by the lovely Degala, whose shameful bondage he had ended by hunting the killer bear . . . his peril-ridden sojourn with the Skidi Pawnee, from whom he had rescued the daughter of a Sioux chief, who had been destined for sacrifice to Morning Star . . . his restoration of her to her father, her profession of love for him, which he had renounced, but which had compelled him to kill the son of the shaman to save his own life . . . and then the flight from the wintry land of the Dakotas with Lije and the cub Lobo to the Jicarilla stronghold in New Mexico, with six Sioux braves on his trail, intent on avenging the death of the shaman's son . . . his acceptance by the Jicarilla and his blood brotherhood with Descontarti, and then his saving Carlos from the mountain lion. It had been a cycle of his own resourcefulness pitted against manifold dangers, and at their end he had known the rapture of love and the responsibility of a family of his own.

He turned to look at Dorotéa and saw the adoration and desire in her eyes, and he trembled in his awareness of how deeply she loved him, how candidly, unashamedly, she showed it with that look. His heart went out to her, and he took her hand and squeezed it, and he whispered, *"Te quiero, mi corazón."*

It was time for the ring to be placed on her finger, and

John Cooper started, remembering that he had not thought of this part of the ceremony, and inwardly furious with himself for such neglectfulness. Suddenly he heard a whisper, "I have it here for you, John Cooper." Raoul put something in his hand. Automatically, he glanced at it, and his eyes widened: It was a magnificent blood-red ruby, mounted on a thin gold band. Raoul whispered, "I gave it to my wife on our wedding day."

John Cooper's throat was choked with emotion, and all he could do was nod, for now Dorotéa was looking at him so trustingly, her hand in his, her lips quivering. He had an urge to kiss her then and there—but it would have been improper. Instead, lifting her right hand, he kissed it reverently, and then placed the ring on the appropriate finger.

Old Padre Rancorda smiled. "Before *el Señor Dios*, by virtue of the authority vested in me, the humble priest of His bidding, I pronounce you *esposo y esposa*, till death and beyond in the Resurrection and the whole of life to come, in His blessed name."

"Amen," John Cooper and Dorotéa said simultaneously. A murmur of delight ran through the audience as he now turned to her, his hands gently grasping her by the shoulders, and his mouth fused to hers. He heard her whisper, just as he began to kiss her, "Oh, my dearest one, my darling, *mi esposo!*"

There followed a flurry of congratulations and good wishes, and Andrew came up beside his father and kissed his new mother, though he blushed to his earlobes.

As John Cooper led his beautiful young wife to the center of the courtyard, the *vaqueros* who had accompanied their *patrón* this long way to Argentina reached out to shake his hand or clap him on the back. At the same time, the *gauchos* were cheering, and when they fell silent, John Cooper addressed them. *"Hombres,* I can't find words to tell you how happy I am to have you here on this day. I have learned in this short time to respect you for your courage and your honesty, for your horsemanship and your valor as loyal friends of my *suegro*. Let me say here and now that he is a dear friend, and I am grateful to *el Señor Dios* for his friendship and for the way he received my son and me when we came to your country. Now, my wife and my son and I invite you to share in our wedding feast, to dance with us, to enjoy the music, and to play and sing the songs of the *pampas*, so that we shall never forget this blessed day."

By then it was nearly sundown, and the household servants were turning the spits over the fires to roast the mutton and the beef and the venison and the quail, while the *criadas* set the tables and decorated them with vases filled with lush tropical flowers. The same musicians who had played on the evening John Cooper had first come to the *estancia* of Raoul Maldones were there again, and they were playing the *fandangos* and other dances of old Spain, together with the languorous melodies of the *pampas*, which they themselves performed in their own *fiestas* far from the *haciendas* of the *patrónes*.

Raoul Maldones had asked Padre Rancorda to join him at the table, where he sat with his daughters, his son-in-law, and the latter's son. Lifting his wine glass, the priest rose to propose a toast.

"My children, God is good to us this day. He blesses this household; He looks down from His Heaven and sees that the world he made is good and that . . ."

There was a shriek as an arrow thudded into the priest's heart. He stood a moment, his eyes glassy, and then the glass dropped from his hand, and he fell forward across the table.

"*¡Los indios, los indios, protéjanse!*" Felipe Mintras cried as he ducked under the table where he and his fellow *gauchos* were seated. Drawing his knife, he flung it with all his strength at the back of the Indian rider who had just galloped by and released the fatal arrow. The Charrúa, a short, stocky man with a grass helmet, leather jacket and breeches, and moccasins made from the skin of the puma, uttered a cry. He flung up his arms, dropped his bow and quiver, pitched off his horse, and lay still.

Nearly a dozen Charrúa galloped through the courtyard, and John Cooper pulled Dorotéa down under the table just as an arrow whizzed by her, imbedding itself in the wall of the wing of the *hacienda*. Raoul Maldones cried out, "*Gauchos*, after them!"

A *gaucho* drew his pistol, squinted along the sight, and pulled the trigger as an Indian horseman lowered his lance toward the *gaucho*'s chest. The Indian, with a gurgling cry, clutched at his throat and fell to the ground.

Felipe barked orders to his men. "You, Juan, to the shed with the rifles! You, Corrado, get your *bola;* you, too, Benito!

Come, you others. Wait till they've ridden through, before they turn back, then to the stable, *pronto!*"

"Get inside the house, my darling," John Cooper whispered to his wife, who crouched under the table beside him, trembling, her face pale. "I'll take you. There, the first wave of attackers is gone! Now, run for it with me, my darling!"

As the last horseman went by with a savage yell, the ten Charrúa who had ridden past in this surprise attack now wheeled their horses to regroup and charge again back into the midst of the terrified guests. Heitor Duvaldo, livid with fury, seized a heavy cut-glass decanter of wine, and as one of them came at him with a leveled spear, flung it with all his might into the Indian's face, smashing his nose and teeth. With a scream, the Indian fell out of his saddle and tumbled onto the ground, reaching for his sharp knife. Instantly, one of John Cooper's *vaqueros* sprang forward, throttling him with both hands until the Indian slumped in death.

John Cooper and Dorotéa gained the safety of the *hacienda* as he ordered, "Go into the bedroom and crawl under the bed, just in case they attack the *hacienda!* I'll get my rifle, *mi corazón!*"

Señora Josefa, emulating the action of the others, had made the other three girls crouch down under the long, rectangular table to be out of harm's way. There was the sound of whirring arrows, and one of them found a *gaucho*'s throat as he was running to the stable. He ran a few steps, clutching at the arrow, his eyes goggling in their sockets, then stumbled down to one knee, and rolled over, dead.

John Cooper emerged, "Long Girl" in his hands, and, kneeling, took careful aim at the Indian who led the return attack. With the crack of the rifle, the Indian was flung out of his saddle, as if by an invisible hand, and his horse galloped wildly on.

Felipe and the other *gauchos* reached the stable and mounted their horses, uncoiling their *bolas*. John Cooper reloaded swiftly just as one of the Charrúa galloped toward him. John Cooper threw down the rifle, drew his Bowie knife, stepped back, and flung the sharp knife into the Indian's heart. He fell at the feet of John Cooper, who rolled him over, wrenched out the knife, and waited for another attacker. From the west, another group of ten Charrúa rode, brandishing their lances and howling their war cry, their faces painted red and yellow, hideous with grimaces.

John Cooper reloaded his rifle, and seeing one of the Charrúa pose his spear and ride after a *gaucho* who was running toward the stable, pulled the trigger. The Indian dropped his lance and fell backward over the tail of his horse, one foot twisted in the stirrup, as the maddened pinto galloped on, dragging its rider's lifeless body with it.

Fifteen of the *gauchos*, led by Felipe, mounted and whirled their *bolas*. Seeing one of the Charrúa come at him, the adroit *gaucho* let his *bola* fly, and the leather-covered stones wrapped around the Indian's throat. Dropping his lance, the Charrúa tried to unwrap the *bola*, blood pouring down his neck from the gash at his left jawbone. The Indian lost his balance and fell from his horse with a shriek of agony. Swiftly, Felipe dismounted, agilely ran, crouching, to the wounded Indian, caught the latter's hand as he was about to stab at the *gaucho* with his knife, and turned it back into the Indian's heart. He tore out the knife, then unwrapped his *bola* from the dead body, hurried back to his horse, and leaped into the saddle. *"¡Adelante, muchachos!* After them!" he shouted.

Calling to his *vaqueros* to look after everyone at the *hacienda*, John Cooper ran to the stable and found the wiry colt that he had ridden during his visit. There was no time to saddle it; he leaped on its bare back and urged it after the *gauchos* who were pursuing the remaining band of Charrúa.

The man who had played the mandolin so beautifully to welcome John Cooper on his first night at the *estancia* had been killed. The courtyard was empty and silent as Señora Josefa clambered out from under the table, puffing and panting, urging her three girls, "Quickly now, quickly! Paquita, stop crying, or I'll give you something to cry about! Get into the house as fast as your legs can carry you, I mean it, Paquita! You go with her, María! Paquita, take María's hand! Adriana, stop gawking! Poor Padre Rancorda, may God take his kind soul! Oh, *Dios, Dios*, what a day this is, and such a day for my *pobrecita* Dorotéa's wedding!" Crossing herself, she waddled after the three girls back into the *hacienda*.

After making their attack on the *hacienda*, the Charrúa turned and headed eastward toward the coastline, then turned again to the north directly into the *pampas*, expecting to lose their followers in the tall, wavy grass. As he rode, John Cooper reloaded "Long Girl" and, catching up with Felipe, who led the charge of some fifteen *gauchos*, called to him, "We must capture one or two alive and find out why they attacked us!"

"That is what I am thinking, too, *amigo*," the *gaucho* shouted back. "These are Charrúa, from the north beyond Buenos Aires. Why they came so far to attack our *estancia*, I, too, am eager to know!" Then, waving his short-brimmed hat, he shouted to his men, "Faster, faster, are you old women that you ride so slowly?"

Spurring their horses and shouting encouragements, the *gauchos* rode swiftly through the *pampas*. They saw ten of the Indians, some of them glancing back to see how near their pursuers were.

"Give me your *bola!*" John Cooper shouted to Felipe, who nodded and tossed it to the American. John Cooper deftly caught it and began to whirl it around his head as he spurred his colt forward, racing after the last straggler in the small band of fleeing Charrúa.

Leaning over the neck of his colt, John Cooper drew every iota of stamina from the wiry horse, and gradually the distance between him and the last Indian was reduced to a few yards. Leaning back, he whirled the *bola* and sent it flying. It wrapped around the Charrúa's middle, stunning him and toppling him from the saddle. John Cooper leaped down and, drawing his Bowie knife, crouched over the fallen Indian, putting the blade against the dark-skinned Charrúa's throat. "Speak now; who sent you to attack us?" he urged in Spanish.

The Indian's eyes were wide with fear, and he squirmed under the prick of the knife. "Not kill! I talk!" he said in guttural pidgin Spanish. "Alfredo Gómez. He bring us. He say we attack *estancia!*"

The other *gauchos* reined in, making a circle around the fallen Indian and John Cooper. One of them leaped down from his horse and, drawing his half-moon knife, was about to stab the Indian, but John Cooper shouted, "No, I want him alive; I want to find out who ordered him and his men to attack your *patrón!*"

"Put away your knife, *estúpido*," Felipe snapped, "or I'll break it over my knee and give you a spanking!"

This sally broke the tension, and the other *gauchos* laughed at their comrade's discomfiture, as he shuffled back, muttering under his breath.

"Go on, speak!" John Cooper urged, and touched the point of the knife to the Indian's throat again to quicken his response.

"I say, it Alfredo Gómez."

"Yes, yes, but *quien es* Alfredo Gómez?" John Cooper pursued.

"He and Salcedo, they are family!" the Indian gasped.

John Cooper straightened, turning to Felipe. "Salcedo's the *capataz* of Ramos, isn't he?"

"*Sí, amigo.* Now I understand everything. That *cobarde*, that *porteño*-lover Ramos, he has had his *capataz* bring in the Charrúa. Now I remember! This Alfredo Gómez, he went to live with the Charrúa, and he is *primo* to this filth of a Salcedo!"

John Cooper grasped the Charrúa's wrist and twisted it, putting the knife to the Indian's heart. "*¿Dónde está Salcedo, capataz de Ramos, hombre?*" he growled.

The Charrúa began to speak in his own dialect, but only a few words, intermixed with Spanish and an unfamiliar dialect, emerged. Yet John Cooper and Felipe were able to understand enough of the garbled Spanish. The Indian said that his companions were going back to the camp where they had stayed since they came from their own village, which was near Campana. It was at this camp that Salcedo, along with a few Indians who did not go on the raid against the *estancia*, was waiting.

"*Gran Dios,*" the *gaucho* ejaculated, "Campana is more than a hundred miles from here. What a *bastardo* this Ramos is, to bring the Charrúa all the way from their village to do his dirty work for him!"

"Where can we find Salcedo? Where is this camp you mention?" John Cooper asked the fearful Charrúa, and quickened his reply with tiny touches of the knife. The Indian excitedly and hoarsely began to talk so swiftly that John Cooper could hardly understand, and he made the Indian repeat it slowly.

"Camp is mile from here and inland. It is near forest of hardwood trees."

"I know the place!" Felipe exclaimed. "We will go there, and we will bring this filth of a Salcedo back to my *patrón* for judgment and punishment. He can be useful, if he confesses his association with Ramos. Once we have him and can use him as a witness, Señor Maldones can bring Ramos before a court of law and have him punished. But I hope that the *patrón* turns this Salcedo over to us, for we have a score to settle with him. Two of our men dead, two of our good friends, who shared our *maté* and our beef and sang songs with us. Both of them have wives and children who will go hungry now."

"I will not let that happen; I give you my promise. Neither will the *patrón*," John Cooper declared. Gesturing to the Indian to mount his horse, he spoke in Spanish, "Take us to the camp. When you see your fellows, tell them that we do not wish to kill them. We wish only to punish the *capataz* Salcedo. Go now, go ahead of us, catch up with your *compañeros,* and tell them what I have told you!"

The sky was cloudless, and the moonlight helped show the way as John Cooper and the *gauchos* rode after the Charrúa. The Indian galloped to rejoin his companions, who had slackened their pace when they saw he was not among them. He told them how he had been overtaken and what had been said to him. John Cooper could tell this from the way the other Charrúa glanced back over their shoulders.

"We must prove, *amigo,*" Felipe called to him, "that it was Ramos and Salcedo. It would be good if we could find that scum who calls himself a *capataz* with *los indios.* Then we would know for certain!"

"I hope that also, Felipe. Look, the Indians are not galloping away. The man I talked to must have convinced them."

The Indians turned and passed beyond a giant *ombú* tree. The last man in the line, the man John Cooper had caught, gestured with his free hand, indicating that his pursuers should follow.

"He's leading us to the camp," John Cooper told Felipe. "Have your *gauchos* get their weapons ready, just in case of a trap."

The *gaucho* replied, "To live on the *pampas,* one is always one step ahead of the beasts of prey and the two-legged beasts who are even more deadly."

"Forgive me, Felipe; it was just second nature to me to say that."

"*Ya lo sé.* But look, *amigo,* I see a fire!" Felipe suddenly called, pointing toward his left. He wheeled his horse in that direction, and John Cooper and the other *gauchos* followed hard on his heels. The Charrúa ahead of them were slowing their pace. All the *gauchos* had their *bolas,* spears, and guns ready for use.

"I will go forward into the camp," John Cooper said.

The Charrúa whose life John Cooper had spared now faced him at a distance of ten paces and, patting his chest, declared in pidgin Spanish and many gesticulated signs, "I am Potormingay of the Charrúa. This is our camp, and the *capataz* who is the *primo* of Alfredo Gómez waits here for us."

"Good! Take us to him, Potormingay," John Cooper directed.

The *gauchos* swiftly dismounted, their weapons readied, as Potormingay held a brief conference with his companions, then gestured, with sweeps of his open arms, to indicate that they should follow him.

They saw domed huts of bent poles covered with the skins of guanacos, deer, and cattle. Felipe muttered to John Cooper, "When the Charrúa move on, they leave these wooden frames for others to use, and take just the skins with them. They came from a long ways. There are not many. There is someone at the very edge of their camp whom I cannot see. Be careful; perhaps it is Salcedo!"

Even as he spoke, the figure in the shadows came forward, crouching, cursing in guttural Spanish, "Dogs, whose mothers were diseased rats, you have come here to die!"

There was the bark of a pistol, and one of the *gauchos* at John Cooper's right clutched his belly, groaned, then fell forward. Instantly, John Cooper flung himself down on the ground and, the butt of his rifle pressed hard against his shoulder, pulled the trigger.

There was a gurgling scream. The shadowy figure stumbled forward, took several steps, dropped his pistol, then collapsed on the ground and rolled over in death.

Cries came from the Charrúa who were in the huts as they hurried out, holding their spears and knives.

"Drop your weapons!" John Cooper cried out in Spanish. "Your friends have brought us here to make peace and to talk; do not waste your lives! We have more men than you, and we are well armed! Drop your weapons!"

The Charrúa braves obeyed, and Potormingay ran to one of them, prostrated himself, and began to talk in a dialect that John Cooper could not make out.

The man before whom he had prostrated himself was

burly, his face painted red and yellow, his nose straight and sharp, his hair coarse and black and falling almost to his shoulders. A rhea feather was thrust through it, and he wore a garland of wildflowers woven around his forehead, while in his right hand he carried a spear.

John Cooper approached, drawing his Bowie knife and holding it ready to throw. Felipe and the other *gauchos* came forward now with their *bolas*, pistols, and knives.

Potormingay crouched on all fours and backed away from the *jefe* of the Charrúa, glancing fearfully up at John Cooper and mumbling in his pidgin Spanish, "Our chief, Micidata, he say he make talk with you. I tell him you spare my life."

"*Bueno*, Potormingay. I will talk with your *jefe*," John Cooper said. Then he came forward, the long rifle gripped in his left hand, his right hand at his Bowie knife, and smiled at the formidable-looking *jefe*. "*Soy* John Cooper Baines, *americano*. We come in peace. But one of your men fired at us and killed one of our *gauchos*. I shot so that there would be no more dead among us, for we come in peace."

The *jefe* grunted. He flung out his right arm toward the corpse who lay obscured in the shadows and declared, "He *capataz*, he *primo* of Alfredo Gómez. He Salcedo. He bring us much rum and guns; he tell us we have women if we attack the *estancia* of enemy of his *patrón*."

"He is the *capataz* of Porfirio Ramos, Micidata," John Cooper declared. "Do you know where the *patrón* of this Salcedo is now?"

"*Sí*, is in Buenos Aires."

John Cooper turned to Felipe. "I might have guessed it. He had his foreman bring these Indians in and then went away so that his dirty work wouldn't be known." To the chief, he said, "This afternoon, I took a wife. Your warriors rode into our *estancia* and killed our *gauchos* and the old *padre*. This was an evil thing. If they did this because Salcedo gave them rum and guns, they should be punished. Do you war against the men of the *pampas*?"

Micidata shook his head. "This *primo* of Alfredo Gómez, he say to us, it is joke. It is to frighten the *mujeres* and the *niños*, and Potormingay say to me, '*Jefe*, we not kill; we frighten them. For this, we receive many goods in trade.' That is true, I say this to you, I, *jefe* of the Charrúa."

"Then you were lied to, *jefe*. Ramos, through his *capa-*

taz and your Alfredo Gómez, has tricked you and made you outlaws, men whom my *gauchos* could easily kill now because we outnumber you. But we come in peace, as I have told you."

"I hear you, *gringo*." Micidata folded his arms across his chest and scowled at the crouching Charrúa, who had come to him to tell of the reason for the pursuit of the *gauchos*. "You have lied to me, as has Salcedo. You knew, as leader of the band of warriors, that I wanted no people to be killed. But you allowed that to happen. Why? Was it because Salcedo bribed you?"

Potormingay lowered his head even more, as if to admit his guilt.

"You, Potormingay," the chief continued, "are banished from our tribe. You will live on the *pampas*, and no man will help you. If a Charrúa sees you from dawn of tomorrow on, he will kill you. Now go!"

John Cooper did not understand the words, for the chief had spoken in his own tongue, not the pidgin Spanish. But he understood their purport, and he said in Spanish, "The *jefe* of the Charrúa is wise." Then he and Felipe strode forward and approached the inert figure beyond in the shadows. The *gaucho* bent down and rolled the man over, then nodded. "Yes, it is that scum, Hermán Salcedo. That is one less enemy, a bad one, *mi compañero*."

Making gestures, the chief spoke again to John Cooper, who turned back to Felipe. "He invites us to eat with him and his men. He swears by his gods that he did not know that his braves would try to kill when they rode into the *estancia* of your *patrón*. I believe him. Let us do as he wishes. It will bring peace. They will go back to their stronghold far from here, and perhaps when Ramos learns that his trick did not work, he will think twice before attacking again."

"Let us hope you are right, *hombre*," Felipe said with a shrug.

The Charrúa chief sat beside John Cooper at the meal of roasted capybara with plaintains, and the roasted meat of a small anaconda, which had been pickled in herbs and brine. John Cooper forced himself to eat a few mouthfuls and to proclaim them tasty. Micidata, who was seated cross-legged on a small grass mat, reached between his thick, muscular legs and lifted a pouch made of deerskin. He took out a polished skull, which had been lined with wax to seal the orifices. The top was open to be used as a drinking cup. Into this, one of the braves poured from a clay jug a foaming, dark brown liquid, which the *jefe* urged John Cooper to taste, handing him the skull. In his pidgin Spanish, Micidata, grinning, explained, "This skull of Raseybuse, once he *jefe* of Puelche tribe. I, *jefe* of Charrúa, kill him with my spear. Now I drink from his skull to you, *gringo valeroso!*"

John Cooper hid his distaste as he sipped the strong brew, which was a native beer and highly seasoned with herbs he could not recognize. Then he said, gesturing with his hands to express those Spanish words that Micidata might not recognize, "I promise to give you a gift of cattle, one for each of your warriors who died in the raid. This is to show you that our *patrón,* who is my *suegro,* does not blame you because the *estanciero* Ramos tricked you and your men into fighting his battle for him."

"That is good. We Charrúa promise not to attack these *gringos* with whom you ride. I swear on this skull of my enemy!"

John Cooper rose, and Felipe and the other *gauchos* with him. Felipe said, "We will drive twenty-five head of cattle out to the *ombú* tree where his men turned to lead us to this camp. It will be done tomorrow, after the *siesta.*"

Micidata nodded his head and sprang to his feet. He clapped his hands, issuing orders in his guttural dialect. Two braves brought out a superb black stallion, snorting and prancing. "My gift to you, *gringo valeroso,*" Micidata said as he handed the reins to John Cooper. "Go in peace. Tomorrow, my men wait at the *ombú* for the cattle you promise. When we find them, then I know that you speak true and are friend to Charrúa!"

After thanking the chief and turning his colt over to a *gaucho,* John Cooper mounted the stallion and called to Felipe, "Back to the *estancia* as fast as we can!"

It was nearly midnight when John Cooper rode into the courtyard of the Maldones ranch. The *gauchos* took care of the horses while he walked back to the *hacienda.* Ruefully, he looked at himself. His fine wedding suit was tattered and begrimed, and he thought what a shabby figure he must seem to his bride. The door of the *hacienda* opened, and Raoul came out, his face taut with concern. Then, with a shout of joy, he exclaimed, "God be praised, John Cooper! We had thought you dead, you and the *gauchos* who went with you."

Swiftly, the American told his father-in-law what had taken place. "I shot Salcedo, and from the Charrúa we learned that Ramos went on to Buenos Aires. In this way, he would seem innocent of the treacherous attack on the *fiesta*. Now I must go to Dorotéa," John Cooper said, glancing down at himself with a disgusted look.

"She is waiting for you. She is still in our little chapel, praying for your safe return."

"But I must bathe—"

Raoul chuckled. "That is easily done, *mi hijo*. I will have some of my *criadas* heat pails of water and bring them to you. Hurry, and I will go tell Dorotéa that you have returned safely to her."

In a blue silk dressing robe, his feet thrust into sandals, cleansed and refreshed, John Cooper approached the chamber at the right wing of the *hacienda* that had been set apart for Dorotéa and him as a hymeneal retreat. He drew a deep breath, raised his hand to the door, and knocked gently.

"Come to me, *mi esposo*," Dorotéa's sweet voice called.

He opened the door and closed it behind him, then locked it. She sat in a four-poster bed, propped up by three pillows, under a canopy. She wore an exquisite white lace-trimmed shift, and her black hair, glossy and curled into ringlets, tumbled below her shoulders. On her lips was an enchanting, bewitching smile.

"Dorotéa, forgive me. . . ." he began in a voice that was hoarse and unsteady from his mixed emotions.

She shook her head. *"Mi corazón*, there is nothing to forgive. *Mi padre* just told me what you did for us all. The Charrúa might have killed you, and I should have been a widow on my wedding day. Come to me; I have waited so long for you. I love you, John Cooper; make me yours in every way. I want to belong to you, I want to give you a child, a son—"

He was trembling as he approached the bed, and Dorotéa smiled at him, without fear or shyness. She held out her arms, and he turned to blow out the candle, but she murmured, "No, it solaced me here while I waited for you, not knowing whether you would return. I wish to look upon you, and I wish you to look upon me, and I hope that you will find me to your liking, my very dear *esposo!*"

With a cry of rapture, John Cooper went to her; he took her in his arms, and she embraced him as their lips met. Thus his new life began, as it was ordained.

A week after his wedding day, in late July, John Cooper prepared to board the frigate *Sea Witch,* commanded by Captain Nicholas Voorter, an affable, red-bearded Dutchman. Earlier, one of Raoul Maldones's *gauchos* had ridden to the port of Buenos Aires, and there made all arrangements.

Accompanying John Cooper, his son, and his new wife were old Stancia, Dorotéa's nurse, as well as Felipe Mintras, his wife, Luz, and their two little sons. Of course the four *vaqueros* who had accompanied John Cooper and his son were also present, anxious to return to Texas.

The cattle had been delivered to the Charrúa, as John Cooper promised; now, at least, his father-in-law need have no fear of another Indian attack. Meanwhile, Raoul Maldones had made John Cooper a present of a dozen strong *pampas* bulls and a fine brahma bull, which he had purchased a year before from Fabien Mallard. In addition, the *estanciero* made John Cooper a present of six wiry, speedy Argentinian colts and a dozen Spanish rifles, the latest issued, and taken from a stock that John Cooper's father-in-law himself had ordered some eight months earlier as a precautionary measure against the possible attack by his vicious enemy, Porfirio Ramos. The fine black stallion of the Charrúa, John Cooper had given to his father-in-law, though Andrew was delighted to take back with him to Texas the colt he had been given by Heitor Duvaldo.

Raoul, Adriana, Paquita, and María accompanied the large boarding party, escorted by a dozen well-armed *gauchos.* The *Sea Witch* crew sent out a dinghy for the passengers, and the frigate's crew lowered hoists and pulleys to lift the bulls and horses, which were driven out from the shore and swam to the *Sea Witch.* John Cooper, Dorotéa, and Andrew waited until the very last moment to board the dinghy, and the American turned to his father-in-law and embraced him. "We shall be close in spirit," John Cooper said, "and I shall write frequent letters to you. I promise to return after Dorotéa has given you the grandson that you are praying for. We both pray to God that our wish will be granted."

"I am sad, *mi hijo*," Raoul solemnly replied with a sigh. "You are like a son to me. My beautiful Dorotéa could not be in better hands, and *el Señor Dios* surely sent you to us."

Again they embraced, and Raoul was misty-eyed as he shook hands with his son-in-law. "*Vaya con Dios, mi hijo*," he said. "Those words are the hardest of all I've had to say in many a year, John Cooper."

"If He so grants, Dorotéa and I will return before you know it. One thing more, Raoul, if there should ever again be trouble between you and this man Ramos, send word to me at once. I'll return to help you. This I swear." Dorotéa linked her arm with his and leaned forward to kiss her father. "Now that there is peace with the Charrúa," John Cooper continued, "and Salcedo is dead, I'm sure that Ramos will think twice before he tries more of his treachery."

"I pray you are right, John Cooper. I'll write you, too, to let you know as soon as Dorotéa's palomino has its foal."

"Good! That foal will be of the purest pedigree."

"When it is old enough, Adriana shall have it," Raoul smilingly promised. Then, turning to his younger daughter, he teasingly said, "Don't you want to say good-bye to the Señor Baines's *hijo?*"

Adriana blushed violently but then, seeing the youth's eager gaze upon her, came forward, took both his hands in hers, and stammered an effusive good-bye. Glancing about and hoping that no one would observe her lapse from propriety, she suddenly kissed him on the cheek. They looked at each other for a long moment, and both were remembering the night when they had been able to kiss each other with far more feeling.

Raoul indulgently laughed. "Perhaps," he said to his son-in-law, "there is another link between our families, yet to come. Now, Godspeed. How I shall miss you both! All that will console me is the thought that you will both return."

"I promise, *Papá*," Dorotéa said, then hugged and kissed him.

John Cooper offered his arm to his young wife and led her to the dinghy. As the seaman rowed them to the frigate, both turned to wave to Raoul, standing on the shore, while behind him, the mounted *gauchos* waved their hats to bid farewell to the *americano* and his bride.

Twenty-nine

Jim Bowie and his friends, who would one day form the nucleus of the Texas Rangers, had left the Double H Ranch many weeks before and were back with their wives and children in the large settlement along the Brazos River. But Jeremy Gaige had not forgotten Jim Bowie's visit, nor his secret gold mine, and at long last he intended to go in search of it.

Just before Bowie and his friends rode off, old Jeremy had hurried out of the *hacienda*, waving his arms and calling, "Say, Mr. Bowie, sir, jista little minute, please!"

The scout had reined in his horse and, winking at his friends, turned to face the old prospector. "What can I do for you, Mr. Gaige?"

"Well, sir, I'm mighty sorry to see you go, but that ain't what I came runnin' out about, nosirree bob. You see, Mr. Bowie, when we had that palaver about treasure 'n the mine you found in the San Saba Valley, I said to myself, 'Jeremy boy, here's your big chance'; that's for certain what I said, Mr. Bowie. Now, what I want to know from you, since I've been honest all my life 'n ain't aimin' to change none this far along the road, would you mind if I took a looksee 'n tried to find that mine? I mean, you wuz the first to see it, so I figger you got finder's rights."

"Well, Mr. Gaige—" Jim Bowie had chuckled and shrugged "—the way I look at it is, I never did get to it. I never staked a claim, either. So far as I'm concerned, more's the power to you if you can find it. I wish you all the luck in the world."

"Now that's what I call mighty neighborly, Mr. Bowie. You have a good journey back home, you hear? I tell you what, if I strike it rich, I'll surely let you know, 'n I'll give you a finder's fee. Now that's fair, ain't it?"

"I can't think of a fairer proposition in the world, Mr. Gaige. Good luck to you."

This conversation had fired the eccentric old prospector's determination. As he had told Don Diego and the others, he had often been so close to a really profitable strike, only to see his chances go glimmering because of some circumstance or other. This time, now that Jim Bowie ceded rights to the hidden treasure, he swore he was going to make a try at it.

Several weeks after Bowie's departure, in late July, he approached Miguel Sandarbal and cagily assumed a confidential air. Glancing around to make sure that no one overheard him, he whispered, "Mr. Sandarbal, do you think you could spare me a wagon? I've got a little jaunt in mind, 'n it'd sure be a big favor to me."

Miguel had taken a fancy to the old prospector and played along with him. "The fact is, Señor Gaige, we don't have too many spare wagons. However, I think I might just be able to find one for you. I assume that you want to carry supplies in it?"

"That's it exactly, Mr. Sandarbal!" Jeremy slapped his hand against his thigh with a delighted expression. "You're a mighty smart feller, 'n I guess that's why they made you the—what's that Spanish word they use—you know, for foreman, the top gun, the big man—"

"Oh, you mean *capataz*."

"That's it, I knew I'd come up with it somehow!" Jeremy chortled. Then drawing closer to the amused white-haired *capataz*, he cautiously said, "Maybe you didn't hear Jim Bowie talk about treasure, but he gave me a pretty good hint where I could find a real strike. It's off in the San Saba Valley."

"That's quite a ways from here, Señor Gaige."

"I'm used to travelin'," he said almost indignantly. " 'Course, I'd need to borrow some supplies. Naturally, when I make my strike, I'll pay you back."

"We've food enough to spare. Don't let that concern you, Señor Gaige. I will undertake to find you a good, strong wagon that will carry plenty of supplies for such a long journey," Miguel declared.

"You're a gentleman, Mr. Sandarbal, that you are, 'n I won't forget you. Fact is, when I make my strike, I'm puttin' you down for a full share of the profits. After all, you're sorta grubstakin' me, 'n in my book, anybody who grubstakes a feller, he comes in for a share of the mine."

"That's very kind of you, and I wish you all the luck in the world."

"Thanks, Mr. Sandarbal, I'm sure gonna need it. Well now, you lemme know when you've got the wagon ready, 'n right now I'm gonna tell Don Diego about my plans. I'm countin' him in, too, on account of he 'n that sweet wife of his; they put me up here as if I wuz royalty. I won't ever forget that."

Beaming at the thought of a last adventure in his old age, Jeremy clapped Miguel on the back and hurried to the *hacienda* to have an audience with Don Diego and Doña Inez.

The *hidalgo* and his wife were still sitting at the dining room table, having just finished a leisurely breakfast. Doña Inez was crocheting a colorful shawl for their daughter Francesca; Don Diego was reading to her from a newspaper published by the American settlers on the Brazos and sent to him by Jim Bowie.

Jeremy halted on the threshold of the dining room, twisting his hat in his gnarled hands. He was beginning to retreat when Doña Inez, looking up, gave him a warm smile and an encouraging, "Good day to you, Mr. Gaige. Do come in, please. Sit down and enjoy some chocolate."

"Thank you, ma'am. I didn't really mean to barge in like this, 'n I'm awful sorry—"

"It is a pleasure to see you. You seem excited about something," Doña Inez smilingly prompted. "Come sit here beside me. I shall have Consuelo bring in some chocolate and biscuits."

"Well now, don't mind if I do, ma'am, if you're sure it's not puttin' you to no trouble?" Gingerly, he moved around the side of the rectangular table, pulled out the chair, and seated himself, fidgeting with his hat, till he finally decided to drop it onto the floor beside him.

"*Buenos días,* Señor Gaige," Don Diego greeted him with a twinkle in his eye.

"The same to you, Don Diego. You'll excuse me if I'm real excited, but you know, Mr. Bowie told me about the lost mine in the San Saba Valley. I've got a real good feelin' about this mine. I wuz just askin' Mr. Sandarbal if he'd mind gettin' me a wagon for supplies. Then I'll traipse off there."

"Why, it is a long journey to that region, *amigo*," Don Diego affably remonstrated.

"I'm tough as nails 'n jist as spry as I always wuz," Jeremy protested, glaring at the *hidalgo* as if to indicate that he would welcome a challenge to prove his statement.

"Please forgive me if I seem to doubt your stamina, *amigo*," Don Diego chuckled. "Ah, now, here come Diego and Francesca. Pull up chairs, my children, and sit down."

Francesca went over to her mother and kissed her on the cheek, then kissed her father, who put his arm around her waist and looked up at her, beaming with pride. "*Buenos días, mi corazón.* Mr. Gaige was just telling me that he wants to go look for treasure in the San Saba Valley."

Francesca turned to stare at the prospector, wide eyed. "Maybe Diego and I could go with you, Mr. Gaige!"

"Now, now," Don Diego said sternly as he shook his head, "that is out of the question."

"That's a darn shame because your kids are jist about as excited about findin' treasure as I am," Jeremy said. "They wouldn't be any trouble at all, 'n I'd look after them real good. You know, I'm pretty good with a rifle 'n a pistol, if I do say so myself. I'd protect them."

"That is very kind of you, Mr. Gaige, but I am afraid I must refuse permission."

Consuelo brought biscuits and chocolate, and Francesca ate ravenously with the appetite of the young and healthy, while sending longing glances at her mother. Doña Inez pretended not to notice, but Don Diego put his hand to his mouth to conceal his amused smile and then gruffly interposed, "Now then, *mi linda,* there is no sense pouting or sulking. We have both said no, and we mean it."

"Maybe I could go by myself with Mr. Gaige," Diego slyly prompted. "After all, I'm a man, and I know how to shoot a rifle and a pistol."

"I think," Don Diego countered, "that if your father were back from Taos and could hear you now, he would disabuse you of the notion that you are already a man. You are still a boy. When Señor Gaige returns, he will tell you all his adventures, won't you, my good friend?"

"That's for certain, Don Diego," Jeremy replied. "It's a shame, though, those kids can't come along. I've got a feelin' they might bring me luck. But what a father and mother think is best." To change the subject, he turned to Don Diego, his face glowing with enthusiasm, as he added, "I tell you one thin', though, when I come back to this ranch, I'll be as rich as a king. 'N I'm goin' to see to it that you and that sweet wife of yours get a share of the treasure. You've grub-staked me all this time, jist like Mr. Sandarbal, 'n you'll all get a share."

"That is very kind, but you owe us nothing." Don Diego lifted his cup of chocolate, by way of toasting the old prospector. "To the success of your venture, and may you find the treasure you have sought so long."

"Amen to that, Don Diego, amen to that," Jeremy said.

Tía Margarita and Rosa prepared food for the old prospector's journey: a slab of salt pork, strips of jerky, sacks of flour, *frijoles,* coffee, potatoes, and onions. Wrapped separately were several large melons from Tía Margarita's own garden.

Miguel had a pair of strong geldings hitched to a Conestoga-style wagon for the old prospector's supplies.

The morning he was to leave, Francesca and Diego went for a horseback ride and discussed a scheme whereby they could accompany the old prospector. "It's very simple," Francesca told the tall boy. "All we have to do is to hide in the wagon. Once Mr. Gaige drives it away from the ranch, they won't find us."

"That's clever, Francesca," Diego commended her. "That's what we'll do, then. I heard him tell one of the *vaqueros* he was going to leave early this morning, so he could get started before the heat of the day. *Diablo,* but it truly is hot already!"

"I wish you wouldn't swear, dear Diego," Francesca primly reproved him. But when he reined in his horse to look at her, for she had used the word *dear* to refer to him, she turned scarlet with confusion and lowered her eyes.

"I promise I won't swear again, dear Francesca," he slyly countered, and saw her blushes deepen still more.

"Oh, you!" she exasperatedly exclaimed. Kicking her horse's belly, she urged it to a gallop back to the *hacienda.*

That same morning the two young people sneaked out the front door of the *hacienda,* circled around the side, and hurried to the wagon and climbed into the back. In addition to the food supplies, there were blankets, a skillet, a cooking pot, and a coffeepot, and Francesca and Diego at once pulled the blankets over themselves and lay motionless.

Jeremy had said his last good-byes, waving to fat old Tía Margarita and thanking her again for her generosity. "When I come back, Miss Margarita," he promised, "I'll buy you a beautiful new dress, see if I don't, 'n some jewelry to go with it. That's to thank you fer the scrumptious meals you've been fixin' fer me durin' my stay here, Miss Margarita."

"Oh, Señor Gaige, it was my pleasure, because I do so like to watch a hungry man eat. *Vaya con Dios,* and may He reward you for thinking so generously about an old woman."

"Shucks, ma'am," the old prospector cackled, "I'm older than you by a darn sight, only I don't feel it, lookin' at you!"

Tía Margarita was scandalized, but she could hardly keep from giggling as she flung her apron over her head and retreated to her kitchen, where she asked Rosa to help prepare breakfast.

"Very willingly, Tía Margarita." Rosa smiled. Because of the wonderful dishes she sometimes prepared when Tía Margarita was too busy or too tired, Rosa had been elevated to assistant cook, second only to Tía Margarita. Thus she had a prestigious position on the Double H Ranch. Moreover, she was now the wife of Antonio Lorcas. They lived together in one of the worker's cottages, looking forward to a bright and prosperous future.

Jeremy clambered into the driver's seat, took up the reins, and clucked his tongue to start the two geldings. Many of the *vaqueros* and their wives and children came out to wave good-bye to him.

As the wagon jostled along the well-worn trail leading to the east from the Double H Ranch, Jeremy looked up at the cloudless sky and exhaled a deep sigh. He said aloud, "By crickety, this is gonna be lots of fun. Well now, lemme see, how far I got to go to get to the San Saba Valley? I got the picture of that mountain pretty much fixed in my mind, so once I see it I can find it."

Inside the wagon, under their blankets, Francesca and Diego put their hands over their mouths to keep from giggling, for the old man was talking to himself as loudly as if there had been someone seated beside him.

"Let's see, now. Close as I kin figger it, it oughta be somewheres around Brady. That's near the Colorado River so, from here to there, would run about—" holding the reins in his left hand, he scratched his head with his right forefinger and scowled in deep concentration "—reckon it's about two hundred miles or so. Oughta be able to make fifteen, twenty miles a day with this team of geldings, the way they prance along 'n don't seem to mind the weight they're draggin' behind them. Well now, say two weeks, we'll be there, Jeremy Gaige, boy. We'll find that mine 'n we'll strike it rich. Who knows, I might even settle down 'n take me a wife. Somebody to cook my meals, good as Miss Margarita does, that's for certain. A mite purty, but I ain't expectin' too much, on account of I'm no prize package myself." He broke out into a peal of cackling laughter, pleased at his own self-deprecation. Then, remembering an old tune he had heard in the early days of prospecting, he began first to whistle it and then to sing it, in a reedy, off-key voice that again taxed Francesca and Diego to keep from bursting into laughter.

The road was bumpy and the stowaways were jostled from side to side as the heavy wheels slid into ruts left by earlier trailmakers. Jeremy was brimming over with energy and hope and drove the pair of geldings at a faster clip than he would normally use during a hot day. Cheered by his excellent start, he again raised his voice in song, the thin, reedy voice alone in the silence of the vast plain. Here and there, clumps of mesquite and chaparral, with an occasional scrub tree, broke the monotony of level ground.

His voice cracked on the last line of the song, and with a grimace, he reached for his canteen, opened it, and took a lengthy swig. "That's a mite better. Jeremy boy, you're on your way to riches. Doggone if I don't bring back a wagon full of nuggets big as a rooster's comb," he gleefully announced.

There was no village or hamlet for miles around him, and the sun was beginning to beat down mercilessly. Jeremy frowned and said aloud, "Maybe I better pick a shady spot to rest for the afternoon 'n think about fixin' some grub."

From their hiding place Diego and Francesca looked at each other, and she whispered, "I'm hungry. Aren't you, too, Diego?"

"Pero sí!"

The wagon rumbled on for another mile, until Jeremy made out a small mesa, with a flat top surmounting steep rock walls rising some fifty feet. At its base and to his right was a huge live-oak tree and a patch of thickly grassed land. "That'll be a fine place to park, Jeremy," he told himself. "There'll be shade, 'n you've come far enough this first day, so you can be mighty proud. Only, now it's time to make some grub. Wonder what I'll have? Beans 'n some of that jerky, most likely, 'n some good, strong coffee." His face brightened as he said aloud, "Darned if I didn't forget those nice melons Miss Margarita sent along with me. That'll be fer dessert. All right, Jeremy, let's find a place to leave the wagon 'n the horses 'n get a fire goin'. I'll make the coffee first off."

He drew in on the reins and called out, "Whoa! That's it, whoa, now," and when the geldings obediently halted, he got down from the driver's seat, unhitched the team, and tied the reins to a low-hanging branch of the huge live-oak tree. "That'll do it. Now you jist stay there nice 'n easylike, boys, 'n I'll give you some oats, jist as soon as I git my fire goin' fer coffee."

He stood looking around, then shook his head, "Mighty lonely out here, all by ourselves, Jeremy. But you're used to it. One thing, though, if you hit this strike, you'll have people around you. That idea of a wife ain't a bad one. She'd be fixin' my dinner right about now, if I wuz married. All right, now, let's git things started."

With this, he walked to the back of the wagon and reached for one of the sacks. At that moment, Francesca lifted the blanket which concealed her and found herself staring into his astonished face.

"By all tarnation, Francesca! What in the world are you doin' in my wagon?" he gasped.

"Stowing away, Mr. Gaige."

"Diego, too?" he gasped.

"That's right, Mr. Gaige," Diego said.

"I tell you what, Mr. Gaige," Francesca said, "we'll help you prepare the meal."

"Well, drat it, if that doesn't beat all!" he happily swore. "You know, Francesca, when I saw you peek out at me from under that blanket right then, I thought I wuz seein' a ghost. It's mighty lonely out here; we've come a long ways from the ranch."

"You aren't angry with us, are you, Mr. Gaige?" she plaintively asked.

"Of course I'm not, honey. I'm jist an old bear who

growls a lot, but I haven't got any teeth to bite anyone with. Matter-of-fact, I'm tickled pink to have you along, you 'n Diego. I'd be mighty obliged if you would help me fix dinner. I'm sure feelin' hungry now."

"So are we," Diego spoke up.

"Since we're all together now, we'll make the most of it. Diego, can you make a fire?" the old prospector asked.

"Of course!" the boy proudly said, and jumping down from the wagon, he collected bunches of dry grass and twigs. Using the prospector's tinderbox, he soon had the fire blazing while Francesca, at Jeremy's instructions, took out the skillet and the coffeepot.

"This is goin' to be a lark," the prospector delightedly exclaimed. "You know, I wuz figgerin' this would be real lonely. 'Course, I don't want you to get into trouble. I bet your folks will be real mad for your sneakin' away like this."

"I hope not," Francesca dubiously said. "But anyway"—this with a bright smile—"we're here, and they don't know which way we came, so we're just going to help you, Mr. Gaige. When we come back with the treasure, I don't think they'll scold us too much."

"Now that's the way to look at it. This is real neighborly, sort of like a picnic. Yessirree bob," the old prospector said with a chuckle, "I'm sure glad you stowed away fer the ride!"

But as they ate their meal that day, Jeremy was uncharacteristically silent. He wondered if it was his duty to return his two young stowaways to the Double H Ranch. Finally, however, his lifelong dream of one great strike overcame his pangs of conscience. And he looked upon Diego's and Francesca's unwavering belief in him as a certain sign that, this time, he was destined for success.

That was why he cunningly decided to change his route when they started out again that evening. His thinking was that by this time their absence from the ranch had surely been discovered, and there might even now be some of the *trabajadores* in pursuit. Thus he intended to get a good head start when he resumed his journey, heading the team due north by northeast.

That evening, Don Diego and Doña Inez supposed that Diego and Francesca had gone out riding all day. They gave this little mind, preoccupied as they were over John Cooper's whereabouts—they had received his letters but had no word about when he was returning—as well as their awaiting news from Carlos and Teresa about when they were coming home. They were also busy with Carlos's other children, as well as their own two adopted youngsters and John Cooper's children, during most of the day. As a result, it was not until suppertime that Doña Inez, with a worried look, said to her husband, who was sitting in the parlor, *"Querido,* I just realized that Francesca and Diego have not come back yet. They have been out all day."

"Never fear, my dearest one," he soothed her. "They are both self-reliant, and I am happy that they are now such good, loyal friends."

"That is all very well to say, Diego, but the fact is that they should have been back by now. If you do not mind, will you go and talk to Miguel?"

"Of course, of course," he agreed, rising from his chair and putting an arm around her shoulders. "Surely you do not think that I am not concerned about them. I shall go find Miguel, and if they are still not back in a little while, I shall have him send some of the *trabajadores* out looking for them."

"Dear one," she said, kissing him tenderly. Then, putting her hands on his shoulders and stepping back, she looked at him with concern. "Do you know, Diego, I am worried about you even more than the children."

"Nonsense! I have never felt better in my life!" he boasted.

"You look tired and drawn. I know how much Catarina's death affected you, dear one. Neither of us is young any longer, and it is best that we realize this and not overtax ourselves."

"Why," he stormed indignantly, "if you doubt me, I am willing to take a horse and go find the children myself!"

"You assuredly will not do that, Diego. I want to be your wife and companion for a good many more years yet. So there is no sense in making heroic gestures that you know I will not permit you to carry out."

He softened at the deep anxiety in her eyes, and uttered a long sigh as he hugged and kissed her. "Inez, Inez, it is high time I told you how much I am in love with you, even more than on the day I married you."

Tears ran down her cheeks as they clung to each other,

and in their eyes was the pledge of undying devotion. Suddenly embarrassed, Doña Inez freed herself and almost teasingly ordered, "Now go find Miguel at once, and that is enough of that! I shall not be able to sleep tonight, until I see Diego and Francesca. I am going to give her a good scolding for upsetting both of us so much!"

In truth, Don Diego was more worried than he wanted to admit as he strolled out to the bunkhouse. The *trabajadores* had finished the last touches of painting it and the church, so that both edifices looked brand-new. One could not have believed that in Francisco López's attack last December, both of these buildings had been ravaged by fire.

Don Diego was relieved to see Miguel coming out of his cottage. Although Miguel was five years younger than Don Diego, he looked at least fifteen years younger. Still, no two men could have been more closely bound than these Spaniards, who had shared bitter disappointment, tragedy, and now, in their twilight years, the fruition of fatherhood and joy.

Don Diego lifted his arm in greeting, forcing a pleasant smile to his bearded lips. *"Hola,* Miguel, I thought you would be supping by now. Just look at that magnificent moon! Ah, Miguel, it reminds me of the Alhambra, of the Moorish gardens in what was once our beloved country."

"That's true, *patrón."* Despite their long comradeship, despite the fact that Don Diego treated Miguel like an equal and a confidant, the *capataz* was always deeply respectful toward this man whom he considered his savior as well as his employer.

"Oh, by the way," Don Diego continued, as casually as his own growing concern permitted, "have you seen either Francesca or Diego today?"

"To tell the truth, no, Don Diego. I thought perhaps they were out riding. They're almost inseparable these days."

"That they are. Just the same, it is really late. We are about to sit down to supper now ourselves."

Miguel touched his forehead by way of salutation at what he considered a tactful order. "I understand you, *patrón.* Why don't I pick some of the *trabajadores* and go out looking?"

"I should be much obliged if you would, Miguel."

"First, I will go to the stables to see if their horses are there." Miguel dashed off as Don Diego stood in the same

spot, waiting for his friend. He let out a deep sigh as Miguel
came running back, shaking his head. "All the horses are accounted for. So Francesca and Diego are not out on horseback. Do you have any idea where else they might be?"

"I think I might at that," Don Diego said slowly. "It
comes to mind—this is only a speculation—that they may
have gone off with Señor Gaige in search of that treasure."

Miguel looked concerned. "I understand, *patrón*. Well,
assuming that they went off with Señor Gaige, they couldn't
have got too far. We will find them."

"I am deeply indebted to you, Miguel. I shall go tell
Doña Inez, so she will not be upset."

"*Sí, patrón*. I'll attend to it at once. We ought to be able
to pick up their trail. The ruts of the wagon wheels should
make it easy, even though it's nightfall now. And we'll take
Yankee along. After all, the wolf-dog is a particular favorite
with Diego and Francesca; he knows them well, knows their
scent, and could certainly be of great help."

So certain was Jeremy Gaige that this time would be
lucky, that at last the will-o'-the-wisp he had pursued for so
many years was within his grasp, that he was careful to outwit anyone who might be following him. He had experienced
several claim-jumping incidents during his more active days,
and he told himself that, if this hidden mine was as rich as
Jim Bowie had said it was, anybody who had ever heard
about it would be making tracks to find it. This time he was
going to be first.

His anticipation and excitement did away with sleep.
For the next several nights, while Francesca and Diego slept
in the wagon, the old prospector drove steadily through the
darkness, switching his direction from time to time, and even
turning the wagon in complete circles. This, he reasoned, was
certain to confuse any pursuer.

Miguel and his four companions assumed that by riding
all day and camping with a full night's sleep, they could easily catch up with the old man. On the sixth day, Miguel
turned to the riders and shook his head, scowling. "I don't
know how he's done it, *amigos*, but he's given us the slip.
We're running out of supplies. Two of you ride back to the
nearest town and buy what you can. We'll go on and hold
down our speed, so that you can catch up with us."

"I thought sure that Yankee would have picked up the

track by now," one of the men grumbled. "But so far even he's been baffled."

A day later, the other two riders caught up with Miguel and his companions, having purchased flour, beans, bacon, salt pork, jerky, and coffee, and all five men set out in pursuit. "Our only chance is to go on to the San Saba Valley area," Miguel told his men, "and hope that we'll catch up with them there. I certainly do not want to go back to the ranch and tell the *patrón* that we couldn't find them. He and Doña Inez would only worry all the more."

Jeremy Gaige made better time than he had hoped and arrived in the San Saba Valley just before dawn on the tenth day of his journey. Though the weather was stormy and oppressive, he clambered down from the wagon in high spirits while Diego and Francesca watched, their faces aglow with excitement. "Is this the place, Mr. Gaige?" Francesca excitedly demanded.

"It sure looks like it, honey. Yessirree bob, rememberin' what Mr. Bowie told me, this should jist about be it. He said it wuz near a big mesa, 'n there wuz a series of hills along one side of it. Right in one of those caves, that's where Mr. Bowie said there wuz that mine."

"This must be it, Mr. Gaige," Diego said enthusiastically.

"All right, now. We're going to set up camp, 'n jist as soon as we've had some vittles, I'm goin' to do some prospectin'. Diego, boy, hand me that shovel 'n that pickax. Francesca, would you mind fixin' us some vittles?"

"Of course. I'll get some bacon and beans and coffee right away," Francesca promised.

After their quick repast, huddled at the side of the wagon to stay out of the mounting wind, the old prospector and the two young people hurried toward the row of small hills, and Jeremy, shouldering pickax and shovel, went ahead of Francesca and Diego, his eyes glittering with anticipation. "I don't know exactly which one it wuz, 'n neither did Mr. Bowie," he explained to them, "but I'll take a look. I'll jist bet this is gold country; I'm sure of it. Won't they be surprised when we all come back with the wagon loaded with those nice big nuggets!"

"They will, Mr. Gaige," Diego replied. "They won't even scold us for being away."

Jeremy's attention was suddenly drawn to a cave at the foothill of the mountain, which stood at the left of the series of small hills. "I'm going to try this one; I got a feelin' about it." He trudged hastily off to his left. Francesca and Diego followed, exchanging wondering looks.

The old prospector left his shovel outside the cave and, pickax in hand, stooped to enter the cave. "Francesca, Diego, make a torch. See if you can find a branch 'n tie some cloth around it, soak it in some of that oil, 'n then take my tinderbox 'n light it. It's dark in here!"

A few moments later, Diego handed him the flaming torch, and Jeremy went back into the cave. A fierce wind was howling as Diego and Francesca stood outside, their eyes wide with wonder. "I feel he's going to find some treasure, Diego," Francesca confided.

"I do, too." Diego could barely contain his excitement.

Jeremy stuck the torch in a little crevice in the wall, projecting it out at an angle so that it would stay fixed and shed sufficient light to work by. He took his pickax and moved to the opposite wall, where he struck three or four heavy blows. Then he uttered a cry. There was a streak of yellow metal, dull and narrow, but assuredly a vein. Dropping his pickax, he hurried outside to tell of his finding. "Francesca, Diego, come inside! Come take a look! It's gold, it's a miracle! I found it!"

The two young people hurried into the cave and Jeremy pointed with his pickax. "See there?"

"It *is* gold, Mr. Gaige," Francesca breathed, turning to Diego. "I just knew Mr. Gaige would find it, I just knew it!"

Outside, the sky grew even darker and a savage wind tore at the mountain. But Jeremy, Francesca, and Diego were too excited to notice. The old prospector, panting with exertion, swung the pickax, dislodging more and more of the rock and rubble around the vein. "Gosh all sakes," he exclaimed, "jist look how high it runs, even beyond the top of the cave. I wouldn't be surprised at all, nosirree bob, if that vein went all the way up the mountain! Mr. Bowie wuzn't fibbin', no he wuzn't, not by a durned sight!"

Suddenly there was the crash of thunder and a drenching rain borne in by the wind. And then, from the top of the mountain, loose earth, rubble, brush, rocks, and boulders began to tumble in an avalanche. There was a crash as tons of matter roared to the ground and blocked the entrance to the cave.

The trio heard the incredible noise, and Francesca, having turned to the mouth of the cave, saw darkness where once there had been light. "Mr. Gaige, Mr. Gaige! Something's happened! We can't get out!" she cried.

Diego ran to the mouth of the cave, knelt, and tried to push away the stones and rubble with his hands. He turned back, his young face twisted in anxiety. "We're blocked in; it's sealed the mouth of the cave! What are we going to do now?"

"Now don't get upset, Diego boy," Jeremy said, trying to act cheerful. "I should of brought the shovel inside, but this pickax will cut through the rock. You'll see."

He set to work, hoisting the ax high over his head and bringing it down with all his might. After six such blows he had made scarcely a dent.

"Oh, what are we going to do?" Francesca hysterically cried, bursting into tears.

Diego moved to her and put an arm around her shoulders. "Never mind, we'll all work at it. We'll clear it away and get out. Don't you fret now, Francesca *querida!*"

Miguel and his *trabajadores* came into the San Saba Valley and found the trail that Jeremy had left during the last day of his journey. They had to pause, huddled together upon their horses while a violent, brief storm passed overhead. Then Yankee, reveling in this long trek, raced ahead of the five men, his yellow eyes shining, glancing back over his shoulder now and again to make certain that they were keeping up with him.

"At last!" Miguel cried as he pointed ahead. "See the wagon near that small mountain? *Adelante, mis amigos!*"

A few moments later, galloping their horses, they reached the wagon and saw the shovel just outside the mouth of the sealed cave. Miguel glanced up at the mountain and shook his head. "There's been an avalanche, *compañeros.* A recent one, probably caused by that storm. They must be in this cave. What horror it would be if they had suffocated! Come, quickly, we must open the mouth of the cave and see if they are still alive!"

There was only Jeremy's abandoned shovel, for the five horsemen had carried no tools. Miguel took the shovel and vigorously scooped and thrust at the rubble and the rocks and the boulders, while his four *trabajadores* used their bare hands to clear away the debris.

Yankee stood barking at the place they were digging. "I'm sure they're in there, Señor Sandarbal," one of the *trabajadores* volunteered. "See how excited the *perro* is! He knows, that one!"

"Let me take the shovel, Señor Sandarbal," the youngest of the *trabajadores* volunteered.

"Very well, then. Hurry! I can only pray that we aren't too late. Oh, *Señor Dios,* in Your mercy, let them be still alive! How can I go back to the *patrón* and Doña Inez with such horrible news?"

The young worker took the shovel and set to work with a frenzy, gritting his teeth and heaving shovels full of dirt and pebbles and little rocks over his shoulder. Half an hour later, he had made a small opening and Miguel pushed him aside, knelt, and cupping his hands to his mouth, shouted, "Señor Gaige, Diego, Francesca, are you there? Tell us, *por amor de Dios!*"

"We're here; we're here; please get us out!" Francesca was sobbing.

Yankee, flattening himself, ears drawn back, hair bristling, now wedged himself through the narrow opening and barked excitedly as Diego and Francesca received him with cries of joy, patting and caressing and fondling him, while he licked their faces. "Thank God for that," Jeremy breathed, shaking his head in wonder. "A coupla hours more, it'd really been bad for all of us!"

Another of the *trabajadores* volunteered to take the shovel and energetically cleared more of the debris, till the opening was broad enough to enable the three captives to crawl out. "Hurry," Miguel exhorted, glancing up at the mountain. "It looks as if there's going to be another rockslide!"

Francesca came first, and Miguel helped her to her feet, exclaiming, "Señorita Francesca, my heart was in my mouth! It is only the mercy of *el Señor Dios* that we found you in time!"

Next came Diego, stumbling to his feet, breathing in the pleasant air, for his lungs had already begun to protest the foulness of the sealed cave. At last, Jeremy Gaige crawled out, coughing and gasping for breath.

Two *trabajadores* helped the old man to his feet. Suddenly, Miguel cried, "Look out!"

Diego, Francesca, and the old prospector stumbled back to the wagon, while Miguel and his four workers led their horses to safety.

There was a sudden rumbling sound, and from the top of the mountain came the avalanche. This time it had dislodged the largest boulders, and they crashed in front of the cave. Inside, the walls of the cave were weakened, and they too began to give way. Suddenly, there was a tremendous crash, as tons of dirt and stone poured down.

The treasure of this lost mine in the San Saba Valley was buried under tons of stone and rubble. The caves alongside were blocked and hidden from view. Now, the treasure would belong to no one and exist only as one of the innumerable legends to inspire men's dreams.

Thirty

The journey of the eleven Dominican nuns and their mother superior had taken far longer than they had estimated. Sister Eufemia had to draw on all her religious faith and patience to shepherd the eleven women who had accompanied her from Parras.

In their journey, the spiritual restoration of Sister Caridad had been a heartwarming example that had strengthened Sister Eufemia's belief that a Divine Providence would watch over all of them. When they had left the tiny village where the elderly nun suddenly cast aside the heavy burden of her guilt and took the illegitimate child of the old man's daughter who died in childbirth, Sister Eufemia had thought that the road ahead would be brightened and eased by this transformation in a nun who had, for years, cantankerously complained over the slightest discomfort.

It had taken them three days to reach the city of Monterrey, in the province of Nuevo León. Named after one of the most famous Spanish provinces in the days of the great monarchs, when León and Castille had vied for power, the Mexican counterpart was rife with poverty, sporadic attacks by outlaws, and even an occasional skirmish with the remnants of the Toboso Indians, who continued to harass *peón* and *hacendado* alike. But it also had a magnificent church that dated back nearly two hundred years, and Sister Eufemia and her eleven companions went there at dawn to hear mass, take communion, and pray for strength and guidance during the rest of their long journey.

Thanks to the silver that Padre Madura had sent to Sister Eufemia, the mother superior was able to buy more food, but there was a violent rainstorm, and the roads were muddy and unsafe. The nuns had to wait another three days in Monterrey until the rains let up.

Then, no sooner had the weather improved than Sisters Dolores, Terneza, and Magdalena came down with the flux, a strange epidemic that had attacked the city. The other nuns and the mother superior spent weary hours tending to their three ailing companions, while Sisters Eufemia, Mercedes, and Consuela approached the local priest and volunteered to act as nurses in such homes as would receive them.

The priest was a man in his early fifties, Padre José Montrascor. He was gentle, old before his time, and he believed in the eternal justice of God, and the virtue of prayer and self-abnegation against the world of vanities and material possessions. He had already antagonized at least three of the rich *hacendados* whose ranches dominated much of the city and who didn't bother to attend mass on Sunday and confess their sins.

Two doctors had been sent from San Luis Potosí, men in their thirties who had spent two years in Europe, where they acquired new medical knowledge, which they passed on to the city practitioners. One of them diagnosed the flux, from which a dozen citizens had already died; it was brought on by rats and he exhorted the townspeople to hunt them down and kill them.

Sister Eufemia aided the doctors. When they held public meetings, she sat with them, made suggestions, and so impressed the frightened townspeople that they hunted down all the rats they could find. They were insular in Monterrey, but they were also terribly frightened of a disease for which there seemingly was not yet a cure, one that struck down apparently healthy young men, women, and children in the dead of night.

Then almost miraculously the flux abated, the three ailing nuns recovered, and Sister Eufemia went to mass to give thanks to a merciful God.

Yet on the day they were scheduled to push on toward the Double H Ranch, a new delay was incurred: The tiny baby, whom Sister Eufemia had named Innocente, began to breathe laboriously and cry with a shrill intensity. Another two days were spent by the nuns in caring for the baby, until at last his fever broke, and he regained his appetite and pleasant disposition.

From Monterrey to Villadalma, a distance of about sixty miles, took more than three weeks. To begin with, the goat that had been furnishing milk for Innocente sickened and died. Then, shortly after they had begun their journey, there was a violent sandstorm, and the new burro was blinded. It staggered erratically, braying shrilly in its pain and terror, fell into a ditch, and broke its leg. Mercifully it died, whether of fright or pain or sheer old age, the nuns did not know.

Once again, the nuns became beasts of burden and pulled the cart with their supplies. If they averaged a few miles a day, they were doing exceptionally well. Those nuns who had been ill were capable of little effort—only prayer, and the hope that, by resting, they would regain their strength and be able to help Sister Eufemia on the final lap of the journey.

Those nuns who were well wound the ropes around their waists and over their shoulders and tugged like laborers drawing a stubborn plow over arid ground. Sister Caridad had been able to get another goat, but the man who owned it had been miserly and, though he admitted himself to be a good and faithful son of the Church, asked far more than the goat was worth. Still in all, there was no choice, and Sister Eufemia counted the pieces of silver into the man's bony hand and blessed him for his charity.

Little Innocente thrived, and Sister Caridad, worried though she was and having lost some of her fat during this arduous trek, was radiant with hope.

Their path led from Villadalma to Candela. This town

was some thirty miles distant from their last stopping place, and less than a hundred miles from the Rio Grande in Texas. They were nearing their destination!

There was a small post of *federalistas* stationed in Candela. These men were under the orders of Santa Anna himself, who behind-the-scenes, continued his cunning game of seeming to be in retirement. Actually he was preparing for the day when he would be called upon to "save all Mexico from oppressors."

On the day in August when Sister Eufemia arrived, with three of her nuns still convalescing, a courier rode into the little fort on the outskirts of Candela with a message from Santa Anna to Colonel Moravada. Esteban Moravada was a lean, gloomy man in his early forties who had, three years before, been demoted from his colonelcy to the rank of captain for an alleged insult to General Jorge Liscanada. Dourly returning to his command, he had led several patrols against bandits, captured the leader, and sent him to a firing squad. The grateful villagers of those towns that had been ravaged by the bandit band sent a letter off to Mexico City extolling his virtues. As a consequence, Moravada was restored to his colonelcy.

Santa Anna's message intimated that Moravada might win even more military acclaim and rank if he were to patrol the Rio Grande and, particularly, apprehend known outlaws who had come into the Texas territory. These men, Santa Anna wrote, wished nothing better than to stir up trouble, and it was already evident that the brash Texans intended to ignore Mexican traditions and customs and go their own offensive way. If, Santa Anna cleverly pointed out in his letter, Colonel Moravada was able to do something to stop this criminal activity, he would win a glowing reputation that would make him one of the foremost officers in all Mexico.

Santa Anna had added a postscript:

> I call upon you, my dear friend and comrade at arms, to remember that in union there is strength, and in harassing the *gringos,* particularly the settlers who are too close to the Rio Grande, you may well avert unfortunate incidents that will bring about a bloody conflict between those accursed *americanos* who call themselves Texans and our own judicious military. In doing this, *mi*

coronel, you will make your name known to me, and I shall not forget your actions.

Although a *católico,* Colonel Moravada had no great love for the pomp and ritual of the church and still less for the sanctimonious attitudes of so many of the priests he had encountered during his military career. Moreover, having risen from a background scarcely above the status of *peón,* he regarded the church in Mexico as a dangerous irritant. The poor contributed tithes to the parishes, and the parishes paid no taxes to the government. They did as they pleased, they were above military regulations and procedures, and it had long been his belief that Church should be subordinate to state.

Colonel Moravada had been kept apprised of the settlements of Moses and then Stephen Austin, both authorized by the Mexican government. He considered this a dangerous precedent, since it brought greedy, self-important *americanos* along the border of land that he believed should be Mexican. It could only lead to a war, and the danger that the Texas territory would join los Estados Unidos was becoming plainer and plainer with each new day.

When his burly, bearded young corporal, Jesus Abierto, entered his office, smartly saluted, then informed him that a party of Dominican nuns had just entered the town of Candela, he glowered with anger. "Corporal, see to it that they are brought in here for questioning. I wish to know whence they have come and where they intend to go. You tell me that they have drawn a cart themselves, and that one of them, a fat old woman, is carrying a newly born child. This is very suspicious. I wish to know if they have passes to come and go freely, or if, as should be expected, they have been assigned to some parish or abbey and have decided to shirk their duties."

"Very good, *mi coronel!*" The corporal saluted, turned on his heel, and strode out of the office, calling for two privates in his platoon to ride with him into the town.

An hour later, Sister Eufemia appeared together with her eleven companions in the office of the irascible Colonel Esteban Moravada. He stared at the elderly nun and then barked, "Where are you from?"

"The abbey of Parras, *mi coronel.*" Sister Eufemia had long ago learned the wisdom of placating overzealous officers by indicating that she knew their rank and was respectful of it.

"All the way from Parras? *Madre de Dios,* but that is an enormous journey! All of you have come this way with a cart and this baby?"

"The baby, *señor coronel,*" Sister Caridad interrupted, "would have died, if we had not taken it from its mother, who lost her life in giving it birth, and from the girl's father who renounced her because she had been the consort of a *bandido.*"

"It would have been better to have let the child die," Colonel Moravada snapped.

"That would be a mortal sin!" Sister Caridad indignantly responded.

"What do you intend to do with this squalling brat?" he scowlingly demanded.

"Begging Your Excellency's pardon," Sister Caridad sarcastically retorted, "he is quieter than most babies, particularly when he is fed with good goat's milk. We are on our way across the Rio Grande, to the *hacienda* of Don Diego de Escobar."

"It is true, *mi coronel,*" Sister Eufemia interposed, "because, you see, our abbey at Parras was confiscated by the *alcalde* there who is in league with a *jefe de bandidos.* We had no choice. Padre Madura of Taos wrote to us that there would be sanctuary at that *hacienda.* There are good Catholics there, *mi coronel,* and we can be of assistance to the needy, the sick, and the children whom we will try to educate in the ways of God."

"Then you have no pass?" he angrily demanded.

"Only the will of God that directs us, *mi coronel.*" Sister Eufemia made the sign of the cross and lowered her eyes.

"A pox on your piety!" he snapped. "There are some who might say that your traveling away from the country that nurtured you is treason. I will not go so far, except to say that we shall shortly go out on patrol as far as the Rio Grande, and I will not allow you to leave Candela until we have returned from our mission. I shall make investigations for myself about this Don Diego de Escobar. If he is not an enemy of Mexico, I may grant you permission to continue your journey. Until then, Sister, you will remain here. That is all I have to say to you. Corporal, see that they go back to whatever shelter they have found, and post guards to make certain that none of them tries to leave, until I return with my men."

From Candela to Laredo, just across the border, was less than a hundred miles. Colonel Moravada and fifty of his troops rode out the next morning. Their patrolling took them past a dozen little hamlets and villages, which they searched for illegal firearms and for *americanos* infiltrating across the border to stir up trouble. Arbitrarily, Colonel Moravada confiscated supplies and horses and allowed his men to arrest for questioning three young women, one of whom had caught his own fancy.

For the week before he and his men returned from their mission, Sister Eufemia and her companions had little to do. Sister Caridad had come down with a fever, and she grew steadily weaker. As Sister Eufemia knelt beside the rude pallet on which the old nun lay, Sister Caridad, in a husky, faint voice, stammered, "I know I am going to die. I wish to confess my sins."

"Sister Caridad," Sister Eufemia said tenderly, "what you have done since we started from Parras is, I firmly believe, blessed in the eyes of our dear Lord. You have saved a human life. I will see to it that Innocente is placed with a family who will give him every opportunity to become a good, useful man."

"I pray for that, Sister Eufemia. I have been slothful, vexed with my fellow sisters; I have sinned grievously. I am heartily sorry for my sins." Sister Caridad closed her eyes and uttered a long sigh. "May God forgive me, and may my brother's spirit forgive me, also. I have tried; I have made mistakes and erred against our Lord. I pray—" Her words trailed off in a shudder. Sister Eufemia put her hand on the nun's heart and then wept silently, tears streaking down her face. She made the sign of the cross, folded Sister Caridad's hands across her bosom, and drew the sheet over the dead nun's face.

She herself would take charge of Innocente. Perhaps in Candela she could buy another goat. The one they had gave very little milk. What troubled her most of all was the military guard posted outside their adobe hovels on the outskirts of the town. Their landlords asked very little money for these miserable dwellings, but Sister Eufemia believed that there was more charity in the world than had been shown her and her sisters. She told herself, "He tests us, as He tested Job in the days of old. We shall not be found wanting, for we believe in Him and we know that He will guide us finally to the place to which we are destined, where we can work and be of use and service to those who need us."

When Colonel Esteban Moravada returned to Candela, he could hardly wait to send off a courier to Santa Anna. In Laredo, quite by chance, he had heard a *vaquero* talking to several companions in a *posada*. The man had been praising the *Hacienda del Halcón*. "I tell you, *hombres,* I wouldn't mind working there myself. I've a cousin there, who was hired by their *capataz,* a certain Miguel Sandarbal, and from time to time when he comes to Laredo to see his family, we meet in this very *posada.* You would not believe the wages that the *vaqueros* earn there!" The colonel had pricked up his ears and moved closer to the table where the *vaquero* and his friends sat drinking *tequila.* "There is a *gringo* there, and they call him *el Halcón.* He lived with the Indians, and it seems that he found a treasure of silver. I know it was taken to a bank in New Orleans. They could buy a dozen *haciendas* and more, from what I am told. Alas, I must work for a wretched old man and his sick wife, who begrudge me even the food I eat and the few *pesos* they give me at the end of every week."

That evening, Esteban Moravada wrote a lengthy letter to Santa Anna and, as soon as he reached Candela, sent it off with one of his swiftest couriers.

Santa Anna swore under his breath when he received the courier's message. The silver, the silver that would have made him absolute ruler of all Mexico, had been taken out of his grasp forever. It belonged to that damned *gringo.* Francisco López must surely be dead by now. He had heard nothing in all this time. Well, the fool deserved to die if he could not overcome these stupid *gringos.* Yet he was grateful for the news. Colonel Esteban Moravada was a man after his own heart, who might well replace Francisco López and go much farther. Ingenuity and resourcefulness he admired above all else, so long as the man who possessed these attributes did not try to advance himself over the next ruler of Mexico—himself.

He would build up his army, enlist more and more volunteers, and wait quietly until the government in Mexico City had confounded and eliminated itself. Then he would make his move. It could be for the presidency, or even for the monarchy. But whatever future Mexico was to have, Santa Anna was certain, it must be directed by him.

The day after his return, Colonel Esteban Moravada ordered his men to bring in the nuns. Sister Eufemia had been feeding little Innocente with milk from the new goat, and there was no time to make arrangements to leave him with anyone, so she brought the child along.

"I shall let you go on your journey. But I warn you; since my men will patrol across the border from now on at orders from the government," Colonel Moravada told her, "I mean to keep an eye on you and to see what you really intend. If you show the least sign of treason to our country, your robe will not protect you, Sister. Now go."

By late August Sister Eufemia and her ten companions had crossed the Rio Grande and reached the little hamlet of Benecia, near Laredo, which numbered about fifty inhabitants. The Sisters had managed to acquire still another burro in Candela, and this animal proved to be cooperative.

Two young Texans had come to Benecia with their Mexican wives and children to settle on a farm. They had no particular interest in a republic of Texas or a war with Mexico to achieve that goal; they had fallen in love with their Mexican sweethearts, and they asked for nothing better than to live in a small village, obscure and forgotten, and not become involved in the growing antagonism that was soon to set *tejanos* against Mexicans.

Sister Eufemia was welcomed by the two young Texans, Ernest Bormeyer and David Sumpter. After she had told them that she and her companions were on their way to the Double H Ranch, Bormeyer, a tall, blond-bearded man of twenty-seven, smilingly exclaimed, "We know that ranch, Sister. We learned about it when we passed through Eugene Fair's town on the Brazos."

David Sumpter, a stocky, brown-bearded man of twenty-eight, added, "Fact is, we're thinking of moving there by next spring because there's good farming land, better than this little spot. But in the meantime, Sister, we'd be honored to put you up for as long as you want to stay."

"God bless you, my son." Sister Eufemia made the sign

of the cross and, seeing that both men bowed their heads in reverence, added, "You are of our faith, I perceive."

"Yes, Sister," Ernest replied. "We don't have a church here yet, but I've built a little chapel on my place, with a little representation of Jesus that old Tomás Mejira made for me, so it'll have to do till more settlers come here and we can raise money enough to build a real church."

"God does not require temples in which to worship Him," Sister Eufemia gently responded. "It is very kind of you to give us shelter. We have had a long and difficult journey. Can you tell me how far we are from the Double H Ranch, which they call the *Hacienda del Halcón?*"

"I'd say about a hundred miles north by northwest, sister."

Sister Eufemia sighed and shook her head. "So far as that! Well, if we may stay here for two or three days until we are rested—"

"Stay as long as you like, Sister. There are three empty adobe *jacales* off to the south edge of the village. You're certainly welcome to them."

"Thank you, my son."

On their first evening in Benecia, the sisters were invited to the house of Ernest Bormeyer. His pretty, young wife, Pía, served them a delicious supper and provided fresh milk from a cow for little Innocente who, since the death of Sister Caridad, had been tended by Sister Eufemia, with the help of Sister Mercedes.

Some of the villagers played music and sang folk songs for the visiting nuns and, after it was over, knelt before them and asked for their blessing.

As Sister Eufemia entered the *jacal* with Sister Mercedes and the little baby and Sister Dolores, she sighed happily and crossed herself. "God is good to us, my sisters. Perhaps, if we are fortunate, we shall arrive within a few weeks at our place of sanctuary. Let us kneel now and pray and give Him thanks for our deliverance."

But even as they bowed their heads, there was the sound of horses' hooves and the angry shouts of soldiers, and then the more terrifying sound of musket and pistol fire.

With a cry of terror, Sister Dolores hastened to the door of the *jacal* and stepped out into the night. There was more gunfire, and her eyes widened with an incredulous look, as she fell like a log. A stray bullet had pierced her brain.

Sister Eufemia, who had come behind her, uttered a horrified cry, swiftly knelt, and felt for the nun's heart. Tears ran down her cheeks as she murmured the prayers for the dead and crossed herself, then slowly closed the nun's staring eyes.

Then, stiffening, trembling with anger, she called as an officer rode by on a black stallion, "Your men have killed one of our Sisters!"

The officer reined in his horse and turned to stare at her. "It's you, Sister Eufemia!" he angrily exclaimed. "I had thought to have seen the last of you in Candela." It was Colonel Esteban Moravada.

"What reason can you possibly have to shoot down innocent people and to kill a holy nun here in Benecia?"

"Reason enough, Sister. There are two *tejanos* here, and they have weapons. These people come to Texas and profess to be farmers, but they are sent here by the government of los Estados Unidos to wage war against my country."

"This I do not believe. You have killed Sister Dolores. May her death be on your soul."

"Enough of your ranting, old woman! My men have arrested the two *tejanos*. Since you're here, you can do them a last service before we execute them."

"No, I protest in God's holy name!"

"Protest all you like; but they are to die," he sarcastically exclaimed.

With a heroic effort Sister Eufemia controlled her anger. Turning back to the hut, she called, "Sister Mercedes, I shall return as quickly as I can."

"I have no horse for you, Sister. You must walk along beside me. But I will not ride too quickly. It will give those *tejanos* a few more minutes of life," Colonel Moravada mockingly declared.

She began to pray, following him, till they reached the little town square. There were thirty of his soldiers on horseback, and another dozen who had dismounted. Of these latter, six had drawn up with rifles at their sides, and the other six were leading Ernest Bormeyer and David Sumpter toward the adobe wall of a large barn. The men were offered blindfolds but refused them. Colonel Moravada called out, "Give them a minute, *soldados,* to make their peace with *el Señor Dios!*" Then, to Sister Eufemia, "Be quick about it!"

Sister Eufemia walked unsteadily toward the wall, her

cheeks wet with tears. "My sons, I would I were more than a weak woman and could stop this murder."

"It's not your fault, Sister," Ernest Bormeyer replied. "Can I confess to you; is there time?"

"I am not a priest, my son, but we can pray together. That officer would not dare shoot you down with me standing here with you," Sister Eufemia tearfully declared.

Both men, their wrists bound behind their backs, knelt down and bowed their heads, as Sister Eufemia prayed with them.

"Ten thousand devils, Sister, make an end of it!" Colonel Moravada shouted.

"We're ready, Sister. God bless you," David Sumpter spoke up. "Pray for us. Try to comfort our wives and kids—"

"I promise you I will, I promise," Sister Eufemia murmured, her voice choked with sobs.

She moved away, making the sign of the cross, as Colonel Moravada made an impatient gesture to the lieutenant who was commanding the firing squad. Just as the volley rang out, Ernest Bormeyer cried, "Long live the Republic of Texas!"

"The Republic of Texas," Colonel Moravada scornfully repeated. "It will be in hell where that *gringo* is now. All right, *soldados*. Take what pleasure you wish. The town is condemned because we have found firearms unlawfully held by these accursed villagers. Even our own good Mexican people, it seems, are corrupted by the *tejanos!*"

"What do you mean to do, Colonel Moravada?" Sister Eufemia cried out, aghast at what she had just heard.

"Why, Sister, what is generally done when a town is sacked because of traitorous citizens. If it offends you, go back to your hovel and pray. My men will not disturb you or your nuns, unless you interfere with our duties."

With this, he wheeled his horse and rode away. The lieutenant of the firing squad, waving his sword, called out, "You are now at liberty, *soldados*. Have your pleasure, but do not take too long. We ride back to the Rio Grande at dawn."

A little group of villagers had gathered to watch the execution. Among them were the pretty, young Mexican wives of the two murdered Texans. The soldiers made for them, dragging them toward the wall where their husbands' bodies lay, flung them on the ground, tore off their clothes, and as Sister Eufemia watched in horror, savagely violated them.

She cried out in protest, but the soldiers blasphemously scoffed at her.

Weary of soul, crushed and agonized, she waited, praying only that they would not kill the women when they had taken their lustful pleasure of them. She could hear cries elsewhere in the little town as the mounted soldiers reined in their horses before the *jacales,* entered them, and dragged out their prey.

Three other women, flung down on the ground beside the two wives of the murdered Texans, shared their fate. When it was over and they lay naked and despoiled, bruised and bleeding, Sister Eufemia hurried to them and did what she could to assuage their shame and agony. "Patience, my daughters," she breathed, "I will find my sisters and bring them here to tend your pain."

Through the night, the other nuns assisted Sister Eufemia in nursing the violated women of Benecia. At dawn, Colonel Moravada and his troops rode out, on to another border town, where they might find more "rebels" to be punished because they would foment war against the Republic of Mexico.

Thirty-one

Fair winds and swiftly moving currents carried the frigate that bore John Cooper and Dorotéa within sight of the Florida Keys by the twenty-second of August 1826.

Andrew discreetly left his father and young stepmother to themselves as much as he could, and often clambered to the quartermaster's deck of the frigate and stood at the rail, wistfully looking back. When he closed his eyes, he could see the piquant, lovely face of Adriana Maldones.

Four days later, the frigate docked at New Orleans. John Cooper planned to use the carts he had originally brought to New Orleans when he came with the livestock for

Raoul Maldones. He would use one cart to transport the prize brahma bull and the other carts, including a few extra from Fabien Mallard, for the *pampas* bulls that his father-in-law had given him. His four *vaqueros* took charge of the horses, tethering them to their own in a kind of remuda. He visited his factor, Fabien Mallard, who warmly greeted him and was enchanted when he was introduced to Dorotéa. "M'sieu Baines, you simply must bring your charming wife to dinner at my house this evening," he insisted. Thus John Cooper and Dorotéa, together with Andrew, old Stancia, and Felipe and his wife, were guests at a lavish supper, at which many toasts were drunk.

The next morning, after a short visit to the New Orleans bank where the silver had been deposited to his account, John Cooper met with Monsieur Beaubien, who headed the bank and who had taken personal charge of his account. He introduced Dorotéa to the banker, and as a wedding gift, opened an account for her with a thousand dollars, which would be hers to spend on any fine clothes or jewelry in New Orleans, when they returned early next year, perhaps for Mardi Gras.

Next he purchased a wagon, since he did not wish old Stancia to be forced to ride horseback, and Felipe Mintras insisted on driving it to the Double H Ranch. "I have not done anything since we boarded the *Sea Witch*, John Cooper, and I am feeling useless. Just tell me the way to go, and I will drive Stancia and my family to our destination."

John Cooper clapped Felipe on the back and laughed, grateful for the *gaucho*'s helpfulness and cheer. He was excited by the prospect of showing Felipe his ranch in the weeks to come, of sharing with him all he had learned about cattle raising and horse breeding. Even more, John Cooper was thrilled at the prospect of being home and introducing his new bride to his family.

On the eleventh day of September, John Cooper and his entourage returned through the gateway and pulled up in the courtyard of the *hacienda*. Yankee was the first to be aware of the return of his master, and he raced from the *hacienda* to John Cooper's side, jumping up on him and licking his face. Laughing boisterously, John Cooper rubbed the wolf-dog on his head and then ordered him to sit as he introduced Yankee to his new wife. Dorotéa smiled, knelt down, and patted the wolf-dog's head, and Yankee licked her face.

When it was learned that John Cooper was home at last,

there was a fever-pitch of activity. The families of the ranch dashed from their dinner tables to welcome *el Halcón*. Carlos and Teresa, Don Diego and Doña Inez, and all the children came out to stare at the sight of the beaming John Cooper with his arm around a beautiful, dark-haired Spanish girl less than twenty years old. Suddenly everyone realized that John Cooper had found a new wife, and Carlos, who had returned from Taos with Teresa not long before this, rushed forward and exclaimed, "I had a feeling that you would bring back the loveliest treasure of all from Argentina, *amigo*. This must be Señora Baines. Señora Baines, be welcome, and come now, the both of you, to see my father and stepmother."

Doña Inez was nearly beside herself with surprise and happiness, and she cried copiously as she embraced the lovely young Dorotéa and welcomed her to Texas. Don Diego stepped forward and said simply, *"Mi hija."*

During the shipboard journey, John Cooper had told Dorotéa about his family. Now she exhibited remarkable poise and self-control as she greeted the adults and then the children in turn. Her greatest delight—more than the embraces of Doña Inez, Carlos, Bess Sandarbal, and Miguel, more than the kisses of all the children—were the words Don Diego used when he greeted her: *"Mi hija."*

Tía Margarita burst into tears when John Cooper brought Dorotéa into her kitchen to introduce her. She embraced the Argentinian girl, and then, impulsively, kissed John Cooper and exclaimed, "I am so happy; I hope your beautiful señora will not be jealous that I stole a kiss from you! I prayed all this time that you would come back safely!"

"It was because you gave me the *ojo de Dios*, Tía Margarita, as well as your prayers, that kept me safe and let me bring back my beautiful Dorotéa."

That evening, there was a great *fiesta*, with music and dancing. Felipe Mintras was the center of attention at the tables of the *trabajadores*, the *vaqueros*, and their families. Everyone had questions about life on the *pampas* and Argentinian livestock and animals.

Francesca, Diego, and Jeremy Gaige had returned, and the three of them were abashed at their violation of Don Diego's trust, as well as over their grave mishap with the gold mine. But Don Diego and Doña Inez had forgiven them, for they were much too happy to have the children—and the old prospector—back in their midst. Francesca and Diego promised never to give another thought to secret treasure, and as for Jeremy, he was spending more and more time in the kitchen helping Tía Margarita and frequently whispering words into her ear that caused her to break into great peals of laughter and to throw her apron up over her face.

Andrew sat with his brother Charles and Francesca and Diego and all the other children at a large table, and he was truly glad to be home as first his brother, then his cousins, told about all their adventures while he was away. In time Andrew would tell them all about his trip to Argentina, though there would be one thing he would keep to himself for now. That was his love for Dorotéa's younger sister, for the lovely Adriana Maldones.

Sitting with John Cooper and Dorotéa were the old nurse Stancia, as well as Don Diego, Doña Inez, and the Sandarbals. Carlos and Teresa were seated at the left of the newlywed young couple. Already Teresa and Dorotéa were chatting happily and easily, as though they were old friends. Indeed, Carlos even leaned over to John Cooper and whispered, "They are kindred spirits, those two, are they not?"

Briefly, so as not to spoil this great homecoming party, Carlos told his brother-in-law about the state of affairs in Taos. "I think for a time there will be no more serious incidents, John Cooper, for that Cienguarda has been put in his place. My greatest sadness right now is that Chief Kinotatay is seriously ill and will be taken from us."

"I know," John Cooper replied. "He was sick when I visited there in what seems like a lifetime ago. We both knew then that it might be the last time we saw each other. I am only sorry that he may not live long enough to meet Dorotéa and know I have found happiness."

"Do not despair, *mi cuñado.* I have a feeling Kinotatay knew your travels would bring you joy and fulfillment."

"I think, Carlos," John Cooper said reflectively as he sipped his wine, "Kinotatay understands that you and I—who have found new happiness after terrible tragedy—are not the kind of men to give in or despair."

Carlos told his brother-in-law the other news of the ranch: how the fine, pedigreed bulls he had bought last January from Fabien Mallard had been mated and how the wolfdog Luna would have a litter sometime in October. "Our community at the Double H Ranch is truly growing by leaps and bounds, John Cooper," Carlos humorously explained.

"My Teresa is with child, and—who knows?—perhaps you and your Dorotéa will soon have a child."

That night, when John Cooper and Dorotéa were alone in their bedchamber, he took out a beautiful inlaid jewelry case, which he had purchased in New Orleans expressly for the turquoise necklace with the silver bells that Kinotatay had given him. He opened the case, took out the necklace, and put it around Dorotéa's neck.

"My good friend and blood brother Kinotatay gave this necklace to me, my darling. It was a prized heirloom of the Indians, and he told me it brings good fortune and happiness. He was right, for I am truly fortunate and happy, my Dorotéa. Now that God has given you to me, the necklace is yours. Remember this, my sweetheart: You and I are new to each other, and our lives begin now that we are back home."

She touched the necklace and smiled as the silver bells tinkled. She put her arms around her husband and kissed him fervently, then whispered, "I am grateful to your Catarina. She brought you love, and because of that I am twice blessed in being allowed to share your life. There are so few men who know how to give love. I knew from the very first, when first we kissed, that you were one of those men to whom a woman can give herself wholeheartedly because she knows that even greater love will be given her in return. Now, John Cooper, I have a gift for you, as well. I know myself to be with child, and we will give my father the son he has always longed for. I will pray to the Holy Virgin to let it be a son, *mi corazón.*"

It was on the day that John Cooper returned to the Double H Ranch that Kinotatay left his wickiup and rode toward a distant summit far from the stronghold, along the range of the Jicarilla Mountains. Since he had parted from Carlos, on that morning when Carlos and Teresa had prepared to ride back to Texas, the valiant Jicarilla *jefe* had been cruelly tortured by the gnawing pain in his vitals. He had survived, pale and drained of strength, yet still able to hold council with the elders and to tell them, as well as the young braves who would soon follow Pastanari's leadership, how they were to watch over their comrades of the pueblo and to make certain that the *alcalde mayor* did not break his vow.

It was twilight. Kinotatay turned to his mustang, drew his knife, and murmured words of gratitude for the animal's loyalty. Then, swiftly and painlessly, he killed it. Sinking to his knees on the summit of the peak, he lifted his arms to the sky and intoned his death chant.

His voice faltered, and the night birds seemed to echo it from the tall fir trees behind him. A last spasm seized him, too agonizing to bear without crying out. His right hand gripped the still bloody knife, and with all his failing strength, he drove it into his heart and fell dead.

Two days after John Cooper's return to the Double H Ranch, the nine Dominican nuns, led by Sister Eufemia, passed through the gateway. Miguel Sandarbal saw them and ran into the *hacienda* to tell Don Diego that they had come.

The *trabajadores* had already built a mission house to welcome them, for Padre Madura had sent word to Don Diego early in the year that they were coming.

Padre Pastronaz led them to the church, after they had moved into their pleasant, comfortable new quarters and rested, then enjoyed a hearty supper that Tía Margarita prepared. The families of the Double H Ranch attended the mass which the young priest held to welcome the gentle, brave women who had endured such hardships. At last, they could look forward to a life of good deeds and prayer among the families of the *trabajadores* and the *patrónes* of this great ranch.

In his final prayer, Padre Pastronaz knelt and said, "Oh heavenly Father, let there be peace between the nations of los Estados Unidos and México; and let those who govern these countries be moved by Thy wisdom and kindness, that they may shun the evil of war and bloodshed."

The church bell tolled as Sister Eufemia murmured a prayer for the souls of Sisters Caridad and Dolores.

Little Innocente was baptized, and Esteban Morales begged to adopt him; and that is exactly what took place.

After a blissful week during which Dorotéa completely won the hearts of everyone at the Double H Ranch, John Cooper proposed that the two of them, together with Andrew and Charles and, of course, Yankee, visit Eugene Fair's settlement on the Brazos. Young Charles was delighted at this mark of favor. With Andrew's return, he had sulked just a bit because he was no longer the center of attention Miguel and Carlos had made him feel during his father's absence.

Dorotéa won him over by saying to John Cooper, "What a fine, tall, handsome boy he is, as strong and brave, I'm sure, as Andrew! Truly you were blessed, *mi corazón!*"

It was a few days' journey to the settlement on the Brazos. John Cooper and his family went by horseback, shooting game for their meals—which Yankee often fetched—and sleeping under the stars. When they crossed the Brazos by ferry and saw the sprawling settlement, John Cooper realized how much it had grown since his last visit. There was a community meetinghouse, where square and folk dancing took place, as well as picnic suppers for the families, and special games and parties for the children. There was a schoolhouse, and the church, which had been enlarged since new settlers had arrived. Simon Brown and his wife, Naomi, welcomed John Cooper and Dorotéa, and Naomi proudly showed them her twin boys, born just a few months before.

Minnie Hornsteder and her husband, Henry, were the self-appointed welcoming committee for all the visitors, and they also were responsible for the parties and dances given at the community hall. Minnie had been in bed with the grippe when John Cooper visited last year, and now when the rancher was introduced to the good-hearted, outspoken matron by Simon Brown, she cackled, "Land's sakes, Mr. Baines! If you ain't the tall, handsome galoot to go along with all your handiness on the frontier! Land's sakes alive, Henry," she went on, turning to her beaming husband, "if you'd been half as good-looking as Mr. Baines here and half as handy ridin' a horse and shootin' a rifle, I mightn't have let myself go to pot so and look like a fat, old woman; nosirree, I wouldn't have."

"You look just fine to me, honey, so don't you say anything like that," Henry stoutly replied. John Cooper and Dorotéa laughed and embraced the good-natured woman, who had so befriended Naomi when her cruel first husband had whipped her at the wagon wheel after he had coerced her into marrying him.

John Cooper, Dorotéa, and the two boys stayed on two more days. In the early afternoon of the second day, Jim Bowie rode in with his friends. He had come to talk to Simon Brown to learn whether Mexican troops had been seen near the settlement. When he caught sight of John Cooper, he let out a war whoop and ran toward him, gripping his hand in a steely vise and grinning from ear to ear. "You old so and so!

If this isn't lucky! Do you know, I came a few days after you'd pulled up stakes and headed for Argentina! You got my Bowie knife safe enough, didn't you, John Cooper?"

"I did, indeed, and I've got plenty of stories to tell you. But first I want to introduce you to somebody." John Cooper caught sight of his wife talking with Naomi Brown, and he called out to her, "My Dorotéa, will you come here a moment, please?"

When she approached, John Cooper smilingly turned back to Jim Bowie. "I brought this young lady back from Argentina. I can tell you that it was your knife that helped make her say yes. You see, they've huge snakes in that part of the world, and one of them would have gotten her if it hadn't been that I had my knife handy and cut her loose. I'll never forget you or the knife."

"Well, now, I'm mighty glad about that. It would have been a crying shame if a beautiful lady like this hadn't been spared to make Texas even more beautiful than it is," the famous scout gallantly said.

"I am very happy to meet you, Mr. Bowie," Dorotéa said to him in her sweet, clear voice. "My husband has told me so much about you. I, too, am very grateful for that knife of yours!"

The two men burst into laughter, and Jim Bowie said to John Cooper, "Darned if I'm not a little bit in love with this girl of yours. Would you cut my gizzard out with that knife of mine if I stole a kiss?"

"I've no objection to just one kiss, so long as I'm watching. But don't make it too friendly, Jim," John Cooper said with a chuckle.

When that amenity was over, much to Dorotéa's blushing amusement, the scout turned to John Cooper. "You know, I've been scouring the country talking to settlers. I'm founding what I call the Texas Rangers. These friends of mine are part and parcel of the first group. We're not legally accepted yet, but I hope it won't be too long. You see, I've had news that Mexico is beginning to put a ban on new American settlers. There's trouble over religion and our views on law and order."

"I was afraid of that," John Cooper said.

"Most of all, the present government seems to think that Texas really belongs to Mexico, and I think they find themselves in the position of wanting to be Indian givers."

"I sincerely hope it won't come to that, Jim. I would like to see your Texas Ranger idea put into practice as soon as possible."

"Well, I'm doing all I can. I might even be able to persuade the Mexican bigwigs that if I had a group of law and order men like these, they'd be sure to have no botheration with outlaws and riffraff. Well, John Cooper, I hope to visit you at the Double H Ranch one of these days."

"You'll always be welcome there. Good seeing you again."

"Likewise. And to you, Mrs. Baines, a long and happy life. This fellow here will make you a good husband; take my word for it."

"I already know that, Mr. Bowie. Thank you. Good luck to you, as well." Dorotéa gave him her hand. Jim Bowie gallantly brought it to his lips, then turned and waved his hand in farewell and went back to his horse.

As the little procession returned to the Double H Ranch, Miguel waved his *sombrero* and came hurrying toward John Cooper and his wife. Andrew and Charles dismounted and led their horses, as well as those of their parents, to the stable to put them in their stalls.

"It's good to have you back again, *mi compañero*, Señora Baines," Miguel beamed. "Yesterday, a courier rode in with a letter for you from New Orleans. It is marked very urgent. Don Diego has it for you."

"I wonder what it could be?" John Cooper mused aloud. "Come, Dorotéa darling, let's go into the house. I'm sure you must be hungry after the long ride we just had."

"You mustn't treat me as if I were an infant, *mi corazón*," she remonstrated, wrinkling her lovely nose at him. "I'm eighteen, I'll have you know."

"I humbly apologize," he chuckled, and then took her by the shoulders and kissed her warmly on the mouth.

They walked arm in arm to Don Diego's study. The white-haired *hidalgo* was sitting in an armchair, sipping a cordial, and Doña Inez was solicitously standing beside his chair, her arm around his shoulders. There was concern on her face, for his health continued to fail, and he seemed weak and listless at the end of the day, though he still maintained his sense of humor. "Dorotéa, John Cooper," she smilingly exclaimed, "you are back safely. Thank the good Lord for looking over you. There is a letter for you."

"Yes, my son," Don Diego said with a weary smile. "It is here in my desk. There you are."

John Cooper frowned as he opened the letter. He read it, then he uttered a stifled cry. "Oh, no—it can't be!"

"What is it, *mi corazón?*" Dorotéa asked as she came up to stand beside him.

"Read it for yourself, Dorotéa. It's the worst of all possible news."

Dorotéa took the letter and read it aloud for the benefit of Don Diego and Doña Inez.

> "Honored Señor John Cooper Baines:
>
> I write this in all haste and pray that a fast ship will bring it to you. My master has been arrested and is now in prison in Buenos Aires. Porfirio Ramos, may his soul rot in hell forever, has taken over his lands and now lives in the very *hacienda* where my master and his wife and children had such happy lives. I myself and some of the other loyal servants are now living in the *jacales* of the loyal *gauchos.*
>
> Señor Baines, if it is at all possible, can you help my master? The other *hacendados* did nothing, in spite of their protests of loyalty to him. Even his old friend Heitor Duvaldo was unable to help, though he is looking after my master's daughters.
>
> I dare not ask you to write back, for the letter may be intercepted by the *porteños* since it would come to Buenos Aires first, and then be delivered by courier. But I pray God that you can assist our beloved *patrón.*
>
> Yours respectfully,
> Fernando."

Dorotéa's eyes met her husband's as John Cooper said, "Are you thinking what I'm thinking, my sweetheart?" When she mutely nodded, her eyes still anxiously fixed on his, he said determinedly, "We must go back at once to Argentina. You and I will do everything in our power to save your father from this vicious, treacherous enemy. We'll take Felipe Mintras back with us, because he will lead the *gauchos,* and he's resourceful and knows the country and will help us do what must be done."

"Yes, yes," Dorotéa agreed, and ran up to John Cooper, who put his arm around her. She looked first at him, then at the anxious faces of Doña Inez and Don Diego. "My dear ones," she said, putting out her hands to them. They came over to her and took her hands.

And so these family members—as diverse in their backgrounds as they were in their ages—held each other for several moments, drawing strength for the ordeals ahead.

★ WAGONS WEST ★

A series of unforgettable books that trace the lives of a dauntless band of pioneering men, women, and children as they brave the hazards of an untamed land in their trek across America. This legendary caravan of people forge a new link in the wilderness. They are Americans from the North and the South, alongside immigrants, Blacks, and Indians, who wage fierce daily battles for survival on this uncompromising journey—each to their private destinies as they fulfill their greatest dreams.

☐	22808	INDEPENDENCE!	$3.50
☐	22784	NEBRASKA!	$3.50
☐	23177	WYOMING!	$3.50
☐	22568	OREGON!	$3.50
☐	23168	TEXAS!	$3.50
☐	23381	CALIFORNIA!	$3.50
☐	23405	COLORADO!	$3.50
☐	20174	NEVADA!	$3.50
☐	20919	WASHINGTON!	$3.50
☐	22952	MONTANA!	$3.95
☐	23572	DAKOTA!	$3.95

Prices and availability subject to change without notice.